Flawed

Caught by the Bad Boys
Book Two

BY RAATHI CHOTA

Flawed

First Print Edition: March 2019

Limitless Publishing, LLC
Kailua, HI 96734
www.limitlesspublishing.com

Formatting: Limitless Publishing

ISBN-13: 978-1-64034-544-7
ISBN-10: 1-64034-544-2

Dedication

To my younger and only sister, Razaanah. I'd do anything and everything for you no matter what gets in our path.

To the quiet ones wanting to be heard, don't worry...I hear you.

Chapter One

Lana

I'd experienced a lot of déjà vu in my life, such as being dragged to the empty part of the school, being babysat by Griffon Bronx one too many times, or Kelly embarrassing me, but this topped all of that. We spent the last five hours in panic mode in search for Jack's body. We dug up the whole area and finally concluded that he wasn't there. We left his jacket underground, not wanting anything to connect to us. None of us spoke since we got into the car. It still rained as I sat in the back with Benny while Nick drove and Liam called shotgun. I called Mom and told her I'd be staying at Miranda's. She's glad since I left a big chaos for her.

"Maybe we just looked in the wrong place?" Liam assumed as he broke the awkward silence. Nick let out a scoff as he turned to his friend.

"Then why was his jacket there?" he asked. Liam shrugged.

"What are we gonna do?" Benny asked as he

looked out the window. To be honest, I was tired of that question. I didn't know how to respond, yet the answer always came to us sooner or later. I turned to Benny and thought about the kiss we shared a few hours ago. I didn't know why, but I enjoyed it, yet whenever something good happened it seemed something terrible topped it.

"I don't know, just keep an eye out for anything and watch the news," Nick said.

"Boring. I'll just ask around," Liam said as Nick scoffed.

"What are you going to ask them, huh? Have you seen a dead body lurking around? I buried him, but he managed to escape," Nick babbled as he turned on the radio.

"Everyone thinks he's missing, dude. You can't just ask that," Benny said.

"Oh yeah…I forgot," Liam responded. Silence took over us, but it soon ended as the radio played weird old music. Liam turned to it and threw his hands up in surrender.

"It's Will from *Stranger Things*!"

Nick hit his radio, and it replaced with the radio station he set it as. He turned to Liam with an annoyed look.

"For the fifth time," he said, "my radio's been faulty, and no, it's not Will from S*tranger Things*!"

"Oh yeah…I forgot."

"Why don't you get it fixed?" Benny suggested.

"Yeah, Blake said he'd help me out," Nick replied.

"Blake?" I questioned.

"Yeah, he's a pro in fixing cars and stuff. No

wonder he's had that motorcycle for so long," Liam stated, then started a new topic. "Who do you think Nancy should be with, Lana?"

"Huh?"

"Nancy from *Stranger Things*? Steve or Jonathan?" I raised my eyebrow at his sudden change of subject. Then again, I'm talking to Liam Sanchez.

"Err…I don't know."

"I like Jonathan. He's cool," Nick stated as he drove through the rain.

"The upside-down thing was cool," Benny added as I raised a brow at their casual conversation even as we'd lost a dead corpse.

"Wish we could've dumped this in the upside-down…" Liam trailed off as he held up his black high tops. My eyes widened as Nick hit the brakes. He turned with an icy glare as he looked at the shoes, then Liam. We brought them with us because we had to get rid of them once and for all. We specifically told Liam to do whatever it took so that we wouldn't see them ever again, yet with his addiction to *Stranger Things*, he thought he'd dump them in the upside-down!

"We told you to get rid of them in the woods!" Nick grunted as his fists tightened.

"Oh yeah…I forgot."

From the corner of my eye, I saw Benny move forward. I tried to hold him back as he continuously whacked Liam. We looked like a bunch of idiots on the side of the road. Liam tried to lighten the mood while Nick mumbled to himself and I told Benny to stop. You wouldn't say that they played football, because after a minute it was quiet, only their heavy puffs to be heard.

"That guy didn't have to mark it, though…these were my favorite," Liam complained as he held the one that had a mark on it.

"What does it say?" Benny asked as we stared at it.

"S1," Nick replied as we observed the white marker on the black Converse.

"What the heck does that mean?"

"Sanchez!" Liam suggested.

"Why would he put your last name and then the number one?" I asked. He shrugged as he looked up and thought for a bit.

"Maybe I wrote it…I tend to forget things," Liam said as Nick sighed and started the car. "I'll get rid of them, don't worry."

Benny shook his head in disappointment as we drove through the city. It looked beautiful, the bright lights followed by the big Christmas tree in the middle. It startled me how close Christmas was. I felt an arm around my shoulder as Benny shifted next to me. I gave him a smile as I rested my head on his shoulder.

"You can stay with me if you want," he suggested. I gave a nod because it was already late and I didn't want to wake Miranda or her mother.

"Aren't you guys glad that we came?" Liam asked after a while.

"Yeah, I'm glad that we came and got our clothes dirty again and found nothing…so happy," Nick replied sarcastically.

"That's the spirit!" Liam clearly ignored his

sarcasm. We pulled in Benny's driveway and got out. We said goodbye to Liam and Nick, and they said we'd meet up tomorrow…well, later today. I followed Benny to the back of his house. Needless to say, his house was big. I remembered at Thanksgiving he said he'd take over the family business. Whatever business it was, it must be going well. Benny took out his keys and unlocked the back door as we snuck in. I followed him up the stairs and into his room. It was pitch black throughout the house, but as soon as he shut his bedroom door and turned the light on, I was blinded. I awkwardly sat on his bed as I watched him rummage in his closet. A few seconds later, he brought out a pair of sweatpants and a baggy sweater. He handed them to me, then ran his hand through his hair.

"Bathroom is right next door; you can clean up, then I'll throw your clothes in the wash for tomorrow," Benny suggested as I stood up. I thanked him as I strolled out of his bedroom and into the bathroom. I looked at myself in the mirror, and I honestly looked dull. My hair was in all directions, and my black sweater had dirt on it. I quickly slipped into the baggy sweater and sweatpants, then put my hair up into a ponytail. I walked out of the bathroom and saw Benny in his sweatpants and shirt. He had a smile on his face as he gestured for me to follow him. We tiptoed down the stairs as Benny took my dirty clothes. He seized my hand in his as we walked through the dark. Once we reached the basement, he turned on the light. It was like Ethan's but looked more like a family room than a man cave. Numerous games were stacked by the TV, as well as consoles. A bar was in the corner, and a pool table stood next to it. Benny put our dirty clothes in the washer and took out blankets and pillows. I watched as he set them on the two sofas. "It's almost two in the morning," he mumbled. "We should probably get some sleep."

"Yeah," I agreed as I rested on the one sofa and him on the other. I set my glasses on the coffee table as I snuggled into the blankets. Once I was finally comfortable, I lay on my back and stared at the ceiling. "Night, Benny," I whispered as my eyes became weaker.

"Good night, Lana Willson."

***

I slowly opened my eyes and noticed a figure towering over me. It was clear that it was morning since the person's head seemed to glow. I squinted my eyes as I fluttered them open to see Benny, although it wasn't Benny. It was a younger version of him with spiky hair and he wore headphones. The boy raised a brow at me but immediately grinned.

"You're pretty," he stated as I slowly sat up.

"Err…thanks," I croaked out, then sat up. He looked to be twelve years old. He held a game controller in his hand as he eyed me.

"Can you make pancakes?" he asked as I glanced around the room. I saw Benny get up as he rubbed his eyes. Our eyes locked as he gave me a sleepy smile. He looked adorable with his morning hair.

"Morning," he grumbled. Oh, his voice sounded deep and groggy.

"Morning," I murmured as Benny turned to the boy and squinted his eyes at him.

"What are you doing here?" Benny asked as he forced the blankets off himself.

"I always play Xbox on Sunday, but I see I'm interrupting something," the younger Benny said as he sent me a wink.

"Lana, this is my little brother Sam; Sam, this is my friend Lana," Benny introduced us as we looked at each other.

"I knew that you'd be too cute to date my brother, but you can call me anytime, cupcake," Sam said with a smirk plastered on his face. Benny let out a groan, clearly embarrassed by his younger brother, while I tried to hold in a laugh. He reminded me of a confident blond playboy. Sam was tall with golden brown hair and bright brown eyes.

"Sorry, but you're too young for me," I stated as Benny and I walked upstairs.

"Wait for me, you beautiful blue-eyed girl!" Sam shouted. I let out a chuckle as Benny shut the door. He turned to me and awkwardly scratched the back of his neck.

"Sorry about that. He plays this game where the female character has bright blue eyes, so I guess he has a liking for any girl with blue eyes," Benny stated as we walked down the hall.

"He reminds me of Carter," I blurted out as we approached the bathroom.

"Yeah, hopefully, he doesn't mix with Carter any

time soon." We laughed as he handed me my clean clothes.

I walked out of the bathroom with my hair neatly brushed. I heard voices at the end of the hall as I walked in that direction.

"Mom, I want peanut butter spread on my toast!" Sam whined.

"Why do we even buy this brand? It's horrible!" Benny complained as I stood in the doorway.

"I like it!" Sam argued as he snatched the jar from his brother. I did an awkward cough as Benny's mother spun around. I pushed up my glasses as everyone watched me.

"Oh my god, it's a girl," she blurted out, then rested her palm against her chest.

"Told you, Mom!" Sam said as I slowly approached her.

"Lucas Nielson, get in here. Your son finally brought home a girl!" she said. My eyes widened as I turned to Benny, who jumped out of his seat and scurried next to me. Lucas Nielson, who I assumed was his dad, walked in with a stunned look.

"Wow, and for once it wasn't Sam," Mr. Nielson commented as he walked to me. "I'm Lucas Nielson, and this is my lovely wife, Amber Nielson."

"Nice to meet you. I'm Lana Willson, a friend of Benny's," I responded and noticed how his mother frowned.

"Are you related to Sheriff Willson?" his dad asked.

"Yeah, I'm his daughter," I answered with an innocent smile.

"How lovely. Would you like to join us for breakfast?" his mother asked.

"I'd love to," I said with a warm smile. I sat next to Benny as we ate in silence. I glanced up and noticed Sam was opposite me. He sent me a wink, and I shuddered because it got weird.

"So, Lana, how long have you known Benny?" Mr. Nielson asked.

"Well, since first grade, I guess," I said as Benny smiled.

"And we're only seeing such a cutie now?" Sam asked as he looked at us. It was awkward to think that he did all those things to me. I didn't like to think about it, and I knew he didn't either. I looked down to my food as Benny glared at his brother.

"Well, err…Lana, what are you doing for winter break?" Mrs. Nielson asked.

"I have family friends coming over from California today, so we're gonna spend time with them."

"I hope Benny brings you over again soon. You seem like a lovely girl!"

"Mom," Benny groaned. I felt sorry for him because it was funny to watch him be embarrassed by his family. The way he continuously ran his hand through his hair and looked away when his mother mentioned us. The rest of breakfast was spent "getting to know Sam's future girl," as he said it. Turned out the Nielsons owned a bunch of seafood restaurants. Benny's dad and Ethan's dad were close friends since they're both in the marketing business.

Afterward, Liam picked all of us up in his

grandma's station wagon. Melissa, Nick, and Miranda were in the car as well, but Marcus was attending a family gathering. After an hour, we finally arrived at my house. The place looked the same before the sleepover, which meant that Mom cleaned up.

"Mom, I'm home!" I exclaimed.

"Lana, could you come here for a sec?" Mom ordered as her voice roared through the house. I raised a brow as Miranda gave me an assured look that they'd be fine. I nodded in response as I bolted up the stairs and into their room. A big smile formed on my face as I spotted Dad at the edge of their bed. Yet it immediately it dropped to a frown as his head was placed in his hands. Mom stood in front of him with a drained expression.

"Hey, Dad," I greeted as I sat down beside him. "When did you get back?"

"This morning."

"D-did you g-get him?"

He shook his head and let out a huff. From the corner of my eye, I saw Mom raise her arms.

"But you know what he did get?" she asked. "A bullet!"

"I was wearing a bulletproof vest!" Dad said as he raised his head.

"But what if you weren't, Harry? You could've been hurt!" Mom yelled, then crouched in front of my dad and took his hands and gripped them. "You could've been dead."

Dad let out a sigh as he brought Mom in for a hug as he assured her that everything was going to be okay. A million scenarios ran through my head at the thought of James killing my dad.

"Lana, don't worry. I'm fine, sweetie. We've been in worse situations, but the Willsons always manage to fight through it, right?" Dad asked.

"Yeah," I breathed out as I wiped a tear away.

"Come on, our friends are coming today…wouldn't want to spoil the mood," Dad said as he got up and walked out of the room. Mom and I followed as he walked downstairs and came face to face with everyone else. "Mood ruined," Dad muttered, then walked into his office.

The rest of the day was spent indoors. Melissa called Carter, but he and the rest of them were recovering from a hangover from a party. I still wanted to talk to Blake about what we almost shared the other night, yet something told me that I shouldn't. That's if I wanted to face more rejection. Ugh, I hated it so much. I didn't know what to feel. Benny and I didn't talk about the kiss last night either, yet what he said still made me squeal a bit on the inside.

"Yeah, his red hair is finally gone," Nick said as we looked at Benny's brown hair. A grin spread across my face as I remembered that day.

"But I liked tomato face Benny," Liam said with a frown. "Hehe, it's funny because when he used to get angry, his face would go all red, so the hair made it even more entertaining."

"Liam, your lips keep moving, but all I hear is bullsh—"

Benny got interrupted when a loud honk erupted through the house. The television was turned off a while back because we were talking.

"They're here!" Mom exclaimed as I groaned. We heard footsteps as Mom rushed through the house while Dad trailed behind. We followed causally as Mom ripped off her apron and fixed her hair. She opened the door, and we went outside. We stood on the porch as Richard and Jade Radcliff got out of their car, but no Levi. I couldn't contain the excitement as I double-checked the vehicle to see if the familiar dark-haired boy was in it. Thankfully he wasn't as Jade and Richard approached us.

"Angie!" Jade exclaimed as she pulled her in for a hug. Somehow, I pictured Miranda and me doing it when we met up on a Monday after not seeing each other for a whole weekend. Jade and Mom did everything together, and they gossiped a lot. Dad and Richard spoke formally yet they'd bonded so well over the years. "Lana! You've grown so much!" Jade stated as she pulled me in for a hug even though we saw each other in the summer of 2015. "Oh, hello, Miranda!" Jade said as she pulled away from me. Miranda gave her a small smile and awkwardly waved.

"Hi, Mrs. Radcliff."

"Ooh, I see you have friends over. Which one of you is Lana's lucky boyfr—"

"That would be me, Mrs. Hagshif—I mean Radcliff," Liam responded as he swung his arm around me.

"Aww, so cute," she said, then pinched his cheeks.

"No, he's not, he's goofy," I said. "This is Liam, Benny, Melissa, and Nick."

"Nice to meet you all. Your mother has talked

about some of you…which one was it? Bl—"

"Why don't you teenagers make yourself useful and help our guests with their luggage?" Mom suggested as she cut off Jade.

"Sure," Nick replied. The adults walked into the house with Mrs. Radcliff in last. They had a lot of stuff in their car because they'd driven. Miranda came up beside me as we walked into the house and carried bags.

"Thank goodness he isn't here," she muttered as we set the bags in the front.

"Where's Levi?" Mom asked as Miranda grunted.

"Oh, you know him." Jade laughed. "Always the adventurous type and likes to travel on his own. He'll be here any second."

I sighed because the chance of a peaceful Christmas was gone. Miranda and I walked out of the house and stood on the porch with everyone else.

"Well, I guess we better get goi—" Melissa cut off when a low roar gushed down the street. We whipped our heads as the familiar sound got louder. It wasn't just any sound but an engine. A familiar 1967 black Ford Mustang came into view as it approached the house. Miranda folded her arms and huffed.

"Spoke too soon," she muttered as we watched him park the car in front of the house.

"Now that's a car," Liam commented. I wanted to roll my eyes as Levi got out of the car as if he knew we watched him. He looked the same as last time except for the new tattoo on his neck.

"Now that's a hunk," Melissa commented. Nick glared at her. His deep blue eyes locked with mine as he neared us. He held his arms out as a smile formed on his face.

"Princess!" Levi cheered as he brought me in for a hug and picked me up. I felt everyone stare at us as Levi's arms wrapped around my waist. He set me down, but his arms were still wrapped around me. He looked down at me with a grin on his face. "What? No hello, my knight in shining armor?" He winked. "Remember?"

I rolled my eyes as I pried his arms off me. He glanced over my shoulder as he smiled.

"Miranda." He gave a curt nod toward her.

"Levi."

He turned his head to observe everyone else, and I swore Levi almost flinched. He slowly walked toward Benny, who gazed at us the whole time.

"Do you remember me?" Levi asked with a fearful look in his eye.

"How can I forget the self-centered jackass known as Levi Radcliff?" Benny hissed as Levi chuckled.

"Yep, and here's the guy who tortured my girl for years," Levi said as I squirmed. "The dick who couldn't control himself whenever he lost it, the woman beater also known as Benny Nielson."

"Well, things have changed," Nick stated.

"Yeah, Levi, we made up," I said and watched as the two glared at each other. Their eyes were filled with hatred toward each other. Levi was an inch or two taller than Benny, but it didn't make much of a difference. Levi let out a dry laugh as he looked at

Benny then me.

"She might've forgiven you, but I don't forgive dipshits like you that quickly," Levi grunted as he clenched his fists. Levi knew that Benny bullied me because he saw it once. Levi beat Benny after that if he ever laid his hands on me, but then Levi moved away. So Benny took advantage, but when Levi visited, he'd always had the last punch.

"Look, can't we just forgive and forget?" Liam broke the awkward silence. "By the way, I'm Liam, and I like your car."

"Oh, would you look at that!" Miranda said as she looked at her watch then grabbed Benny's arm. "Tomorrow's school. Gotta go. Bye, see you in the morning, Lana!" She rushed out as everyone else caught on. In a minute, they were in the station wagon and down the driveway. I turned to Levi, who had a satisfied look. I glared at him, and he tilted his head.

"You're a jerk! Don't act like you're the innocent one here!" I yelled, then stormed into the house.

***

We sat around the dining table and had dinner. I sat next to Levi with our parents around us. The discussion was mainly about Christmas and memories.

"Oh, remember when Levi taught you how to ride a bike?" Jade cooed as she looked at us. "Then you fell, and he kissed the bruise on your knee."

I felt a hand being placed on my thigh and

winced. From the corner of my eye, I saw Levi smirk.

"That's not the only place I've kissed," he whispered, then stroked my thigh. I swallowed the piece of chicken and glanced around the table to see that our parents were too engrossed in each other to even acknowledge us.

"Speaking of old times, how's Griffon?" Richard asked.

"He's good…still working at the high school and found himself a girl," Dad replied with a grin.

"Who's the chick?" Levi asked, his hand still securely placed on my thigh.

"My English teacher," I mumbled.

"Go, Uncle Griff," he said as everyone laughed. Dad introduced Griffon to the Radcliffs a while back, so we often spent a lot of time together.

"Oh, remember when Griffon babysat that one night and when we came home he was washing them in the bath?" Jade babbled on as everyone laughed. I cringed at the thought of five-year-old Lana and six-year-old Levi in the bath together.

Suddenly his hand went further up as he whispered, "Can't wait to recreate those memories."

I looked around the table because no one noticed anything. He only did it to annoy me like he always did. I took my right leg and placed it on top of my left and made sure to squash Levi's hand. He let out a yelp as he pulled his hand away.

The rest of the evening was spent unpacking as the Radcliffs got settled. I was on the La-Z-Boy, rocking back and forth as I watched Levi prepare his bed for the next few weeks. Thankfully they came often, so the sofa could turn into a couch bed.

"Griffon still staying in that apartment of his?" Richard asked my dad.

"Yep, ten years and going," Dad replied as he handed Levi some blankets. "Wanna pay him a visit?"

Out of the corner of my eye, I noticed Levi tried to hold in a smirk as our mothers entered the room.

"Levi, honey, are you sure you have enough blankets?" Jade asked as she handed him another.

"Yes, Mom. Besides, I'm sure Lana won't mind if I pay her a visit for more," he said, then winked at me. I rolled my eyes as Richard nudged his wife.

"Wanna check Griffon's place out?"

"Sure!" Jade exclaimed as she turned to my mother.

"We're all going?" I asked.

"I'm chilling here," Levi stated as he collapsed on the sofa bed. "Go and enjoy yourselves, Bobby," he said, using my dad's middle name. "You're certainly not getting any younger."

Dad scoffed as he turned to the rest of the adults. For years, Levi called him Bobby, and he finally concluded that he wouldn't stop.

"We'll be back soon, and Lana is in charge!" Mom called out as they grabbed their belongings.

"What? I'm older!" Levi protested as he stood up.

"Girls mature faster than boys!" Jade stated as they walked out. I stuck my tongue out at him, and I stood, watching as our parents walked out of the house.

"Say hi to Uncle Griff for us!" Levi said as he

observed them through the window. I raised a brow as I had my gaze on him. He eyed them as the car pulled out of the driveway and to the street. Once they were gone, he slowly spun around with a mischievous look. I squinted my eyes as he slowly approached me. I backed away, and he smirked at me.

"Levi, what are yo—" I cut off when he trudged toward me. My eyes widened as I picked up my pace and bolted upstairs. I heard his loud footsteps behind me as I ran into my room.

"Gotcha!" he yelled as his muscular arms wrapped around me. We fell onto the bed with him on top of me. He tickled me in various places as I chuckled. I loved to laugh but not like this. I hated it when someone tickled me, and he knew that. It's like a million pinches that made me squirm.

"Levi, stop!" I giggled and screamed at the same time. He ignored me and snickered. He hovered over me as we laughed hysterically. He suddenly stopped as he rested his arms on either side of me. His dark blue eyes stared into my round blue ones. I took in his facial features. His nose ring was in the exact place as Blake's, and I couldn't help but think of him. I was brought back to reality as Levi's face inched closer to mine. He kept his eyes on my lips. My eyes widened as I pushed him off me. He landed on the bed as I jumped up.

"Aww," he said as I backed away.

"How dare you try to kiss me?" I yelled as he rested on my bed as if it were his own.

"It's not like we haven't done it before."

"You try and kiss me after you treat Benny like

shit?"

"Oh, that reminds me," he said. "What the actual fuck? Why the hell are you hanging out with him, princess?"

"Don't fucking 'princess' me! We made up. Things have changed, Levi! Fuck 'princess!'"

"I already did," he said with a wink. I rolled my eyes and mentally slapped myself for that. He got up and sat on the bed. "What could he possibly do to let you forgive him? If I'm not mistaken, he almost put you in a coma once."

"Now you're just dramatic. Stop holding a fucking grudge!"

"Oh please!" he said. "So nobody remembers how that asshole ruined your life, and you all just carry on being best friends and shit? I bet you someone still thinks of what he did." He pointed to nothing in particular. I rolled my eyes and avoided contact as I looked around the room. He got up and approached me. I faced him as he leaned in and stared me dead in the eye. "There is someone!" He pointed his index finger in my face. I let out a snort as I rolled my eyes. "Please, Lana, I've known you for more than thirteen years. I know when you're lying." He followed my gaze. I remained quiet as he kept eye contact, then a sudden spark appeared in his eyes as he smiled. "It's a he!"

"What? No!" I squinted my eyes at Levi.

"Was it that weird guy who liked my car? The dude with blond hair? Your boyfriend?"

"No, no, and no. I don't even have a boyfriend!"

"Not yet," he muttered. "I'm gonna find out what happened, Lana," he said with his back faced to me.

"Remember, I always find out. You can't keep anything from me."

I shook my head as I watched him approach my closet. He opened it and looked inside. "Get ready. We're going out," he said as he went through my clothes.

"Where are you going?" I asked.

"We're going for a drive," he said with a smirk plastered on his face. My eyes widened as he pulled out casual clothes. He then pulled out a pair of black lingerie and whistled. My cheeks flushed as I grabbed them from him and stuffed them in my drawer. "Damn, I need to find out what happened while I was gone."

"You're acting as if you're the innocent one here, coming to save everyone when you've done much worse with no explanation!"

"Can't we talk about this another time?"

"No! You left me, Levi, and I had to find out from your mom that you were too busy even to pick up the phone and call!"

"I did call the other day!"

"Yeah, one fucking year later to say you can't wait to see your princess!"

"Why must the guy always call when he fucks up?"

"Well, since I called a million times and sent dozens of messages, it wouldn't hurt to call or text back!" He let out a dry laugh as he threw his hands up in exasperation.

"You wanna know why I didn't call? Because I felt guilty for doing that to you! When I wanted to apologize, it was too late, and I wanted to do it in person but never had the balls to! That day when Griffon yelled at me, I knew I fucked up badly, and I didn't want to be more of a bad influence on you, so I left," he screamed. "Each day went by as I looked at the phone, wanting to call you, but I didn't know where to start. I'm sorry, I shouldn't have left you." His voice dropped to a whisper. There was silence as I stared at him. His tall figure slouched, and he held a gloomy expression. I watched as he took out a dress from my closet. "I was hoping that this would make you forgive me." He held the dress by the hanger as my eyes widened. It was the same dress I found on my bed on Thanksgiving; I always wondered who got it for me.

"I-it was you."

"Yeah. I asked one of my friends to drop it off, but they said you weren't home, so he snuck into your room and placed it on your bed."

"Thank you," I whispered as I thought of Keene Stoner in my room.

"Did you wear it yet?" He put it back in the closet. I nodded, and he slowly bit his lip. "You must've looked stunning," he mumbled, then turned to me. "Since I bought it."

I playfully rolled my eyes as he took out an outfit and tossed it onto my bed. He looked at me, then at the clothing as he licked his lips.

"You're gonna look hot tonight." He winked. I watched as he walked out of the room and told me to meet him by the car.

I locked the house, then walked to his car and got into the passenger seat. The White Stripes played as we drove. I got some of my music taste from Levi. One day I came home, and he had his friends over and "Still Waiting" by Sum 41 played, and I couldn't help but bob my head to the music. When his friends left, I asked him what song it was, and from that moment I found bands on my own.

The drive was quiet as we arrived in a familiar area. The streets were piled with cars as people chatted. I've been here with Levi before, but something else made my stomach turn. All the buildings were closed for the day, which made it the perfect spot for the youth.

"I can't believe you still do this," I said as he parked the car.

"You know me, I love to see my baby on the road," he said as we got out of the car. Whistles and cheers surrounded us as people approached.

"He's back!"

"Now the show's getting started."

"Levi Radcliff, what a surprise," a familiar voice said as I looked over my shoulder to see Keene. He's Levi's friend who always tagged along when he raced. Keene and I hung out, but only when Levi was around. When he left, I never saw Keene again. His messy brown hair fell onto his face as he smiled at his friend. He was two years older than me, and when it used to be the three of us, I'd always look at him as an older brother. He appreciated it since he lived in a rundown apartment. "Thought you left us for the babes in California," Keene joked as he hugged Levi. His eyed landed on me as he let out a low whistle. He eyed me up and down as I blushed. "But I see you already got yourself one."

"Back off, dude. She's mine," Levi replied as he slung his arm around my waist. I raised a brow at him as I pulled out of his hold and approached Keene.

"Hey, Keene," I greeted as we hugged.

"'Sup, Lana? Almost didn't notice you there. Love the outfit."

"Thanks."

"Yeah, I found a whole lot of new things in her closet," Levi said as he winked at me. I rolled my eyes as I glanced around at the few people who watched the race. It was illegal, and I died on the inside, but what the heck? I had a rough weekend, and so far, things were going well. Levi would win like always, and we'd go home. I turned back to see Levi gone and Keene next to me. I raised a brow as I frantically searched for him but only found his car lined up for the next race.

"Where's Levi?" I asked.

"He'll be back, just sorting out a few things before the race," Keene said as he placed his hand against the wall and leaned on it. "So did you like my gift?"

"Yeah, but you could've left a note or something." I laughed at the thought of Keene climbing into my window.

"Where's the fun in that?" he rhetorically asked as Levi approached us with a pack of cigarettes. I watched as he opened the pack and took out one and gave it to Keene, then one for him.

"Remember how to smoke, princess?" Levi asked as he held a cigarette. I reached into my pocket and took out a lighter as I took the cigarette.

"How could I forget?" I grinned. I lit it and took a drag. Levi smirked as Keene took the lighter and lit his. He blew out a smoke ring as we watched the cars. Girls passed by and eyed Levi, but once they saw me, they sent daggers. Levi was a well-known racer, he used to do it a lot in the summer, and people loved him.

"Don't worry…I won't tell anyone about the pack in your room," Levi whispered as he stood next to me. I turned to him with my brows squinted and was about to ask when a loud roar erupted. We turned our heads to see a crowd cheer. I squinted my eyes as I watched a Lamborghini Aventador turn a corner, followed by a Subaru STI, yet I noticed how touched up they were. "Who the hell are they?" Levi asked as they parked and people crowded their cars as they checked them out.

"They've been coming here for the past few weeks, and they're kind of good, man," Keene said as we watched them get out of the car.

"Well, they certainly haven't gone up against me," Levi said through gritted teeth. I almost did a double take as I saw Ethan and Carter get out of the Lamborghini and Aidan and Blake get out of the Subaru.

"You're versing them tonight," Keene stated as girls crowded around them.

"Then let's go and introduce ourselves," Levi said with a smirk plastered on his face.

Chapter Two

Lana

Levi was well known in elementary school for his pranks and humorous gestures. Ethan and Aidan knew him, but Carter came in the freshman year. Blake arrived this year, so they wouldn't know each other. I squinted my eyes as I watched everyone remark on them. Girls crowded around them as guys checked out their cars. From the corner of my eye, I saw Levi and Keene stroll toward them. I threw my cigarette on the ground and crushed it as I leaned against the wall. Levi spun around with his brow raised.

"You coming or are you waiting for an invitation?"

I gave him an innocent smile as I shook my head. No way would they know I was here, especially with Levi Radcliff.

"I'm comfortable here," I said as my eyes flicked toward the crowd. "Good luck."

Levi raised a brow as he took in my strange

behavior. He rolled his eyes as he gestured for Keene to follow him. I wandered along the wall as I watched Levi. As soon as people spotted him, they parted like the Red Sea. Ethan leisurely leaned on his Lamborghini as Aidan sat on the hood of his Subaru. All eyes were on Levi and Keene as they approached the cars. Keene stopped in the middle as he gazed at Carter, who had a girl wrapped around his waist. I watched as Keene smirked while Levi walked around their cars and took in every detail. Aidan got off the hood of his vehicle and stared at Levi in suspicion.

"Nice car. Too bad it's a piece of shit," Levi stated as he touched the Subaru.

"Interesting," Aidan said as he tilted his head. "Let me add that to the things I don't give a shit about."

There were a few snickers and whispers as Levi strolled up to Aidan. He let out a dry laugh as he towered over him.

"Who the fuck are you?" Aidan demanded. Levi must have found the situation hilarious as he laughed. I glanced at Ethan and noticed him eyeing Levi apprehensively. Carter received strange looks from Keene while Blake smoked.

"Wow, your memory must suck, Rowley."

I couldn't stand to hear them any longer. There was a bistro where everyone hung out while the races took place. I decided to go in there while they bickered. I entered the bistro and saw guys who appeared to be around my age and older. They gave me flirtatious looks. I rolled my eyes at them. I walked to the counter and sat down on a stool.

There was a flatscreen TV displayed above showing what was going on outside; they had cameras all around the area. I could see Levi and Ethan talking, and I noticed the tenacity in their eyes. A random guy appeared and broke the two up. He must've said something about the race. Levi gave a simple nod as he turned to Ethan and Aidan.

"What can I get you?" the guy behind the counter asked.

"Water please," I said. He smiled as he handed me the glass then turned to the TV.

"He's back." The guy laughed as he looked at Levi. I glanced up to see them ready at the starting line. There were four cars at the traffic light: Levi's Mustang, Aidan's Subaru, Ethan's Lamborghini, and a guy in a Chevrolet. I heard their engines from outside as they looked at each other. The camera showed each car and how it ignited. The flag girl came in the center wearing what normal flag girls did to catch everyone's attention. Everyone in the bistro stared at the TV as she took a white flag out of her crop top. She held it up as she glanced at each racer. I sipped my water eagerly at the thought of who'd win. Keene said they're good, but Levi's raced for three years. It's like everything happened in slow motion as she bent down and lowered the flag. Then they sped off.

Chevrolet was second as Aidan led the way. Levi trailed behind, but I knew him. The Chevrolet took a right turn, and out of nowhere Ethan popped out and bolted past him. Cheers filled the room as I looked around to see a familiar blond walk in. Oh no. I looked forward as I heard Carter's voice echo through the room. I placed my hand on my forehead to make myself less noticeable. I heard him approach girls and couldn't help but eavesdrop. When I turned, I saw the girl slap Carter then walk out of the bistro. I laughed at his probably lame pick-up line and decided to watch as he approached another group. He said a few lame ones but ended it off with a dirty one. I almost choked on my water as I looked over my shoulder to see that the girls gaped at him. The one he said it to stomped his foot with her heel then walked off with her friends. He yelped in pain as he spun around, which made me turn back quickly. I think he caught me as I heard footsteps behind me.

"Oh, girl, after tonight you'll never forget my name," he whispered. I tried so hard not to react but couldn't help it as I spat out my water. Out of the corner of my eye, I saw Carter raise a brow as he sat down next to me. I turned to him, and his eyes widened. "*Lana?*" he exclaimed. "What the hell are you doing here?"

"I should ask you the same thing. What's with the dirty pickup lines?"

"I'm bored, and I have needs." He winked. I scoffed as I turned back to the TV.

Ethan was in the lead as he tried to block Levi. The Chevrolet took a chance and bolted past the both of them. Carter scrunched his nose up as he took a sip of my refilled water. I knew he thought of the pick-up line he told me, and I couldn't help but grimace. I watched as he chugged down the whole thing then turned to me with a wicked look in his eye. "Look, Lana, you're my friend, but I simply cannot have sex with you even though I wan—"

"I don't want to!"

"Do you know how hard it was that time when I slept over?" he asked with a flustered look. "You move a lot in bed. That's why I had to go shower before you saw my friend."

"Too much information there, Carter."

"You're hot and everything, but I can't bang you—besides, bro code."

"Ugh!"

"Strict bro code, even though I want to."

"I'm going to sit over there now," I stated as I hopped off the stool and walked to the other side. I sat down and still got a view of the TV. Thankfully, Carter didn't follow as he saw another girl. People threw profanities at the TV as I glanced up. I could tell Levi was pissed since Ethan blocked him. Levi swerved onto the sidewalk as he squeezed his way past Ethan. I smirked as I watched Levi catch up to Aidan and the guy with the Chevrolet.

"Well, you seem lonely." A deep voice snapped me out of my thoughts. I spun around to see a guy who looked to be a few years older than me. He had long brunette hair and a pointy nose.

"Nope," I replied, then looked at the screen but noticed that he took a seat beside me.

"You look pretty bored." He placed a hand on my shoulder. "I can keep you comp—"

"There you are, gorgeous!" a familiar voice said as the guy dropped his hand. I watched as Carter squeezed in between us and literally blocked the guy from physical contact with me. "Who's your friend?"

"Brooke."

Carter let out a snort as he took in Brooke's appearance. "Brooke?"

"Yeah got a problem?" Brooke asked. I face palmed myself because I knew what was coming.

"That's a girl name," Carter stated as I rolled my eyes.

"No, it's not. Do I look like a girl to you?"

"Well, err…yeah," Carter said as he pointed to the long hair. Brooke stood up and towered over Carter as he clenched his fists. "I have slept with two Brookes, and they were definitely females, so I don't know what happened to you, bro."

Brooke let out a dry laugh as he ran his hand through his hair. I stood up and hid behind Carter, who seemed as big as his freaking ego.

"I'm going to give you three seconds to run, and if you're not gone, I'm going to beat the shit out of you, Blondie," Brooke hissed.

"Surprised you can actually count that high."

"Carter!" I yelled as I tugged on his arm.

"One."

"You're almost there."

"Two!"

I grabbed Carter by the ear and dragged him out of the bistro. I mouthed a "sorry" to Brooke, who glared at us. Once we were outside, I let go of him and watched as he rubbed his ear in pain.

"You have a tight grip," he moaned as he caressed his ear.

"And you are the stupidest person ever! Brooke is a unisex name!"

"I know, I just wanted to have fun." Carter

winked.

"Come on, let's go inside, and if he's there, I'm leaving you," I stated, since the race was almost finished and I wanted to see who won. Carter nodded and walked in front of me as we strolled back to the pub. He raised a hand and told me to wait while he peeked inside for Brooke.

"The she-male is gone," he whispered. I rolled my eyes at his immature behavior as we walked into the bistro. We decided to sit in a booth where we'd still see the TV. Everyone was occupied with the television as the race went on. I watched as Levi sped past Ethan and drove side by side with Aidan. The finish line was close as both cars leaped forward. Ethan caught up too as I bit the inside of my cheek. The guy with the Chevrolet was nowhere to be found as everyone focused on the three.

"Come on, Levi," I mumbled. Then what happened next took us by surprise as Levi swerved into Aidan's car and made him hit the brakes. All sorts of reactions spread through the room as people gasped, cheered, yelled, and some even ran outside. I watched as Ethan hit the brakes too because if he didn't, he would've driven right into Aidan.

"What the fuck?" Carter yelled as he rose to his feet. Then like always, Levi sped past the finish line as people applauded. I watched as Carter stared at the TV in disbelief, and I grinned. I approached him with a blank look on my face as I tapped him on the shoulder. "I'm gonna check if they're okay."

"No, wait!" I said, then pulled him back. "You can't let them know that I'm here."

"Why are you here in the first place, Lana?"

I anxiously licked my lips as I looked at the TV, then Carter. He followed my gaze as his eyes widened.

"You're with him?" he demanded as he pointed to the screen, which showed Levi.

"Well, no and yes. Please, Carter, I don't want any more trouble," I begged. He let out a deep sigh as he looked at me, then the TV. I watched as he ran his hand through his blond locks and shrugged.

"Fine, but then we act as if this whole 'pick up line' moment never happened, okay?" he asked with a grin.

"Deal."

He smiled as he walked out of the bistro, and I bit my lip agitatedly. I glanced back at the TV and saw Aidan's car stopped. As soon as it was parked, Aidan jumped out of the vehicle, followed by Blake, who sat in the passenger seat. They darted toward Levi, who smirked as people congratulated him. My eyes widened, as I knew what would happen, so I bolted toward the exit. I stood in the shadows as I watched Aidan approach Levi with a furious look.

"The fuck was that?" Aidan yelled as he pushed past the people.

"That was street racing…" Levi sarcastically replied.

"Dude, not cool," Blake said as he checked out Levi's car. I watched in amusement as Blake took out a cigarette and lit it, then took a drag and blew in Levi's face.

"Well, then, tell your titan-ass friend over there to not block like a freaking granny." Levi pointed at

Ethan.

"That doesn't mean you have to ruin my car!" Aidan yelled as he stood in front of Levi.

"Told you it's a shit car." Levi shrugged. Aidan was about to punch Levi, but Blake stopped him. I raised a brow as Blake slowly shook his head and glared at his cousin.

"Who are you?" Ethan piped up.

"You'll find out soon, Eth." Levi winked as Aidan rolled his eyes.

"Whatever. Come on, guys," he said as everyone followed him toward the bistro. I tried to mix in with the crowd as they passed yet looked at Blake. He had a cold look as he gazed at Levi's Mustang. They locked eyes as they gave each other a once over. They were similar in a way. Both had tattoos, leather jackets galore, and a nose piercing in the same place, undoubtedly giving the bad boy façade. The only difference was the color of their eyes…Levi had blue eyes, and Blake had brown. Blake gave a nod to Levi as he walked away. Once the coast was clear, I approached Levi and Keene. They leaned on the hood of the car as they smoked.

"I still got it!" Levi sang as he spotted me.

"You're an ass."

"Oh, come on. I spiced things up, didn't I?"

"You're not even here twenty-four hours, and you're already making enemies."

"Hey, at least that guy with the tattoos is cool." He winked. "Remind you of someone?"

"One asshole recognizes another asshole."

"You know him?" Levi asked as he tilted his head.

"Unfortunately," I mumbled. Levi nodded liberally as he dumped his cigarette on the ground. Keene hopped off the hood and hugged Levi.

"Bye, Keene," I said, then let his arms wrap around me.

"See you guys later," he said and backed away. "And stay out of trouble, Radcliff!"

"Can't make any promises!" Levi said as I chuckled. We got into his car and drove home. I was surprised he didn't have a girl with him before we got home. When he won, he usually had a girl in the backseat, and they'd bang. Ugh. I'd be off with Keene in the bistro until he was done. The thought of him in the back with another girl made me cringe. "Man, I never thought Ethan Baxter would do racing," Levi broke the silence. It was kind of interesting that Levi remembered Ethan and Aidan yet they couldn't recognize him.

"What do you expect? He literally comes to school with a new car every week," I said as Levi frowned.

"Sad they don't remember me."

"Well, you've changed. You have tattoos, a piercing, and you're taller and muscular."

"Hmm, so I'm muscular, hey?" he asked with a grin. I playfully punched him in the shoulder, and he laughed. I glanced at the time and saw that it was almost eleven p.m. If our parents were home, they'd be furious. Yet Levi was the eldest, so I'd blame it on hi—*oh, wait, I'm in charge.* I bit the inside of my cheek as we turned onto my street. My house was completely dark with only the porch light on. They must've piled into one car since Dad's police car was in the driveway along with Richard's car. Levi parked his car in front of the house, and we got out. From the corner of my eye, I noticed a light approach us.

"Oh, shit," I muttered as I quickened my pace.

"No! You locked the whole god damn house," Levi said as he gripped my wrist. "Let's go around the back."

He pulled me toward him as we ran around the house to where my window was. I glanced at the big tree in front of it and gulped.

"Come on, quick," Levi said as he crouched down by the tree and held his hands out.

"I've never climbed a tree before. You know I'm afraid of heights!" I called out.

"Well, now it's time to face that fear or our parents!" Levi hissed as he entwined his hands together. I let out a sigh as I stepped onto his hands so that he'd push me up. I grabbed onto the branch as I swung my leg over it and crawled to my window. The tree shook as Levi's weight was put on it. I heard voices from the front. I let out a yelp as I felt him smack my butt. "Today still, princess!"

"Hold your freaking horses and don't spank me!" I scoffed as I reached my window. Thankfully, it wasn't locked as I pushed it up and open. I quickly snuck inside and immediately ran toward my closet. I heard voices downstairs as I hunted for my pajamas. I ripped the leather jacket off as soon as I could.

"Well, you're eager," Levi said as he saw my underwear. I rolled my eyes as I slipped on my pajamas and put my hair up into a ponytail. I heard footsteps from outside my door as I turned to Levi. He was there a second ago. I glanced at my bathroom and noticed a shadow underneath it. My room door flew open as Dad and Jade came into the room. My eyes widened, as the first place they looked was the bed.

"Where's Levi?" Jade asked as I plopped down on my bed.

"He's in the bathroom."

"Okay, well, err…goodnight, honey,"

"Goodnight, Dad, goodnight, Aunt Jade," I responded. As soon as they were out of the room, my bathroom door burst open with Levi in a white tee and jeans. His hair was in all directions as he grinned at me.

"Wasn't that fun?"

"Sure, even though we almost got caught," I muttered as I crawled into the warmth of my bed.

"Uh huh…there's more where that came from." He winked then walked out of the room. I rolled my eyes for what seemed to be the millionth time today as I turned on my side. I turned the light off, and somehow, I fell asleep faster than any other night.

***

It's weird that on Friday night everyone came to sleep over and we ended up in the living room, thus allowing me to sleep. On Saturday night, I slept in Benny's basement like a baby. Now I'm up in my room, and it's the first night in weeks that I've gotten real sleep in this room. My eyes fluttered open as I stared at the ceiling. I haven't slept so well in a very long time. The sun shone through the window. The sweet cologne lingered through the air as light snores filled my ea—*wait, what?* I turned my head to see black hair beside me, my eyes widened as I glanced down to see his tattooed arm wrapped loosely around my torso. I flicked Levi's hair, and he groaned. I let out a huff as I pried his arm off me and got up. I literally groaned as the thought of school entered my mind.

"What the hell are you doing in my bed?" I demanded as I got up. I folded my arms over my chest as I stared at him. He turned over so that he was on his back as he rubbed his eyes. Once he was done, he stretched his arms and placed them behind his head as he watched me.

"It's cold down there."

"And you couldn't ask for more blankets?"

"I didn't want to wake you up, plus you looked so warm and cuddly I couldn't resist."

I shook my head as I walked to my closet and took out an outfit for today. As it was a Monday, I didn't want to play dress up, so I decided on a black and white striped sweater with blue jeans. I gathered my things and went into the bathroom. I showered as quickly as possible and slipped on my clothes. Levi was nowhere to be found, so I figured he was downstairs. I put on my white Converse and grabbed a jacket along with my backpack. I walked downstairs and into the kitchen where Mom made coffee and Levi casually sat by the small table.

"This is new." He gestured to the pair of glasses in his hand. They were the Ray Bans that Ethan got me after Benny destroyed my others.

"Give them back," I demanded as I plopped down on the seat opposite him and reached over. He pulled the glasses away. He continued to laugh at my failed attempts but soon handed them to me.

"How did you sleep on the sofa bed, Levi?" Mom asked as she placed a cup of coffee in front of me.

"Lovely, Angie. It was so comfortable and warm." He sent me a wink.

"Enough blankets?"

"Uh huh, I snuggled into them, making it even warmer."

"I'm glad," Mom commented as Dad entered the room.

"Morning, Bobby!" Levi belted out as Dad groaned.

"Not in the mood, Levi."

"Honey, why don't you take the day off? You've been quite busy these past few days," Mom suggested.

"Even if I wanted to, I can't. We have to do a follow-up, and I have a short meeting with Detective Kale," Dad said as I quietly sipped my coffee. A familiar honk broke the silence as I stood up. I chugged down the coffee and approached my parents.

"Well, good luck, Dad." I kissed his cheek, then hugged my mom.

"Don't I get a hug and a kiss?" Levi cooed as he opened his arms and pouted. I slowly shook my head as I waved, then dashed out of the house. Benny flicked through the channels on his radio as I heard footsteps behind me.

“What the fuck is he doing here?” Levi hissed as I walked toward the car.

“He’s my ride to school,” I said as Benny glanced up.

“You’re not riding with him!” Levi ordered, then squinted his eyebrows. “Shit, that came out wrong.”

I ignored his protests as I climbed into the car and shut the door. Once I was buckled in, I told Benny to drive and ignore Levi’s protests.

Chapter Three

Lana

There were a few people inside as Mr. Bronx rested behind his desk with his legs propped up on the table. I walked past him as he sent me a mischievous smile.

"The devil has arrived," he said, and I only thought of one person, Levi Radcliff.

"Uh-huh," I said as I walked to the back of the class and sat in the corner. Aidan hopped into the classroom and waved at Mr. Bronx as he passed. Mr. Bronx raised a brow at Aidan's weird actions but gladly waved back. He plopped himself in front of me with a big grin spread across his face. "You look happy."

"Well, I'm not!" Aidan said with a tight-lipped smile. "My car is freaking damaged, so the only way to feel better is to do something stupid."

"Aren't you supposed to be angry?" I asked.

"Lana dear, people let out their anger in different ways," he assured me as he stood up and glanced at the window. "I need your help. When I say go, you must open the window but make it look as casual and good girl as you can make it, okay?"

"Err…okay," I said as he went to sit at another table, not too far for him to talk to me. As everyone else piled into the classroom, I glanced at the window. Nick sat in front of me, and I greeted him. Mr. Bronx took the attendance as I took out my stuff for Calculus. Aidan turned to me and then mouthed a go. I squinted my eyes as I glanced at Mr. Bronx. He was busy with a student, so I took it as a chance and walked to the window, then opened it. Out of nowhere, a bottle was thrown into the class, yet I ducked in time.

"Ouch!" a familiar voice roared. I scurried back to my seat as I searched for the bottle. It must've landed on Austin's head, as he held it in one hand and rubbed his head with the other. It looked to be a spray can, but there was nothing written on it.

"Okay, we're doing the warm-up sheets first," Mr. Bronx announced as he walked to the chalkboard. From the corner of my eye, I saw something move. I snapped my head to see Liam climb in; he must've thrown the bottle. Nick glared at his friend as we watched Liam rise into the classroom. He landed with a big thud on the floor as Mr. Bronx turned around. Liam lay flat on the ground as I watched Mr. Bronx scout the classroom.

"Austin, if you're going to have water bottles in the classroom make sure they don't distract you," he said, because Austin still held the bottle with a puzzled look.

"Mr. Bronx, this isn't a wate—"

"Drink your water, then set it on the table so you can get on with your work." Aidan let out a snort as Mr. Bronx watched Austin. As soon as Austin opened the bottle, an odd smell filled the air. Mr. Bronx scrunched his nose up as he waved his hand in front of his face.

"Eww, what's that smell?" Austin gagged.

"All right, who was that?" Mr. Bronx demanded as he grabbed a stack of worksheets.

"Whoever smelt it, dealt it," Aidan said as he pointed to Austin. It must've been a fart can. Austin spun around and glared at Aidan as he threw the bottle in the trashcan at the back of the classroom. The odd odor still lingered through the air as people covered their noses.

"If I throw a stick, will you leave?" he asked Aidan.

"Is the stick from up your ass?" Aidan shot back. Everyone watched as the two glared at each other, but my focus was on Liam, who crawled behind my chair. He slowly sat in the desk behind Aidan and winked at me. Austin and Aidan continued to bicker as I rolled my eyes. Mr. Bronx approached the two with the stack of papers in his hands.

"Both of you shut up, or I'll send you to the office and Principal West can deal with you." He gave all of us a paper, including Liam.

"Ugh, not this again," Aidan groaned as he looked at the Pythagoras sheet. "Mr. Bronx, I could've sworn we did this in like seventh or eighth grade."

"That's why it's called a warm-up sheet, Mr. Rowley. To wake up that thing you call a brain,"

Mr. Bronx replied.

"Why can't we get work that's our grade level?"

"I did at the beginning of the school year, but you were the one who said, and I quote, 'Bronx should give us easy work since it's so freaking early in the morning.' Remember?"

"Nope," Aidan replied as he stared at the sheet.

"Wait, so we've been doing seventh grade work all along?" Liam piped up. "And here I thought I was a freaking genius since I was getting them all right!"

"See? Even Mr. Sanchez gets it right. All you need is a brain and a calculator, right, Lana?" Mr. Bronx asked as he turned to me.

"Wha—that's not fair! You're asking the smartest girl in the class! She even remembers how she was born!" Aidan said before I could reply. I sent him a glare. "I can't even remember how I got to school this morning. Do you wanna know why?" he asked Mr. Bronx, who stared at Aidan with a blank look.

"Why, Mr. Rowley? Please tell me because I'm so interested."

"Thanks for asking! Some douche who looks oddly familiar decided to dent my freaking car with his black vintage Mustang!" Aidan exclaimed. When Aidan said black vintage Mustang, I felt Mr. Bronx's eyes on me. "So I had to get a ride with this guy and his girlfriend." Aidan pointed at Nick.

"Great life story!" Mr. Bronx cut off Nick before he'd argue. "Now finish the warm-up sheet then we'll move on to today's work."

I watched as he ran a hand through his hair in

frustration as he walked back to his desk. Before he sat down, Mr. Bronx spun around and squinted his eyes at Liam.

"You're not even in this class!"

Liam shot up in his seat as he looked around the classroom with a dumbfounded look on this face. "Wait, so this isn't Social Studies?"

***

The rest of the day was spent with people fooling around. Especially Aidan and Liam. Thanks to them, we had a ton of homework for winter break, but I was going to start on it when I get home. I walked with Miranda and Melissa to the locker rooms.

"So is Levi keeping his dick in his pants so far?" Miranda asked as we entered the locker rooms.

"Uh huh," I hummed as the thought of him almost kissing me entered my mind.

"Oh, sweet Jesus, Lana, he is hot," Melissa said as we got undressed.

"Good to know," I mumbled as I slipped on my polo shirt. Once we were done, we walked out and into the corridor to join the rest of the class. I watched as Ethan and a few other guys helped Coach Harris get a few things out of storage.

"Since I'm in a good mood today, we'll be playing badminton!" Coach yelled as he motioned for us to follow him. We followed him into the gym. Once we arrived, I stood with Melissa and watched as they set up.

"What am I? Flypaper for freaks?" a familiar

voice screeched. I turned my head to see Jennifer's glare at a guy who tried to give her a shuttlecock. He threw his hands up in innocence and backed away.

"What's up with Miss Gold-digger?" Miranda asked as we watched Kelly try to comfort her. I noticed Kelly dyed her hair again since the ombre highlights faded. She now had red tips.

"Her brother got arrested again," Melissa muttered as we watched the two comfort each other. No family was perfect, that's for sure. Jennifer Brighton might be rich, but she had many problems in her family. Her dad had a mistress, and her brother was a huge drug addict.

"What are you three posing here for?" Coach Harris voice roared as he passed us rackets and two shuttlecocks. "Get practicing. There will be a short game later in the lesson."

I let out a huff as we walked to the other side of the court and practiced. I hit the shuttlecock with my racket and watched it make its way toward Miranda. She effortlessly hit it back, but me being lazy, I never thought it'd pass me. I groaned to get the shuttlecock and looked over my shoulder to see that she played with Melissa.

"Looking for this?" a deep voice asked. I turned my head to see Blake sitting at the end of the stands while Carter leaned against it. I let the racket hang loosely by my side as I held my hand out. Blake shook his head as he observed the shuttlecock.

"Aren't you guys playing?"

"Badminton isn't my thing," Blake said as he tossed the shuttlecock up in the air and caught it. I let out a huff as I marched to him and crouched down for the shuttlecock. He leaned back and caught it behind his back. I tried to reach over him and bent down.

"Come on, Blake, just give it to me!" I demanded as I stretched out even further and dropped my racket.

"Oh, so you want this shuttlecock?" he asked as Carter laughed. I cursed under my breath as I tripped over his foot and fell on top of him. His light dog chain was in my mouth, so my face was buried in his chest. I let out a groan as I glanced up with my glasses falling to my nose. He smirked then pushed them back up. "I like this position," he said as my cheeks flushed. I quickly grabbed the shuttlecock, ignoring his smirk. I pushed myself and straddled him, looking at the shuttlecock. He lay there on his back as if he were on the beach. I stared at him as he placed his hands behind his head and winked at me.

"PDA," Carter coughed, and I instantly stood up. I looked at Carter, and my eyes widened. His beautiful face was jacked up. He had a swollen eye, a bruise on his cheek, and a cut on his jaw.

"What the hell happened to you?" I demanded.

"By that tone, shows how much you care," he said sarcastically. "Turns out Brooke had a few friends, and guess what their names were?"

"What?"

"Leslie and Perry."

"Let me guess, you've slept with a Leslie and Perry and they were both girls?"

"Yeah, and they weren't too happy when I told

them that."

"Dude, your fucking name is even unisex," Blake chimed in as I threw my hands up in exasperation.

"Thank you!" I said as Blake raised a brow.

"Wait…how do you know who Brooke is?" he asked. Before I answered, we heard loud footsteps approach us. I spun around and saw Aidan. I squinted my eyes as I took in his badminton outfit.

"Bro, what are you wearing?" Carter asked as he skipped to us. Aidan wore the school polo shirt, yet he borrowed a pair of shorts that were apparently too short for him along with blue runners and knee socks. I watched as he posed in front of us and stretched.

"I love badminton!" He smiled, then made lunges.

"Oh my god, those shorts are too short for you!" I shrieked and turned away since his crotch moved.

"I can't believe I'm related to you," Blake muttered as Aidan straightened. He looked at me, and I tried so hard not to look down. The worst part was that the shorts were white.

"Eyes up here, sweet cheeks." Aidan whistled as I rolled my eyes. He took the shuttlecock and racket with a grin. He threw the shuttlecock up then walloped it. I watched as it flew across the gym and hit the wall. My brows raised in amazement as I turned to him. I watched as Aidan held the racket back as he aimed for Carter. He let go with the other hand, and it smacked against Carter's butt.

"Fuck, that hurt, you ass wipe!" Carter yelled as he ran after Aidan. I let out a chuckle as the two ran around the gym and decided to sit down next to Blake, since I didn't have a racket. The last encounter I had with Blake was when he told me everything would get better. Before that was the kiss we almost shared. It was weird. I couldn't figure him out. He acted as if nothing happened, like always.

"Yo, guys, watch out!" someone yelled as we looked up. It was too late as the shuttlecock came and landed on my thigh. Blake gave me a concerned look as I awkwardly rubbed my thigh. "Sorry, Lana." The guy shrugged as he took the shuttlecock from Blake.

"Don't be sorry, be careful," Blake hissed as the guy raised his arms and walked off. "You okay?"

"Yeah, it still hurts, but I'll be all right."

"Anything exciting happen in the last twenty-four hours?"

"Err…not really."

"Your dad back yet?"

"Yeah, he arrived yesterday morning." I frowned at the thought of my mother freaking out when Dad got shot.

"You don't seem happy."

"I'm barely happy anymore."

"Why is that?"

"Dad got shot, but thankfully he was wearing a bulletproof vest," I mumbled as I turned to Blake. His jaw tightened as he looked at the ground. I then remembered that his dad died and cursed under my breath.

"Is he okay?"

"Still overprotective, but he's good."

"He might be the overprotective dad but," Blake said as he stared me dead in the eye, "he's the only guy that's ever going to be there for you."

"Tell me about your dad," I blurted out as he raised a brow. "T-that's if y-you want to."

"Okay. He was the best dad in the world," Blake began as I crossed my legs and got comfortable. Somehow, I liked when Blake spoke about personal things. He talked with such need and emotion that it felt like someone else spoke. "I bonded with him more than Axel did. He owned a motor shop in Minnesota, and I hung around there a lot. Axel bonded with my uncle more, who was an alcoholic." Blake let out a laugh. "We used to do everything together and talked about anything and everything. He even helped me get my first girlfriend.

"All the guys wanted her because she was so beautiful. Loads of guys asked her to prom, I asked my dad for advice, and in the end, she chose me. I was surprised because I looked like shit back then.

"We dated for a couple of months, and in that time my dad became distant. I didn't know if it was because of my girlfriend or his work, but we rarely talked. I always asked him what was wrong, and he replied with, 'I'm okay, just living in the moment.' I took it as nothing, but Axel didn't.

"There were constant fights between my dad and Axel, so he left to go and live with my uncle in another city. The house became quiet, and Mom told me that's it's nothing, yet I knew she was lying. That's when I started smoking; I couldn't handle all the stress and the quiet, so I found a pack in Axel's old room.

"Before summer break, there was a huge fight between my mom and dad. I overheard them, and that's how I found out that my dad was diagnosed with prostate cancer two years before." He did that thing again where he laughed. "Turns out that's how my great-grandfather and all his siblings died. Runs in the family, I guess," Blake muttered with a depressed look. "It was too late, though; he had a month. One fucking month, yet he didn't tell me.

"I went over to my girlfriend and told her, and instead of comforting me, she told me to man up. She didn't like that I smoked or that I owned a motorcycle…like I can't fucking help it if my dad owned a motor shop.

"The bitch told me to call her when I decided to 'man up.' Summer came along, and we all flew down here to visit Aidan. That's how I got this tattoo because I lost some bet." He pointed to the feather. "We flew back, and after all the tests and chemotherapy, Dad was put into the hospital. I couldn't take it anymore, so the cigarettes increased, I got mood swings, tattoos, and went to juvie. I even had a special cop who always knew me," he said, then laughed bitterly. "One day I visited my dad and told him that she broke up with me, and all he said was that she was never the one." Blake shook his head. "I was fucking pissed because he never even met her, so I left. Little did I know that was the last time I'd hear my dad's voice."

Silence surrounded us as I took in Blake's words. Prostate cancer was common, and I had a family member who died of breast cancer. I didn't know what to say. Yet Blake sucked in a deep breath and continued.

"Axel came back for the funeral, along with our uncle. He didn't even cry, but I did because through everything, Dad tried to be strong for me. Someone had to be the strong one in the family, and it was always him.

"Our uncle wanted the motor shop even though I wanted it because I basically knew everything. He wanted to take my mom to court, but she wasn't up for that, so he got it. We were left with his will, but the money was gone soon after. No doubt Axel took it." He reached into his pocket for a cigarette. He gave it to me, and I held it as he took out his matches. I held it up to my lips as he lit a match and flicked it over the cigarette. Tobacco filled our noses as I inhaled then gave it to him. "So I took the bitch's advice and decided to man up. I touched up my motorcycle, wore my dad's jackets, smoked, slept around, and most of all didn't give a flying fuck what people thought about me.

"Because through everything, nobody helped me to cope. Axel was gone, and Mom worked her ass off so I basically could do anything I want. Then Aidan's mom said we should move here to get away from everything, so we did."

I figured he was done as silence took over us. I didn't know what to say because that was a lot to go through on your own. I didn't want to apologize because I knew he'd scowl.

"Wow, so that's how Blake Gunner became a bad boy," I said after a while. I watched as he blew out the smoke and sent me a grin. We sat in silence as we stared at each other. Sadness mixed with secrecy filled his brown eyes, and that somehow made me captivated.

"Hey, you two!" a familiar voice boomed as I tore my gaze away from Blake and saw Coach Harris. My eyes widened as I stood up. "Gunner, you might look cool, but you're not. No smoking on school grounds!" he shouted, then turned to me. "And you, Willson? I thought better of you than hanging out with a delinquent like him," he said, then handed me a racket. "Then again, you were in detention for slapping West's daughter." He shoved a racket in Blake's chest.

"That was a good slap," Blake commented as he dropped the cigarette on the ground.

"No one asked for your input, Gunner. You both get detention for tomorrow afternoon," Coach said as my jaw dropped. "One for not participating, and two for smoking! Now get your butts on the court before I report you two!"

"Thanks a lot," I mumbled as we walked toward Carter and Miranda.

"You're welcome." Blake smiled as he twirled the racket in his hand.

"We'll be doing short games now!" Coach yelled.

"Can he get any louder?" Kelly asked.

"Imagine him in bed," Carter said, which resulted in everyone throwing profanities at him.

***

I didn't think Coach was serious when he said that Blake and I had detention tomorrow. I sighed at the card that I had to get signed. Dad was going to kill me. I groaned as I dumped the card in my backpack and walked out of the school building. Everyone lingered downstairs as I approached them.

"Please, dude, I don't want to ride with them. They're like those clingy couples, and it's so awkward," Aidan nagged Benny.

"Hey!" Nick said as he put an arm around Melissa's shoulder.

"I'm already taking La—"

"Hey, Aidan, look—it's your friend." Carter laughed as he pointed across the street. We whipped our heads to see Levi parking his car on the curb. My eyes widened as Miranda stared at me.

"Shit's about to get real," she whispered as I sent her a glare.

"I think I'll walk. Yeah, that's a good idea. See you guys tomorrow!" I rushed out then ran toward Levi. Being the prick that Levi was, he got out of the car and leaned against it. Once he noticed me, he opened his arms. I ignored him as I went around his vehicle to the passenger seat.

"Aww, sad she doesn't wanna get in your car?" Levi cooed as I glanced up. It turned out they followed me. They looked at Levi and me. As I dumped my bag in Levi's car, I noticed Blake squinted his eyes.

"Dude, what you did last night was not cool," Aidan said.

"Yeah, sorry about that, Aidan," Levi said.

"How do you know my na—"

"It's Levi, you idiot!" Miranda cut off Aidan, and his eyes widened.

"I don't think we've officially met. Heard a shitload about you. My name is Blake." Blake stuffed his hands in his pockets.

"Levi. Cool tattoos," Levi said as he looked at Blake's arms.

"Nice bird," Blake said as he looked at the tattoo on Levi's neck.

"Okay, if we're done with the introductions, what are you doing here?" Miranda asked as she stared at Levi.

"Just here to get my princess," Levi said as he sent me a wink.

"Well, no need since I do that already," Benny muttered. I glanced at Blake, who seemed interested at the looks Levi and Benny gave each other.

"Well, too bad. I'm here now, and I don't think she wants to drive with a psycho," Levi stated.

"Levi, give it a fucking rest. We all made mistakes, right?" I glared at him. I didn't know why, but whenever he was here, I cussed a lot. He knew precisely when and where to push my buttons.

"At least mine were forgivable," he sang as his eyes flicked toward Benny.

"What'd you do?" Blake snorted as he took a drag from his cigarette.

"Fucked her then I left her," Levi responded as I scoffed. Blake's amused expression changed as his jaw tightened.

"Fuck you." I rolled my eyes at Levi, who laughed.

"Okay," Melissa said as she entwined her hands

with Nick's. "See you." She pulled him toward his car. She turned back and gave me the thumbs up. I sighed.

"Look, can't we all be friends?" Liam asked as he looked at Levi and Benny. Benny glared at Levi, who took a cigarette from Blake. I knitted my brows as I watched them; they'd only met and already acted like friends.

"Nope," Levi responded.

"Never," Benny muttered. Liam groaned as he backed away. I watched as the school grounds got emptier, and silence overtook us. Levi leaned against his car as he turned to Aidan with a grin.

"How's your shit-ass car doing?" he asked.

"Sorry, I didn't get that. I don't speak bullshit," Aidan stated in a frustrated tone.

"Would you all just stop?" Miranda demanded. "Can't you see he's doing this to piss you off, to get under your skin and then use you?" She let out an annoyed scream and marched toward her car, Marcus following close behind.

"Thanks a lot, jackass," I said as we watched Miranda viciously get in her car and drive off.

"I knew she liked me," Levi stated. The guys laughed except Benny and Ethan. I noticed Liam checked out Levi's car and raised a brow.

"Dude, what's the horsepower on this thing?" Liam asked.

"Three-thirty-five to three-sixty, I guess." Levi shrugged.

"To be honest, this thing was a beauty last night," Blake commented as he leaned against it.

"Uh huh, and when I win again, we're all going

out and celebrating," Levi said as he sent me a wink.

"How do you know that you'll win?" Benny asked. Levi leaned off his car as he let out a chuckle. He stood right in front of Benny and held a poker face.

"Because I always win."

***

I gave Levi the silent treatment as we drove back home. I was beyond pissed that he'd treat Benny like that when he was just as guilty! Then when he dropped me off, he drove on and said he wouldn't be back for dinner. Good, because he didn't deserve my mother's freaking delicious food!

It was already after ten, and I was busy with homework. I'd done four pages of work already when a knock on my door disturbed me.

"Lana, you still busy?" Richard asked as he tiptoed into the room.

"Yeah, I'm almost done though," I said.

"I heard you want to go to Yale," he said as he took a seat on my bed.

"Yeah, but I'm looking at other universities too."

"Well, hopefully everything goes well and you get into there. Over the years I've known you, Lana, you've built yourself up well," he said as I bit the inside of my cheek. "We've all made mistakes and you either accept it or learn from it."

"Yep," I said as I avoided eye contact. "Where's Levi?"

"He's downstairs, came back a few minutes ago.

I think he was out with Keene," Richard said as he stood up.

"Okay, well, goodnight," I said as I stood up from my desk chair.

"Goodnight." He walked out of the room. I went to the bathroom and decided to put on my pajamas. I put my hair up into a bun then walked out of the toilet. I took my glasses off and set them on my bedside table and looked at my phone. Miranda hadn't messaged me yet; Melissa said she needed to cool off.

"I'm sorry," a familiar voice said as I spun around. Levi leaned against my doorframe in his sweatpants and shirt. I crossed my arms over my chest as I looked down. He let out a frustrated sigh as I heard him come into the room and lock the door.

"You can't expect me to forgive you just like that if you're just gonna treat Benny like shit the whole time." I raised my voice. He put his index finger to his lips and took his other hand to point to next door to where his parents were.

"He deserves it for doing that stuff to you," he said and stepped closer.

"Can't you just move on?" I yelled in a whisper. "You're in the wrong too for acting like a dick last year, so don't just think you're off the hook because Benny is my friend now."

"At least I didn't hurt you!"

"You have some nerve to say that! I mean, Aidan didn't do anything wrong, yet you act like a douche toward him!"

"We're just fucking around. I went over to

Blake's house, and they were all there, so we caught up."

"Then why do you have to act like such a dick the whole fucking time? It's like you're waiting for me to yell at you, asshole!"

"Fine. I'll try to be nicer from now on, but you gained a clever mouth over the past year."

"Wonder where I got it from?"

"Sssh, you better keep that mouth of yours shut," he yelled in a whisper.

"Or what?" I asked as he inched closer. I backed away, but my legs hit the edge of the bed.

"Or I'll shut it for you, my princess." He smirked as he pressed himself up against me.

"I'd like to see you try."

It's like he waited for me to say something like that because as soon as I said it, he wrapped one arm around me. He put it the other hand on my cheek and smashed his lips against mine. The kiss was forced yet filled with need as he groaned. I lost my balance as I tried to pull away from him, so we fell on the bed. Our lips were still attached as he hovered over me. I used my fists to hit his chest. He grabbed my wrists and pinned them on either side of my face as he pulled away. Our breaths filled the room as he pressed his forehead against mine. His grip tightened on my wrists as he bit my bottom lip then kissed me again.

"Levi, what are yo—"

"Please, just one last time before I lose you," he breathed out as I looked into his wild blue eyes. Somehow, I felt weak under him as I slowly closed my eyes. I parted my lips as I felt his brush against mine.

Chapter Four

Lana

The feeling of something that is bad, but in a way, it's okay? I always wondered what it meant. I finally understood as I lay in my bed and stared at the ceiling. I probably woke up ten minutes ago. Through my window, the sky looked gray and dull, another sign that it's a cold, miserable day in winter. I glanced to the side and watched Levi sleep next to me, his black hair in my face. He was shirtless and only wore his sweatpants while I wore his shirt—just his shirt. I hated him so much yet last night said otherwise.

My alarm went off, but Levi turned it off. He let out a hoarse groan as he turned to face me. I watched as Levi took his arm and wrapped it around my torso as he brought me closer. I squinted my eyes as he snuggled into my neck, but I immediately pushed him away. I forced myself up and looked at my alarm clock. It was six-thirty as I hopped out of bed. Thankfully, Levi's shirt ended at my thighs as I walked to my bedside table and grabbed my glasses. I quickly put them on and tied my hair up into a bun. I felt a smack on my butt, and I spun around to glare at Levi. He rested leisurely on my bed with his hands behind his neck as he smirked at me.

"Stop it!"

"You never said anything last night when I did it."

I flipped him off as I walked to my closet. I didn't know why, but I felt guilty. He always controlled me and got what he wanted. It made me confused because I'd never hate him. Last night felt so nostalgic as I remembered the past when it was just the two of us.

I grabbed a warm, comfy outfit for the day, then walked into the bathroom. I shut the door and made sure to lock it, then turned on the shower. Once I was done, I quickly put on my clothes and walked out. Levi was still in my bed. He had a wicked look in his eyes as his lips pulled up into a smirk. I ignored him and spun around to face my mirror. I brushed my hair, noticing his stare through the mirror. Then I saw it. I stared at it. At first, I didn't think it was real as I ran my hand on it, but it was pure and tender. Right above my collarbone was a hickey. I heard Levi snicker as he realized I had noticed it. I spun around and flung the brush at him.

"Hey, watch it!" he exclaimed as he ducked.

"Why?" I hissed as I pulled off my sweater, then rummaged through my closet for the right shirt that covered the hickey.

"Leaving my mark on the world."

I took a thick gray scarf and put it on along with

my glasses. Okay, it's covered, but if the scarf moved, then the whole world would see. I grabbed my backpack, forgetting it was open from last night. Something fell out, and as I was about to get it, Levi beat me to it.

"Damn. Smoking during periods and not participating. What happened, princess?"

"Nothing, and I wasn't even smoking! Blake was!" I said, then put on my brown boots.

"You gonna let your parents sign this?"

"I have to, otherwise I'll get another dete—" I cut myself off as I watched Levi take a pen from my desk. He scribbled on the paper and handed it to me once he was done. "H-how do you know my dad's signature?"

"Uncle Griff taught me how to forge signatures years ago. How do you think I barely got into trouble at school?"

I let out a chuckle as I stuffed the paper in my bag. We strolled downstairs, and thankfully nobody was there. Levi went into the living room as I walked to the kitchen. I made myself coffee and toast, then sat by the island. I nervously tugged on my scarf as I sipped my coffee.

"Morning, sweetie," my mother's voice boomed through the kitchen.

"Morning," I replied. Mom kissed me on the forehead, then walked to the fridge, all dressed and ready for work. I watched as she took out a tub of yogurt and spoon. She spun around with an upset look on her face, then sat opposite me. "Everything okay?"

"Not really," she sighed. "Lana, I have to talk to

you."

"Okay."

"I know that we had this talk when you turned sixteen, but you're eighteen now, and at this age, teenagers are quite busy," she emphasized.

"Err...okay."

"Your hormones are everywhere, and I understand that you just want to experiment," she whispered. My eyes widened because she must've heard us last night. My parents' bedroom was down the hall, and Levi's parents were right next door. "It's the talk...the birds and the bees." Oh no. They heard us. We're doomed. Yet I could've sworn whenever I wanted to say something Levi muffled it with his hand or mouth. "Or as Miranda says, 'Netfix—"

"It's Netflix, Mom."

"Yes! Yes! Netflix and chill!" she said.

"What about it?"

"Ever since I saw Carter in your bed, it gave me chills. A million scenarios ran through my head, but I saw that both of you had clothing on and a pillow separating you two," she explained as I gripped my coffee mug.

"Then why did you say 'How was your night with Mr. Blondie' instead of shouting at me?" I asked as the thought of Carter entered my mind.

"I trust you, Lana, and well...I didn't see any protection in the bin."

"*Mom!*"

"I'm sorry, but I just wanted to let you know that I'm here for you, honey, and we've all been through that phase!" she added as I scrunched my nose.

"You've been hanging out with a lot of boys lately, and one of them is bound to fall in love with you, so just remember."

"I don't want to fall in love ag—"

"I'm a doctor, and I don't want to deliver a baby from you when you're so young."

"Why do you bring this up now?"

"Well, your father and I wanted to talk to you about it, but he's stubborn, so I had to sooner or later."

"So not for any other particular reason?"

"Nope. Oh, and next time let me know when you're having a boy over. Other than Levi, of course…we trust him," she said as a smile broke onto her face.

"I feel like a whore now." I frowned.

"Oh, don't worry, dear, we've all been through it," Mom assured me as she stood up. I sat with a puzzled look on my face as she walked out of the room. That's one way to start a Tuesday. I grabbed my backpack and walked into the living room. Levi was on the sofa. He was casually playing his electric guitar. He offered to take me to school, and I gladly accepted, because I had to tell him about the conversation I had with my mother.

***

When I walked down the hallways of Jefferson High, I was still ignored but conscious about the scarf around my neck. Anyone who towered over me could peek at it. I kept my head down as I strolled to my locker. I opened it yet wanted to get to Miss Rosa's class as soon as possible.

"Morning, gorgeous." I looked over my shoulder to see Carter.

"Hi, Carter."

"You okay?" He leaned forward as I squirmed.

"Yes!" I turned away, but it was too late, because being the annoying player that he was, he saw it.

"No freaking way, and here I was going to tell you what night I had!" Carter exclaimed as he tugged on my scarf. I smacked his hand away as I turned to him.

"Not helping!"

"Aww, Lana wants to cover it up so she won't get into twouble," Carter cooed as he pinched my cheeks.

"Are you gonna help me or just make fun of me?" I asked as I slapped his hands away.

"Ugh, please, Lana, you're talking to Carter Halls, professional hickey star and sex god." I rolled my eyes. "You wanna see mine?" He raised his shirt.

"No thanks."

"This is how you do it," he said as he began to fix my scarf. He lifted it up and took a quick glance at it. "Damn, that'll take a few days to go away." He whistled.

"Just fix it, please," I begged. Carter continued to adjust my scarf as I glanced over his shoulder. My eyes widened as I spotted Blake walking down the hall. "Shit!" I muttered as I pulled away from Carter and looked at my locker.

"Wha—oh, 'sup, bro?" Carter greeted.

"What are you two doing?"

"Oh, nothing! Just enjoying this lovely day!" Carter laughed nervously as I shook my head in disappointment. My thoughts went back to the day of the drugs, and he tried to play cool, yet he was the worst liar ever.

"It's raining outside," Blake stated.

"I don't care. It's still a lovely day," Carter said uneasily. Blake raised a brow at his friend's weird behavior.

"Are you trying to hide the fact that you didn't get laid last night?"

I scrunched my nose up at the thought of why Blake assumed that, of all things.

"No! I did get laid, in fact by twins. Goddamn, bro, you mus—"

"Okay, eww! I don't want you guys standing by my locker and talking about that stuff."

"Yeah, you got plenty of that last night," Carter mumbled as Blake walked to the other side of my locker. I sent Carter a glare as Blake leaned on the locker next to me.

"You coming to detention?" he asked.

"Like I have a choice."

"How'd you get it signed?" he asked, and I tried so hard not to grin.

"Levi forged my dad's signature," I said, then turned to Blake. "I heard he came to your house?"

"Yeah, turns out we have a lot in common, and he's not such a bad guy, right, Carter?" Blake asked. Carter nodded.

"He said something happened between you two?" Carter asked.

"Yeah, one day he was here, and then the

next…he was gone," I mumbled, then pressed the books against my chest. Carter's eyes flicked to Blake then me as the silence stretched between us. The bell rang as I shut my locker. Blake walked off while I went with Carter to Miss Rosa's English class.

***

I stared at the detention slip in my hands as I walked to the classroom. I thought Thanksgiving would be the last. It was all Blake's fault; I did nothing. Well, I did do nothing as in not participating. I let out a sigh as I pushed open the door. There were a few people already there. It was the same girl and boy from the last time who asked if I was in the right place, then a few other people along with Blake. I glanced at the teacher's desk and resisted the need to roll my eyes. I'd prefer Mr. George who slept, or even Coach Harris, but Mr. Bronx?

"Lana, you need an invitation to sit down or what?" he asked as I handed him the slip. I gave him a blank look as he read the sheet then let out a chuckle. I spun around and sat behind Blake. He stood up, then sat on his desk, putting his feet on the chair to face me. "Hey, redhead?" Mr. Bronx piped up as he looked at us. Everyone turned to look at the girl and boy who were in the back of the classroom. She bobbed her head to absolutely nothing. The guy widened his eyes as he stared at Mr. Bronx. Blake and I turned back to the teacher, only to see his arm stretched out. We watched as the guy rose from his seat and strolled to the front. On the way, he stumbled and almost fell as people snickered. I watched as he pulled out a bag from his jacket and gave it to Mr. Bronx, who had his legs on the table. My eyes widened as I glanced at the bag of weed. "Don't know why West hasn't expelled you two yet," Mr. Bronx said as he shook his head.

"Word would get out that his students are smoking weed and shit," the guy stated, then slowly walked back.

"You should consider going to church once in a while," Mr. Bronx said as he observed the bag. "And while you're at it, dunk your head in the holy water."

I watched as Mr. Bronx stuffed the bag in his jacket, probably to get rid of it later. He then went back to his phone as I looked up at Blake. He already stared at me with a blank look. I raised a brow in which he squinted his eyes. I awkwardly fiddled with my scarf because I was worried he might see.

"Err…so you and Levi are getting along quite well, I see?" I asked.

"Yeah, he's all right." Blake shrugged. "Cool car, though."

"Uh huh. He loves racing with it," I said as Blake turned to me.

"How do you know?"

"He told me."

"Oh, okay…damn. I'd love to drive his car in a race."

"I thought you were the typical motorcycle guy?"

"So you think I can't race?"

"I never said that!"

"You were implying it."

"No, I wasn't," I replied. I felt someone's gaze on us and wasn't surprised when my eyes flicked toward Uncle Griff.

"Okay, then I'll prove it to you that I'm not just the 'typical motorcycle guy' and can actually race," Blake said.

"How?" I asked, suddenly interested that he wanted to prove something to me.

"By racing," he said with a smirk. "Against Levi."

I let out a snort as Mr. Bronx watched us in amusement. Blake didn't seem to find it funny as I stared at him.

"With what car?"

"I'll borrow one of Ethan's."

"You'll never win. Like Levi said yesterday, he always wins, and he's been doing it for years."

"Well, he hasn't gone up against me."

"Even if he did, he would win," I stated with a smirk molded onto my face. It was the truth; Levi loved his car, and he was damn good.

"Okay, tell you what…next time there's a race, we'll go against each other with a few other people. When I win, then you'll know I'm not a typical motorcycle guy."

"And what if you lose?"

"Me losing is like Carter not getting laid in the past forty-eight hours…impossible."

"Okay, but don't come crying to me when you have to get out of that car and see everyone cheering Levi on."

"You want a bet, Willson?" Blake asked as the corner of his mouth rose. From the corner of my eye, I saw Mr. Bronx wave his arms and mouth the word *no*. I turned back to Blake and nodded with a smile. "If I lose, which will be a tiny chance, then you can decide on the punishment."

"And if you win?"

"Then you have to kiss me."

Chapter Five

Lana

I walked down the empty hallways as I thought over what I had agreed to with Blake. I knew Levi would win, so that I wouldn't have to kiss him. I didn't want to mainly because of the night when we were about to kiss, he pulled away. Now suddenly, he wanted to kiss me. I'd make sure Levi wins. I exited the school to see Blake on his motorcycle. Once he noticed me, he tossed the helmet toward me—I caught it.

"Wanna take the scenic route home?" he asked as he got onto the bike.

"Err…sure," I answered as we put on our helmets. Blake started his motorcycle, and off we went. I didn't even know that there was a scenic route to my house. Thankfully the weather cleared up as Blake went through a back road. The sky faded with a few clouds, yet it looked so aesthetic. Trees rushed past us as we drove on the smooth road. Blake looked over his shoulder as if he wanted to say something. He pointed forward so I leaned to the side. The view was fantastic with a straight, flat open road. There were very few cars as we drove on. I leaned in to Blake and said, "It's incredible."

"You get a better look if you see above," he yelled. I sat back with a puzzled look on my face as I tried to think of a way to see above. I sat for a few seconds until my face broke into a smile. The craziest idea ran through my head as I lifted myself up. "Be careful!" Blake called out as I stood on the foot peg. Once I was balanced, I glanced up to take in the view. With the beautiful skyline and never-ending road, it looked breathtaking. A bright smile crept up on my face as I sat back down and laughed. All good things had to come to an end as we soon arrived at my house. A smile was molded onto my face as we took the helmets off.

"That was amazing!"

"Uh huh."

"Well…I guess I'll see you tomorrow then," I said, then spun around. I glanced up and saw Levi against the porch frame with a grin.

"Harley Davidson. Nice one, dude," he said and looked at Blake's bike.

"Thanks," Blake replied. They started talking cars, so I walked into the house. Mom and Jade were in the living room watching a soap opera. I greeted them, and they silenced me as their focus was on the TV. I rolled my eyes as I walked upstairs and into my bedroom. I shut the door and turned, only to see that the bed wasn't made up. I scoffed because Levi must've gotten back into bed after he dropped me off. I quickly made up the bed and arranged my room a bit. I sat down in my desk chair and began my homework. I turned on my Beats Pill and hit shuffle.

'Primadonna' by Marina and the Diamonds echoed through my room as I did my homework. I put the book in my lap as I propped my legs on the desk. I bobbed my head to the beat as I filled in the formulas. The sooner I got it done, the better.

"What crap is this?" a stinging voice asked. I glanced up to see Levi enter my room. I squinted my eyes as he collapsed on my bed. I also noticed Blake leaning against my doorframe.

"It's not crap! Marina and the Diamonds is fantastic."

"You do realize that's due next year?" Blake asked as he entered the room.

"Yeah, but I don't want to do it during winter break." I shrugged as he stepped closer. Levi took my phone, and I rolled my eyes and turned to Blake. He strangely inched closer and towered over me as he rested his hands on my desk. We locked eyes as I saw his left arm. I heard a drawer open then close as Blake raised his hand. I stared at him and then at the pack of cigarettes in his hands. Our faces were inches away as he stared at me with a blank look.

"What is this?"

"From the shape of the box and the smell, I guess it's cigarettes," I sarcastically replied as Levi snorted.

"These are mine," he said as he twirled them in his hands.

"You gave them to me," I said as I shoved him away with my pen.

"Nope. These are the ones I bought from the store months ago, then Parker started getting them for me," Blake stated as he stood up straight.

"Well, then I must've got it somewhere else," I lied as I took off my glasses.

"Sneaky," Levi added. I watched as Blake opened the pack and saw that there were only three gone. I hadn't used that pack yet, even though I had it the longest. I finished my others, then I'd probably use his.

"Get ready." Levi snapped me out of my thoughts.

"Where are you going?" I asked as they stood in front of me. Levi still had my phone in his hand as he scrolled through it.

"My house." Blake smirked as I sighed.

"I don't think there's a need for me to go," I said, then turned back to my work. A second later, "Stacey's Mom" by Fountains of Wayne played. I looked up to see Levi bobbing his head.

"Now this is incredible," he said as the song played. I watched in amusement as he lip-synced the song. Levi used my phone as a mic as he swung his arm around Blake's shoulder. Blake soon joined as they belted out the lyrics.

"Stop," I whined as they sang the chorus.

"Will you come with us?" Levi asked as they rocked back and forth. I shook my head and crossed my arms, then Levi turned up the volume. My eyes widened as I reached for my phone, but he ran away as the music played. "Blake!" Levi called out, then tossed my phone. Thankfully, Blake caught it as he raised his arm so I couldn't get it. They laughed as I jumped for my phone.

"*Lana, turn that music down!*" Mom yelled as I groaned.

"*I will!*" I replied. Blake threw it back at Levi as I spun around. I watched as Levi jumped onto my bed and sang. Very soon, Blake ran up and joined him.

"I just made the bed up!" I yelled as I tried to push them off. "All right, I'll go!" I yelled over the music as they jumped. They immediately stopped, and Levi turned off the music. They jumped off and walked toward the door.

"I'll be waiting in the car," Levi said, then exited the room. I let out a sigh as I ran my hand through my curly hair. I picked up my phone and shoved it in my pocket, then put on my glasses. I walked down the stairs and into the living room to be met by my mother and Blake.

"Where are you going?" she asked as Jade sat down beside her.

"Blake's house."

"Okay, don't stay out too late."

"Axel will be there," I blurted out. Blake had a puzzled look on his face as Jade stared at him. My mother smiled as she gave a curt nod.

"Tell your brother I say hi," Mom said.

"Err…yeah, his birthday was a few days ago," Blake said in an ominous tone.

"Well, tell him we say happy belated birthday," Mom said, then turned back to the TV. I squinted my eyes as I watched her. I followed Blake out the door as we walked to Levi's car.

"What was that about?" he asked as he got onto

his motorcycle.

"I have no idea…my parents know Axel."

"Hmm…must be because he got arrested or something." Blake shrugged as he started his bike.

"Yeah," I mumbled as I walked toward the black Mustang.

***

"Make yourselves at home," Blake said as we stepped into his house. It looked the same as last time. It seemed cleaner. The vase that Blake and I fixed stood above the fireplace. Blake soon disappeared, which left Levi and me alone, yet I heard voices from the other side of the house. "All right, come on," Blake said as he came into the room with a toolbox in his hands.

"Why are we actually here?" I asked as Levi and Blake walked to the kitchen.

"Touch up my car for the next race." Levi winked as he accepted a bottle of beer from Blake. He offered me one, but I kindly declined as I sat on a stool by the island. I watched as the boys opened their bottles with their teeth. I laughed. The garage door was right next to the fridge. Blake opened it, and they walked out and left me in the kitchen as they touched up Levi's car. I became suspicious as to why Blake wanted to help with his vehicle.

"Fancy seeing you here, pumpkin." I glanced up to see Axel Gunner. He sat opposite me with a guilty look. I raised a brow as he spun around and opened the fridge. Once he took out a bottle of beer, he faced me. "Look, about the other night, I was drunk and stupid." He sighed as he twisted the top off. "My bad, pumpkin."

"You're not good with apologies, are you?" I asked, and he chuckled.

"You know me so well, pumpkin."

"Heard it was your birthday a few days ago," I said. Axel's eyes lit up as he took a sip of beer, then nodded eagerly. He stood up and walked to the back door.

"Guess what I got for my birthday?" he asked. Before I even thought about it, he waved it off with an excited look. "Wait, don't guess…his name is Scruffy." He opened the door.

"What kind of name is Scruffy?" I said and tilted my head. My eyes widened as a black greyhound entered the kitchen. My hands gripped the edges of the island as the dog jumped on Axel. The dog barked, which showed his sharp, scary teeth. I loved dogs and preferred them to cats, but this dog seemed to frighten me. The dog's appearance was beyond scary as I bit the inside of my cheek.

"Scruffy, meet Lana." Axel shifted Scruffy's head toward me. With one look, Scruffy released himself from Axel and darted toward me. My eyes widened as Scruffy ran toward me as he barked. He jumped on me, and we fell to the ground. I let out a scream as Scruffy hovered over me and barked uncontrollably. I thought he'd bite me as I shut my eyes. "Bad Scruffy!" Axel called as I opened my eyes. Levi was above me with Blake on my left and Axel on the right. They pulled Scruffy away from me as I frowned. Blake held his hand out, which I gladly accepted. He pulled me up as I glared at him.

"You could've told me you got a dog," I grumbled as Levi and Axel put Scruffy outside.

"You never asked," Blake stated as he brushed me off. I shook my head as Levi and Axel laughed. Axel didn't have many tattoos like Blake and Levi. In fact, he only had a few on his hands. "I didn't know you two knew each other."

"We met at a party once." Axel shrugged as he sat back down. Levi and Blake walked back into the garage and left me alone with Axel, who tried to hurt me twice. The quietness was soon interrupted with an engine.

"That's my girl," Levi cheered, and I pictured his smirk. I noticed someone entered the room—a female who looked to be my mother's age. Her dark brown hair was tied up in a bun with a few strands stuck out. She wore black glasses and a formal black suit.

"Hey, Momma," Axel greeted as she set her bag on the island. It made sense as the standard features seemed to come from Blake and Axel. Yet I didn't imagine her with glasses.

"Hi, baby." She smiled as Axel got up to kiss her on the forehead. She turned to me with a warm smile as she took in my appearance. I shifted awkwardly as I held my hand out.

"Hi, I'm Lana Willson," I said as she gently shook my hand.

"Roxanne Gunner and I know who you are; my sons talk about you all the time," she said as my eyes flicked toward Axel, who winked at me. I turned to his mother. She smiled at me.

"You have a lovely home, Mrs. Gu—"

"Momma's boy!" Levi yelled from the garage. We turned our heads to see Blake jog in. He was shirtless, and the sweat made his body stand out. The tattoos on his arms seemed to glow as he ran a hand through his hair. I watched as Axel went over to the kettle and switched it on. Blake walked to his mother and kissed her on the cheek.

"Hey, Momma, how was work?" he asked, then sipped on Axel's beer.

"Tiring as always." Mrs. Gunner sighed as she sat on a stool. "Axel, did you feed that dog your uncle bought you?" she asked as she removed the hair tie and let it flow on her back.

"Yes, Momma," he mumbled as he fiddled with the crockery.

"Good, because I'm not going anywhere near that thing."

Levi walked in, and it was no surprise that he was also shirtless. He had more tattoos on his body rather than his arms.

"Dude, your car will be ready by tomorrow night, but you should go for a new paint job," Blake said as he put his arm around his mother's shoulder.

"I know, I know." Levi sighed as he waved to Mrs. Gunner.

"What are you two doing?" she asked.

"Busy with his spark plug…oh, and you need a new battery," Blake said, then walked out. "I think I have one in the back. Come on."

"He has a car battery?" I raised a brow.

"He has everything," Axel stated as he placed a cup of tea in front of his mother.

"He loves motors," Mrs. Gunner said, then

turned to me. “Do you know what he wants to be?”

“A mechanical engineer,” Axel said as he joined them in the garage.

“Wow, that’s amazing.” I smiled.

“Indeed, my boy has dreams,” she said, then sipped her tea. “Now I just have to find a way to make them come true.”

***

A raspy yawn escaped my lips as I walked through the hallway. After Mrs. Gunner and I talked in the kitchen for a while, Levi and I had to go. It was nice to talk to her, and they were a genuinely nice family. It was Wednesday, and as I turned the corner, I saw Benny by my locker. He acted strangely lately, and I really didn’t know why. I felt like it had to do with Levi. I slowly approached him, and his face immediately lit up.

“Hi.” I smiled, then opened my locker.

“Hey, err,” he mumbled, then let out a frustrated sigh. “Do you wanna go on a date?”

“O-on a date?” I repeated.

“Yeah, but if you don’t want to, I unde—”

“No.” I quickly cut him off as I placed my hand on his arm. We looked down, and I removed my hand. “I-I’d love to. It’s just I haven’t been on a date before.”

“Well, if you don’t feel comfortable, just think of it as two friends hanging out.”

“Okay, but what do I wear?”

“Anything. What you’re wearing is even perfect.” He stuttered as he glanced down at my outfit. I let out a chuckle as I glanced at my gray hoodie and faded black jeans.

"So comfy and casual it is," I said as the bell rang.

"Yeah, I'll pick you up at seven." He laughed as we walked to Physics class. I couldn't stop smiling as we entered the classroom. I couldn't believe I was going on my first date tonight! I didn't even know what to wear. I didn't know where we're going or what we're doing, but I hoped it turned out perfect.

"Good morning, class!" Mr. Gorton smiled as he entered the classroom.

"Well, good morning to you too," Liam replied as he sat in front of me.

"Look, I know winter break is in two days and your brains are probably fried by now, so free period," Mr. Gorton said as the class cheered.

"There must be a reason," Nick said as he raised a brow.

"Well, as you know, there are other Physics classes, and all your results have been tallied. Our class received the highest!" he exclaimed as everyone clapped and cheered.

"Can we practice?" Liam asked as Mr. Gorton took the attendance. He nodded then propped his legs on the table.

"Yo, Ethan!" Nick called as he held his hands out. Ethan miraculously had a basketball in his hands, then he tossed it to Nick. Since most of the team was in the class, they spread out so that they could throw the ball to each other. Coach told them to practice a lot since there's no practice today and there's a game soon.

"Careful with the ball. I don't wanna be a witness for when you guys break the window…again." Mr. Gorton sighed. I leaned back in my chair as I watched the boys goof around. Liam stood on a chair as he formed a hoop with his arms. I laughed as Ethan flung the ball into his arms. The door was wide open, and Aidan casually strolled in. He ducked as he walked over and plopped down in the chair in front of me.

"What are you doing here?" I asked as he smirked at me.

"English with Mr. Basil is annoying." Aidan frowned. His posture seemed to straighten as he looked over my shoulder. I raised a brow and followed his gaze, only to see Tiffany Martin. Her long red hair fell to her hips as she tugged on the sleeves of her sweater. She laughed with her friends, which made her eyes squint. I spun back around to see the big smile molded onto his face.

"Why are you staring at Tiffany?" I asked.

"Just thinking back to Homecoming," he sighed. "We had an awesome time, and she looked stunning in that dress."

"You like her, don't you?" I tilted my head.

"Yeah, but she won't go for a troublemaker like me." He frowned as I rolled my eyes.

"Don't say that, Aidan. You're a great guy who's fun—"

"Rowley, what the heck are you doing here?" Mr. Bronx's voice cut me off as he poked his head into the room. Mr. Gorton shook his head in disappointment but welcomed Mr. Bronx. Aidan let out a sigh as he stood up and walked to the door. He spun around and stared at our teacher with a mischievous look.

"Can I stay please?" he whined, and Mr. Gorton shook his head.

"Aidan, catch," Ethan said as he threw the ball to him. I sighed as I slowly got up to go and talk with Mr. Bronx.

"Lana, watch out!" Ethan yelled as I froze. It was too late as I felt a solid basketball connect with my cheek. I stumbled back as my legs hit the desk. The ball landed on the floor as I settled down on the desk.

"I'm so sorry, Lana!" Aidan exclaimed. I peeked up to see him by the door with a panicked look. Mr. Bronx glared at him as he looked around the classroom, then ran out.

"Are you okay?" Benny asked as he, Liam, and Ethan rushed toward me. Mr. Gorton rose to his feet, but Mr. Bronx stopped him.

"That's a big bruise," Liam said as he tilted his head. I raised a brow as they stared at me. Mr. Bronx shuffled toward us as his eyes widened. I squinted my eyes as I touched my cheek. A small bump lay beneath my fingers, but Ethan shook his head and motioned down. My hand slowly moved down until Ethan told me to stop. I didn't feel anything, but they seemed aware of the bruise. Liam let out a sigh as he took out his phone and opened his camera. He gave it to me as I stared at myself through his phone. My eyes widened as I saw it. They thought my hickey was a bruise. I gave Liam my phone as I pulled my hoodie up and sat down on the chair. Benny, Liam, and Ethan gave me weird looks, but Mr. Bronx shooed them away as he sat in front of me.

"I know that's not a bruise, Lana," he said with a concerned look.

"I can't help it," I whispered as I rested my head on the desk.

***

"*Oh my god!*"

"*I know!*"

"*Oh my god!*"

"*I know!*"

"Would you two shut up?" Melissa grumbled from the backseat. Miranda drove me home, and I told them about my date with Benny.

"What, Singe? Upset because Blake didn't have the balls t—"

"Whatever! I'm still team Blake long and strong!" Melissa confessed.

"Any tips, guys? This is my first date." I frowned as I nervously twirled my hair.

"Don't talk too much about yourself. Give him a chance."

"Don't order any finger food even though I know you love that food."

"Don't talk about any other guy."

"If you're gonna order pasta, don't take the spaghetti, because once you slurp it up, it whacks you in the face."

"Smile and laugh at his jokes, but not too much."

By the time they were done, we had arrived at

my house.

"All in all, be yourself and have fun," Miranda said as I got out of the car. "Tell us all about it tomorrow!" I anxiously ran my hand through my hair as I walked into the house. Mom and Jade were in the kitchen as I quietly entered.

"Hey, Lana, how was school?" Jade asked.

"It was good, err…listen, I won't be home for dinner tonight," I mumbled.

"Why not?" she asked as a smile formed on my face.

"Benny asked me out on a date!" I squealed as I rushed toward my mother. Mom and Jade let out a squeal as we jumped up and down and talked about tonight. I knew Mom would be happy because I've never been on a date, yet Jade had a son, so she was obviously delighted since I was like a daughter to her.

"Whoa, what are we celebrating?" Levi asked as he walked in.

"Lana's going on a date!" Jade squealed as she pinched my cheeks.

"With who?"

"Benny."

"Fucking cunt!" Levi's blank expression changed as he rushed out of the room and into the garage. I followed him only to see Blake on the floor right next to Levi's car.

"Shit, dude. Sorry, I forgot you were under there." Levi laughed then helped Blake.

"What's all the fucking commotion about?" Blake asked.

"Lana's going on a date with Benny." Levi

huffed as he leaned on his vehicle.

Blake squinted his eyes at me as he gave me a questioning look.

"Get back to your cars." I waved them off with a smile then skipped out of the garage.

***

I stared at myself in the mirror as I tugged on the cream sweater. Benny said casual. I let out a sigh as I slipped on my over knee boots and red scarf. Jade straightened my hair rather nicely, so I decided to leave it loose. I was nervous because it was my first date, and I didn't know what to expect. I trusted Benny, and he wouldn't do something extreme, especially for the first date. That explained why he was so quiet the past two days. I glanced at my clock, and in time the doorbell rang. He must be nervous too, since it's six fifty-eight. I walked downstairs, and I saw my dad by the door. I let out a groan as I watched him interrogate Benny. He looked cute in his jacket, black sweater, jeans, and high tops. I approached my dad, but my eyes were on Benny. Once he spotted me, he smiled. I looked at my dad, yet his gaze was already fixed on me.

"Don't worry, Dad, we won't be out too la—"

"No, you kids have fun," Father said as he smiled at Benny. "I'm trusting you with my daughter, Nielson. Don't mess it up."

"Yes, sir," he mumbled as I stepped out of the house.

"But don't stay too late, otherwi—"

"Bye, Dad!" I cut him off with a tight-lipped

smile. Once the front door shut, I heard Benny sigh. I chuckled as his pace quickened so that he could open the door for me. “Thanks.” I smiled as I got into the car. Once we were buckled in, he started the engine. We drove in silence as I stared out the window.

“You look beautiful,” Benny blurted out.

“Thanks you too,” I mumbled, but my eyes widened as Benny snorted. “Wai—I mean you look…”

“It’s okay, Lana.” He chuckled then turned to me with a grave look. “Are you nervous?”

“A little,” I mumbled, then shook my head as Melissa and Miranda’s advice kicked in. “We shouldn’t be nervous. We’ve known each other for years. Tonight, let’s just have fun and be ourselves.” I shrugged yet mentally slapped myself. I was never the romantic type, yet I’ve watched every romance movie there was.

“Because being ourselves is the best we can be.” Benny smiled then took my hand in his as he drove on.

We had dinner at a restaurant downtown, yet it wasn’t fancy or anything. Once we sat down and talked, the awkwardness subsided as laughter filled our ears. I decided on pasta but not the one where it whacked me in the face. Then we shared a dessert and talked. We walked, and he draped his jacket over my shoulders. The streets were quite busy for a Wednesday night, but most people took transport home.

“Can you hear that?” Benny asked as he stuffed his hands into his jeans pockets. We stopped as I listened for the peculiar sound. A sweet, persistent sound filled my ears as it got louder. Benny entwined my hand in his as he ushered me forward. "Come on," he said, then jogged down the streets. The music got louder until I saw a man with a saxophone. He was so into it—his one leg was propped up on the bench as he swayed. His fingers moved elegantly over the keys, which created a beautiful sound. Benny took my other hand in his as he pulled me closer to him. We started to go to the beat of the saxophone as I looked up at him. He smiled down at me then twirled me around. His hands moved down to my waist as he securely wrapped his arms around me. I locked my arms around his neck as we danced. The saxophone soothed and relaxed us as I rested my head on his chest and closed my eyes.

***

Benny's car came to a stop as he parked in front of my house. We haven't spoken since we danced as we absorbed tonight's event. I turned to him with a smile and said, "I had fun tonight."

"Me too." He smiled as we stared at each other. It seemed like an eternity until I finally looked away and gripped on the door handle. I looked back once more into his brown eyes and bit my lip.

"Goodnight," I murmured as I pushed the door open.

"Night, Lana," he mumbled as I got out then shut the door. Without looking back, I walked up the porch and heard his car start. Once I was at the door, I spun around to watch him go. I noticed his stare on me through his tinted windows as he drove off. Once he was down the street, I spun around to unlock the door. A familiar smell lingered through the air as I froze. I gazed over my shoulder and into the night. The smell was so familiar and vigorous it compelled me to follow. I walked down the porch steps and followed the scent. I raised a brow as it ended by Levi's car. I crouched down and stared into the tinted windows. The window rolled down as a face appeared, and I jumped in surprise.

"*Boo!*" Blake yelled, then laughed. I let out a huff as I stared at him and the driver that was, in fact, Levi.

"What the hell are you guys doing?" I yelled.

"Hop in, princess," Levi replied as he took a drag of his cigarette. So that's what the familiar smell was. "You do realize he wanted to kiss you?"

"Were you guys watching us?" I asked as my face twisted.

"Believe me, we tried not to," Blake said as he rolled his eyes.

"Why didn't you kiss him?" Levi asked as I shrugged.

"I don't kiss on my first date."

"Yet you've kissed him before," Blake muttered as I scoffed. Levi started the car as Blake lit his cigarette with Levi's lighter. He turned to me with a smirk plastered on his face and spoke. "We're going racing. Hop in, princess."

Chapter Six

Lana

The continuous cheers of people made me edgy as I watched the monitor. Blake did practice races with a bunch of other racers, and let's just say he might win. I sat on the hood of Levi's Mustang as Ethan stood next to me. Ethan brought a Porsche 918 Spyder for Blake to use. The way he drove rapidly down the streets made me nervous. Every turn he took the tires screeched as the engine roared. Last time I saw Levi and Keene were when we got here. Then they went into the bistro followed by a bunch of girls. The reason why they hadn't raced because they were waiting for Aidan. He got his car fixed by someone Blake knew. It was weird that Blake didn't fix his cousin's car. The word fix made me uneasy at the thought of Blake sabotaging Levi's car so that he'd win. Levi was smarter than that, so I didn't know what would happen. I didn't want to kiss him. I was still in my date clothes, and the thought of Benny and I dancing over an hour ago made me feel guilty. I liked Benny, I honestly did, and he's so sweet to try and make up for everything he's done.

"There they go again," Ethan sighed as Blake drove past us.

"He's good," I murmured as the other cars trailed behind him.

"Yep, he loves cars," Ethan said. I turned to look at the big jock beside me. His pierced jawline stood out as he gazed over the crowd. Ethan was like a big brother to me who's caring and protective. Miranda said he's more of a gentleman, and I smiled in agreement. "You do realize he's gonna win, right?" he asked as I tore my gaze away from him and looked at Blake on the monitor.

"He hasn't gone up against Levi."

"If he wins, then you must kiss him."

"I don't want to!" I whined, and Ethan laughed.

"How was your date with Benny?"

"Amazing," I breathed out as the thought of us dancing to the saxophone entered my mind. I smiled, thinking of when Benny gave the man money and told him he's got talent. That immediately disappeared as Levi entered my mind. *We had sex a few days ago.* I didn't know why I let him do it, but in a way, I liked it. I missed him yet something told me not to. He broke me, yet somehow, I always forgave him. Miranda's right; I was a softie who's forgiving. I couldn't help that I forgave too easily and cared too much. I let out a sigh as I thought back to when Ethan apologized to me at Rodney's store. That was where it all began, how I became soft and forgiving. "You know that day in the cafeteria when you said that if I wanna talk…"

"Yeah, and I'm here, even to listen."

"Do you ever feel like you hate someone because they've done something horrible to you yet…you always find a way to forgive them because you missed them so much and just craved them?" I turned to Ethan with a frown.

"Look, Lana, I haven't found that special someone yet, but when I do, I know that we'll have arguments leading to us not talking for a few days, but if I really cared…" He trailed off as his chocolate brown eyes met mine. "Fuck yeah, I'll crave for their presence. Like you said: Everyone deserves a second chance." He playfully nudged my shoulder.

"What if you've been through so much together and everything seems fine, but you don't actually know if they care?"

"If he didn't care, he wouldn't be part of your life anymore," Ethan said. Silence took over us after that. I pursed my lips at the thought of who Ethan referred to, I knew who I did, but I was curious.

"There's my favorite lingerie buddy," a familiar voice erupted as I glanced around. I raised a brow as Axel walked toward us. His hands shoved in his jeans pockets as he smirked at me.

"What are you doing here?" I asked as he greeted Ethan.

"You have a favorite lingerie buddy?" Ethan piped up as Axel grinned.

"Keene invited me, and yes," Axel answered both our questions.

"I'm not going to even ask how you know Keene." I sighed.

"That's why I like you, pumpkin," Axel said, then ruffled my hair. I scowled as Ethan raised a brow at the two of us.

"You call her pumpkin?" he asked as Axel leaned against the hood.

"At least it's better than Levi calling her princess and Carter calling her cutie or hot stuff." Axel shrugged as my cheeks reddened.

"Have you guys ever tried calling me by my name?"

"Where's the fun in that, pumpkin? Makes you unique to us." He chuckled.

"Sure." I laughed. "Can't you be like Ethan and call me Lana?"

Axel opened his mouth to reply, but the sounds of an engine booming cut him off. We whipped our heads around to see a crowd forming. I jumped off Levi's car as I followed Axel and Ethan. We joined the group to see that they circled a vehicle. It wasn't just any car; it was Aidan's. It looked different. Whoever Blake sent knew his stuff. A new paint job made the Subaru stand out with its shiny white color. The hood scoop stood out, which made the car even more striking with the gold rims. Axel let out a low whistle as we stared in awe. Aidan hopped out of the car with a wide grin spread across his face. He walked toward us, then hugged his cousin. Ethan and I watched in amusement as Axel and Aidan joked around.

"You look like a winner tonight." I grinned as Aidan smiled.

"Uh huh. Like the rims?" he asked. I nodded, impressed, as we talked. A loud siren went off, which signaled the end of a race. I nervously spun around to see Levi and Keene approach us. Blake got out of the Porsche, and people congratulated him as he walked toward us.

"This should be exciting," Keene mumbled beside me as we watched the people gather around the start line. All the racers lined up their cars, and I anxiously watched Blake as he smirked at Levi. We stood behind the vehicles as they went over the rules. I didn't even know why they even bothered with rules since they broke half of them. It was Blake, Aidan, Levi, and this other guy who drove a Mercedes SLS.

"Good luck, dude," Aidan said to the guy with the Mercedes.

"Yeah, looks like you'll need it," the guy responded as Aidan raised a brow.

"Pucker up," Blake cooed as he made kissy faces. I scrunched my nose up as I stared at him. Somehow, he'd became cockier in the last few days. I didn't know if it was Levi or his ego that showed the most.

"Wait," I blurted out as Levi and Blake shook hands. Aidan and the other guy were already in their cars as people cheered. I nervously bit my lip as I approached Blake.

"If you're gonna give him a good luck kiss, I think I deserve one too," Levi piped up as I faced Blake.

"You said you wanted to drive his car in a race," I said. "Why don't you?"

"I'm down." Levi shrugged as he looked at the Porsche. I casually folded my arms as I turned to Blake. He looked at me curiously, as if he knew what I was on to, but shrugged.

"Cool with me," he said, then walked off. Before Levi walked to the Porsche, I gripped his arm. I looked him dead in the eye as he raised a brow at me.

"You better win this, Radcliff."

"Whatever you say, princess." He chuckled, then pecked me on the cheek. I was taken back from his action as he ran toward the car. I walked to the side and stood with Keene, Ethan, and Axel. Aidan's Subaru was in front of us as they got ready. People surrounded the area, cheering, mainly because the best racers went up against each other. A strange feeling whirled inside of me as their engines thundered. I didn't know why, but I had a feeling that they'd play dirty and jack up Aidan's car again. The crazy notion seemed to jerk me forward as I gripped the handle of Aidan's passenger door. I quickly opened it and slipped inside. I ignored Ethan and Keene's complaints as I shut the door.

"Lana, what the hell are you doing here?" Aidan demanded as he stared at me.

"Please, can I ride with you?" I begged.

"No, it's too dangerous!" Aidan stuttered as he glanced at the road.

"Please, Aidan…if you let me, I'll talk to Tiffany for you!" I offered. Aidan's eyes lit up as he stared at me. Before Aidan spoke, the flag girl strolled toward the center of the cars. My eyes widened as I realized what was happening. I'd only ridden twice with Levi, and both experiences terrified me. I quickly put on my seatbelt as Aidan watched me as if I were a freak. "Safety first!" I exclaimed as the girl raised her flag. That's when they hit the accelerator. A look of determination filled Aidan's face as he turned to look at Levi and Blake. I leaned forward so that they'd see me. Their reactions were priceless as Levi's eyes widened and Blake had a blank look. I gave an innocent wave, which only made them angrier as their cars boomed.

As soon as the girl lowered the flag, we were off. Blake being the show off that he was, he hit the accelerator pedal until a screech came out of the car. My eyes widened as the car rose as he dashed forward. I gripped on to my seatbelt as we zipped down the street. The Mercedes led the way as we trailed behind him. I glanced at the side mirror to see Blake and Levi gain on us. A turn came up as Aidan hit the gas pedal. He swerved past the Mercedes and took the turn. Out of nowhere, Levi turned with us as his tires screeched against the concrete.

I glanced in the mirror and saw no sign of Blake. A sigh of relief escaped my lips. I looked up to see that Levi was trying to block us. As we drove past a street, Blake appeared out of nowhere, as if he'd come out of the shadows. Both blocked us as they tried to push each other off. Blake bumped into Levi as he did the same. A smirk danced on my lips as I looked at our surroundings. One advantage of driving with Levi was that I'd learned his tricks, patterns, and ways. "Go onto the sidewalk." I pointed to the walkway that had a few stores, but thank goodness it was night, so nobody was there.

“What?” Aidan yelled as he hit the gas pedal and hit Blake’s bumper.

“Sidewalk!” I rushed out as the car swerved. Everything happened so fast as we drove onto the sidewalk and past Levi and Blake. The car wobbled as we drove onto the uneven sidewalks. Once we were far away from the two, he drove back onto the road. We drove at an alarming speed as my eyes flicked from left to right. We turned right into a random street, yet something about it made it seem familiar. Realization hit me as I recognized the familiar alley on our right. “Go left!” I yelled because I didn’t want to pass the alley, as it had police tape surrounding the area, which meant it was still under investigation. The car curved to the left, making me regret saying that. Up ahead was a main road which made Aidan go faster. I pushed my glasses up, then gazed at the traffic light. It changed to yellow as Aidan picked up his pace. I turned to look at him and noticed the sweat running down his forehead.

“Hold on!” he shouted. I glanced up to see the light was red as all the cars stopped. We needed to get to the other side of the intersection because we went left instead of right. My nails dug into the seat as the car swerved to the right. Dozens of headlights passed us as the drivers stared at us. I let out a shaky breath as we drove on and saw Blake and Levi in the distance. Aidan caught up with them as I watched the two. Suddenly they went opposite ways further into the industrial area as I raised a brow. I looked straight ahead to see why. My eyes widened as I saw a bridge open. I glanced at Aidan and noticed a wicked look in his eye.

"Aidan, no!" I demanded as we were now on the bridge.

"It's a shortcut, Lana, and you want to win, right?" he asked, then hit the gas pedal.

"If we survive, I'm so going to kill you after this!" I yelled as we inched closer. "This isn't *Fast and Furious*!"

With one final push, the car went up in the air. Aidan laughed while I screamed for dear life. Then like a humongous speed bump, we flopped back onto the ground. I breathed so loud that I didn't even notice that we were on the road again. I glanced up to see no sign of Blake, Levi, or the Mercedes. We might win. Construction work was up ahead, yet Aidan drove right past it since the rest of the street was clear. Aidan took the last right where we saw the finish line two blocks away. Out the corner of my left eye, I saw a car approach us. It was Blake. Levi was nowhere to be found, which made me nervous. The sounds of the Mustang approaching us made me look at Aidan. We were the only two cars as people cheered. I saw Keene raise his head and overlook us. Axel and Ethan howled as we inched closer to the finish line. It's like a hit of adrenaline swept through Blake as he bolted past us. My jaw dropped as we passed the finish line seconds after Blake. Aidan and I got out of the car and were thrown with noise. Blake stood against the Mustang as the people cheered him on. Keene ran past us before I could ask him what's wrong. Blake walked toward us and congratulated his cousin then turned to me. My jaw clenched at the thought of the kiss.

"No way!" a loud voice shouted as I tore my gaze away from Blake. Everyone watched the monitor as it played the recent event. I suddenly paled as I watched Levi and Blake. It was the empty street with the construction. Levi was in the same lane as the road works with Blake next to him. Blake contested Levi as he drove against him. Then at the right moment, Blake swerved to the right as he saw the roadworks. Levi looked ahead as he spotted it too, then hit the brakes, but it was too late. At speed, the Porsche's left side of the hood hit against a concrete block and the car tilted. I watched in horror as the car flipped in the air, the wheels spinning as Levi swayed inside it. It landed on all fours but jolted forward as Levi hit the brakes. The car came to a complete stop in the middle of the road as Levi sunk in his seat. I whipped my head back to Blake to see the concerned look. His eyes met mine, and I had the sudden urge to punch him. Apparently, he wouldn't need to sabotage a car, because to play dirty was all he needed to win.

I spun around and ran toward Levi. I heard footsteps behind me as well as Aidan's and Axel's voices, but I didn't care. I sprinted down the street. My boots would probably be ruined by the time I got home. After what seemed like forever, I stopped when I saw the Porsche. It had a massive dent on the side, and I immediately felt sorry for Ethan. I approached the car to see a laid-back Levi in the driver's seat. His eyes were shut as he leaned against the window. I gritted my teeth as I tried to get the door open. After a few attempts, I got it open, and Levi almost fell out of the car. I instantly lifted him up and put him back on the seat. I cupped his cheeks as I searched for injuries. He let out a hoarse groan as I saw the cut on his forehead.

"Are you okay?" I asked as he scrunched his nose up. He groaned again but gave a short nod. Seconds later, Keene approached us.

"Dude, you okay? Should I call an ambula—"

"No, I'm fine," he muttered then took my hand in his. "Just take me home."

I nodded as Keene and I helped him out of the car. Ethan and Aidan stayed by the vehicle and cleaned up. I helped Levi into the passenger seat of his car, then left Keene to do the rest. Out the corner of my eye, I saw Blake and Axel. I clenched my fists and squinted my eyes at him. I marched toward them as I pushed my way through the crowd. Axel noticed me and grinned as he elbowed Blake. He spun around with a wicked look in his eye as I approached him.

"You want your kiss?" I grumbled. Blake raised his brow as he slowly nodded. I took the palm of my hand, kissed it, then gave him one hard slap. Oohs and snickers surrounded us as I quickly spun around and walked toward Levi. Without another word, I got into the driver's seat and drove off with Levi beside me. We drove in silence as I glanced at Levi. He rested against the seat as he looked out the window. "How's your cut?"

"Not that deep, Keene touched it up. Don't worry." Levi sighed. "How was your date?"

"It was good."

“So are you guys a thing now?”

“I-I don’t know.”

“So you guys just gonna go out and fuck like the last few years didn’t happen?”

“No, what the hell? We’re not even a couple yet.”

“Blake agrees with me that he’s just playing you.”

“Like you two haven’t,” I muttered. I glanced at the time and noticed that it was almost midnight. Dad didn’t give me a curfew, though.

“You still holding a grudge?” Levi groaned.

“Look who’s talking.”

“Fine, okay, I get it. It’s just we don’t like him. Never have, never will,” he admitted as he raised his arms.

“We? You’ve known Blake for three days, and you grew on each other. Conceited and egotistical,” I muttered as we pulled into the driveway.

“What can I say? I’ve found my people.” He chuckled.

“It doesn’t mean you guys have to act like a bunch of assholes. At least he’s trying to make up the eight years, unlike some people who are so self-centered. Can you guys at least try to act friendly in front of him?” I sighed then made a pouty face. “For me?”

“Fine, but only because I don’t want to see you get hurt.” Levi sighed. “Just so you know, I don’t believe in that ‘as long as you’re happy that’s all that matters’ bullshit, because if he hurts you, I’m gonna strangle him,” he continued as I sighed. “Like I did every year when you cried in my arms.”

"Well, things have changed, Levi," I said as we sat in the car. "A lot. I've been doing things on my own, and it's scaring me. The most unexpected people can come into your life and make a difference."

"Wonder what Benny did to make you feel this way…that's the thing Blake and I can't get," he muttered as we sat in total darkness.

"There's nothing to get. I like Benny a lot, and there's nothing that you and your new best friend can do that will change that," I said as I gripped onto the door handle.

"All right, just don't come crying to me when he breaks your heart."

"Bullshit. It's already broken."

***

The rest of Thursday, I ignored Blake, which wasn't hard since I barely had any classes with him. Lunch wasn't so bad since everyone talked and he sat across the table. Liam and Aidan went on and on about *Stranger Things,* which resulted in Nick and Benny spoiling the last episode for them. As promised, I spoke to Tiffany for Aidan. It turned out she had a crush on him since sophomore year and swooned when he asked her to Homecoming. After lunch, he asked her out on a date, which she evidently said yes to. I joined her girly moment as we squealed.

I walked down the quiet hallway on my way to the gym. Benny said he'd give me a ride home after practice. I didn't mind sitting and working while they practiced.

"So you're going to ignore me now?" Blake said.

"He could've been severely injured, Blake! You didn't even stop to see if he was okay," I snapped.

"I called him last night, and he said no problem, happened before, no biggy." Blake sighed as he threw his hands up in exasperation. "We're not like girls who bitch around and sob for every little thing," he added as I let out a dry laugh. "I'm still waiting for my kiss." He leaned forward. Blake towered over me as his dog chain stuck out. I really wanted to take it and choke him. I glanced down at his black Doc Martens, then up to his leather jacket.

"Screw you," I hissed, then stepped back. Blake tilted his head as he put his hand on his chest. I rolled my eyes, entirely aggravated by him.

"Ouch, that hurt, Willson," he sarcastically said.

"Ugh, I hate you."

"That's funny. At the beginning of the school year, I heard I was your favorite."

"Yeah, that's before I got to know the egotistical, selfish, backstabbing, cold-hearted, mystifying bastard know as Blake Gunner," I said as I placed my hand on his chest. "So yes, Blake, I don't hate you. I just hate the arrogant, self-centered, and confusing side of you," I said, jabbing my finger in his chest at each word. "In fact, I like you, Blake. Just not the way that you like me."

We stared at each other for a moment. An emotionless look filled Blake's face as I stepped back. He watched as I walked away. I entered the gym and saw all the basketball players practice, yet Benny was nowhere to be found. I glanced at Liam,

Nick, and Ethan and strolled toward them.

"Hey, guys." I smiled.

"Hey, Lana, looking for someone?" Liam wiggled his eyebrows. I gave him a strange look as Nick swung his arm around Liam's shoulder.

"Her boyfriend," Nick answered with a sly grin.

"We're not a cou—"

"Boyfriend!" Liam called out as he glanced around the gym.

"Liam, what are you doing? If he's no—"

"Why aren't you saying *Benny*?" Ethan asked as he raised a brow at me.

"Oh no, she only says his name when they're alone," Nick emphasized. My eyes widened as they smirked at each other, then moaned out Benny's name.

"Benny!" Liam groaned in what seemed to be a seductive way.

"Oh Benny!" Ethan joined in as my cheeks flushed.

"You guys!" I whined as I playfully punched Ethan.

"Benn—"

"What?" a familiar voice asked, and I turned to see Benny. He walked to us in a muscle tank top and Adidas shorts. I turned back to the three guys, who laughed. I swear I was red as a tomato when Benny stood next to me. We stood there as the rest of them fooled around. Coach Harris entered the gym, and the guys cursed.

"Eight laps around the gym, now!" he yelled, then blew the whistle, making Liam jump. He tugged on his friend Tyler, and they ran. I watched as they jogged around the gym but felt a hand entwine in mine. I looked over my shoulder to see Benny. We walked out of the gym and stood in the empty hallway. I leaned against the wall as he glanced down at me. He nervously licked his lips, then rested one arm on the wall next to me.

"I had fun last night," he murmured.

"Me too." I smiled.

"Look, err…I want…" he stuttered, then took a deep breath. His brown eyes met mine as I saw the nervous look. "I know we've only been on one date, but Thanksgiving when you kissed me, I-I wanted you. I like you, Lana, and I want to be with you more. With Levi here, it just makes me nervous, and…what I'm trying to say is…" Benny trailed off as he looked at me. "Lana, would you be my girlfriend?"

My blank expression immediately changed as a smile grew onto my face. I slowly placed my arms around his neck as I brought him closer to me. Our foreheads were pressed together as I smiled at him.

"I'd love to," I whispered. Benny let out a sigh of relief, then smiled. He leaned in as he pushed my glasses up, then gazed at my lips. He pressed himself against me as he leaned on the wall for support as our lips met. I smiled against his lips. The thought of Benny Nielson being my boyfriend couldn't register, but it was genuine. We could kiss in public, hold hands, and feel comfortable around each other. The kiss was soft at first as his lips pecked mine but soon filled with admiration. His body clung to me as my mouth parted. Benny took the chance as he deepened the kiss, and I raked my fingers through his hair. He let out a hoarse groan as the kiss became gentle.

"Stop that before I hose you two off," a loud voice interrupted as I pulled away. I glanced over my shoulder to see Coach Harris. Benny awkwardly scratched his neck as I blushed. Coach shook his head then walked back into the gym. As soon as he was gone, Benny came up beside me and smashed his lips against mine. It was quick yet sweet as he pulled away, then grabbed my hand. We walked back into the gym together, and I noticed Liam and Ethan grinned as they ran. I sat in the stands as I did homework yet I couldn't focus or slap the smile off my face. I had a boyfriend!

"Benny!" Liam and Ethan moaned as they ran past us. I swore at them, and Liam gasped. Then Benny passed, and I smiled at him. He sent me a wink, which apparently made my cheeks warm up. I still couldn't believe that I had a boyfriend.

Chapter Seven

Lana

I stirred in my sleep as the memories of that night entered my mind. I suddenly calmed down as an arm wrapped around me, and I was brought closer to the person's body. I smiled at the thought of Benny, who had me securely in his arms. Before I went to bed last night, he called and said he missed me. Then we talked for two hours until I fell asleep. My eyes shot open as I remembered that Benny didn't come over, he dropped me off, but that was it. I glanced over my shoulder to see Levi's face buried in the pillow. I got up too quickly and fell off the bed. I landed on my butt as I squinted at my window. It was already morning. I sprung up as Levi sat up and stretched. I ran to my closet and took out casual clothing. I ran into the bathroom and showered. Five minutes later, I was out in a plain white tee, jeans, and denim jacket. Levi was in the same spot as before. I glared at him the whole time as I slipped on my boots and glasses.

"What the hell were you doing in my bed?" I demanded.

"In the middle of the night, I needed to take a piss, so I used your bathroom, then came out to see you mumbling stuff in your sleep," he began. "You tried grabbing something, so I just extended my arm and, well…you pulled me in."

"I'm locking that door from now on. I have a boyfriend!" I exclaimed as I took my phone. I glanced down to see that I'd received a message from Benny. Without giving Levi a second glance, I sprinted down the stairs and into the kitchen. Mom and Jade had coffee, and I could've sworn I ran past Dad. "Hey, Mom. Hey, Jade," I said as I grabbed an apple. Benny's car honk echoed as I dashed through the house. "Bye, Mom. Bye, Jade!"

I scrambled into Benny's car and shut the door. I turned to face him as he leaned forward. I smiled as we kissed then drove on.

"Listen, since the game is tonight and there'll probably be a party afterward, I was thinking maybe we ditch the party?" he suggested as I took a bite out of my apple.

"And do what?" I grinned.

"Chill at my place, watch movies, y'know, since it's the last day of school."

"Fine with me." I smiled. We arrived at the school on time. Since we had Physics first, Benny and I walked together to class. I sat at the back of the class with Benny in front of me. Ethan sat on my right as the teacher roamed in the front. Once everyone was in class, Mr. Gorton picked up a bunch of papers and handed them out. Everyone groaned at the thought of doing work on the last day of school.

"It's not my fault that someone piped up that we didn't do work the other day," he mumbled and snatched the basketball from Tyler. We sat in silence and did the sheet on Nuclear Physics. I finished earlier than everyone else, so I looked around the classroom. I noticed Benny sunk in his seat. He leaned back and rested his head on my table. I smiled as I sat up straight and leaned forward so that he'd see me. Benny smiled at me as I ran my hand through his dark brown hair. I kissed his forehead. He let out a sigh as he leisurely shut his eyes. Out of the corner of my eye, I saw Liam raise his arm. I propped my chin on the palm of my hand as I rested it on the desk and watched Liam.

"Yes, Mr. Sanchez?"

"Have you seen Jack August?" he blurted out as Benny's eyes snapped open.

"Who the heck is that?" Mr. Gorton asked as he spun the basketball with his index finger.

"Wait—is he that hobo on the news?" Ethan asked as Nick turned around to glare at Liam.

"Yeah, he's missing. Wonder why the police are making such a big fuss about it," Britney explained as Benny slowly sat up. I nervously bit my lip as whispers and murmurs spread throughout the classroom. Liam turned to us as he gave an apologetic smile. Benny groaned as Nick flicked him. Mr. Gorton stood up from his seat and went to the front of the classroom.

"Quiet down!" he exclaimed. Once everyone was settled, he turned to Liam and raised a brow. "Why do you ask, Liam?"

"He's just missing..." Liam shrugged as he avoided eye contact. Mr. Gorton sighed as he told us to get back to work. I sighed. Jack. Yeah, he's missing, and it doesn't look like he's going to be found very soon.

***

"The best thing about Nick is that he always gives me his jacket." Melissa smiled as we entered the gym. The rest of the day flew by in an absolute blur. Blake and Carter didn't come to school, and Ethan told me that they never went on the last day. Park Town High was opposite us, and Liam was right. They were tall and massive. I sat down in the stands with Miranda on my right and Melissa on my left. Marcus and Parker were next to her as they talked. We got the perfect view as both schools got ready. Benny's eyes met mine as he sent me a warm smile.

"This has Levi written all over it," Miranda said. I raised a brow as I followed her gaze to my faded hickey. I descended in my seat as they stared at me with questioning looks.

"It happened before Benny asked me out, okay?" I mumbled. Miranda let out a sigh as she glanced up at Benny, then me.

"I adore that you guys are finally together, but I just have this strange feeling that Blake is going to ruin it."

"Or Levi," Melissa added.

"Oh, shit. There goes my happiness," I said.

The game started and everyone quieted down. Benny played well; the way he dribbled the ball across the court and passed to his teammates showed how skilled he was. Ethan played center as he directed his team while Nick was shooting guard and Liam was the point guard. The rest of the game went well, but Park Town High was full of surprises with a better tactic. Ethan, Benny, and Tyler were the ones who scored the most, as well as the taller guys from Park Town High. One of them was benched for foul plays, yet he seemed familiar. Miranda and Marcus bought food while Melissa scolded them to stop and actually focus on the game. When they finally did, I noticed that there were thirty seconds left.

"They just need to score two points then we'll win!" Marcus said since the score was 45-45. I watched eagerly as the big guy from Park Town High stole the ball from Nick and ran the opposite way as he dribbled the ball. Ethan came out of nowhere as he flipped it out of his hand. Giants surrounded Ethan as he tried to score.

"Pass it to Sanchez!" Coach yelled as Ethan snapped his head toward Liam. I glanced at the clock to see twenty seconds were left. Ethan threw it to Liam, who caught it with ease as he dribbled the ball past the Giants. People were at the edge of their seats as we watched the brunette run across the court like there's no tomorrow.

"Come on, Liam!" Parker yelled as he stood up. Soon everyone followed as we stood up and cheered Liam on. He stopped at the three-point line and glanced at the clock. Eight seconds left as he looked at the hoop. The opposite team came as Liam angled his hands to score. We watched as he threw the ball in the air. It soared and hit against the backboard. Everyone suddenly froze as we watched the ball drop on the ring. It did a semi-circle and at the last second fell in the hoop. As the ball landed on the ground, the buzzer went off as we cheered. Everyone made his or her way down as the team congratulated Liam. Park Town High glared at us but was immediately snapped from their stares as their coach yelled at them. Benny ran up to me and engulfed me in a hug as I stood on my tippy toes.

"You were amazing," I said as we pulled away.

"Let's go party!" Nick cheered as we walked out of the gym.

"Err, we'll see you guys later," Benny said as he gathered his things. They didn't mind at all and walked on. Miranda spun around and pointed to her neck while Benny grabbed his stuff. I gave a short nod as I buttoned up my jacket. We walked to Benny's car, and I was glad that we didn't go to the party. I wasn't in the mood, and I heard that those after game parties got wild like the last time when Benny and I did a body shot.

We arrived at the house and noticed that his parents were home. We entered the house to see no one in the living room.

"They must be sleeping," Benny mumbled as he put his things down. I followed him into the basement and was immediately thrown with noise. Once we reached the bottom of the stairs, I glanced up to see Sam on the sofa with a controller in his hand as he stared at the TV.

"Sam, go play in your room." Benny sighed as he took off his jersey.

"Aw, I thought you wer—" Sam said as he paused the game and spun around. He cut himself off as his eyes met mine. His blank expression changed into a smirk as he walked over to us. "Hey, sugar, came back because you realized your life wasn't so good without me?"

"Sorry, little bro, but she's mine," Benny stated as he slung his arm around me and kissed my forehead. Sam's jaw dropped, then he scrunched his nose up as he turned to me.

"You went for the ugly Nielson?"

Benny glared at his little brother as I chuckled. I sat on the sofa as I watched Benny try to persuade his brother to go upstairs, yet Sam ignored him and turned to me.

"Why? Of all people, why did it have to be my own brother?" he fake sobbed as Benny pushed him toward the stairs. "Can't Lana and I play video games?" he asked as he pointed at the controller. "I'll even let her use my special controller, but just know I'll always be in control!"

I laughed as Benny grunted, then literally threw his brother over his shoulder. Yet that didn't stop Sam as he continued with his sorry pick-up lines.

"Dude, you're not hanging out with Carter anymore!" Benny exclaimed as he pulled his brother up the stairs.

"Can I at least get her picture? I want to show Santa, and hopefully he'll take me off the naughty list!"

With one last attempt, I heard a door shut, then

Benny's footsteps down the stairs. He looked at me with flushed cheeks as I laughed.

"Your brother is quite something," I said as he plopped down next to me.

"It's Liam and Carter who keep influencing the poor kid," Benny added as he reached over for the remote. He flicked through the shows on Netflix as I rested my head on his shoulder. "What you feel like, babe?" he asked as I looked at our choices. I bit the inside of my cheek at that word, *babe*. I'd never thought I'd ever hear it from Benny Nielson.

"Zac Efron," I casually replied as I looked at *Seventeen Again*.

"Sure, let's order pizza." He chuckled as he threw the blanket over us and took out his phone. The rest of the night we watched movies and cuddled. It was nice to relax with someone and have no worries. It got late, and I sensed Benny was tired, so I decided to go. I wanted to take an Uber, but Benny insisted that he'd take me because he didn't want a total stranger to drive me home at this time of the night. So he drove me home and said he'd see me tomorrow as we kissed. I hopped out of the car and walked to the front door and saw Benny waited for me to get inside. I smiled as I quietly unlocked the door and went in. I slowly shut the door and tiptoed through the house.

I walked into my room to see that it was neat and tidy. Hmm, maybe Levi finally decided to clean up his mess. I shook the thought away as I began to undress. I slipped on a pair of sweatpants and an old sweater, then tied my hair up in a loose ponytail. From the corner of my eye, I saw movement. My head snapped to that direction as I saw a figure by my window. My eyes widened as the person began to knock. I slowly approached my window and grabbed the first thing I saw for protection. With the scented candle in my left hand, I opened the window to my right. I was about to hit the person until I froze.

"Blake? What the hell are you doing here?" I stared down at the teenage boy who dangled by my tree.

"Lana, I need your help," he rushed out as I took in his appearance. He seemed flustered with a panicked look in his eyes. The sleeves of his leather jacket were rolled up, and his Linkin Park band tee was creased. "Weren't you at the party?" He raised a brow at me. I shook my head as he nodded, then ran his hand through his dark brown hair.

"What's going on?"

"It's Levi. We were at the party, and he got drunk and started to yell and argue with people, so we got kicked out," he said as I looked over his shoulder to see Levi's Mustang parked by the street.

"Well, where is he?" I asked. Blake anxiously licked his lips as he stared at me.

"I don't know."

***

Levi

I gathered a vast amount of spit, tilted my head back, and spat on the ground. I chuckled at the saliva mixed with blood and shook my head.

Asshole couldn't punch correctly, that's what. I recalled the random guy hit me because I made out with his girlfriend. *Yet he punched me?* He should go all ape shit on her for coming on to me. I shook my head as I walked down the streets. I continued to walk as I sipped the remains of my beer bottle. I saw the familiar sculpture up ahead and walked toward it. I stared at my reflection and saw how lifeless I looked. The beer bottle dangled beside me as I inched closer to get a better look at myself. My hair was in all directions, the cut from the other night faded because I didn't want a Band-Aid on, eyes bloodshot and droopy, not to mention the bruise on my cheek from that fight.

I suddenly straightened my posture as I stared at myself. I gripped the beer bottle in my hand as I raised it and threw it against the sculpture. The harsh noise of the bottle hitting against the structure made my jaw clench as I watch it shatter to the ground. I looked straight ahead as I walked. Thank goodness I wore combat boots as the glass crushed under my shoes. Once I was under it, I crouched down and rested on my back. I gazed up and took everything in. A sudden chill brushed against my body as I received goosebumps. It snowed earlier, yet I still froze because I misplaced my jacket. I raised my left arm and stared at it. Right below my wrist was a small hole where they injected me. I ran my fingers over it and nervously bit my lip. I didn't mean for it to happen; thank goodness it only happened once. Yet that one time fucking ruined everything.

I quickly got up and dusted myself off and

jogged through downtown in search of the simple building. Once I reached my destination, I gazed up at the stairs. They still haven't built a fucking elevator for the place? I cursed under my breath as I walked upstairs. My head spun more the further I walked. I felt my tummy twist as something lurked up my throat. I leaned over the fifth flight of stairs as everything I had from the party hurled out. I gagged as I tried to get everything out. I looked down to see the massive puddles of barf on the stairs and walls. I let out a hoarse groan as I continued to walk until I got to the seventh floor. I strolled to the old wooden door that read thirty-eight and banged on it. After a few attempts, it flew open with an exhausted Keene.

"Dude, what the hell are you doing here? It's like…" he croaked, then looked over his shoulder. "Late."

"Well, hello to you too," I said, and Keene scrunched his nose up as I walked past him into his apartment. I flopped down on his couch and took in the scent of his pillow.

"You smell like shit," he said from the kitchen.

"Oh yeah, err…you need to clean the stairs," I stated as I adjusted myself so that I was on my back.

"Dude, not again." He sighed, then came into the room with a can of beer and a glass of water.

"You're so kind." I sighed as he set the glass on the table.

"Nuh-uh. Go wash your mouth. I don't want you to talk when your breath reeks like shit," he said as he opened the can. I groaned as I got up and walked to his bathroom. I washed my face as well as my mouth, then walked back into the living room and noticed that he was smoking a cigarette.

"Where's your roommate?" I asked, because the last time I came here, his roommate went all ape shit on me being too drunk to handle.

"Gone for the weekend," he replied as I sat on the sofa. "What the hell you doing here?"

"Went to a party," I said, then grabbed the can.

"No shit," he retorted as he exhaled the smoke.

"Are you gonna be sarcastic the whole time and complain or listen to my shit ass night?" I slammed the can down in annoyance.

"Dude, I always listen. Remember that one time you were ranting about this guy who thought he had a bigger dick than you?"

"Oh yeah, thanks, bro." I giggled then sent him a wink. "Well, we went to this lame-ass party, got into a fight, and, well…got kicked out."

"We?" He raised a brow. My eyes widened at the thought of Blake entered my mind.

"Oh, shit…I forgot Blake." I chuckled. "He'll find his way."

"Mm…dude, you okay from the other night? I thought you'd be dead," Keene said as he stared at me.

"Well, I think I'm alive."

"Unfortunately," he said, to which I laughed. "How's Lana?"

"She's dating the fucker now." I squinted my eyes. "Why didn't you tell me before that they're friends?"

"I'm not your spy," he said, then crushed the cigarette in the ashtray.

“They’re not gonna last,” I muttered.

“Dude, would you stop? She’s not yours…never was, never will be,” Keene snapped as he glared at me. “That night when you two fucked, you knew it would be the last time you could control her, now she’s wit—”

“Shut up, Keene.”

“No. Last year you had your chance, and you let it slip right through your fingers.” He pushed himself off the seat so that I looked up to him. “I know you don’t believe in love and all that shit, but girls do, and you acted like a dick!” His chest rose as his huffs filled the room. I stared at him with a blank look, which made him angrier. “Now you’re all protective and shit just because you hate the guy.”

“Because I care about her!” I yelled.

“Yeah, in that way,” he mumbled.

“What the fuck is that supposed to mean?”

“You care about her in that protective fuck buddy, best friend way, but she…” He trailed off then collapsed into the armchair and stared at the opposite wall. “Dude, that night when the car flipped, you should’ve seen her reaction…she wanted to kill Blake. The way she ran to the car like it was the only way to escape and then the look she had when she saw you…she cares about you, Levi. A lot.”

“I know she does. I just don’t see an us. She deserves so much better,” I mumbled, then turned to Keene. “My life is too fucked up right now, and I don’t want to involve Lana. She has her whole life ahead of her. She’s even going to Yale.”

"How do you know?"

"I just know," I said as a smile appeared on my lips. "She's been dreaming about Yale since ninth grade."

"Maybe this Benny dude is the one."

"Fuck no," I snapped. "My princess deserves much more."

"Okay, you're still drunk. You better not call her that in front of Benny," Keene snorted.

"Whatever, but she'll always be my princess. I'll just have to accept that there'll be more than one knight trying to save her."

The room filled with silence as I stared at the ground. I thought this year would be like any other year when we visited, yet this year had been absolute shit for me. Then coming back to Illinois suddenly felt better and more like home. A loud knock broke the silence as I glanced up to see Keene walk to the door. He opened it and let out a long groan as he left it open and walked back to the armchair. I watched as Lana stormed in with Blake behind her. They looked pissed.

"Hey, guys!" I waved.

"Dude, we've been looking for you for the past hour," Blake stated as he leaned against the wall.

"How'd you find me?" I chuckled as I drank the beer in one gulp.

"I figured you were with Keene, plus we just followed the barf smell." Lana gagged.

"Aww, you know my barf smell." I rested my hand over heart. "I'm touched, princess."

"Well, come on." Lana sighed as she walked toward the door then spun around. I let out a loud groan as I stood up too quickly, and I lost my balance and fell. I face planted on the floor and heard the faint snickers.

“Not funny. Help me,” I mumbled into the floor as I raised my arm. I was pulled back onto my feet as Blake wrapped my arm around his shoulder, then his arm around my waist as he held me up. “Thanks, bro.” I gave him a faint smile. He grumbled beside me as we walked toward the door. We greeted Keene, and he said he might see us tomorrow. I blinked rapidly as we walked toward the stairs. We reached the stairs, and Lana suddenly stopped as she looked ahead. We followed her gaze to see the barf everywhere.

“Dude, you’re gross.” Blake chuckled as he tried to walk through the barf. It took us five minutes to get down the stairs as we tried to avoid the barf. I glanced up to see my car, and my blank expression immediately changed as I forced myself off Blake and darted toward it. I pressed myself against the car as I embraced it.

“I thought I lost you,” I cooed and squished my cheek against the window.

“Wait, so you ran off because you were looking for your car?” Lana asked as she opened the door. I nodded and climbed in the back with her while Blake walked to the driver’s side. He let out a dry laugh as we got comfortable in my car.

“Dude, your car was right in front of the house,” he said as he started the engine. I threw my head back and laughed as we drove through downtown. Lana was quiet beside me as she rested her head against the window. I glanced up in the rearview mirror to see Blake's stare. I sent him a questioning look as I gestured to Lana, but he shrugged. He turned on the radio to break the tense atmosphere. I placed my hand on her shoulder, and she turned. It was the first time tonight I got an actual look at her. She looked exhausted, the bags under her eyes darkened. I motioned her to come closer as I raised my left arm and placed it on the seat. She raised a brow as she pushed her glasses up. I rolled my eyes as I sank in my chair.

"Come on, you're tired, and that looks uncomfortable," I pouted. "I won't tell Benny."

Lana let out a sigh and rolled her eyes as she shifted next to me and placed her head on my chest. I smiled as I ran my fingers through her hair. When I looked up, I saw Blake with a cigarette between his lips. I tapped him on the shoulder as he looked at me through the mirror. I held two fingers up as I blew through them, and he grinned, then threw his pack over his shoulder. I took out my lighter as Lana took out a cigarette from the pack and held it between her lips. I lit it and took it from her after she took a drag. I threw the box in front, and Blake caught it as I held the cigarette between my lips. I blew out smoke rings until I felt a poke on my chest. I glanced down to see Lana patiently waiting. I playfully rolled my eyes as I removed the cigarette from my lips and lowered it. She took a drag. I smirked. Ten minutes later after driving with the radio on and sharing a cigarette, we arrived at the Willsons' home. I got out to see Blake's Harley parked in the front.

"All right, see you guys later," he mumbled as

we stood on the porch.

"Thanks," Lana replied as he walked to his motorcycle. Blake smiled as he got onto the bike. I raised a brow. I turned to Lana by the door. We walked into the house, and I immediately collapsed onto the sofa. Lana leaned against the doorframe as she stared at me.

"Did you guys fuck in my car then come and get me?" I asked. Her eyes slanted.

"What the hell? No! We were arguing most of the time, and he almost drove into another car," Lana grumbled as she spun around and walked toward the stairs.

"Thanks for tonight," I called out. "Love you."

I glanced over my shoulder to see her. A blank expression filled her face as she backed up the stairs. A sigh escaped from her lips as she glanced up at me and said, "Love you too."

Chapter Eight

Lana

I pushed myself off the bed as I let out a yawn. After last night's event, I went to bed immediately. I walked to the bathroom and brushed my teeth as well as my hair, then opened the door. Voices filled my ears as I strolled into the kitchen.

"Morning, everyone," I greeted. Everyone except for Levi sat at the table eating eggs and sausages. I sat down next to my dad as I dished up.

"Morning. What time did you come home last night? I heard a commotion downstairs," Mom asked as she set a fresh plate of bacon on the table.

"Err…I had to go and get Levi from Keene's place," I mumbled, then drank my orange juice.

"What was he doing there?" Richard asked at the same time Levi walked in. I shrugged in response, then turned to Levi. He sat opposite me with a tired look as he ran a hand through his dark hair. He let out a yawn and turned to my dad.

"Morning, Bobby!" He grinned. Dad rolled his

eyes as he sipped his coffee.

"Lana, dear, you have to start making those cinnamon rolls soon. We bought all the ingredients," Mom said.

"That's another reason why we still come every year," Richard said. Jade hit him with the dishcloth. I made different cinnamon rolls every year, and everyone loved them, but they took time to make since I made them from scratch.

"Ooh, can you make those ones with the chocolate sauce over them?" Levi chimed in with a bright look on his face.

"I like the ones with the nuts," Richard added.

"What about the ones where there's custard insi—"

"Christmas is, like, in a week. I don't think I'll finish it all this weekend," I said.

"Well, then you better start soon, dear," Jade stated.

"Yeah, I'll go shower now," I said, then got up. I walked into my room, made my bed, and took out an outfit for the day. I decided on something dull but warm since our house wasn't that warm, even with the heaters. I pulled my hair up into a bun as I looked at myself in the mirror. I wore a white, long-sleeved shirt and a maroon skirt with black leggings. I slipped on a pair of black ankle boots and my glasses, then walked down.

Two hours later, we were still busy. We were on the fourth batch with the other two in the oven. Keene came over, but he didn't help at all and said he's only here to keep us company and get free cinnamon rolls. Dad and Richard were in his study since Dad had a TV set up, so they watched sports while Mom and Jade went Christmas shopping. Keene bobbed his head to a song on the radio while I folded the dough. I felt my thigh vibrate as "Teenagers" by My Chemical Romance played. I tried to get my phone from my skirt pocket, but my hands were dirty. Levi approached me with a smirk plastered on his face. He pressed himself against my back as his hand ran up my thigh to get to my phone. A shiver jerked up my spine. He pressed his chest against my back and answered my phone.

"Lana and Levi's disposable dildos, she sucks 'em, and I chuck 'em. How may we pleasure you today?"

My eyes widened as I pushed him, then spun around to hear the person's response. I paled at the thought of it being Benny, Miranda, or even Uncle Griff.

"Well, yes, I haven't received mine yet. Can I get a refund? Cash won't do. I think I'll need her to com—"

"Oh my god!" I shrieked as Carter spoke in a horrible British accent. They laughed as I shook my head and got back to work. "Get ready, we're coming," Carter said as Levi put the phone on speaker.

"Are we still on the sexual jokes or are you actually coming?" Keene asked.

"I wish…Aidan and Liam want to go to that stupid Wonderland shit," Carter muttered.

"It's not shit!" Aidan yelled in the background.

"See you sexy fuckers in five," he said, then ended the call. Keene helped me clean up while

Levi took selfies on my phone. We were done just in time as we heard cars honk. I slipped on my coat and a maroon scarf, then followed Keene and Levi out the door.

"Shit!" Keene yelled. I glanced up and noticed Keene fell, reason being that he was met by snow. A smile crept on my face as I glanced around the snow that surrounded our garden.

"Dude, snow angels!" Liam exclaimed as he ran up to Keene and plopped down beside him. Keene glared at Liam, who leisurely made snow angels while he struggled to get up.

"Dude, you suck." Aidan piped in as he ran toward Liam and Keene. We watched as he let out a frustrated groan then stared at the two brunettes.

"You both swallow!"

I laughed as I walked toward Aidan's car where Benny and Miranda were. She started to sniff the air as Benny wrapped an arm around my waist.

"You making cinnamon rolls?" Miranda wiggled her brows.

"Yeah, my dad is keeping an eye on them so we can have some when we come back." I smiled.

"Hey, Lana," Tiffany greeted as she waved from Miranda's car. I waved back as I spotted Melissa and Nick by the vehicle. I glanced at Aidan and Liam, who walked toward us.

"I see your date went well," I said to Aidan, who smiled at Tiffany. His cheeks reddened when he thanked me again, then walked to her.

"Yeah, it's easier," Ethan said as I tilted my head. He saw my confused look and laughed. Benny turned to me as I rested my head on his shoulder.

"We're going in three cars, so it's quicker," Ethan mumbled as everyone got into a car. All the girls piled into one car while Benny, Liam, Nick, and Marcus got into Aidan's car. Levi decided to take his car as Keene, Blake, Ethan, and Carter drove with him.

"You guys are all dating jocks now, wow," Tiffany commented from the backseat. Her date with Aidan must've gone well since she decided to come.

"I know, right?" Miranda smiled. "Everyone goes for the basketball players, but I enjoy my soccer player."

"Speaking of our wonderful boyfriends…" Melissa trailed off as she looked at me. "Where were you two last night?"

"We didn't feel like a party, so we just chilled at his place and watched Netflix."

"Netflix and chill already?" Tiffany gasped as Miranda squealed. My eyes widened as I furiously shook my head at the three girls who squealed and asked the most inappropriate questions.

"No, it wasn't like that! We just watched a few movies and cud—"

"Yeah right," they said in unison. I buried my head in my hands from embarrassment as they laughed.

We arrived at the park to see the huge Winter Wonderland. Booths sold almost everything, there were carnival food, rides, an ice skating rink, and shows took place. We walked around and took in the atmosphere. I walked hand in hand with Benny as we followed our group.

“Oh my gosh, Lana, look—those hats I was telling you about!” Miranda squealed as we walked through the booths.

“I like the black one,” Melissa referred to the Russian hats.

“The white one will look beautiful with your hair,” Miranda said to Tiffany.

“You think so?” She chuckled as the guys groaned.

“Are you guys literally gonna stop at every booth, trying on things yet not buy anything?” Aidan asked.

“Err…yeah. You brought us here for a reason,” Melissa pursed her lips.

“Dude, just don’t say anything. You’ll get used it. In the end, you’re the one carrying all the bags,” Marcus assured him.

“Well, I’m hungry as hell. See you guys later,” Liam said as he walked off with Ethan and Aidan.

“Hey, we should all get one!” Miranda squealed as she turned to the three of us.

“All right, see ya,” Levi said as he walked off with Keene and Blake.

“Which one do I take?” I asked. I picked up the dark brown one and took out my hair tie as I tried it on. I turned to Benny, who smiled at me.

“You look beautiful,” he said, then approached me.

“Hey! You wear, you buy!” the woman behind the booth said as Benny planted a kiss on my lips.

“We’ll take these.” Miranda pointed to the hats we wore. Miranda bought them for us as she put on her red one; Melissa wore a black. Tiffany had a white one, while I stuck to my brown one. "Carter, make yourself useful and take a photo of us," Miranda said as she gave him her phone. I laughed as he gave her a look but raised the phone anyway as we posed for the picture. We continued to walk as Carter gave Miranda's phone back and went to go catch up with the rest of the guys.

"Please, baby!" Miranda whined beside us.

"You wanna throw up?" Marcus asked.

"No, but by the time we get to the rides, the food will already be digested!"

"Fine…the usual?" Marcus asked as he glanced at Benny.

"Uh huh." Miranda nodded.

"Come on, dude, the lady wants food," Marcus said as he tugged on Benny's arm. I laughed as Nick, Benny, and Marcus walked in search of food. Out the corner of my eye I saw a booth that sort of lured me into it. I approached the booth and took in all the different types of vinyl on the table. My eyes scanned through the genres of music as I felt a presence beside me.

"You got that one," Levi said. I followed his gaze to see that I held ABBA's vinyl.

"How do you know?" I set it down and looked through the others. I picked up The Wanted as my lips formed into a smile.

"And that one," Blake said as he appeared on my other side.

"Do you guys hang out in my room while I'm not there or what?" I asked, then put the vinyl down.

"Sometimes," Keene replied as he stood next to

Levi. I let out a sigh as I flicked through the vinyls until I came across one I was sure I didn't have. It was a special one since I loved the album.

"Bastille," I said to myself as I looked through the song list. I noticed Keene, Levi, and Blake lingered around the booth too as they checked out other music. I wanted the vinyl yet I wasn't sure, because I already had so many types. I sighed as I put the vinyl down and walked to the girls. Thankfully Benny was there with two crepes in his hands. He spotted me as a smile crept onto his face.

"Strawberry or bananas?" He raised his hands.

"Strawberries." I grinned and accepted the crepe from him.

"Do you guys have change?" Ethan asked with an irritated look. We shook our heads, and he groaned and walked off. We followed his gaze to see Liam and Aidan by a game booth as they yelled in frustration. We followed Ethan and approached the two.

"Benny, I need a dollar," Liam demanded as he eyed the buckets.

"I don't have change. All I got is a five dolla—" Benny held up the note. Liam snatched it as he shoved it in the guy's hand.

"Thanks, dude," Liam said as he picked up a ball. Aidan threw balls by the moving buckets; however, he missed.

"Ugh!" he groaned as the guy placed another bucket of balls between the two. We watched in amusement as the two angrily threw them. "I shall not rest until the balls have reached their destination!" Aidan exclaimed as he gave the guy another dollar.

"It's rigged, you idiots," Carter stated as he offered me some of his cotton candy, but I kindly declined.

"Step aside, losers. Let the pro handle this," Levi said as he flicked his hand over his shoulder as if he had long hair. Aidan and Liam backed up as Levi grabbed a ball. We watched as he focused on the buckets, then at the right moment, he threw it with all his strength. We followed the ball and watched it hit the table. Miranda let out a snort as Liam and Aidan laughed, then continued.

"When's the pro getting here?" Miranda asked. Levi flipped her off. We finished our food yet still watched the two toss balls toward the tent while the guy counted his money. We decided to leave them as we walked on. I entwined my fingers with Benny's as Melissa and Nick stopped at a booth.

"Want to know your fortune? Join Madam Saga's Fortuning Telling special techniques to seek your destiny!" a woman said from her booth. I raised a brow at her outfit as she mystically moved her arms.

"Sounds fun," Benny muttered sarcastically.

"Can we go?" Melissa chirped as the woman stared at us.

"It's complete and utter shit," Keene said as the woman glared at him.

"Let's just go for fun," Miranda groaned as she dragged us to her.

"Excellent!" Madam Saga exclaimed as Miranda gave her a few dollars. Aidan and Liam returned with grins spread across their faces.

“What did you two do?” Nick blurted out.

“Oh nothing, just kicked the guy in his balls and threatened to throw them in the bucket if he didn’t give our money back for the stupid game,” Aidan replied as Liam showed his money. I laughed as Miranda tugged on my arm. We eventually followed the woman into her booth as she raised the curtain. It was much more elaborate on the inside. A carpet was thrown on the floor to make the tent look dark and mysterious as we sat down in a circle. I sat next to Miranda and Benny while everyone else followed.

“All right, join hands,” Madam Saga commanded as she sat in the middle of the circle. We did as told, then watched as she brought her crystal ball out. I resisted the urge to roll my eyes as she waved her hands around it. Out of the corner of my eye, I noticed Blake stare at her. We locked eyes as I motioned to the woman. He rolled his eyes and gestured to headbutt her, and I snickered. “Who would like to know their fortune?”

“Ooh, me!” Miranda piped up.

“Okay, child,” Saga said, then shut her eyes as she waved her hands around the crystal ball. “I see good things coming your way, yet you’ll go over hurdles, but in the end, you’ll be happy with love,” Madam Saga said, which made Miranda smile as she kissed Marcus on the cheek, but Saga’s eyes seemed to linger around the circle.

“Who’s next?”

“I’ll go.” Carter shrugged. She did the same thing as earlier. A smile molded onto her face as she spoke.

"You'll be welcomed by the opposite sex and your good is yet to get even better in the future."

"I already knew that." Carter snorted as we laughed.

"Why don't you try, Lana?" Tiffany suggested.

"Err…okay," I mumbled as I watched Madam Saga do her thing. After a few seconds, her eyes squinted as she let out a raspy sigh.

"Things are not clear," she began. "Everything seems okay one minute, and then the next…"

Madam Saga's breathing quickened as her eyes flickered. Murmurs and whispers spread through the tent as someone reached over to her.

"Don't break the circle!" she exclaimed as her hands gripped the crystal ball. Ethan quickly sat down as we watched in horror. Benny's grip on my hand tightened. "No, no, no…" she trailed off. "Great dangers are coming to you, child, yet it's unclear when and h-how, but some people in this room are i-involved."

Madam Saga's eyes shot open as she backed away from the crystal ball. It was quiet as everyone stared at Madam Saga and me. My eyes flicked to everyone as they held blank looks.

"That's bullshit," Levi said as he and Keene laughed. I watched as they got up and walked toward the exit with everyone behind. I walked past Madam Saga but felt her grip on my arm. I whipped my head around to see her stare at me with a frightened look.

"Trust your gut," she said as her gripped stiffened. "And be careful, Lana."

I then felt Blake's hand on my arm as he tried to

pry the woman's hand off me.

"Crazy," he muttered once he got me loose. I gave him a wary look as we walked out, and he looked away. We walked out of the booth, and I felt Tiffany wrap her arm around my shoulder.

"Don't worry, it's not real," she assured me as I nervously pushed up my glasses.

"Yeah, sometimes they just say stuff like that, so you'll pay more." Marcus shrugged.

"Yeah," I whispered as we walked on.

"So what do you guys wanna do now?" Melissa asked as Nick slung his arm over her shoulder.

"Ice skating anyone?" Aidan pointed up ahead to the ice rink. Everyone agreed just to get rid of the tense atmosphere. We walked to the arena, where we paid for half an hour and got our skates.

"Dude, race you to the opposite side," Liam said as he got on the ice.

"You're on," Aidan said as they bolted past the people. I carefully stepped onto the ice and gripped the pole for support. I'd never ice skated before, yet I always wanted to. It's easy to say things, but to do it was something else. I glanced up and saw everyone else enjoying him or herself while I leaned against the pole. Out the corner of my eye, I saw Levi approach me.

"Come on, princess, another thing to tick off the list." He winked.

"What list?" Blake asked as he stood next to me.

"When we were little, we made this bucket list, and every year when he comes, we try to do the stuff on it," I said.

"Dude, some of the stuff on there is fucking

crazy." Levi chuckled as I glanced at Blake. I noticed that he also held onto the pole, yet he played it off while my arms trembled.

"We only got half an hour. Come on," Keene said as he and Levi skated off. I glanced around to see Benny in the center with everyone else. I felt Blake stare at me, so I turned to him.

"Ladies first." He motioned with his head as his grip on the poles tightened.

"Age before beauty," I stated with an innocent smile. Blake let out a frustrated sigh then pushed himself off the pole. I tried not to laugh as his legs wobbled as he balanced himself. He slowly spun around and placed his hands in his pockets as he stood up straight.

"See? It's eas—" he began but lost his balance as he fell backward. Luckily, he regained his balance then came back to the pole. "I'm not doing this shit ever again." I laughed. "You're up, nerd." He gave a supportive smile. I turned to the ice and noticed Miranda and Benny staring from across the rink. I anxiously licked my lips as I glanced down at the ice.

"Come on, Lana!" Miranda cheered. I pushed myself forward as I kept my head up high and moved. For once, I didn't fall over.

"There you go!" Blake cheered. I felt like I was going to fall sometimes, but I looked straight at Benny. I laughed at myself as I approached the center. Benny opened his arms as I dashed forward. Suddenly, my left foot decided to swerve as I lost my balance. Thankfully, Benny caught me in time as his arms wrapped around me. We still moved as he brought me closer to him.

"Hey, don't worry…I got you." He smiled as we stopped. I held his hands then straightened my posture. Once I was confident, I looked at him, only to see that he smiled. I gave a stiff nod as he pulled me forward.

"Lana, watch out!" someone yelled behind me. Benny's eyes widened as he tugged me forward, but it was too late as I was pushed down. My chin hit the sharp ice as I felt another body land on top of me.

"You idiots!" Miranda yelled. The person got off of me.

"Oh, shit! I'm so sorry, Lana!" Liam rushed out as I attempted to get up.

"Last time we're playing human slingshot." Aidan sighed.

"Dude, what the fuck?" Benny growled as he helped me up. Liam apologized as I regained my balance. Benny handed me my glasses, and I thanked him. I glanced up at my friends and noticed their apprehensive looks.

"That's gonna leave a mark," Tiffany said as she stared at me. I squinted my eyes and glanced down. I was perfectly fine. Suddenly, a red spot landed on the ice, and I touched my face.

"Come on, babe, let's get you to the doctor," Benny said as he wrapped an arm around my waist.

***

I shut my eyes as I felt the thread being pulled through my chin. Turned out the impact Liam had on me when we tumbled managed to cut my jaw open.

"All done," the doctor said as he applied the bandage over the cut. There was an Emergency Clinic gazebo not too far from the ice rink, so we went there. Everyone else went back to the cars while Levi, Miranda, and Benny stayed with me. "After five to seven days you can get the stitches removed, but there will obviously be a little scar." The doctor rummaged through his bag.

"Nothing a little makeup can't fix," Miranda stated as she smiled at me.

"Yeah, just don't chew like a camel or horse, then it will obviously affect the healing process." The doctor gave me a lollipop. I think I lost my enthusiasm for the candy when he said that.

"Thanks, Doc," Levi said as I got off the bed. We walked out of the gazebo and was swept by the cold wind. My fingertips grazed over my stitches and sighed. How would I explain this to my parents?

***

We arrived at home, and Levi invited everyone inside and said that there was dessert. I sighed because they ate all the cinnamon rolls and I'd have to make more.

"Damn, these are amazing," Blake moaned as we ate the hot cinnamon rolls that I reheated in the oven.

"Dude, you should taste the caramel ones," Levi said as I joined everyone in the living room. I sat next to Benny, and he wrapped an arm around my shoulder. We shared a cinnamon roll since they were big and I helped everyone else. From the corner of my eye, I saw Aidan. I turned to him and Liam and noticed that Levi whispered to them. Suddenly they turned to me then laughed.

"Lana, don't chew like a camel or else," Aidan said as he and Liam ate like a horse. Their jaws went around and round that made me squirm. I shrugged them off when Dad and Mom walked in. Dad saw the last cinnamon roll on the table and quickly snatched it before anyone else could.

"Hey, Mr. Willson." Marcus greeted.

"Hey, it's Lana and Levi's friends in my living room…as always." He muttered the last part as I laughed.

"At least it's better than the jail cell," Aidan said, and Ethan nudged him. Dad took a bite out of the roll then turned to me with a blank look.

"What happened to you?" he asked, glancing around the room for the culprit.

"Madam Saga predicted danger," Liam answered as everyone laughed.

"Should we be worried?" Mom asked as she literally lifted my face and examined my cut.

"Not at all, Bobby. She's in safe hands," Levi said.

"Who's Bobby?" Ethan asked. Levi pointed to my father as the guys laughed.

"I like that…Bobby." Carter beamed as he chewed his food.

"Bobby," Liam sang. I let out a sigh as I got up to refill the empty plate. The doorbell rang as I entered the kitchen. I put a few cinnamon rolls onto the plate then walked back to the living room. Blake leaned against the door as I raised a brow. His jaw clenched as his eyes squinted. I followed his gaze to see Axel on our sofa.

"What is he doing here?" I whispered as Levi and Keene joined him on the couch.

"I don't kn—"

"Lana, let Axel try your cinnamon rolls," Jade said as she gestured to the plate. I walked to the coffee table and placed the dish on the table. I backed away and stood next to Blake. Out the corner of my eye, I saw Richard enter the room. A baffled look filled my face as Richard smiled at Axel.

"Hey, Mr. Radcliff," Axel greeted as Richard leaned against one of the sofas. I raised a brow and tried to fit the pieces together of the adults' weird behavior toward Axel. Suddenly they looked at me with blank expressions. I squinted my eyes as I watched Axel and Levi turn to Keene. He shook his head, and Axel and Levi shook their heads at the adults.

"Something's going on," I whispered to Blake as we watched the adults' weird behavior.

"Yep." Blake sighed as my mom offered Axel another cinnamon roll. "Tonight should be interesting."

Chapter Nine

Lana

I stared at the last cinnamon rolls because I had to make more in the next few days. I placed them in a container as the laughter from the living room disturbed my thoughts. Everyone was still here, and the adults even treated Axel like a freaking king. The curiosity killed me, and I mentally reminded myself to ask them about it later. I placed the container in the fridge then shut it. Our double door fridge had many things on it, pictures of when I was young, my parents on their wedding day, Levi and I when we were little, a grocery list, and a calendar. The thing that caught my eye was the small mirror held up with a magnet. I took off my glasses as I stared at myself in the mirror. Even though it was a bit blurry, I still saw the stitches on my chin. I slowly traced the stitches with my thumb. The sound of crockery being placed in the sink brought me back to reality as I spun around. A tall figure stood by the sink and stared at me. I slowly put on my glasses to see Blake.

"These are really good." He pointed to the cinnamon rolls.

"Thanks," I mumbled. I watched as Blake's gaze suddenly dropped. I followed his gaze to see that he stopped by my neck. My eyes widened in embarrassment as I thought of the hickey. I tied my hair up earlier but only took my scarf off when I entered the kitchen. I grabbed my scarf and slowly put it on. I packed the other cinnamon rolls and took out another container. I felt his eyes burn the back of my skull as I stacked the rolls into the container. Multiple footsteps entered the kitchen as I packed away the second to last container. I spun around and leaned on the fridge to see Axel, Keene, and Levi. I watched as Keene swiftly put on his jacket while Levi rummaged through the drawers. "What are you looking for?"

"The lighter fluid that I bought. Have you seen it?" Levi asked. I walked to the island and reached over by the fruit bowl. Dad barely ate fruit, so it was the perfect place to hide it. I snatched the bottle out and tossed it to Levi. We watched as he whipped out his Zippo and refilled it with the lighter fluid. Out the corner of my eye, Miranda and Benny entered the room.

"Pumpkin's dating a jock now?" Axel piped up as Benny stood next to me. I gave a curt nod as Axel smirked. "Didn't see that coming." He sighed then glanced at his brother. "But hey…you know what they say. Expect the unexpected." Axel winked at Blake as I raised a brow. I wearily rested my head on Benny's shoulder as I watched Levi.

Once he was done, he put the bottle back between the fruits.

"Thanks, Prin—Lana," he mumbled.

"Where are you guys going?" Miranda asked as they walked out the back door.

"Out. Come on, Carter!" Keene yelled as he grabbed Levi's keys. We watched as the blond boy skipped into the kitchen and put on his beanie. With one last wink, he walked out the door then shut it. I let out a sigh as I took a seat on the island. Miranda grabbed another cinnamon roll, and I groaned as Benny sat opposite me.

"You okay?" he asked, then placed his hands over mine. I nodded yet gave him a sleepy smile as he took my hands in his then raised them. Our elbows rested on the table as he left a gentle kiss on my knuckles. "Liam apologizes again for what happened earlier."

"It's okay…accidents happen." I chuckled. "Remember when you got stitches in ninth grade?"

"How could I forget? She was out of the class for one minute then came back to the whole class talking, leading to all of us to stay during lunch to clean the storeroom."

"Yeah. Remember the dead bird we found in the cage?"

"Yeah, then Nick and Tyler took out all the fish tanks, which I didn't see."

"How did you not see a gigantic fish tank on the table?"

"Not my fault the table was right behind me! They took the lid off, and I cut my arm on the freaking sharp edge," he muttered, then pulled up his sleeve. I stared at the large scar on his forearm where six stitches were once put in. "It's not a nice thing to have."

"But it's a good memory and funny story to tell," I said as he glanced at me. His brown eyes locked with mine as the corners wrinkled up to form a smile. I gave a smile back as he took his thumb and rubbed circles on my palm. The doorbell rang as we turned our heads toward the living room. We saw Dad walk to the front door and open it. Two men stood by the door that I didn't know. Dad must've known them since they spoke. Benny and I exchanged a few looks, then walked toward my father. Dad let out a sigh as he ran a hand through his hair.

"Marcus, someone's here to see you," Dad said as he stepped aside. My eyes squinted as I took in the appearance of the man in a suit and the police officer beside him. Marcus stood in the hall with Miranda beside him as they stared in confusion. The two men stepped out of the cold and into the house as we went into the living room.

"Marcus Sanders," the man in the suit said as we took our seats except for the two men and Marcus. "I'm Detective Kale, and this is officer Owen. I'd like to ask you a few questions."

"Err…sure."

"This is related to the case of Mr. August, who went missing on October 1, 2016. We'd just like to know where were you last night?" he asked as the officer took out a notepad. I glanced at Nick and Benny and noticed their stares on the detective. The room suddenly went quiet as everyone listened.

“I was at a party,” Marcus said in an ominous tone.

“How far was this party from the industrial area…the crime scene?” Detective Kale asked.

“I-I don’t know it was at Tyler’s hou—” Marcus said as he looked at Liam.

“Tyler lives in the suburbs, probably about half an hour from there.”

“Were you anywhere near the crime scene, boy?” Detective Kale asked as he raised a brow. Marcus shook his head, and the Detective laughed. “You better not be lying, Sanders, we have evidence, and he can take you in.” He pointed to the officer.

“Whoa, whoa, Kale. Nobody’s getti—”

“Wait. I remember going there the other day…” Marcus cut off my father.

“Uh huh.” Detective Kale smirked as he pulled out a bag that had the word **EVIDENCE** written on it. My eyes widened as everyone stared at Marcus than the Detective. “Now explain why this was found in the alley that is under investigation and has your prints all over it.” Detective Kale held up the bag. I never thought I’d see it again. However, Blake and Aidan flushed down the last two bottles that I ever had.

“I—I—” Marcus stuttered as he looked at the bag then Detective Kale.

“He needs a lawyer!” Aidan blurted out. We turned to Aidan and stared. “Sorry…I’ve always wanted to say that.”

“Come on, Sanders, I haven’t got all day. The prints on the bottle match yours precisely,”

Detective Kale growled. I raised a brow as I thought how they had his prints. Marcus was eighteen but still, the only time he had my bottle was when he walked to the trashcan and threw it away. I glanced at the pills inside and, how ironic that there were fourteen in there.

"Well, the, err…my friend was taking those, and I wanted him to stop, so I grabbed them from him and ran down the street," Marcus began. "He followed, and I tossed it somewhere…that must've been the place where it landed."

There was absolute silence as Detective Kale stared at Marcus. I barely knew Marcus, only the things Miranda had told me. Other than that, we barely spoke.

"All right," the detective said as he turned to my dad. "Sorry to bother your little party, Willson."

Dad gave a short nod in return as we followed them to the door. I leaned against the staircase as Dad opened the door for them.

"Any leads yet?" Dad piped up as the police officer walked out the door.

"Not really. With scarce evidence and a clueless family, it'll take a while to find him," Detective Kale answered as the lump grew in my throat.

"What do you mean by clueless?" Nick asked.

"That's classified information, boy," Kale said as he eyed Nick. Dad let out a sigh as he watched Detective Kale walk out into the snow. Everyone else returned to the living room, but Nick, Benny, and I stayed in the hall.

"Dad, what happened to Jack's family?" I asked as Dad shut the door. Dad let out a deep sigh as he spun around and looked at us. Benny stuffed his hands in his pockets while Nick folded his arms, apparently not going anywhere until my dad gave an answer.

"Saw Kale questioning them in the interrogation room the other day. They didn't know where he was, and it's like they barely knew him, considering he's an alcoholic," Dad answered.

"Thanks, Dad," I mumbled. Dad gave us a skeptical look as he walked to his office to join Richard as they continued the game in there. Benny stood next to me as Nick stood in front of us. I looked up to see his eyes squinted as he stared at the ground. "Maybe I should just tell," I murmured. From the corner of my eye, I noticed how Benny looked at me as if I'd grown a second head.

"We can't; we don't even know where he is," Nick said. Benny intertwined his hand in mine as I rested my head on his shoulder. He left a gentle a kiss on my forehead as Nick tugged on his hair.

"It's just weird that his family doesn't know anything," Benny said.

"Let's just see how the rest of the week plays out. If nothing comes up after Christmas…" Nick trailed off as he looked at the living room.

"Then what?" I asked.

"I-I don't know." He shrugged, then joined everyone in the living room. I stared at the floor in guilt because I didn't want anything to come until Christmas. I wanted to have a typical Christmas like every year.

"Hey, don't worry," Benny whispered as he brought me in for a hug. I wrapped my arms around his torso and gently placed my chin on his shoulder. He rubbed circles on my back as he brought me closer to him. "Everything's gonna be okay."

***

Blake

Using Levi's Zippo lighter, I lit my cigarette and put it between my lips. I tossed it in the back where Carter, Axel, and Keene sat. Green Day blared through Levi's car as he drove.

"Where's this lame-ass party?" Levi asked as he drove with one hand on the wheel and the other to dump the ash out the window of his cigarette.

"Dude, do you remember that frat party last year? Jaden's house," Keene replied from the back. I turned to Levi and noticed how the corner of his mouth rose. I glanced up into the rearview mirror and saw the looks my brother and Keene exchanged. Earlier when he decided to join us, I didn't take note, but Lana got suspicious, and I understood why. Axel bonded with Keene and Levi way better than I ever had. It was as if he knew them already.

By the time we arrived at the party, it was already packed. The house was located on top of a hill, and I heard the music from the bottom. Wasn't really in the party mood since Levi, Carter, and I were already at a party last night.

"Levi Radcliff!" a guy exclaimed as we entered the house. A dark-skinned guy who wasn't the tallest approached us, dressed in a muscle tee, black sweats, and Nike shoes. He held a drink in one hand as he hugged Levi with the other.

"Jaden, long time no see," Levi said as Jaden hugged Keene.

"I know…I'll visit soon," Jaden said as he looked at Axel, Carter, and me.

"This is Blake, Axel, and Carter," Keene stated. We greeted Jaden as he gave us a once over. He then looked at the door, then back at Levi.

"Where're those little girlfriends of yours?" Jaden asked as my eyebrows rose.

"Err…they couldn't make it," Levi mumbled as he avoided eye contact. Keene shook his head as I folded my arms.

"Ugh, what a shame. Last year she blew the fucking roof off!" Jaden laughed. "Ain't that right, Keene?" he added as we turned to Keene. A puzzled look filled my face as I stared at Keene. What I'd heard from Keene was Levi didn't date. So there could be only one person Jaden referred to. Yet I didn't understand how it affected Keene. "Enjoy the party, gentlemen, and if you need something, hit me up," Jaden said, then disappeared into the crowd with Keene behind.

"All right, see you guys later." Carter smirked as a girl approached him. I let out a sigh since we'd be here for a while. Axel and Levi disappeared, and I suddenly felt thirsty. I walked through the full house to find a drink. The living room seemed to be the spot for dancing, yet it was the only way to get to the kitchen. Ten minutes later, I was finally in the kitchen where people did beer pong, body shots, and made out. I scanned the different types of bottles until I found a pack of beer.

As I drank, I glanced around and took in the party atmosphere. Opposite me was a couple doing a body shot. I mentally cringed at the thought of Benny and Lana doing it a few months ago.

"Hey," someone said beside me. I turned my head to see a brunette with a bright smile on her face. I glanced down to see her in a yellow neon tank top and her underwear. I raised a brow at her as I looked straight and took another sip of my drink. "Dope party, right?" she asked. I turned to her again, stared her dead in the eye, then turned away. She groaned as I took another sip. "Are you one of those smirky-ass bad boys who're looking for his good girl?" she asked as I rolled my eyes. I stayed silent as I continued to drink my beer, hoping that she'd get the message and go away. "Look, dude, you're hot. My friends over there dared me to kiss someone." She pointed to her group of friends. I gave a fake smile as I waved at them. The girls squealed as the one in front of me jumped. Her boobs bounced as she twirled her hair. "So?" She stepped closer and rested her palm on my chest.

"This house is packed with perverted guys looking for a girl in her panties, yet you decide to come and disturb me?"

"You weren't even doing anything." She stepped back and folded her arms.

"I am now," I said, then took another sip. Sudden wetness was felt on my jacket as I glanced to the side to see someone messed their drink on me. "Fuck," I muttered as I put my beer down.

"So sorry, Blake!" someone said. I looked up to

see Erwin. We were usually lab partners, but other than that, I rarely spoke to him. I realized what an outcast he was at the party since he was too dressy and didn't even wear his glasses.

"Erwin, why aren't you wearing your glasses?" I groaned, then took off my jacket, which left me in my Blink 182 tank top.

"Tattoos," the girl on my right whispered. Shit, she's still here.

"I'm wearing contacts," Erwin mumbled, then looked at the girl. "Did I interrupt you guys?"

"Yes!" the girl said as she glared at Erwin.

"Nope," I replied as I gave Erwin my jacket. I turned to the girl, who gave me an irritated look. I fake smiled in return. "Now if you don't mind, my buddy Erwin and I are gonna go get high." I swung my arm around Erwin's shoulder.

"You'd rather hang out with a loser than with me?" the girl demanded as we walked away.

"I know this loser!" I said, then showed her the middle finger. We continued to walk through the crowd until we found an open space by a window. The window was smashed open as I moved all the broken glass then took a seat. Erwin leaned against the wall as he handed me my jacket. I thanked him for taking care of it for me.

"What was her problem?" he asked after a while. I shrugged.

"She wanted to kiss me, and I didn't want an STD."

Erwin nodded as he anxiously glanced around the room full of wasted people. I raised a brow as he tugged on his collar and fixed his gelled hair.

"So what brings Erwin Chambers to this side of the world?" I asked, then took out a cigarette.

"Err…I'm actually here with someone," he said as I took out my matches and lit the cigarette. I offered him a cigarette, but he declined.

"Who's the lucky girl?"

"Bianca."

"Bianca…Bianca…Bia—is she the girl in our Bio class?"

"Y-yeah."

"Lucky you," I said. "You can go. I'm sure you don't want to have a virgin asshole forever."

Erwin chuckled as he thanked me, then walked back into the living room. I finished my cigarette and threw it out the window. The party seemed like it'd go on forever. I put on my jacket as I pushed myself up. I walked around, and I saw Axel making out with a girl on the sofa. I shook my head and walked to the first door I saw. I opened the door, stepped in, and shut it behind me. It's as if the party stopped. The room must've been soundproofed because the music suddenly changed. A few other doors surrounded the rectangular room. Two poles on either side of the room had girls dancing on them. I glanced around the room and saw Jaden sprawled out on the sofa with a girl on his lap. Levi sat in the armchair with a hookah pipe beside him. I plopped down on the end of the couch where Jaden sat. Levi handed me the pipe, and I took it, then vaped.

"Parker!" Jaden exclaimed as I whipped my head in his direction. Keene walked with Parker and Austin. Parker pulled out a brown bag and tossed it toward Jaden. I watched as Jaden gestured to the coffee table, probably for his money.

"So you're Parker," Levi stated as he sunk in the sofa.

"Nice to finally meet you, Radcliff," Parker said with a smirk.

"How do you two know each other?" I asked.

"Oh, we don't, but Keene always talks about getting shit from this guy," Levi said as Parker laughed. Carter came downstairs and sat down next to me.

"How's business?" Keene asked as he took out a cigarette.

"Err…I've received my pay for this year," Parker responded.

"Bro, the money rolls in when everyone's busy with finals," Jaden said as the girl got off his lap and walked off.

"I know." Parker smirked at Carter and me.

"Does she…" Keene trailed off as he stared at Parker. Parker shrugged in response as Carter and I exchanged a look.

"Does she what?" Carter asked.

"Nothing," Keene mumbled as he took a drag and looked away.

"Does she what, Keene? Tell us. I'm sure we'd love to know," Jaden said as Keene sighed and avoided eye contact.

"Parker and I were friends. Being the nerd that Lana is, I watched as she stressed about finals last year," Keene mumbled. "So I introduced her to Parker."

My jaw clenched as the memory of flushing all

those pills down the toilet entered my mind.

"So you were the one who started her on the pills?" Carter demanded.

"Yep, and her other option were cigarettes," Austin stated.

"Oh, thanks, Captain Fucking Obvious," Levi added. Austin glared at Levi, yet I stared at Parker. At the beginning of the school year, I remembered Aidan always hung out with them. The more we hung out with Lana he found out what they truly were. Then I saw him freak out when we found out about the pills, which interested me.

"Why did Aidan lose his shit when you guys came out of the janitor's closet that day?" I asked.

"What?" Levi asked.

"Lana was overdosing on that crap you first gave her. Found her in the janitor's closet with these two." I looked at Keene.

"Were you guys having a thre—"

"No!" Austin cut off Jaden as I let out a sigh of relief.

"Not that time…" Parker trailed off as he glanced around the room. We stared at him as Austin squinted his eyes.

"What the fuck is that supposed to mean?" Levi barked.

"Lana didn't want anyone to know that she was using pills so…"

"You guys were fuck buddies?" Carter demanded.

"I kept her happy; she kept me happy," Parker replied with a shrug. I swallowed the lump in my throat as the thought of Lana Willson with Parker entered my mind.

"That's why Aidan was pissed. He's seen you two come out of the janitor's closet before, yet it didn't bother him because he and Lana weren't friends back then…" Carter said as he put two and two together.

"But it doesn't make any sense. You two came up with the bet," I said.

"Yeah, it was fucking hilarious waiting for which one she'd have sex with first, only for one of you to realize she wasn't a virgin in the first place." Parker laughed. It all made sense that Aidan didn't try to kiss her or hit on her; he suspected that she wasn't a virgin. Out of the corner of my eye, I saw Levi push himself off the sofa and march toward Parker. He violently shoved Parker, then grabbed his collar.

"You cunt!" Levi yelled as Jaden jumped up and separated the two.

"Jealous you're not the only guy who fucked her, Radcliff?" Parker asked as he tilted his head to the side.

"You used her by fucking in the janitor's closet just so that you wouldn't tell about the pills!" Levi shouted.

"Remember that time she'd do anything to get out of school, to get away from us—especially him?" Parker emphasized.

"Who?" we asked in unison.

"Benny," Keene mumbled. It was quiet as the music played in the background. I couldn't believe she'd do such a thing. She must've been so desperate to get away from him.

"She didn't care about sex at that time. As long as she got her pills and A's, then she'd be the happiest person in the world," Parker said. "But now the tables have turned...she hasn't talked about Yale. She's applied to colleges in Illinois because he's here," he added. Levi grumbled as he removed Jaden's hand from his chest and lunged at Parker. Multiple punches were thrown as I got up to help Jaden. Jaden held Parker back as I pushed Levi away from him. His blue eyes were dark as he huffed.

"Don't you ever fucking touch her again!" Levi shouted.

"Can't help it, she keeps coming back to me!" Parker said, and my jaw tightened. "What's wrong, Blake? Jealous that two guys fucked Lana and neither of them were you?" Parker asked. I let out a bitter laugh as I glanced around the room. I didn't realize that a crowd had formed around us. Some held phones up as they waited. I spun around to walk away, then whipped back around and threw a punch at Parker. All sorts of reactions spread throughout the room as people yelled, cheered, and whistled for more. I shoved Parker to the ground as I straddled him and punched him straight in the jaw. No one held me back, so I continued to beat him. All my anger and stress that I felt for the past few weeks suddenly fell out. The fact of almost killing Levi in a street race, almost kissing Lana again, Lana and Benny dating, then seeing the hickey. They weren't even dating for a week, and they'd already fucked. Now to hear that Parker fucked her last year seemed to hit a nerve. I didn't know what happened to us. I blinked as I realized Parker passed out. I let out a huff as I stood up and watched the unconscious curly blond on the floor.

"He fucking deserved it," Carter said as he nudged Parker with his foot.

"Fucking pervert," Levi muttered.

"Do you know Lana and Benny already fucked?" I asked out of the blue.

"How do you know?" Carter asked.

"The hickey on her collarbone…it was faded, but it was there," I said. Carter and Levi exchanged looks as I raised a brow. Levi whistled as he glanced around while Carter hummed. "What?"

"Nothing," Carter replied as his eye twitched.

"Dude, I can see it on your face. You're the worst liar ever," I said.

"Lana and I had sex before she started dating Benny. The hickey was from me," Levi mumbled as I clenched my fists.

"What the fuck, man? Yet you punched Parker!"

"Well, at least she wanted to have sex with me!" Levi exclaimed. I shook my head in disbelief as I glanced at my best friend.

"And you fucking knew," I said to Carter, then walked toward the door.

"Blake," he called out, but I ignored him as I pushed open the door, back to the regular party.

***

I let out a sigh of relief as I reached the second floor. It took me ten minutes to get up; I didn't know why. I only had a few drinks. I looked for a bathroom to wash my hands because I realized there was blood on them. I walked down the halls, and the only thing to be heard were moans or furniture hitting against the wall. I entered the bathroom to see a couple passed out in the bathtub. I shook my head as I glanced in the mirror. My eyes were red and droopy, hair in all directions, face jacked up. I looked like shit. I washed my hands under the faucet and ignored the sting when I flexed my hands. Once I was done, I walked out of the bathroom, only to bump into someone.

"Sorry, dude," a girl said as she placed her hands on my wrists.

"It's cool," I murmured, then looked down at the blonde. Even though she wore a miniskirt and crop top, she was hot.

"I don't know why, but I have this sudden urge to kiss you," she said, then rested her palm on my chest.

"Why don't y—" I cut off when she smashed her lips against mine. My back hit the wall as her hands lingered. I placed one hand on her waist and the other on her ass. As we kissed, I spun around and pinned her against the wall. She moaned against my lips as her arms wrapped around my neck. My hands trailed down to her thighs as I raised them. She jumped up and wrapped her legs around my waist. I removed her hands from my neck as I pinned them against the wall. I kissed down her neck as she puffed. Out of the corner of my eye, I saw an open door next to us. I kissed her again as I placed my hands on her ass while I walked. I went into the empty room and kicked the door shut with my foot. I threw her down on the bed, and she looked up with a smirk. I took off my jacket and shoes to join her.

"You're a fucking good kisser," she said as I hovered over her. I smirked as I kissed down her neck. I swiftly pulled off her skirt and no surprise—she didn't have any underwear. I removed my shirt as she undid my belt. I took off my jeans and tossed them aside. We kissed again, but this time it was more energetic as our breaths filled the room.

***

I blinked rapidly when a pillow hurled toward me. I sat up and saw the blonde anxiously getting dressed. There was a huge commotion downstairs as the music stopped.

"The fuck is going on?" I groaned as I put on my clothes.

"Cops," she said. My eyes widened, and I quickened my pace. I glanced to the side and noticed that it was one in the morning. The previous event entered my mind as I realized we fucked half an hour ago. The door was suddenly pushed open as an officer ran into the room.

"Don't move!"

We raised our hands as he ushered us out the room. I watched the many teenagers being escorted out of the house, and my first instinct told me to find the guys. I finally found Levi against a cop car. I jogged toward him with an anxious look.

"Dude, what happened?"

"Someone snitched about the drugs," Levi

replied as he shook his head. "Now they're taking tests with those machines."

I followed his gaze to see a bunch of people lined up as a cop used a mouth machine to test for any usage.

"Let's go," another cop said as he handcuffed Levi and me.

"What the he—"

"Apparently the person who fucking snitched said we were with Jaden at the time." Levi shrugged as we walked to a van. The police officer shoved us in the back of the van where we found Parker, Jaden, Keene, Axel, Carter, and two girls. I thought of Austin because he was the only other person with us who wasn't here.

"Hey, brother." Axel winked at me. I sat next to Keene as the police shut the doors while the other started the car.

"I need to piss," Parker whined. I glanced at the two officers in front to see the one drank a bottle of water. Once he was finished, he threw it behind him.

"Piss in this."

Parker caught the plastic bottle with ease, then observed it. He shook his head as he threw the bottle back.

"The thing that I wanna do will not fit in that bottle," he said as we groaned.

"Well, keep your shit, because you'll have plenty of time to get rid of it," the police officer grumbled. We arrived at the station, and thankfully I didn't see any familiar faces. We were put into one cell as the police took the girls.

“Whoa, whoa, whoa,” Axel said as he stopped the officer from taking the girls. “There’s still space in here, Officer.” He pointed to our cell. Carter laughed as the officer rolled his eyes and continued to walk with the girls. I leaned against the bars and glanced around the cell, the place I promised myself not to go again.

“What the fuck?” Keene trailed off as he walked toward the bench. We followed his gaze to see a guy in a clown costume. The clown didn’t move; he sat there with a big smile on his face.

“Yo, dude, Halloween’s over.” Jaden inched closer. He was two feet away when the clown turned to him and laughed. It was that annoying clown laugh, as if he’d do something crazy. “Shit,” Jaden said as he threw his hands up and backed away. The clown stopped but still looked at us with that freaky smile.

“Yeah, err…he’s a weird one,” the police officer who sat at his desk opposite us retorted.

“I hate clowns,” Carter said as he stood next to me. “Dude, guess what I just found out?” he asked as we crouched down to sit on the floor.

“I don’t know, but I think you’re gonna tell me,” I said.

“Jennifer Brighton is a lesbian,” he said as I raised a brow.

“That’s not true. She’s friends with Kelly. Probably fucked you more than once, and maybe even that clown,” I said as Carter shook his head.

“Dude, I saw her making out with a chick at the party.”

“Maybe she’s bi.” I shrugged.

"Yeah…if she is a lesbo, I wanna ask her if she ever liked my di—" Carter cut off when the clown laughed again. We watched as he threw his head back and laughed like a psycho.

"Dude, shut the fuck up," Parker groaned as he took a piss.

"Why are you in here?" Axel asked as he stared at the clown. The clown didn't reply; he just laughed even louder. Axel threw his hands up in defeat as he leaned against the wall. From the corner of my eye, I saw Levi walk toward the clown, a pissed look on his face as he raised his fist. He must have still been angry from earlier.

"Whoa!" Jaden exclaimed as he blocked Levi from the clown. I stood up and dusted off my clothing.

"Hey, don't start, boy," the police officer said as he propped his feet on the table.

"Why can't you take him to another cell?" Keene asked.

"I'm not going near him," the officer replied as he shivered. Loud footsteps were suddenly heard as I spun around. I placed my hands on the bars as I tried to peer through. A familiar man who wore a suit stepped into the building. Axel stood next to me as he put his hands on the cell.

"No way," he mumbled as the guy looked at us.

"Fuck," I muttered as he smirked and walked over to us.

"The Gunner brothers, nice to see you again."

"Officer Kale, what are you doing in Illinois? I thought you only work in Minnesota," Axel said as I glared at the guy who I hated back in Minnesota.

"I moved, and that's Detective Kale now," he said, then turned to me. "I'm watching you, Gunner."

I watched him walk off and immediately ran my fingers through my hair. He's the cop who always busted me back in Minnesota. While I waited for someone to bail me out, he'd sit in the cell with me and talk. I hated him.

"All right, you boys get two phone calls," the police officer said as he handed Levi the card for the phone. We watched as Levi walked over to the phone in the corner of the cell and put the card in. He put in the number and placed the phone to his ear.

"Who you calling?" Carter asked.

"Someone who owes me a little favor," Levi replied with a smirk.

Chapter Ten

Miranda

I covered my face with my hair as I laughed and looked at Marcus, who smiled at me through my laptop.

"Can you blame him? It's a good show! It even takes place in the eighties," I said, since we talked about Liam's addiction to *Stranger Things*.

"True, true," Marcus said as he pulled off his shirt and sat on his bed.

"Ooh, are we getting to that part of FaceTime?" I asked and looked at his toned abs. He chuckled, then ran his hand through his curly brown locks. Marcus's bright expression changed when he frowned. "Baby, what's wrong?"

"It's just weird…that detective at Lana's house," he mumbled.

"Why would he ask you, though?" I tilted my head. Marcus shrugged, then looked into the distance. "Is there something I need to kn—"

"Oh, wait! That day in the cafeteria when Aidan

and Lana were fighting, then she took out the pills," he began. "I was the last person to touch it because I threw it away in the trashcan, remember?"

"Then how the heck did it get there? At a freaking crime scene?"

"Maybe when the garbage collectors were emptying the trashcans it fell out when they got to the alley."

"Yeah, maybe…" I sighed, then looked at him. "Hey, err…thanks for covering Lana, though. I appreciate it, babe."

"Anything for my girlfriend's best friend." He bit his lip.

"What's wrong?"

"It's just—Nick and Benny seemed quite surprised when that detective questioned me."

"Well, it's not every day that a detective comes and asks you about a guy who's missing."

"True, but don't they seem off to you, babe?"

"Off?" I raised a brow.

"Yeah, like they've become very…distant. I don't know how to describe it, but you get me, right?" Marcus asked.

"They do seem a bit off. I thought it was only me. Especially that night when we all slept over."

"Yeah, that night still gives me the chills. I wanted to call the cops, as any sane person would, but Aidan said I shouldn't. And that's coming from the guy who used a frying pan as a weapon."

"That night was weird…also when Benny and Lana were yelling. It's as if they knew—"

"That it was coming!" Marcus and I said in unison. I sat on my bed for a moment as I tried to remember everything that happened that night.

"Wait—Nick, Liam, Benny, and Lana were in the room when they were yelling. Then how does it involve Aidan?" Marcus asked.

"Remember they went to follow the guy who climbed out of Lana's room? Maybe the guy threatened them or the—"

I got cut off when a squeaky voice came through the laptop. Marcus turned to the side as he smiled.

"Mom wants you to come and massage her back!" I recognized the voice as Marcus's little sister, Elenore.

"It's past midnight. Is she crazy?" Marcus asked as I laughed. Elenore came into view and waved at me. Marcus groaned as he stood up and slipped on a hoodie.

"Hey, El," I greeted as she smiled at me, which displayed the little gap. Her tooth had come out recently, so Marcus and I took her to the park to see her friends.

"Hi, Miranda. Don't worry, bro, I'll stay with your girlfriend," she said as Marcus smiled.

"I think Miranda's tired n—"

"You always say that," Elenore whined as I chuckled.

"I'll leave you two alone," I said as she pouted.

"Night baby. Sweet drea—" he said, then ruffled Elenore's hair.

"Hehe, you said baby." Elenore laughed as my cheeks flushed. Marcus and I laughed as Elenore stared at us. I shook my head then ended the FaceTime as I shut my laptop. I placed my computer on my desk then walked to the light switch. Suddenly, my phone went off as "Fireworks" by Katy Perry played. I raised a brow because who would call at this hour?

"Hello," I answered the phone as I sat on my bed.

"Hey, sweet cheeks," Levi greeted as I squinted my eyes.

"Why are you calling me?"

"Aww, can't I talk to my best friend's best friend?"

"What do you want?"

"I need you to pick us up," he said, to which I raised a brow.

"From where?"

"The station," he mumbled as I snorted. "Look, the officer will explain when you get here…"

"And why would I want to help you and your buddies?" I muttered.

"You owe me a little favor, Stevens. I spoke to Marcus the other day, and he seemed quite proud. Does he know what happened last year?"

"You wouldn't, Radcliff," I said through gritted teeth as I gripped the phone.

"Oh, you know me, sugar. I like people knowing the truth. You know what they say: honesty is the best policy," he sang as I pushed myself off the bed.

"Fine, I'll be there soon," I muttered, then ended the call. I was frustrated and tugged on my hair. I quickly put on a sweater and Converse, then walked downstairs, where I saw my mother on the sofa. The Cooking Channel was on as my mom sipped her brandy.

"Where you going?" she asked, her gaze still

fixed on the television.

"Bailing someone out," I answered as I put on a coat.

"Okay. Just make sure the car is returned in one piece," she stated.

"Okay," I said, then walked out the door. I climbed into our car and drove off. We could only afford one car, so Mom used public transport to get to work. It was the usual routine when I went out; Mom asked where I went and then told me to return home safe with the car. She still hadn't gotten over Dad, who left us fifteen years ago. I tried to get in contact with him, but Mom said I shouldn't. I realized she still loved him. From what I remembered, I got my blue eyes from him and that he loved baseball.

By the time I arrived at the station, it was almost three a.m. It looked creepy. I entered the building where I saw a woman sitting behind the desk. Her tag read Jackson.

"H-hi…I'm here for, err…" I mumbled because I hadn't done this before.

"Name?" she asked.

"Err…Levi Radcliff and…"

"You haven't done this before, have you?" she asked as she grabbed a clipboard. I nodded, which made her chuckle as she read off the clipboard. "No charge."

"What? I thought I was supposed to bai—"

"Honey, half these people here are from that party up on Lewis Street. It turns out there were drugs, and some of them are in here because of that."

"What about the others?"

"We did tests, and some of them only had drug usage, while others were just drunk as hell."

"So who didn't do drugs?" I asked, then folded my arms. The woman sighed as she read off the clipboard again.

"Axel Gunner, Blake Gunner, Carter Halls, Levi Radcliff, and Erwin Chambers, who got dropped off by Deputy Paul because he was crying too much. Poor kid."

"Who did drugs?" I asked as she swung the keys in her hands.

"Err…Keene Stoner, Parker Collins, and Jaden Reid," she said as my eyes widened.

"Umm…I'll take the first four, please," I said with a tight-lipped smile. The woman nodded and motioned me to follow her. We walked through the building past random cells filled with people in a drunken state.

"Do your parents know that you're here?" the woman asked.

"Surprisingly, yes," I mumbled as we stopped. I took in my surroundings to see an officer sitting behind a desk with his legs propped up on the table. He ate a bag of chips. I followed his gaze to see that he stared at the guys who were in the cell.

"These four kids are free to go." The woman dropped a note on his desk.

"Cool," the guy replied as he stared at the note. The woman threw her arms up as the man ate his chips.

"Well? Go get them!" she demanded. He jumped from his seat. He took the keys from her and stared at the cell. The guy squirmed as he slowly put the key through the hole. "Hurry up!"

"Hold your horses, Jackson! I don't like clowns, and this one has been laughing non-stop," the man blurted out as I looked at the clown. He honestly looked scary in the dim light as he smiled. I diverted my eyes somewhere else to where I saw Keene and Jaden. While the officers argued, they walked over and leaned against the bars.

"Hey, Blondie…you're looking good." Jaden smirked as he eyed me up and down.

"I got a mirror." I folded my arms.

"Feisty as always." He winked at me. I rolled my eyes and looked at the officer, who finally opened the cell. He pulled it opened and flicked his wrist.

"Hurry, hurry! Before he does some weird shit again!" The officer rushed out as Levi, Blake, Carter, and Axel walked out.

"You forgetting someone?" Keene asked with a smile.

"No space, sorry," I said with a fake pout. Jaden chuckled as Keene stared at me. I shifted my gaze to the officer who talked to the guys. I let out a deep sigh as I walked down the hall.

"Hey, err…thanks," Carter said as he appeared beside me.

"No problem," I sighed as we walked out of the sheriff's station and toward the car.

"Thank goodness Bobby was on night patrol." Levi chuckled as we got in. Carter sat in the passenger seat while the others sat behind us. As I drove, I thought where I'd dropped them off. I didn't want to play their driver, so I decided to drop them off at the Gunner household. The alternative music brought me back as I glanced down and saw Carter turn up the volume. The familiar smell made me scrunch my nose up as I looked through the rearview mirror.

"Hey, no smoking!" I growled as Axel exhaled at me. They ignored me as the tobacco smell spread through the car. My nails dug into the wheel as my jaw clenched. "I'm not gonna drive until you stop smoking."

Levi laughed as Blake blew out smoke rings. I let go of the wheel and folded my arms. Out the corner of my eye, Carter threw his cigarette out as he grabbed the wheel.

"What the hell, Miranda?" he demanded as he looked at the road. We swerved a bit as Carter tried to drive while I controlled the pedals.

"You trying to kill us?" Axel asked.

"Are you trying to kill me?" I demanded. I looked out my window and into the side mirror, where I saw Axel throw out his cigarette. I kept in a grin as I looked over my shoulder to see Levi and Blake do the same. "Thank you." I then put my hands back on the wheel.

"What made you come and get us?" Carter asked.

"I-I don't know," I said as my gaze locked on the road.

"Really? I think you know damn well why. I'm sure Jaden would love to see you at his parties again," Levi said as he leaned forward.

"Never going to his parties again. I mean, look what happened to you guys," I scoffed as I membered last year when Levi dragged Lana and me to Jaden's party.

"What are you guys talking about?" Blake asked.

"Just what Jaden said about last year." Levi smirked. "How she blew the fucking roof off. Do you think they'll know tha—"

I cut off Levi when I hit the brakes. His head hit against Carter's seat, and he groaned while the guys laughed.

"We're here," I mumbled. They thanked me, then piled out of the car. "Just be glad that you're friends with Lana and I care about her. Otherwise, I would've punched you so fucking hard right now," I confessed as Levi got out.

"Goodnight to you too, Miranda." He laughed then shut the door. I turned the radio off and drove in silence. One thing was for sure—Levi and I never got along. Lana tried to make us enjoy each other's company, but I knew it was never going to happen. I stuck by her because I knew that when he left, I was all she's had. Well not now, obviously, but there were times when we hung out because we were tired of the opposite sex.

I arrived home safely in the car in one piece. When I entered the house, I wasn't surprised to see my mother in the same position as earlier.

"Is the car in one piece?" she asked as I took off my coat.

"I'm okay, Mom, and yes, the car is in one piece, but it will have a weird smell, though," I mentioned and walked upstairs. Mom muttered something under her breath which I didn't hear. I let out a sigh as I walked into my room.

***

Lana

The springs in my mattress bounced while my ear was on the bed, which meant my pillow disappeared during the night. I let out a groan as I opened my eyes.

"Wake up!" the annoying voice yelled.

"Why? It's Monday," I whined. The mattress sank as I felt a weight on it. I turned so that I was on my back to see Levi on my bed in his pajamas. "Levi, no," I warned as I reached for my glasses. As I put them on, Levi jumped on the bed. He laughed as I bounced. He collapsed right beside me with a grin spread across his face. "Where were you yesterday? You didn't come home."

"I hung out at Blake's place. We were all pretty hungover from the party on Saturday," he responded. Out the corner of my eye, I saw Dad enter the room, already dressed.

"Well, I better get ready," Levi said as he got up and walked to my bathroom.

"Use the bathroom downstairs," I said as he shut the door.

"I can't hear you because of this one being better," he said, then turned on the shower. I let out a chuckle as Dad rolled his eyes. I watched as he sat down beside me then placed his hand on my shoulder.

"Get ready. We're going Christmas shopping," he said.

"I don't want to go to the mall with my parents,"

I groaned. “Add that to the list of embarrassing things.”

“How is it embarrassing? What list?” Dad questioned.

“Nu-nothing.”

“Lana.” Dad pressed as he looked at me.

“Well, people at school talk, Dad. Especially since you arrested half of them Of course they’ll gossip,” I admitted.

“You think I’m embarrassing?”

“No! No! It’s just…this is high school, Dad. People used to pick on me. There’s always those kinds of individuals at school.”

“Lana, dear, sometimes they only do that because they’re either jealous or raised like an ass.” Dad sighed as he swung my legs over his lap and brought me closer to him as I rested my head on his chest. “And if they still pick on you when you go back after winter break, call me. I’ll whoop their ass, put them in jail, and maybe afterward your mother can help them to the hospital.”

“Why would they be jealous?” I giggled.

“Well, if you look at it…your mom is a doctor, I’m a sheriff, and you have Griffon as your uncle. Obviously, people would be jealous because you have those advantages. Plus, you’re brilliant. Take me, for example. Believe it or not, I was the cool guy back in high school,” he said as I snorted. “I was friendly and very careless like that one friend of yours…that always cleans our fridge?”

“Liam?”

“Yeah, that one…does he get fed at home? Because he ate my doughnuts that I brought home from the station the other day," Dad grumbled.

"Yeah, Dad, he just loves food."

"Okay then…well, once I got to college, I became serious about what I want in life. Then when I became a cop, my friends started to say how I was changing, especially since I arrested one of them." He sighed. "Griffon was one of my real friends who stood by my side. I met your mother, got married the next year, and then a few years later I became sheriff." He sighed. "What I'm trying to say is…there'll be people in your life who will bring out the good and bad in you. But stick with the ones who bring out the best in you."

"Thanks, Dad." I smiled.

"You said used to. What happened?" he asked after a while.

"Well, let's just say the senior year really does determine who you'll be graduating with," I admitted as I stood up.

"Don't think so far ahead, kiddo. You still got the rest of the school year…which will obviously be a breeze for you."

"I hope so," I whispered. From the corner of my eye, I saw a figure clap their hands. Dad and I looked at Levi, who was shirtless in sweatpants with a towel around his neck.

"That father-daughter moment was just so moving," he pouted. I playfully rolled my eyes as Richard stood by the doorway.

"Ready to go?" he asked, then looked at my appearance. "Let me rephrase that. Everyone out of bed?"

I let out a laugh and nodded as I walked to my

closet and picked out an outfit for the day.

"All right, this is how it's gonna work. Angie and Jade think we're all going shopping, but it's just you two," Dad clarified as I held my clothes in my hands.

"What about you guys?" I asked. Mom and Jade went shopping yesterday, but I woke up too late and they were already gone. So today had to be the day we go.

"We're going to watch a football game at a bar," Richard answered.

"Badass, Sheriff." Levi smirked.

"Not really, I just don't want to shop..." Dad whined.

"What if they find out?" I asked.

"Griffon will be there, so we'll just say that he invited us and we couldn't let him down." Richard waved off as he walked into the hall.

"Bobby, just remember...they always find out," Levi sang as Dad cursed under his breath. I awkwardly stood in front of Levi as he took the towel and dried his hair. He put the towel back on his shoulder, then grinned at me.

"Well, looks like it's just you and me, princess."

"Yep." I sighed, then walked into the bathroom. I locked the door and undressed. I took a quick shower as I thought of the gifts I'd get everyone. I already got Benny a gift, and I'd receive it soon. I turned off the shower and grabbed the towel. Out the corner of my eye, I saw movement. I quickly wrapped the towel around me as I squinted at the person.

"Levi?"

"Yes, princess?"

"What the fuck? How'd you get in? I locked the door," I groaned as I joined him at the sink counter. I put on my glasses and watched as he gelled his hair.

"Yeah, you need a new lock."

"Déjà vu," I mumbled as I gripped on my towel.

"What?"

"Nothing."

"Not nothing…someone doesn't just say déjà vu for no reason. Especially in a situation like this." I shook my head as I avoided eye contact then grabbed my toothbrush.

"Did someone else see you naked? Was it Benny? Carter? Parker? Keene? Ax—"

"What the hell?" I demanded. Levi let out a forced laugh as he stepped closer. I backed away and hit against the shower door. I bit the inside of my cheek as his hand grazed over my towel.

"Told you I'd find out. Remember you can only be bad for me, princess."

I pushed Levi off me and glared at him. I roughly opened the door and gestured for him to get out.

"I have a boyfriend now, Levi. Don't touch me, and in the kindest way possible, fuck off," I muttered as I pushed him out the door. I slammed it shut and walked to the sink. I brushed my teeth as quickly as possible, then ripped the towel from me. I glanced up and looked at myself in the mirror. I bit my lip as I ran my fingers over the outline of my body. My poor used, damaged body, yet the only person to blame was me.

***

I stepped into the passenger seat of Levi's Mustang then shut the door. He started the car then dumped his cigarette out. He wasn't even finished. Except for the music that blared through the car, we drove in silence. Out the corner of my eye, he threw his head back in frustration. He turned down the volume and sighed.

"Look, I'm sorry for what happened earlier. It's just every year when I came, it would be you, Keene, and me. And it's not easy to move on. I-I just have to get used to the fact that you're with someone else now," he muttered. "I really have to get used it because you're with Benny Nielson. I mean, him of all people. It would've been fine if it were Blake or even Carter. But Benny fucking Nielson."

"Look, I know you don't like each other, but you just have to get used to it." I smiled. "I like him…a lot."

"Ugh, okay," he growled, then turned to me. "Nice jacket, by the way."

"Thanks." I smiled because I missed the leather jacket.

"I just threw out my cigarette for the whole effect, y'know, because I was pissed," he said, then took two cigarettes out of his pack. I laughed as he handed me one. I put it between my lips as I lit it then inhaled. "This our song, princess!" Levi cheered as "Howlin' For You" by The Black Keys played. I laughed as we began to blurt out the lyrics.

***

For the past three hours, we walked through the mall and bought gifts for everyone. I was glad because I got everyone that I needed to get.

"I still can't believe you bought that," I said as we walked out of a shoe store.

"It was on sale!" he whined as he held up the black Palladium boot.

"Don't you already have black boots?" I asked.

"Yeah, but they're a different shade of black," Levi said. Since his new boots were all in my face, it caused me to bump into someone. He stuffed the shoes back in the box as I glanced up to apologize.

"Ugh, you," Kelly said. Her red tips were gone as her ashy blonde hair went over her shoulders.

"My bad." I sighed, then looked over her shoulder at Jennifer.

"What's your name?" Kelly asked Levi as she bit her lip.

"Ranger Long Sausage. That's my stripper name," Levi said as he dramatically flicked his long hair. Kelly gave Jennifer a weird look then turned to me with a wicked look in her eye.

"I see you have a new guy every week. Wait…you weren't even dating Benny for a week, and now you're with him."

"Lana, you're becoming such a bitch. Like, not everyone likes you. Saturday night I saw Blake making out with this girl," Jennifer said.

"As if I care?" I tilted my head as they rolled their eyes in unison.

"How's our little betrayal, Melissa? That bitch

changed."

"She didn't change. She just stopped acting the way you two wanted her to."

"Glad she joined the bitches' squad along with your other blond friend."

"She and Marcus are something else." Kelly sighed.

"Is your guys' drama gonna have an intermission soon? I need to take a piss, but I don't want to miss some bitch slapping," Levi said.

"Shut up, you freak!" Jennifer yelled.

"Damn, who yanked your tampon out too early?" Levi asked. Kelly hit him with her shopping bag.

"Hey, don't hit him!" I yelled, but Jennifer joined in.

"Ouch! You're hurting princess's nipples!" Levi exclaimed as I slammed him.

"Does she even have real boobs th—"

"You guys should come with a fucking warning label," Levi grunted. We pulled their bags away, and one ripped in two. The boxes fell to the ground, and my eyes widened. I thought it'd be shoe boxes, but no, they were adult toy boxes. Levi and I sniggered as Jennifer went down on her knees and picked up the boxes. Kelly watched her friend in disbelief as we slowly backed away.

"Jennifer, what the he—"

"They're not for me, okay?" Jennifer blurted out as she held the boxes in her hands. Kelly scrunched her nose up as she looked at Jennifer.

"I can't have a lesbian friend! What if you fall for me?" Kelly whined and stomped her foot.

"I think we need to go," Levi whispered beside

me.

"Yep." I laughed as we took our bags and walked out of the mall. We put all the bags in the trunk, then got into the car. While we drove, I told Levi about the time when I kicked Kelly in the face, and he laughed.

"Hey, I need you to drop me off at Benny's house," I said as I read the text on my phone.

"Why?" Levi asked as he blew out a smoke ring.

"Well, Melissa wanted to do something competitive, so we're going bowling. Yippee." I sighed.

"A double date?" he asked.

"Nah, triple…Miranda and Marcus are coming too," I said as we drove through the streets.

"Cool," he mumbled.

"Yeah, err…what are you gonna do?"

"Probably head over to Blake's place."

"Cool."

Other than showing Levi the directions to Benny's house, it was quiet, yet the silence was comfortable. We arrived ten minutes later, and I realized everyone else was already here.

"Thanks, enjoy," I said as I got out of the car.

"You too," he mumbled. I walked toward the front door and raised my hand to knock on the door. It flew open with a very cheery Melissa.

"Finally!" she said, then pulled me into the house. Melissa dragged me all the way into the living room, where Marcus, Nick, and Benny watched a soccer game. Miranda was sprawled out on the sofa with her phone in her hands.

"YES!" Nick and Benny cheered as Real Madrid

scored. Nick teased Marcus, who frowned because Barcelona hadn't scored yet, while Benny jumped up. He spotted me then pulled me into an embrace.

"You're a lucky charm. Just when you stepped into the room, they scored," Benny said as I laughed.

"Lana, who do you think is better? Ronaldo or Messi?" Marcus asked as he pushed Nick away.

"Obviously Ronaldo," I stated as Benny stood behind me and wrapped his arms around me.

"That's why she's a beautiful girlfriend," Benny said as he kissed along my neck.

"All right, since this is a shit-ass game, shall we go?" Marcus asked as he stood up.

"Date night!" Melissa squealed as we walked toward the door. Benny and Nick teased Marcus and said that he just didn't want to see his team lose. I glanced over my shoulder to see Miranda trail behind. Once she caught up, I entwined our hands together, and she looked up.

"You okay?" I asked.

"Yeah…I didn't have a good night on Saturday. Barely got sleep," she said, then let go of my hand and walked out of the house. I tilted my head at Miranda's weird behavior. It must be the fact that Detective Kale questioned Marcus. She didn't have to worry, though; I sent a message to Marcus, and he said it was okay. Somehow, he acted weird, too.

The triple date at the bowling alley was just fantastic and all in all fun. It turned out Benny and I came second, while Marcus and Miranda came first because they were very competitive. Melissa didn't care, though, because she said sports were never her thing, even if Nick did all the work.

***

I squinted my eyes and let out a groan as Dad opened my curtains. The daylight scorched through the room as he walked to the door.

"Get up, kiddo. It's already after one," he said, then exited the room. I forced myself out of bed and rubbed my face. I instantly froze as my hand rubbed against my stitches. I cursed under my breath as I walked to the bathroom. I raised my nightgown, ready to take a piss, but immediately dropped it as I stared at the toilet roll holder. No freaking toilet paper, someone was full of shit. I walked out of my room and strolled down the stairs. Suddenly two hands wrapped around me to prevent me from colliding into them.

"We gotta stop doing this, pumpkin." He helped me downstairs. It had to be Axel because he oddly called me pumpkin.

"Not to be mean, but why are you here?" I asked as he leaned on the staircase.

"Hanging out." He motioned to the living room full of guys. My cheeks flushed as I lowered my nightgown and fixed my hair. I didn't want anyone to think I was a slob. "What are you doing?"

"Well, it's my house, but I came down here for toilet paper. I need to take a shit." I whispered the last part.

"That's the most flattering thing I've heard from a girl." Axel laughed as I walked down the hall. Everything seemed to blur. I opened the hall closet and glanced up to see the crumpled bag. I stood on my tippy toes and snatched the bag.

"What the heck?" I muttered, because the bag was empty. Someone was apparently full of shit in this house. Out the corner of my eye, I saw a tall figure enter the room. I looked over my shoulder to see Ethan walk in with an empty plate in his hand.

"Hey, Lana," he greeted.

"Ethan! My great friend, buddy, captain…hey." I smiled and playfully punched his shoulder. He raised a brow at my weird behavior, and I laughed, then pointed at the bag, which was further away. "You're kind of tall and…buff. I just really need to take a shit."

"Err…okay," he mumbled, then stretched his arm to get the bag. I clapped as he ripped it open and gave me two rolls. I thanked him, then skipped upstairs and into my bathroom. Once I was done, I collapsed onto my bed and snuggled into the sheets. The comfort only lasted about ninety seconds until I felt things being thrown onto my bed.

"Ouch! Dad!" I complained as I looked up to see Dad throwing pepper spray cans.

"Get up, Lana, and I forgot to give you those cans. There are quite a few boys down there, and I'm heading to the station," he said as I pushed myself out of bed again. I mumbled something under my breath as I grabbed a casual outfit and headed into the shower. Afterward, I changed the bandage on my stitches since Mom was at work. Jade was visiting a friend while Richard slept.

I tied my hair up in a bun because I had to make more cinnamon rolls since everyone enjoyed them on Saturday. I opened the fridge and pulled out the containers yet noticed that they were empty. I squinted my eyes as I gripped the empty container and stormed into the living room. Music blared through a Beats Pill as the guys spoke.

"Who ate all the cinnamon rolls?" I demanded as I held up the container. No one answered or moved as I groaned. Out the corner of my eye, I saw a figure move. I snapped my head to see Dad walk with a cinnamon roll in his mouth. Our eyes met, and he instantly froze. "Dad, did you eat all of them?" I asked. He gave no answer as he stood with the roll in his mouth. I threw my hands up in exasperation and groaned as I walked back into the kitchen. I heard the guys laugh as I forcefully put on my apron. Dad came into the room with empty plates in his hands as I took out the ingredients. "Daddy, can't you do something about them?"

"I'm not your mother; she's the miracle worker. I'm a sheriff," he said as he poured himself a glass of water.

"Then arrest them!"

"Have they done something illegal?"

"N-not really, but they will!"

"Sure, Lana. Call me when they do. Even though they've all been arrested, I must go to the station now…which means I'm leaving my daughter all alone with five males. Should I be worried?" he asked. "Nah, I trust Axel, and I like Ethan. Stopped by his dad's store yesterday and bought a few things."

"Cool."

"Why aren't you with him?" Dad asked as my

eyes widened.

"I'm with Benny," I said.

"Oh, yeah…but Ethan's captain, and I heard they did pretty well last game."

"Dad, Benny is on the team."

"You guys go to the same school?" he asked, and I nodded. "Wait…what school do you go to? I never know because I don't get any phone calls."

"Jefferson High."

"Right. But I like Ethan more."

"Dad, you're just saying that because you get a discount from Mr. Baxter," I scolded. Dad shook his head, then set his glass in the sink. Richard entered the room with an empty plate in his hand, and I groaned.

"Rick, who do you prefer? Benny or Ethan?" Dad asked.

"That's an easy one," Richard said. "Ethan…captains all the way!" I threw my hands up in frustration because they were big sports fans.

"Benny's dad owns a chain of seafood restaurants," I pointed out.

"I'm allergic to seafood, honey," Dad said. I groaned as they laughed. Dad walked to me and kissed my forehead. "I like Benny. He's a good kid. We're only joking."

"I'm not allergic. Maybe I can get discount," Richard said. I playfully rolled my eyes then said goodbye to them. Once they were out of the house, the music suddenly got louder. I sighed as I shut the kitchen door, yet it didn't help.

I baked. I loved to bake and sometimes preferred it to cooking, but to do the same thing repeatedly bored me. I spent the next two hours making the cinnamon rolls from scratch. I was on my fourth batch as I placed another pan in the oven. The music hadn't stopped, and neither did the boys when they came into the kitchen for a roll. I literally had to take the rolling pin to get them out of here. They finally gave up and decided on pizza. If I didn't go into the living room earlier then I wouldn't have gotten any.

I cleaned up until I heard weird noises from the other side of the house. I raised a brow as I took off my apron and walked out of the kitchen. The music still played, but none of the guys were in the living room. I turned it off and listened. I spun around to see the front door wide open. Axel stood on the porch as I walked outside into the cold weather. My eyes widened as I saw Blake punch someone. Levi stood next to him with a murderous look. I squinted my eyes and noticed the curly hair under the guy's beanie.

"Let him do it," Axel said. "He deserves it, and you know it."

My breath suddenly quickened as Blake pushed Parker into the snow and kicked him. Out the corner of my eye, I saw my neighbor walk out of her house to see the commotion.

"Blake," I called out as a car drove past and watched us. "Blake!" I yelled as he continued to kick Parker. I stomped down the stairs, then approached Blake. I placed my hand on his shoulder and whipped him around and noticed how his eyes darkened. "Stop!" I yelled in his face. Levi tried to get to Parker, but I stepped in front of him and blocked the way. Parker was unconscious, and I squirmed at the blood on the snow. "What the hell are you doing?" I demanded.

"Oh, sorry, didn't want to get in the way of you and your friend," Levi snapped.

"Quit the act, Willson. We know that you guys were fuck buddies back in junior year," Blake muttered, and I suddenly paled.

"Yeah, we know how you kept each other happy, so you can take your curly-haired freak over here and go fuck somewhere else," Levi mimicked as I let out a dry laugh.

"If your definition of happy was being forced into the janitor's closet before class, threatening me, watching me undress, then using me, then yeah…I'm happy," I sarcastically said. I noticed how Blake's features softened as the realization hit him. I swallowed the lump in my throat to prevent myself from crying. I didn't want to cry, especially in front of them. Not again. "This asshole used me in junior year, and I had no one. Miranda was there, but she wouldn't understand. I was all alone because someone didn't have the balls to pick up the fucking phone!"

"What about them?" Levi pointed to Carter and Ethan.

"Benny wasn't the only one, Levi," I informed him, then looked at Parker. "But it doesn't matter anymore. The damage is done."

I glanced up as I looked at all of them. Looks of guilt and remorse filled their faces as I laughed. Yet it was a laugh filled with pain, agony, and envy, like I couldn't believe it.

“You all believed him. Now I know what you really think of me,” I croaked out, then spun around. I locked eyes with Axel to see his shameful look. I clenched my fists as I walked up the stairs. I opened the door and bit the inside of my cheek to prevent the breakdown. I went into the house and tried to block out their arguments.

Chapter Eleven

Lana

Arguing. Curses. Shouts. That's all I heard for the past thirty-five minutes. The neighbors got annoyed, so I told them to come inside. Being the bunch of assholes that they were, they left the unconscious Parker in the snow. So, after arguing for five minutes of who should go and get him, Ethan and Axel manned up and got him. I felt like Edward from *Twilight* as I watched Parker rest on my sofa. I sat directly opposite him as my nostrils flared. The sensation to cry vanished as rage filled my body. I wanted to punch someone. I wanted to throw something against the wall. I even wanted to throw the TV out the window. The guys were in the kitchen, and I specifically hid the cinnamon rolls before they went in. The recent event played in my mind as I took in Parker's appearance. His face was beaten, yet no pity or sympathy came from me, just anger and hatred.

I remembered in junior year Aidan, Parker, and

Austin walked by. We had Science together, and my locker was the closest to the janitor's closet. Austin and Aidan passed me, but Parker stayed. I didn't want to enter that part of my life again. It was buried, deep down, with everything else. I promised myself I wouldn't talk or think about it ever again. The first bottle I ever got was from Keene, which I later found out was from Parker. When Parker found out that I had used his product without paying, he used it against me. He said he'd tell the whole school, the principal, Mr. Bronx, and my parents. I couldn't let that happen; my life was already depressed. Levi left without a goodbye, and I didn't hear from him for a year, so of course I'd think it's my fault. To hear what he thought of me made me feel lifeless. It made sense yesterday when he said I'd be bad for him. He'd never said something like that before, so naturally I suspected something.

"Ugh," Parker groaned as I glanced at him. His eyes fluttered open as he stared at the ceiling. He turned and gave me a lazy smile. I bit my lip and crossed my arms as I stared at him.

"Why?"

He seemed confused by the word as he squinted his eyes. A second later, he let out a sigh and slowly sat up.

"I was drunk, and they were going to find out sooner or later, Lana. Besides, aren't you glad that it's not haunting you anymore?"

"You said we'd never bring it up. That day in the library behind the shelves, you promised that you wouldn't touch me! You kept your promise, but you still gave me the pills. Why?" I asked. When he gave me the pills in the library, I waited for him to push me into the nearest room. He didn't, but when he and Austin did a few weeks ago, I expected the worst. Thankfully they didn't do anything but confess that they stole the two parcels.

"Look around, Willson. Things have changed. You're not alone anymore, so naturally, I stopped. Look at me." He pointed to his face. I gave him a vacant stare as he picked up the ice pack from the coffee table and put it against his cheek. We stared at each other for a few seconds until he sighed.

"Look, I'm sorry that I…I sexually assaulted you back in junior year. I was new to Illinois and mixed with the wrong crowds," he whispered. "I can't believe I did that to you. I'll never forgive myself for that."

"Why are you even here?" I ignored his apology. Parker let out a groan as he dropped the ice pack. I watched as he reached into his pocket and pulled out a small envelope. He slid the envelope across the coffee table, and I slammed my hands down to stop it. I raised a brow as I ripped the envelope open. My eyes widened as I recognized the tickets. I put them back in the envelope as I slowly stood up. I forced the envelope in my back pocket as Parker watched me. "I-I'll get your money," I whispered. Out of the corner of my eye, I saw him jump up and walk toward me.

"N-No, that won't be necessary," he said, then placed his hand on my arm. I stared at it, and he dropped his hand. "It's on the house. Since this will probably be the last that we're doing business together."

I gave a curt nod as I returned to my seat. The guys entered the living room. I watched as Levi stood right in front of Parker while Blake leaned against the wall. Axel leaned against the doorframe as Ethan and Carter sat on the sofa opposite me.

"You're a sick asshole, you know that?" Levi spat. Parker threw his hands up in surrender and motioned to me.

"I apologized."

"And you forgave him?" Blake demanded as he glared at me. Everyone stared at me as they waited. I looked down and slowly shook my head because I'd never forgive Parker Collins. He sexually assaulted me once, and the rest was harassment, but still, I'd never forgive such a selfish monster.

"Aidan was right. You're a fucking perverted freak," Carter hissed.

"On the bright side, it was stand up missionary. Hence why before class," Parker mentioned as I dug my nails into the couch.

"Get the fuck out, or else I'll rip your fucking face off and feed it to big-ass Scruffy!" Blake yelled as he pushed himself off the wall.

"What's a Scruffy?" Parker asked, and Axel raised his hand.

"My dog," he answered with a flashy smile. Parker threw his hands up in innocence as he strolled to the door. He stopped right in front of Blake and took something out of his pocket. Parker held out a box of Marlboro cigarettes for Blake to take.

"Take this as a sort of peace offering. No hard

feelings?" he asked as I rolled my eyes. Blake didn't move as he stared at Parker with an emotionless look. Parker let out a sigh as he slipped the box into Blake's pocket. He took his index finger and placed it on Blake's cheek. "If it makes you feel any better, Gunner, I'm not the one who stole her virginity."

I suddenly snapped as I pushed myself off the armchair and stood onto the coffee table. When Parker spun around, I jumped on him. We fell to the ground, and I took off my glasses and tossed them aside.

"*Fuck you!*" I screamed as I punched him. My right fist connected with his face as my left wrapped around his neck. "*I hate you!*"

"*Lana, stop!*" Carter yelled as he tried to pull me away from Parker. My grip suddenly tightened on his neck as I continued to yell out what a sick person he was and how he ruined me. Levi was opposite me as he tried to release my grip off Parker. Axel and Carter tried to pull me off as Parker and Levi sought to remove my hands from his neck.

"*Lana, let go!*"

His Adam's apple hit against my palm as he struggled to breathe. I immediately removed my hands as I stared at him. His heavy breaths filled the room as I watched his chest rise while he puffed. Ethan crouched down as I looked at him. A horrified expression filled his face as I stared into his brown eyes. He raised his hands while I breathed heavily.

"This isn't you. Beating him up won't change

anything," Ethan whispered as Carter and Axel hooked their arms with my own. They pulled me off Parker, but I stayed on the floor as I leaned on my knees. We watched as Parker slowly stood up and touched his neck.

"Get the fuck out," Blake muttered as he shoved Parker's beanie in his chest. I watched as Blake pushed him out of the house, then slammed the door shut. I picked up my glasses and sat on the armchair. A stone hard look filled my face as I stared at Levi. His jaw clenched as he tried to avoid eye contact. No one spoke, which made the atmosphere tense. Levi let out a sigh as he straightened his posture. He looked me with weary eyes as he played with the ring on his index finger.

"Look, uh, I'm sorry, princess. We didn't know. I'm sorry you had to go through that alone," Levi mumbled as I leaned forward in my seat.

"*Yeah...fuck you for leaving me when I needed you the most!*" I screamed as I blinked away the tears. "You didn't think twice, yet you all fucking assumed."

"Yeah, well, we've all been through shit, Lana," he stated. I didn't know what to say, so I glanced at Blake, who reached for Levi's lighter. I watched as he took it from the coffee table and put a cigarette between his lips.

"What we experience triggers change," Blake said as he exhaled.

"Yet you still bought from Parker after he did those things to you. Why?" Ethan asked as I stared at the ground. *Well, let me think...* I got involved with a drug dealer. Killed someone, then buried him. Had nightmares of him haunting me, then found out that the drug dealer knew that I killed the guy. *Then* found out he's not in the place that we buried him.

"I don't know."

"Well, I need a beer." Axel sighed as he stood up. Ethan and Carter trailed behind as they walked to the kitchen.

"Lana, I get that you want to get into Yale, but not like this. Something tells me you're not doing this for yourself. You don't want to disappoint your parents because you've always been their little girl," Blake said. "Stop doing this to please others. Do what is right and what you want. This is your life. Don't fuck it up. Just bring out the side that no ever sees. You're too afraid to, because you'll be judged. Just like me."

"We let our appearances get the best of us," Levi said as he lit a cigarette.

"Yep. The bad boy and the nerd." Blake chuckled as he shook his head.

"In the end, we're all human trying to live in this brainwashed society," I croaked out. Yet I shook my head as the lump in my throat grew. The sudden urge to cry got stronger as I attempted to speak. "I-I don't know who I am anymore. I-I don't know what to…what to do anymore. The sudden feeling to live and carry on with life is grim. Especially since your demons always follow you." Blake and Levi stared at me as I let out a pathetic laugh. "I don't even know what to do with my life anymore. I'm not sure if I'll get into Ya—"

"It's because of him, isn't it?" Levi cut me off as

he dumped his cigarette in his ashtray. I squinted my eyes as Levi's jaw clenched and he shook his head. I noticed Blake didn't speak; he just kept his head low and let the ash fall into the ashtray that Levi had. "You're letting Benny fucking Nielson get in the way of your dream school. Just because you're dating now," Levi said as I stood up.

"Stop blaming him for everything!" I demanded as I walked past him. Levi stood up and threw his arms up in frustration.

"Angie said you applied to schools in Illinois and dodged Yale. The only reason would be him, right?" Levi stated as I spun around and glared at him.

"*No! Just fucking stop!*" I shouted, which echoed through the house. "It's not him, it's me! I don't even know if I'm right for that school. Fuck, I don't even know what I want to become anymore!"

After I said that, the house fell into a profound silence. Obviously, Axel, Carter, and Ethan heard from the kitchen. Over Levi's shoulder, I saw Blake stare at me with a concerned look. I turned back to Levi to see a frown spread across his face. Levi opened his mouth, but nothing came out. I slowly shook my head and walked upstairs to my room. I slammed the door, then walked to my desk. I opened the drawer and took out Blake's pack of cigarettes. I took one out along with the lighter that Keene left for me. I sat against the wall as I put the cigarette between my lips. The house was quiet; if someone dropped a pin, I'd probably hear it. I raised my head and noticed myself in the full-length mirror. I looked ruined.

I took off my glasses and threw them on my bed. Even though the mirror was across the room, I knew what I looked like. The stitches on the chin, hair looked dead as ever, dark, miserable blue eyes, and the cigarette. *I hated myself.* I always fucked up. Everything that had happened to everyone I cared for was my fault. I wish things were back to when it was Levi and I when we were kids. Then, Uncle Griff babysat us, and we'd have a fantastic time. Or when I first met Miranda in the girls' restroom and she thought I was intriguing. Even the time when Benny and I were dance partners. He was so nervous that day and kept stepping on my feet.

I looked at myself again at the blurry image in the mirror. The smoke came out of the cigarette and disappeared into the air as I took a drag. I clenched my knuckles as the thought of Parker entered my mind. I hated him. I'd never hated someone so much as almost to choke them. I pinched the cigarette with my index finger and thumb then threw it toward the mirror. I watched as the cigarette hit the glass and the ashes fell to the ground. Then the cigarette fell to the ground. I looked down at my hands and realized they trembled. These hands had done some terrible things. They'd been used to kill, take pills, smoke, and almost choke someone.

I balled my fists then sat up. I walked to the bathroom and took out a pair of contact lenses. I stared at myself in the mirror as I slowly put them on. Last time I wore contacts was when we made a bet. However, appearances didn't matter anymore. As Blake said, I should show the side that I was too afraid to show, whatever that was because I didn't even know who I was anymore.

I took the envelope out of my pocket and placed it in my drawer. I grabbed the air freshener from the bathroom and sprayed my bedroom, then grabbed my coat. I walked downstairs to see the guys in the living room either smoking or on their phones. I walked right past them as I approached the door. I grabbed Mom's car keys then walked out into the cold weather.

***

I walked toward the brightly decorated Christmas house and took in the atmosphere. Wow. My own boyfriend's house decorations were better than mine. We decorated, but it's not as good as the Nielsons'. I nervously knocked on the door and waited. The door whipped open, and Benny's mom stood in front of me with a bright smile on her face.

"Lana, hi!" she said, then motioned for me to come in. I gave a kind smile as I stepped out of the cold and into the warm house. She wore a red jersey, blue jeans, Ugg boots, and an apron. I followed her into the kitchen and looked around for Benny.

"Sorry to disturb you, Mrs. Nielson. I just wanted to know if Be—"

"Oh, it's no problem, Lana. I enjoy some female company. It's not easy living with three men." She chuckled and walked to the oven. I awkwardly stood by the door and watched her cover something up, then put it in the oven. Once it was in, she clasped her hands together then turned to me. "Sit down, honey." She pointed to the chair by the island. "Here, taste this."

She held up a spoon of what seemed to be a particular dessert. I found it weird that Benny's mom spoon-fed me something.

"Mm," I said as my eyes widened. "This is really good."

"Homemade pudding." She smiled as she dished me a bowl.

"Thank you." I smiled. I ate in silence as Mrs. Nielson wiped the counters.

"You know, Lana, I'm glad that Benny has someone like you. I'm not just saying that because you two are dating but…" She trailed off as I looked at her. "When Benny was young, he barely socialized with people. He only had Nick and Liam. He was very quiet growing up. Yet he used to come home and tell me all about his day." She laughed as I smiled. "I told him to write letters since he was so quiet. I don't know if that was a good idea because after he got into the routine to write a letter once a month, he kind of became distant." She stared at the ground and let out a sigh, then continued. "Then high school started, and he became accepted but still stuck to his little group of friends. I wonder if he still writes after all these years."

"Why are you telling me this, Mrs. Nielson?" I asked after a while.

"You make my boy happy again. Sam even gets jealous of Benny talking about you," she said, and I felt my cheeks warm up. "Well, I suppose you want to see him now."

“Thanks, Mrs. Nielson,” I said, then walked out of the kitchen. I knocked on the door, then slowly opened it. When I peeked through, Benny’s back faced me as he sat by his desk.

“I already tasted your pudding, Mom, and it’s lovely,” he said as I tiptoed toward him.

“Guess who?” I asked in a deep voice and cupped my hands over his eyes. His hands instantly touched mine as he felt them.

“Hmm, it can’t be Sam because he isn’t here…Liam?” he jokingly asked as he stood up. Benny quickly spun around and engulfed me in a hug. I laughed as his arms wrapped around my waist while he picked me up. We fell onto his bed as we chuckled. He hovered over me as I stared into his brown eyes. A smile spread across his face as he put a lock of hair behind my ear. “What brings you here, gorgeous?”

“I missed you,” I whispered as I stroked his cheek and took in his facial features. “Remember when you came to my house and said that long thing about me being a fragile piece of glass that you kept breaking but you’re willing to put the pieces back together?”

“Yeah.” He raised a brow.

“Quite cheesy, Nielson.”

“Well, it’s true.” He laughed. “How am I doing so far?”

“I don’t know…the cracks still show.”

“The cracks will always show, but it proves that you’re strong and that we don’t heal overnight,” he whispered. Benny kissed my forehead as I smiled at him. He stared at me then raised a brow. “You’re not wearing your glasses."

"Yeah, I was too lazy to put them on."

"I think it takes longer to put on contacts than to put on your glasses." Benny laughed. "Either that or you didn't want them to get in the way."

"Get in the way of what?" I asked.

"Of me doing this," he mumbled, then kissed me. I locked my arms around his neck as I smiled. He rested between my legs as his hands traveled down my body. My arms went around his torso as I brought him closer. He kissed down my neck as I ran my fingers through his hair. I wrapped my legs around his torso, and he flipped us so I was on top. I brushed against him, and he moaned. I cupped his cheeks as I deepened the kiss. I felt his hands go inside my back pockets and he squeezed my ass.

Just then, Benny's phone went off. I straddled him and watched as he took his phone. "Hello." His eyes locked with mine as he gave me the phone. "It's for you."

"Hello." I raised a brow.

"Lana! I've been calling your phone for the past five minutes. I figured you'd be with Benny," Melissa said as I watched Benny.

"Yeah," I mumbled as Benny sat up. His one arm wrapped around my torso as he held me up. He buried his face in my neck as he left sloppy kisses on them.

"We're having a girls' night at Miranda's house. I've called Tiffany, and she'll be coming too," she said as I sucked in a breath.

"Uh—okay. I-I'll be there…soon." I sighed as Benny pecked my skin. Melissa ended the call, and

I threw the phone on the other side of the bed. Benny wrapped both arms around me as he continued to kiss me. “I need to go. I promised a girls’ night before Christmas.” I moaned as he nibbled on my collarbone. Benny let out a sigh as I got off the bed. I straightened my clothing then turned to my boyfriend. I put my arms around his neck then pecked his lips. “I’ll see you soon.”

***

The whole night, we talked about hot actors and complete nonsense. I borrowed Miranda’s clothes since I didn’t want to drive back home. I noticed the guys gave me space since I hadn’t heard from any of them.

“Where’s your mom?” Tiffany asked Miranda.

“Oh, she’s at a friend’s thingy.” Miranda shrugged her shoulders.

“Hey, hey, is it true that Carter and them are hogging your house?” Tiffany snickered.

“Yeah, like they’re freaking attached to the living room,” I scoffed.

“How are they?” Miranda suddenly asked as she turned the volume down of the TV.

“Err…they’re all right,” I mumbled, yet Melissa and Miranda didn’t seem convinced as I sighed. “I’m not on good terms with them. Levi keeps blaming Benny for everything.”

“Because he knows he can’t control you anymore. That you have someone else that they don’t like,” Miranda said.

“What do you mean by them?” I asked.

"Levi and Blake. You can see on their faces that they hate Benny but won't do anything…not yet."

"What does this have to do with Blake?"

"Oh my god, girl," Melissa said as she looked at Miranda and me.

"They're selfish and think they can get anything they want. Levi's a dick, Lana. He'll just keep on ruining you and make you feel like shit." Miranda raised her voice.

"No, he's not!" I snapped. "Deep down he still feels guilty and ruined. He's a cocky bastard, but he cares. I know he does."

"No, you care!" Miranda exclaimed as she stood up. "He sees that you're doing fine without him, so they're trying to mess with you. To fuck with your feelings!"

"Yet on the first day of the bet, you loved Blake and me. So freaking goals! Now, you hate both of them."

"That's before he got you back on smoking! Before he brought the old fucking Lana back, which Levi created!" She pointed her index finger at me. "Yet the new one made a promise not to bring the old Lana back! You broke our promise, Lana. You said you wouldn't get addicted again, but you fucking did!"

"It's not that fucking easy when you're going through so much shit!" I shouted and pushed her finger away. Miranda let out a pathetic laugh as she tugged on her hair.

"*Stop being so self-centered!*" she yelled. "The people around you are being affected too! They're going through their own shit! Mom isn't even at a friend's house; she's probably at a fucking bar hoping the guy who loved and abandoned us fifteen years ago will come back!"

Everything went quiet after that. I stared at Miranda with drained eyes as I thought of her and her mom. I knew Miss Stevens went through a tough time, but I didn't realize that it got worse. Miranda barely spoke about her mom.

"Miranda, I—" She cut me off as she raised her arms. We watched as she spun around and walked upstairs.

"Give her some time," Melissa mumbled as I stepped forward. A door slammed shut, which echoed through the house, and I couldn't help but think of earlier today.

Miranda didn't come out of her room the rest of the night even though I knocked multiple times. The rest of us decided to sleep on the sofa after we watched movies. I walked into the kitchen and turned on the light. I squinted and noticed that it was three in the morning. I was thirsty, so I poured myself water.

Out the corner of my eye, I saw Melissa walk in. She wrapped herself in her gown as she squinted at me. I gave Melissa a sleepy smile as she went for a drink too. She leaned against the counter and drank her water. I set my empty glass on the table, then turned to her. She raised a brow at me as I bit the inside of my cheek.

"Do you think I'm a whore?" I blurted out as her eyes widened.

"No, you're just surrounded by horny bastards who are selfish. They do things to put you under pressure," she said and sat beside me. "In the end, they want you to choose…"

I didn't know what to say, so I played with the glass. Melissa finished hers and set it on the table.

"Why does Miranda hate Levi?" she asked.

"Long story." I laughed.

"I love stories." She smiled. I let out a sigh as I tried to recall the memories from the previous years.

"Levi just turned seventeen and spent it here. All his friends came over, and they left around midnight. The next few nights were the same, so I decided to follow him since he'd sneak out. That's when he started racing," I began. "Ever since that night…my life changed. He told me to live a little since my head was always in my books. I trusted him, so I agreed to race with him. It was honestly so much fun, and I felt free. We went home and got busted. I had to make up a lie on the spot so we weren't grounded.

"As each night passed, the lies got bigger. I still remember going to this party with him and having my first drink. It was only a sip of Levi's, though. Keene offered me a cigarette, but I kindly declined, saying alcohol was enough for the night. I still remember making a bucket list with Levi when we were young. One of the things he put on it was smoke a cigarette because we saw Mr. Bronx smoking and we were intrigued.

"The thing I liked about it all was that Levi didn't tell me to change my appearance. I still wore my big glasses and oversized cardigans. He said, 'We're showing the world what a nerd can do,' but I wanted to change. I told him, and he took me shopping and bought me a whole new wardrobe with clothes that I was comfortable in."

"So that explains your glow up in junior year," Melissa joked as she nudged my shoulder.

"Finals came, and I sunk into my books again. The old Lana only came out when Levi was here. I couldn't focus, and I was stressing out a lot. Keene knew this guy who could help, and how fucking ironic that it was Parker," I mumbled. "Yet he only gave me one bottle. When Levi left, I didn't have any more, but he left me something."

"Ooh, what was it?" Melissa asked as she stared at me.

"Cigarettes. Somehow, they helped me when I didn't have the pills. Levi said he was sad that he couldn't see my first drag. Yet Miranda wasn't very impressed when she caught me in the back of school before our History final," I mumbled. "She hated that he was trying to change me and that he was a bad influence, but I wanted to change. I wanted to take risks.

"Then summer break of 2015, he said that we're going to finish the bucket list. We tried to by going skinny dipping, street racing, threw a TV out the window at a party, road trip to California, and even took a picture with a snake. We did all the crazy stuff in California. We were inseparable. He was the risk taker, and I was the excuse maker. After we came back, I'd tell our parents an excuse for coming home so late, and sometimes it would work."

"Wow, so you were his good girl, and he was your bad boy."

"Yeah, I guess."

"So when you made a bet, it was all an act because you did half of the stuff already?"

"Yeah, I didn't want to mix with another group of bad boys and leave with the same result, but I guess things didn't go as planned." I mumbled the last the part.

"What did you guys do in Summer 2015 before Levi left?" she asked.

"Miranda, Keene, Levi, and I went to a party. This guy Jaden hosted it, and his parties are wild," I mumbled. "That was the night I lost my virginity to Levi. Next day I woke up and he was gone. End of the story—"

"Wait…you said you tried to finish the bucket list. What was left?" Melissa asked as I let out a dry laugh.

"Quite a few. Levi is a person who doesn't believe in love. He specifically wrote *Do not fall in love*…I could never ever tick it."

"Now I know why Miranda hates him. He left you right after he took your v-card, but you couldn't tick it bec—"

"I fell in love with him," I whispered. "In a way, I let him control me. We used to fight, but I forgave him easily because I didn't want to lose him. He wasn't even mine in the first place."

"Did you ever tell him?" Melissa asked as she gently placed her hand on my knee for comfort.

"Yeah, and the worst part is he said it back, but not in the way I said it to him."

"Do you still love h—"

"What are you guys doing up so late?" Miranda's voice echoed through the kitchen as she cut off Melissa.

"Should be asking you the same thing." Melissa gestured to Miranda's attire. She was dressed in a gray coat, jeans, and Converse. Car keys dangled in her hands as she tugged on her beanie.

"I-I'm going out quick," she mumbled, then put on her beanie.

"At three in the morning," I said. Miranda ignored me as she walked past us and out the back door. I hastily slipped on my shoes and grabbed a hoodie as I followed her.

"I'll stay here," Melissa said as she looked at Tiffany, who was fast asleep on the sofa. I gave a curt nod and walked out the door. I saw Miranda get into the car as I quickly opened the passenger door. When I got in, I noticed Miranda's stare.

"I'm not letting you go out alone at this time," I said as I buckled myself in. Miranda let out a sigh as she started the car then drove out the driveway.

Silence filled us as I rubbed my arms for warmth. The windows fogged up from the coldness, and the road was barely visible.

"I'm sorry for snapping at you earlier. I didn't mean to…" Miranda blurted out.

"It's okay, and I'm sorry too. I didn't know about your mom." I turned to her.

"I hate it when we fight. I mean, you're practically my sister," she said as I smiled at her.

"Love you, Miranda," I said as I playfully punched her shoulder.

"Love you too, Willson."

"Where are we going?" I asked as we drove into the industrial area.

"Mom phoned. She needs me to pick her up."

"Oh," I mumbled. We drove through the streets, and surprisingly, they weren't empty at three in the morning. Mostly drunk people and gangsters lurked. We turned a corner where the club was.

"There." Miranda pointed to where a few people walked around. I squinted my eyes as I searched for Miss Stevens. She leaned against a lamp post as she looked around. Miranda parked the car a few yards away, and we got out. Just then, someone approached Miss Stevens. He touched her, and my eyes widened. "Hey, don't touch her!" Miranda shouted as she ran toward the man. I followed as Miranda tried to pull the man away. The man aggressively pulled away and stroked Miss Stevens' cheek. Miranda kicked the guy as I tried to push his hands off her.

Out of the corner of my eye, I saw a bouncer approach us from the club across the street. He was big and muscular. He ripped the man off Miss Stevens. Miranda went to her mother's side as I watched the bouncer punch the guy. I suddenly paled as I got a view of his face. The words "we're watching you" echoed in my head as the two men fought. Suddenly, he turned to me, and I went stiff. One of James's men stood right in front of me. What frightened me the most was that it was the one who'd been in my room.

Chapter Twelve

Lana

Everything suddenly stopped as I stared at the men fighting. It had to be a coincidence. The memory of him when he entered my room frightened me. He was tall yet muscular, and I heard a little accent.

"*Lana!*" Miranda yelled. I blinked rapidly and turned to see Miranda limping toward the car.

"Get the hell out of here!" the bouncer yelled as he kicked the guy. The man wiped the blood from his mouth, then looked at me. He still dared to smirk as he straightened his posture and ran away. The sudden urge to follow him and ask him questions grew in the pit of my stomach.

"*Leave us alone!*" I yelled as he glanced over his shoulder to look at me. I watched as he ran and turned the corner right into the alley. I was confused as to why he'd want to go there.

"Kid, get out of here. It's dangerous," the bouncer said. I thanked him, then spun around. I ran to the car, where Miranda helped her mother into the backseat.

"I'll drive," I said as I took the keys from her. She nodded, then got in the back with her mother. I started the car and quickly drove out of the area because I hated this place at night.

"Who the hell was that?" Miranda demanded. I looked up into the rearview mirror to see her in the center while her mom was asleep on her chest. I shrugged, then looked back at the road. "No, Lana. The way you looked at that guy…like you've seen him before."

"He was the one who was in my room."

"*What?*"

"Calm down, okay?"

"No, I will not calm down! You should tell your dad. He can help, Lana," she said as I rolled my eyes. "Either you tell him or I will."

My eyes widened at the thought of my dad aware that one of James's men had been in our house. He didn't even know that I was at the cottage that day.

"Fine, I'll tell him." I sighed.

"Good. Thanks, by the way," she murmured.

"No problem," I mumbled as we drove and silence tramped in our thoughts.

***

I stared at my dad's office door and debated on whether I should enter. I could tell him that Miranda and I saw one of James's men. Not the whole room thing. Christmas was in a few days, so I'd rather tell him now than when it's Christmas or New Year's. I opened the door to see my father behind his desk. He was so focused on going through papers that he didn't even notice me. Afterward, he stood up and grabbed his jacket.

"Dad," I said, and he raised his head.

"Lana, hey. How was the sleepover?" he asked as he put his jacket on.

"I—it was good," I mumbled as I looked down.

"But…" He trailed off. I let out a sigh as I looked up. I shut my eyes.

"We were in the industrial area, and I saw one of James's men," I admitted. I slowly opened my eyes to see Dad's knitted brows.

"What? How?"

"Well, we were getting Miranda's mom from a club, then he approached her. This bouncer came and helped us. Then he ran off into the alley."

"The alley?"

"The alley that's under investigation."

"Are you sure it's him?"

"Yeah, his face matches the one at the station," I said. That part was right because some of James's men had been spotted, so there were identities.

"All right," he said after a while. "Come with me."

"Where to?" I asked as we walked out of his office and into the living room.

"The alley. I'll call Detective Kale, and you'll tell him what you said to me," Dad stated as he put on his beanie. My eyes widened as Dad ushered me out of the house after I grabbed my coat. I took out my glasses and put them on as I got into my dad's car.

We arrived at the alley, yet it was covered in tape so we couldn't pass. The thought of being here in broad daylight terrified me. Everything looked the same from the day Benny, Liam, Nick, and I was here. A policeman guarded the alley as Detective Kale approached us.

"Morning, Willson," he greeted. "It's a few days before Christmas. Why'd you call?"

"My daughter here was in the area early this morning and spotted this man. He's one of James Cornelius' men," Dad said as he showed the photo on the iPad.

"He came through here?" Kale questioned as he looked down the alley. I followed his gaze to the alley. There wasn't much since the snow arrived. Most of the evidence was either with them or gone. They still checked every day in the hope that Jack would come back to his home.

"Yeah," I replied as I avoided eye contact.

"What's the latest report?" Dad asked as I folded my arms. Detective Kale looked at my dad, then me. "She's my daughter and a witness," Dad said as he swung his arm around my shoulder. Kale let out a sigh as he looked over his shoulder at the policeman. He gave him a nod and the policeman returned the gesture, then walked off.

"We've done all the questioning, and they all say the same. Something's not right. They keep saying he was an alcoholic, came here and worked in the café," Kale admitted.

"What café?" Dad asked.

"Behind the alley. We've been there and interviewed them. None of them have heard of Jack

August."

"In the news, they said his co-workers weren't fond of him. What about them?" I asked as I remembered when Jack first came on the news.

"They're journalists and news reporters. They change it around and brainwash you to believe anything they say," Dad replied.

"Yeah, and the surveillance cameras are no help either." Kale sighed.

"Wha-what cameras?" I asked as I looked down the alley, yet there were no cameras.

"This wasn't always a bad area. It was okay. Yet they still had their cameras," Kale said as he motioned across the street. I paled as I looked at the camera that was in the building right opposite us. It faced directly at us and got a perfect view of the whole alley. "Spoke to the owners and they said it stopped working a few weeks ago and everything was wiped. Probably a fuse or something."

"And they can't fix it?" Dad asked as I stared at the camera.

"They're working on it, but it's a low chance that we'll get the footage back from September when he went missing," Kale responded.

"Okay, thanks. Merry Christmas," Dad said as he placed his hand on my back.

"Merry Christmas. Oh, and Willson, we need to have that meeting soon," Detective Kale said as we walked to the car. Dad gave Detective Kale a blank look, then a nod. I raised a brow as we got into the car.

"What was that about?" I asked as we drove.

"Nothing, just wanting to discuss a few things,"

Dad mumbled. Silence filled the car as I thought over what Kale said. Who knew how long those cameras were out? I wanted to text Benny and tell him, yet I didn't want to ruin the holiday mood. Maybe I'd tell them after Christmas.

"Do you think you'll ever get James?" I asked after a while.

"Yes, we will," Dad said, then turned to me. "I don't want you to worry. We'll get him."

"I know you will, Dad." I smiled.

"Listen, err…I'll drop you at home. Someone should be there now. I don't want you to be alone," he said as we drove into our neighborhood.

"Thanks, Dad, for everything. I love you," I said.

"Anything for my little girl. Love you too," he said as he stopped in front of our house. I looked past him to see Blake's motorcycle and Levi's Mustang in the driveway. I didn't want to be home with them. Not now. "Well, I gotta head to the station. See you at dinner," Dad said, then kissed my forehead. I got out of the car and walked to the front door. The door was unlocked, so I pushed it open. When I got home this morning, Dad and Richard were the only ones home. Mom and Jade were probably out, and I didn't know where Levi was. Well, he should have been here since his car was here. I walked in. The sound of the television played through the house as I took off my coat and placed it on the hook. I strolled to the kitchen but felt a tug on my arm.

"Where were you? You just drove off like that yesterday," Levi stated as he spun me around.

"I slept over at Miranda's house. Chill," I said,

then pulled my arm back.

"You could've said something instead of just walking out of here," he said with an irritated look.

"Look who's talking," I said, then spun around. I think I bumped into a wall or something because I immediately backed away and rubbed my nose. When I looked up, I saw Blake.

"Sorry," he mumbled. I looked over my shoulder to see Levi. He let out a deep sigh as he awkwardly scratched the back of his neck.

"Look, err…we're sorry again for yesterday. We didn't mean the stuff we said about you being a whore and slut," Levi mumbled.

"We never said whore or slut, but we were thinking it," Blake added.

"You guys fucking suck at apologies," I muttered. "You apologize every damn time yet you still find a way to fuck up."

"Well, Parker made it sound like you two were boning. He literally said you kept each other happy." Blake raised his voice.

"The problem is you believed him. It shows that you'll believe someone you barely know without even asking for my side of the story!" I exclaimed.

"I'm sorry, okay? I'm sorry for always fucking up. We're sorry for always fucking up your life!" It was the first time Blake shouted at me, and it frightened me. I was used to Levi and Miranda, but not Blake Gunner. He always spoke in a neutral or hoarse tone. A vein stuck out in his neck as he yelled, his eyes bloodshot, probably from the lack of sleep, and he smelled of cigarettes along with Levi. "We'll make it up to you, baby girl," he whispered after he calmed down. I folded my arms as I stared at them. I was not his baby nor his girl.

Levi's eyes widened as he approached Blake. He whispered in his ear as Blake smirked. It intrigued me how Blake's cold expression changed within a minute. His smirk seemed to grow as he locked eyes with me. I squinted my eyes as Levi continued to whisper. Blake slowly bit his lip as he eyed me up and down. I felt uncomfortable as I wrapped my arms around my body and waited.

After a minute, Levi was done, and they smirked. "Well, you know what they say, actions speak louder than words."

I squinted my eyes because I didn't know what they were up to. Levi awkwardly coughed, then walked upstairs. "You hungry?" Blake asked as he walked to the kitchen.

"Err…yeah, but this is my house. I should be asking you that," I said as we entered the kitchen.

"Sorry for trying to be thoughtful, nerd," he said, then walked to the fridge. "I'm hungry too, so I'll just whip up something."

"Whip?" I asked as I propped myself up on the counter. I couldn't help but think of his change in moods. I didn't like to be angry at them, and they knew that. I watched as Blake rummaged through my fridge and took out random stuff, then shut the door. He spun around with a smirk plastered on his face. He took off his leather jacket and placed it next to me.

"Whip." He wiggled his brows. I watched as he pulled his sleeves up of his Iron Maiden crewneck. He walked toward me, but I raised my leg and placed my foot on his chest.

"Kinky," I stated, and Blake threw his head back and laughed. His hand wrapped around my ankle as the other went on my calf. Out the corner of my eye, I saw Levi walk down, but he went into the living room. I felt a sudden tickle as I turned back to see Blake stroke my calf. I jerked away, and he used it as a chance to step in between my thighs. I placed my hands on his chest to push him away, but he didn't move an inch as he looked down.

"Is the mark still there?" he asked. I glanced down to see him caressing my thigh.

"Obviously," I said, then shoved him away from me. He chuckled then stood next to me and made sandwiches. I looked straight out the window and noticed our backyard was covered in snow.

"Why did your dad drop you off?" Blake suddenly asked. I shrugged my shoulders as I swung my legs back and forth by the island.

"Just."

"Just…" He trailed off as I sighed.

"James is back. Well, the guy who was in my room," I stated. I thought I'd get a reaction out of Blake, but he continued with the sandwiches.

"How do you know that?"

"Miranda and I saw him last night. She said I have to tell my dad, so I did."

"Now what?"

"Now…we wait."

After a few more minutes, Blake was done with the sandwiches. I glanced to see various little pieces of bread with the crust off and cut into stars.

"Wow." I laughed as I picked one and ate it.

"Made by yours truly."

"They're cut so perfectly."

"Thanks." He chuckled then ate one. Levi entered the kitchen in his coat. He tossed us our beanies and gloves. I gave him a questioning look as he approached us, then took a sandwich.

"We're gonna play in the snow!" he cheered, then walked to the back door. "Come on, Keene!"

I looked over my shoulder to see Keene enter the kitchen with a pissed look.

"Hey, when did you get here?" I asked as he leaned against the counter.

"Before you, and what friends you are!" He gestured to Blake and me. Levi was already outside doing God knew what.

"What?" Blake and I asked in unison.

"I was locked up for three fucking days with that stupid-ass clown. None of you came to get me," Keene said as my eyes widened.

"I didn't know," I admitted. "If I did I would've co—" I was cut off when something was thrown at the window. Keene spun around as we watched Levi.

"Come on!" he yelled as he threw another snowball. Blake let out a sigh as he took the last two sandwiches. He put the one in his mouth then stared at the other. I gave him a weird look as he looked at me, then the sandwich. He took the sandwich in his hand and stuffed it in my mouth, then ran out. I threw my hands up in exasperation and let out a groan as I ate the sandwich. I glanced over at Keene, who stared at me.

"What?"

"I…err…they told me what happened yesterday," he mumbled. I looked down because I didn't want to talk about it. Keene stepped closer and stood between my thighs. "When Parker told us at the party, I didn't think it was true. I know you, Lana, and you wouldn't go for a weirdo like him." Keene ruffled my hair. I glanced up at him to see a confused look fill his features. He let out a sigh as he placed each hand on either side of the table and looked up at me. "This all my fault. I shouldn't have given you those pills at the beginning of junior year. Then you wouldn't have been raped by him."

"It's my fault for letting him do that to me." I sighed, and he shook his head.

"It's understandable that you couldn't tell anyone. I get it; everyone expects you to be the perfect girl with straight A's and always listening to your parents. It's hard because you're put under pressure to be this type of person when you just want to be yourself."

Keene looked down as I watched his brown hair fall in his face. He was much more responsible than Levi. He was the mom out of our trio of him, Levi, and me. He was a foster kid who was removed from his dad and went to many foster homes. I didn't know what happened to his mother, though. During the past few years, he brought himself up, then got a casual job and shared an apartment with someone.

"How many times did he…" Keene trailed off.

"Only once…the rest was harassing," I mumbled.

"Why didn't you just stop taking the pills?"

"I don't know; I just wanted to get away from

everything…from everyone. I didn't mean to hurt the people I cared for."

"It's not your fault, Lana," he said, then looked over his shoulder at Levi and Blake. "It's ours; we did this to you."

"No, it's my fault. You guys just wanted to show me the fun side of life. I took advantage of it and did all this shit."

"Lana, we've all done things we've regretted."

"Yeah, and I'll always hate myself for that," I stated. Another snowball was thrown at the window. Levi and Blake's heads popped up as they squinted at the two of us.

"When you two are done boning, we'd like to play," Levi yelled as he looked at the position Keene and I were in. Keene flipped him off as I wrapped my legs around his waist and locked my arms around his neck. He gave me a piggyback ride all the way out to the backyard.

"Shit, it's cold," he grumbled as his grip tightened. Out of nowhere, a snowball was thrown at us. I looked up to see Levi and Blake were on the other side.

"Take cover!" I yelled as they threw snowballs. Keene ran as I used my one hand to hold on and the other to dodge the snow. He stopped behind a tree and put me down. In unison, we glanced around the tree and realized they'd built a fort. "They're so childish. Why can't we go inside and drink some hot cocoa?" I asked as we turned back to lean on the tree.

"Actions speak louder than words," Keene stated, then crouched down to make snowballs. I raised a brow because Blake said the same thing.

"Are you guys up to something?" I asked.

"Nope, just having fun." He grinned, then dragged his fingers in the snow. "Suck on these balls, dipshits!" he yelled, then threw the ball toward their fort. I watched as Levi raised his head to see and, on cue, the ball hit him right in the face. Keene and I laughed as Levi groaned. My hands froze throughout the game. Keene ran off to get closer to their fort. Out the corner of my eye, I saw Blake. I locked eyes with him as I roughly dragged my hands through the snow.

"There you are, nerd." He smirked and raised his arm. Using all my strength, I threw the snowball at him. It hit him directly in the face, and he staggered back. He dropped the snowball in his hand and wiped the snow off his face. My eyes widened as I watched the snow mixed with dirt fall from his face. I got up and walked over to him as he continuously rubbed his eye.

"Are you okay?" I laughed as he cleaned his face.

"Next time, make sure you know what you're throwing at me." He gestured to his eyes which were red. "Because I don't remember having stones in snowballs."

"Oh my gosh, I'm sorry." I snickered.

"You don't look sorry." He crouched down and made another snowball. I did the same thing and made sure to only use snow. As I stood up, Blake marched toward me, wrapped his arm around my waist, then dumped the snowball on top of my head.

"It's cold!" I shrieked as I wrapped my one arm

around him. Using the same hand, I pulled his jeans and threw the snowball down his butt.

"Fuck!" he yelled as I squirmed out of his hold and ran away. "I'm coming for you!"

"Dude, that's sounds so wrong in that tone!" Levi said as he walked to the other side.

"Shut the fuck up," Blake exclaimed. I ran toward their fort since they weren't there. I found snowballs stacked up ready to be used, and I smiled.

"Every man for himself!" Levi yelled.

"That's not fair. She's got all the balls," Keene shouted as I threw them.

"Yep, I got all the balls!" I laughed as I threw at Levi. They shouted and ran around for cover. They darted toward the tree, but it was no use since they were three six-foot guys. I laughed as Keene and Blake pushed Levi in front of them and used him for cover.

***

The next few days we got ready for Christmas. I baked all my cinnamon rolls while Mom and Jade took care of the food. Dad and Richard went out to a hockey game, then got scolded by their wives because they were supposed to get ingredients. Levi, Blake, Carter, Ethan, and Keene oddly hung out with me, yet when I asked them why, they'd say the same thing: *Actions speak louder than words.* Benny and I went out to a cooking session where we cooked for the homeless shelters, and we had so much fun. Afterward, we spent the rest of the day there and gave out food.

It was now Christmas Eve, and I stood in front of my mirror in a pair of gray jeans, camel-colored boots, and the Christmas sweater Jade knitted me. Every second year she'd knit Levi and I matching sweaters.

"Aww, don't you look cute," Levi said as he stood beside me.

"Where does your mom find the time to knit these?" I looked at my red one and the blue one that he wore with a pair of black jeans and high-top Vans.

"I have no idea, but guess what? She made Uncle Griff one too." He laughed.

"What color is his?" I chuckled as we walked downstairs.

"I don't know, but since the both of us have elves on the front, he should be…" He trailed off.

"Santa!" I laughed. We walked in to see my dad and Richard in the living room. Dad stared at the Christmas tree that Levi and I decorated, and he instantly cursed under breath.

"You had to buy these ones?" Dad asked Levi as he pointed at the Christmas balls. Levi raised his thumb up as I squinted my eyes and looked at it. I let out a dry laugh as I read the green Christmas ball. *Merry Fucking Christmas.*

"Son," Richard said as he got up from the sofa and gestured for Levi to follow him. Levi rolled his eyes and stuffed his hands in his pockets as he followed. I gave Dad a questioning look, to which he shrugged. The doorbell rang, and my mother rushed into the living room with an apron on. She pushed a plate of cookies in my chest as I groaned.

"It's Linda and her children. They're doing Christmas carols. Give one to each," she said. The oven went off, and she bolted back into the kitchen. I turned to Dad and noticed his stare on the tree.

"Who's Linda?" I asked.

"I don't know. I think she's our neighbor." He shrugged. It showed how much time we bonded with our current neighbors yet invited the ones we had from eight years ago. Out of the corner of my eye, I saw Levi and Richard at the end of the hall. They seemed to be in an intense conversation since Richard had his arms folded as he scolded his son. Levi leaned against the wall with his arms folded, head thrown back, and eyes shut as he listened to his dad. The doorbell rang again, and I walked over with the plate of cookies. When I opened the door, I saw five children in front of me, and a woman who I assumed was Linda.

"Just like how we practiced, and no, Luke, you can't rap," Linda said. They sang "Silent Night," and it was honestly the cutest thing ever. They were so short and adorable that I wanted to give the whole plate to them. Levi approached us, and I gave him a look that he ignored.

"Have a lovely Christmas," Levi said after they finished. He took a cookie from the plate, and I smacked his hand away.

"Levi, it's for them!" I moved the plate away from him and toward the children.

"Wait…Levi and Lana?" Linda asked as she pointed at us.

"Who wants to know?" Levi asked as he raised a brow at the woman.

"You two have grown so much! I still remember when you guys were little and used to take lemons from my tree," she cooed.

"That's because we started a lemon stand in the summer," Levi stated.

"Aww, it's so great that you two are finally together. I love the matching outfits."

"Oh, we're no—"

"Thank you, we just love spending Christmas together!" Levi cut me off as he slung an arm around my shoulder.

"Well, thank you and Happy Holidays!" Linda said, then grabbed a cookie.

"Merry Christmas!" the kids cheered. Levi and I said goodbye, then shut the door. I looked down and noticed the plate was empty.

"Who the fuck was that?" Levi asked.

"I think she's our neighbor," I stated, then walked into the dining room.

"Lana, set the table, please!" Mom yelled from the kitchen.

"Will do," I said as I gave the plate to Levi. I walked into the dining area and noticed that the plates were stacked up along with everything else. I set on each of the eight table mats. I took out the glasses and put them out. The doorbell rang, and I saw Dad open it. He sounded happy, and there were a lot of voices to be heard. Once I was done, I walked into the living room to see Uncle Griff.

"Where's your little lady friend?" Levi asked.

"She'll be here soon." He waved off then stared at Levi. "So how's it being back in Illinois?"

"It's cool, sometimes there are surprises, but it's

cool," Levi responded. I gave them each a weird look as they stared at each other.

"Griffon, thanks for coming!" Mom beamed as she entered the room with Jade. Mom had a tray of finger food while Jade had a plate with wine.

"How was the football game?" Jade asked.

"It was gre—" Griffon cut off when Richard and Dad glared at him. "What football game?"

"Told you." Mom laughed as I took a mini bread roll. Levi reached out to grab a glass of wine, but Jade smacked his hand away.

"Nice sweater, Uncle Griff, totally brings out your eyes," Levi joked as we looked at the sweater Jade knitted him.

"Yeah, and yours totally brings out how little everyone thinks of you," Uncle Griff pointed to the little elf. My jaw dropped as Levi's jaw clenched. Griffon awkwardly laughed as everyone followed. By their odd stares, I knew something was up.

"Levi, could you please put these on the table? I know you got one," Mom said as she held up the candles that needed to be lit. He smirked as he took the candles then walked to the table. I followed and watched as he lit each candle with his Zippo, then placed it on the table.

"Something's wrong with Uncle Griff," I mumbled as I stood opposite Levi.

"What makes you think that?" he asked.

"Well first, you guys didn't do that weird handshake you always do, and second, he said 'she.' He always exaggerates about Jenny Rosa." I looked over Levi's shoulder to Uncle Griff, who smiled at my mom yet the smile didn't reach his eyes. "Or it was the look you gave each other?"

Levi looked over his shoulder to see Griffon, then turned back to face me. He forced a smile then said, "I think it's the woman one."

"Yes, I'll be dishing up soon!" Mom said as she walked into the kitchen.

"I'll help," Griffon offered as he trailed behind her. I glanced back at Levi to see his squinted eyes. A few seconds later, my mother came out with salad and placed it on the table. Jade called her over as she walked to the kitchen but quickly spun around to join them in the living room. Levi and I shared a look, then went into the kitchen, where we found Griffon. His back was facing us as he leaned over the sink.

"She's not coming, is she?" Levi asked as he sat by the island. Griffon spun around with a flustered look as he stared at us. He looked down and sighed.

"No, it's not gonna work out between us."

"What happened?" I asked as I rested my arm on Levi's shoulder.

"Nothing, it's just…we weren't meant to be."

"There's plenty of fish in the sea, Uncle Griff. Any woman would want you," Levi said.

"Yeah, I think I'll lay off the whole dating thing for a while. Have to focus on my class, my family." Griffon smiled. "I'll always have you guys…unfortunately…but yeah, I'll always have you two."

"For that, we'll always love you," Levi said as I nodded in agreement. Uncle Griff laughed as he pulled us in for a hug.

***

Afterward, we ate the delicious food Mom and Jade made. When Levi and I spoke to Griffon in the kitchen a bit more, he was back to his old self.

"I don't think they need babysitting. Well, Lana doesn't. Don't know about you, though." Griffon pointed at Levi.

"I've matured!" Levi raised his arms in exasperation.

"Yeah right," Dad, Richard, and I said in unison.

"Remember when I was babysitting you two and I brought that girl Samantha over and she wanted to watch *Legally Blonde*?" Griffon asked as Mom and Jade turned to him.

"You brought women to our house when you had to babysit them?" Jade asked.

"Yeah, Mom, we were like his wingmen," Levi said as I laughed.

"That's not the point!" Griffon rushed out. "As I was saying, these two watched that romantic comedy with us, and Levi kept asking why Lana wasn't blonde."

"Oh, I remember." I glared at Levi.

"Then what?" Richard asked.

"Then he wanted to make me blonde, yet he didn't know how, so he lit my hair on fire!" I said as everyone laughed.

"I was only ten!"

"I had a bald spot for four months!"

"I even offered to cut my hair to give to you."

"Oh, you two." Jade laughed.

"Then when Lana first mentioned Yale, you

though it was some church group," Griffon said. Everyone laughed as Levi shrugged.

"Speaking of colleges, I've heard you applied to a few here in Illinois, Lana," Jade said.

"Have you heard from Yale yet?" Mom asked.

"No, I didn't app—"

"Oh, since you were sending in applications to the other colleges, I sent one to Yale."

"You what?" I demanded as I dropped my fork.

"Lana," Dad warned, and I mumbled a sorry to Mom.

"Since you were sending in so many, I thought you forgot," Mom said.

"I-I didn't forget. I don't even have all my results yet, Mom. Why didn't you say anything?"

"Don't you wanna go?" Levi asked. When I looked at him, I felt as if he still blamed Benny.

"Every year we come you talk about it, Lana," Richard said.

"Applications close the first of January, so I just assumed," Mom mumbled.

"Don't worry. As long as you've sent in an application, you can send the rest of the stuff in throughout January," Griffon assured me.

"Yeah, Griffon can help you, and I'm sure your school has counselors," Dad said as I stared at the table.

"Yeah, sorry." I sighed, then continued to eat. After that, there was small talk between the adults. No one spoke to me as they decided to give me space. I felt Levi's hand on my thigh, yet I instantly shrugged it off.

***

Christmas morning was spent opening gifts and finally having my cinnamon rolls for breakfast. I asked Mom and Dad if I could go to Ethan's house to exchange gifts, and they were okay with it if I returned for lunch. So we sat in Ethan's living room and swapped gifts. Aidan and Blake weren't here because they were too busy with family. Liam insisted that we get into the Christmas spirit, so we had on Santa hats. Ethan got Miranda, Melissa, and me Nike Air Max Thea, and the guys got Adidas Zx Flux. Liam literally pecked him on the cheek and said that he was the real Santa.

"I know that you've been eyeing this for a while now." I gave Melissa the bag she always looked at in the mall yet still debated on whether she should get it.

"Oh my god, Lana!" she cheered, then gave me a hug.

"Here's your gift. That night of Homecoming you looked fabulous in heels, so…I got you these." She gave me a shoebox. I opened it to see a pair of red ankle-strap heels.

"Wow, these are high, high heels." I took one out and observed it.

"I know, right? You can wear it to the New Year's Eve party." She wiggled her brows.

"Party?"

"Yeah, it's your boyfriend's turn to host," Melissa said.

"Don't you just love my boyfriend? He got me a Naked 3 Urban Decay kit!" Miranda squealed as she plopped down between us.

"I was going to get you two, but you're already pretty so I didn't want you looking prettier than me," Melissa said as she looked at the kit.

"Wow, you're a real friend," I said as Miranda stared at her.

"Dude, no way!" Liam yelled. We turned our heads to see Liam with a piece of paper. Benny stood next to him with a grin plastered on his face.

"Yeah, so you'll tone down on your addiction to the show," Benny said as Liam smiled.

"Hug me, brotha!" he quoted from *Drake and Josh*. We watched in amusement as Liam literally picked up Benny as they hugged.

"What is it?" Miranda asked.

"Tickets to Comic Con, dude!" Liam jumped up like a five year old. He continued to cheer and boast about his tickets for the next five minutes. I stood up and walked over to Benny, then wrapped my arms around his waist.

"Merry Christmas…again." I chuckled as I took out the envelope from my back pocket then handed it to him. He pecked my lips, then opened the envelope. I stepped back and eagerly bit my lip as I watched him open it. He read the tickets. His expression immediately changed as his eyes widened.

"No fucking way!" he exclaimed.

"What?" Ethan asked.

"Tickets to the Chicago Bulls versus Brooklyn Nets game on Wednesday," Benny said, then looked at me. I wish I had my phone out to take a photo of his reaction. Ethan snatched the tickets, then observed while Benny pulled me in for a hug. “Shit. Thank you so much!” he said, then cupped my cheeks. He left a long, persistent kiss on my lips, then stared at me. “It must’ve cost a lot for those type of tickets.”

“Don’t worry about it.” I waved off then hugged him again.

“You want your gift?” he asked as he dragged me out of the room.

“Sure.” I shrugged and followed him into the hall. There was a table in the hall where I saw a medium-sized box. Benny took it and nervously handed it to me. I thanked him and took the lid off the box. There was another box inside that had images on it.

“Aww, you got me those pearl bath bombs.” I looked at the bath bombs.

“Yeah, the lady said there’s something inside them,” Benny said as he awkwardly scratched his neck. He pointed to the box where all the bath bombs had a charm in to form a bracelet. “There’s more.”

“Oh.” I put the first box down then took out the other.

“So you’ll look cute when we cuddle,” he said as I examined the mermaid tail blanket.

“Thanks,” I said as my cheeks warmed.

“One last thing.” He sighed and stepped back as I took out a brown package. I raised a brow as I put everything on the table, then looked at the brown bag. It was tied up, so I loosened it. Multiple letters were neatly stacked, and each had a grade on them. I turned to Benny, who leaned against the wall.

"Just read one of them, Lana."

I thought back to a few days ago when his mom told me about the letters. I took a random one and noticed that it was from fourth grade.

Dear...

School wasn't so bad today. Even though I sat in the back of the class as always, Liam made me laugh. I saw her again. She's so pretty. I like her eyes and glasses. She always talks to Ethan and says he can do it. She never notices me. But that boy Levi is always with her. I don't like them. Ethan is good at everything. Everyone loves him. I wish I were like him. Daddy says everyone likes him because he's rich. It's true, his birthday party was the best! We all went laser tag. I don't want to have a birthday party. Nobody would come. I'm a loser.

From Benny

I glanced at him to see that his eyes were shut and his hands stuffed in his pockets. I frowned as I took out another letter. This one was from tenth grade.

Dear whoever gives a fuck,

Today has been one of the worst days ever. I made the basketball team, but Ethan fucking Baxter became captain. He's even dating this chick, Melissa. He's popular, tall, muscular, and rich. If it weren't for his rich ass daddy, he wouldn't even be where he is now. I bet he got personal trainers or some shit. I deserve to be captain! I've wanted to be captain since fifth grade! I worked hard for shit! And then I take my anger out on the person who encouraged him. I hurt her again. I didn't mean to. She's so beautiful, and her eyes get bluer every time I see them. Yet I always have to fuck it up and ruin her. I fucking hate myself. Yet someone gives me the punch I deserve. Levi Radcliff. I let him do it. I fucking deserve it. I don't want to do it anymore. I hurt her then I end up hurting me. Last time I was so close...

From Benny

A lump ached in my throat by the time I finished. I turned to Benny and noticed he had tears.

"B-Benny, what do you mean last time you were so close?" I hugged him. His arm wrapped around my shoulder as the other went around my waist. The hug was tight as he sniffed like he didn't want to let go.

"You deserve so much better," he whispered, then raised his sleeve. A tear ran down my face as I stared at the faded scars. It all made sense. He was alone. He was depressed. He hated himself, so he cut.

"Benny, please," I croaked out and gently placed my hand on his scars. His legs buckled as he slid down the wall. I put the letters on the table and sat next to him. I cupped his cheeks and saw his watery eyes and distressed look. Tears fell as I shook my head. "Please stop. I'd hate myself if you didn't. Please don't do it ever again."

"I stopped the day you forgave me," he whispered. A sad smile crept up on my face as I took my thumbs and wiped his tears away. "Every day when I got home, I'd beat myself up. I'd do it, thinking how ruined you must be because of me. Then when Levi and Keene came, I'd let them beat me up because I knew that I deserved it," Benny said as he stared at me. "I fucking hated myself for doing that to you. I don't deserve you. I mean, what will people say when they see us in school? They'll obviously thi—"

"I don't care what people think about us. Yes, we're not the perfect couple. We're going through shit, but we'll get through it together. I care so much about you, Benny. You make me happy, and I don't want to be the only one happy in this relationship," I said, then kissed his forehead as I ran my fingers through his hair.

"I'm happy now. You're the greatest thing that's ever happened to me. You're my everything, Lana," he said as we looked straight. He swung his arm around my shoulder as I leaned into his chest. "I wish I could be the perfect boyfriend for you."

"And I wish I was the perfect girlfriend, but

perfect people aren't real," I mumbled as my fingertips grazed over his scars. "And real people aren't perfect."

Chapter Thirteen

Lana

The next few days were spent with family and the Radcliffs. Griffon came over too, and we'd bond since the Radcliffs were leaving soon.

"Are you sure you don't want to come?" Benny asked for what seemed to be the millionth time. After our little talk in the hall on Christmas, we left early, then sat in the car and talked. Well, some of it was talking. It still scared me that he used to cut. I didn't want it to happen again.

"I'm a hundred percent sure. I got it for you and your friends. Besides, I'll be busy with my Yale application tomorrow," I said as we walked hand in hand.

"Okay. It won't be fun without you, though." He frowned as we entered the diner.

"If you get bored, you can snapchat the whole thing. I'll watch." I chuckled as we slid into a booth.

"Yeah, and then later you can come over..."

Benny trailed off as he kissed my neck.

"Not here." I chuckled, keeping an eye on the old lady who watched us. "I heard you're throwing a party on New Year's Eve."

"Yeah, every year one of the basketball players hosts a party. Liam was supposed to, but he moved into an apartment," Benny said.

"Where?"

"Somewhere downtown. That's why he's always with his skateboard."

"Oh," I mumbled, because if Liam lived downtown, he must've heard or seen something about the alley. I glanced up from the menu and saw Nick walk toward us. Liam trailed behind, yet I squinted my eyes when I saw him with glasses.

"So you do wear glasses," I said as they sat opposite us.

"Well, hello to you too, Lana." He smiled.

"And your eyes are brown?"

"Yeah, I mostly wear blue contacts." He shrugged as I tilted my head. He looked so different with glasses.

"Brown eyes suit you," I said.

"Thanks. So what are we here for? If it's for eating, then I'm your guy," Liam stated as he took the menu. The waitress came, and the guys ordered while I thought over what Benny said. A few minutes later, she left, and I looked at Liam again.

"You live downtown?" I asked.

"Yeah, now I have to take the freaking bus to school," he mumbled.

"Do you pass the alley?"

"I don't skate past that side of town so early in

the morning." He shook his head and nibbled on his stud piercing.

"What is it?" Benny asked as he placed his hand on my thigh and rubbed it for comfort.

"I-I went with my dad to the alley, and we spoke to Detective Kale. There are cameras," I whispered.

"I never saw one that day," Nick said as he shook his head.

"Yeah, because we focused on the alley, not what's around it. There are cameras on the opposite building."

"Shit," Benny muttered.

"But they're not working anymore, and they were wiped, so unless they find a way to get everything back and fix it, we're good," I mumbled.

"Damn, we should get new identities and move to Guatemala. I'll be Lana, Nick will be Benny, Benny can be me, and Lana will be Nick because it's short for Nicky," Liam said as we stared at him.

"I think they'll still catch us, genius." Nick squinted his eyes at the brunette.

"Yeah, you're right. I'd make a better Benny," Liam said, and Benny sighed.

"We were just…we panicked," Nick croaked out. "We're teenagers. The last thing we wanted was to get into trouble. We were so stupid."

"Yeah, and now if anyone finds out, we're in trouble. We don't even know where the fucking body is." Benny sighed.

"Man, we should've burned the dude and the evidence," Liam said, and I shook my head.

"No, if we burned the evidence, it would've given off plumes of smoke. Plus, we're in Illinois. It gets windy in the fall. If any embers were blown by the gusty winds, chances were it could've ignited tinder or dry leaf litter and set the whole forest ablaze," I stated.

"Holy shit, then we should've watched *How to Get Away with Murder*," Liam commented. Nick and Benny glared at him.

"Okay, you have to admit we should've done that." I high-fived Liam.

"We wouldn't have been in this situation if it wasn't for you." Nick pointed at Liam. "We were in the alley staring at the dead body. Then we heard someone coming, so we hid. Yet this idiot decides to hide next to the freaking body!"

"He was behind the dumpster, best hiding place," Liam stated.

"We could've left the body and called Lana's dad, but no, you decided to touch him to check if he's dead. I think having his eyes open, having sat there for more than twenty-four hours in dried blood, proved that he's fucking dead," Benny said as he glared at Liam. I remembered that day and Benny was quiet while the three of us freaked out.

"I'm sorry, okay? I don't wanna be in this situation any more than you guys." Liam frowned.

"Wait, you said 'behind the dumpster,' right?" I tilted my head.

"Yeah, that's where he tried to harass you, right?" Nick asked.

"I remember walking to the alley then spinning around to see him. We never go deep into the alley."

"Maybe when you hit him, he was trying to

walk, but the blood was too much, so he just collapsed on the ground," Liam suggested. I nodded my head as we sat and thought. I saw the waitress approaching. She placed our food on the table along with our milkshakes then walked away.

"Wait," Benny said as we ate. "When we saw him, he was propped up against the wall, eyes wide open and holding your other shoe while you had the one you hurt him with."

"So?" Nick asked.

"He was holding onto it very tight like he was forced to. I'm pretty sure he knew he was going to die, so why keep his eyes open?" Benny asked.

"Maybe that's all just some big coincidence." Liam waved off.

"And Liam's shoes along with the missing body…" Benny trailed off.

"Benny, what are you trying to say?" I asked.

"Assuming…" He trailed off.

"Well, what are you assuming?" Liam asked.

"I get it," Nick said as he nodded at Benny. "You're assuming that someone's trying to frame us."

***

When I put on my black coat, I turned to my desk. Since Mom was eager to send an application to Yale, I was busy with the rest of it.

"Ready to go?" Levi asked as he leaned against the doorframe.

"Yeah." I smiled as I grabbed my phone. Benny went to the basketball game, so Levi was going to visit Blake. I decided to tag along since I had to give him his Christmas gift. I walked downstairs, where I saw Jade and Richard in the living room. Their suitcases were placed on the sofa as they packed. I raised a brow as I stared at Levi's stuff, which was all over the room.

"When are you guys leaving?" I asked.

"Since I must get back to work and it will take three days to drive back to California, we must leave on the first of January," Richard said.

"Tomorrow's your last day." I frowned at Levi.

"We're leaving around noon, though," Jade added.

"Yeah, and Levi…" Richard trailed off as he gave his son a look. Levi slowly shook his head, and Richard scoffed. "Whenever you're ready, son," Richard said, then walked out of the room. Jade walked up to Levi and put her hand on his cheek.

"Not bit by bit. Everything, Levi Ramone Radcliff," she said in a serious tone. I watched as she walked out of the room, then turned to Levi. He already had his gaze on me as he bit his lip.

"What was that about?" I asked. He let out a sigh, then approached me. He placed his hands on my arms as I stared into his deep blue eyes.

"Some things in California happened, and I…I'm not ready to tell you, princess."

"Are they bad things?"

"Awful," he said, then wrapped his arms around me. I rested my head on his shoulder as we swayed. "But we shouldn't let that spoil the day. Come on."

***

We drove in silence at first as I looked out the window to see everything covered in snow. I turned to my left, where Levi was focused on the road.

"Hey, look in the back," he said after a while. I raised a brow as I looked over my shoulder to where a gift bag was on the seat. I reached over and picked it up. I put it on my lap and oddly stared at it. "Since you already gave me my Christmas gift, here's yours. It's a bit late, but I could only get it yesterday."

I picked up the object and gasped when I saw the vinyl of Bastille I admired at the Winter Wonderland.

"Oh my god. Thank you, Levi," I said as I took in every detail.

"No problem, princess." The corner of his mouth rose as he looked at me. I playfully punched his shoulder since I couldn't hug him. I didn't think I'd get a gift from Levi; he always joked around and said he was my gift.

After ten minutes, we arrived at the Gunner household. It seemed like everyone was home since there were three vehicles. We got out and walked to the front door. I rang the doorbell and stepped back while Levi stood behind me. A sudden noise came as I looked over my shoulder and saw Scruffy.

"Oh no," I mumbled as I crept behind Levi.

"Hey, buddy," Levi greeted as he crouched down and patted Scruffy. The dog turned to me and barked. I yelped from his noise as I slowly backed away. "What the heck did you do, princess?" Levi laughed as he held Scruffy back.

"Nothing!" I exclaimed.

"Ha, watch this," Levi said as he crouched down and formed a ball from the snow. "You want it?" he asked Scruffy as he threw it up and down. Scruffy jumped as he eyed the snowball. "Go get it!" Levi ordered, then threw the snowball. We watched as Scruffy ran after it. The snowball landed flat in the snow. The dog stopped as he searched for it.

"Shame on you!" I said as we snickered. We watched Scruffy as he spun around and watched us. He let out a growl as we froze.

"Shit," Levi cussed as I ran to the door and rang the bell again. "Yo, Gunner, open up!" Levi exclaimed as the dog ran over to us. Scruffy continued to bark as I rang the doorbell. It flew open with a confused Mrs. Gunner.

"Axel, come and control your dog!" she yelled, then pulled us in. Axel entered the room with a wide grin spread across his face. He gave us a cheeky wave, then walked out the door.

"Hi, Mrs. Gunner. Hope you had a lovely Christmas." I smiled as she pulled me in for a hug.

"Nice to see you two again. Oh, we had a lovely Christmas! Always good seeing the Rowleys," she said as she motioned us to follow her. She continued to talk about Christmas as I tried to listen. Levi tapped my shoulder, and I looked at him. He whipped out her present. He was so eager to get her the gift, which confused me. We barely knew Mrs. Gunner, yet he got her such an expensive gift. "I made Blake's favorite. He loves red velvet. Want some?"

"Yes please," Levi said as I nodded. As she took out bowls, Levi placed the envelope next to the cake. I nervously bit my lip as she spun around and stared at it.

"Merry Christmas!" Levi and I said in unison.

"Oh my God," she breathed out. "Thank you, but you didn't have to."

"We wanted to," Levi said as she slowly opened it. To see her reaction was priceless. She covered her mouth as her eyes widened.

"Sending me away for the weekend to a beach resort." Mrs. Gunner wiped moisture from her eyes.

"Yeah," I stated as she walked around the island and hugged us.

"Oh, thanks, you two!"

"You're welcome, Mrs. Gunner. We know how hard it is to have a full-time job, be a single parent, and having two beasts to feed," Levi said as I gave him a strange look.

"Thank you again. I don't know when I'll use it, though," she said.

"You can use it any time before spring break," Levi said.

"Thanks." She cut us a piece of cake. We took a seat and ate the delicious red velvet cake.

"Where's Blake?" I asked.

"He's in the shower," Mrs. Gunner replied.

"Hey, pumpkin," Axel called as he entered the kitchen with a plain box.

"Axel?" his mom asked as he set the box on the table.

"Yeah, Momma?"

"You don't refer to a woman as 'pumpkin,'

especially that kind of word," Mrs. Gunner reprimanded as Levi snorted.

"Wha—she likes it, don't you?" he asked.

"Err…" I trailed off as I shook my head.

"She even has a boyfriend, Axel. I don't think he likes that you call his girlfriend a vegetable," Mrs. Gunner added as I chuckled.

"Momma," Axel whined.

"Call her by her name," Mrs. Gunner said in a neutral tone. Axel turned to me with a blank look. He bit his lip and tilted his head.

"Y-you don't know my name?"

"I do. How could I forget?" He mumbled the last part as he took a quick glance at Levi and his mom. I raised a brow as I watched Mrs. Gunner shift in her seat uncomfortably as Levi turned away. "It's Lana. Lana Jane Willson," Axel said as he smiled at me. I gave an awkward smile back as I watched him move the box closer to me. "You forgot your vinyl in my car the other day."

"Thanks," I said as I looked at the Mayday Parade and Alt-J label.

"Well, I gotta get to work. You kids enjoy, and baby, don't call her a vegetable again," Mrs. Gunner said as she stood up and kissed Axel on the cheek. Levi and I waved, then watched as she walked out of the kitchen. In the hall, I saw Blake walk out; he stopped when he saw his mother. She spoke to him, then gave him a kiss too. I looked opposite me to see Levi stand up as Axel motioned him to follow. I watched as the two walked in the direction of Blake. Levi greeted him with a handshake and pointed at me. I immediately went back to my cake when they turned to me. Out the corner of my eye, I saw someone enter the kitchen. When I glanced up, I saw Blake cut himself a piece of cake.

"Hey, baby girl." He bit his lip as I scowled. He called me that recently, and it annoyed me.

"Please…don't call me that," I said.

"Why not? My brother can call you pumpkin and Levi calls you princess, so why not?"

"It's just—no. Why do you call me that?"

"Because one day you'll be my girl. Then I'll call you baby."

"Never." I held my fork back and shot the cake in his face. It landed on his nose as I laughed. His finger reached up and wiped the cake off then ate it. "Ew," I groaned. I shook my head at his immaturity then continued to eat my cake. I glanced up and noticed Blake's stare. I raised a brow yet diverted my eyes to his crewneck. It was black and had The Killers on the front. "Nice crewneck."

"Thanks, Axel got it for me," he said.

"Cool. What's your favorite song?" I asked as we locked eyes.

"Smile Like You Mean It," he said. "Favorite My Chemical Romance song?"

"The Light Behind Your Eyes," I replied. Blake nodded, then returned to his cake. I finished, so I stood up and walked to the sink. When I placed my plate in the sink, I remembered why I came.

"Oh. Your Christmas gift," I said, then spun around. He got up and walked over to me with his empty plate. He stood in front of me and reached behind to put his plate in the sink. Blake looked down at me with a smile.

"Yours too," he said, then walked out of the kitchen. I quickly followed behind him as we walked down the hall. Music blared through one room, which I assumed was Axel's, followed by laughter. I entered Blake's room and took everything in. Even though I've been in here once, it was during the night, and the next morning was an absolute blur since I ran to his bathroom to puke. It looked the same with the many posters on the wall. He had a clean desk and shelves built above with a bunch of tools displayed. Blake had his back turned to me as he rummaged through his drawer. I took out the little box from my coat pocket and waited. He spun around with a small box too, but he had a little bow.

"You go first," we said in unison. We laughed as I raised a hand to stop him.

"I'll go," I mumbled, then gave him the box. I nervously watched as he opened it. "I've noticed that you didn't have one and you always used Levi's or matches so…" I trailed off as he took out the Zippo lighter.

"Thanks." He chuckled.

"Also, the guy said I could get it engraved, so I put your name, because it's for you, and my name, since it's from me." I pointed to our names.

"Cool. Now my gift will be sorta cheesy." He sighed then took out a cigarette. I watched in awe as he flicked open the Zippo and lit his cigarette. He inhaled the smoke then blew it in my face. He put the lighter in his pocket and handed me the cigarette. I put it between my lips as he held out my present. I took a drag and exhaled it in his face. He slowly bit his lip and laughed. “You do realize we indirectly kissed,” he said as I gave him the cigarette.

“Whatever,” I said, then took the box and opened it. I raised the familiar chain and observed it.

“I noticed that whenever you check me out, you look at my dog tag. So I got you one. Well, I always had more since my dad used to collect them,” he said.

“Thank you, but it’s your da—”

“I have quite a few. He used to travel around the country and collect one from each state. That one’s from home.” He pointed at mine.

“And yours?” I looked at his.

“Connecticut.” He smiled, then took the dog tag from me. “Yeah, so err…I did the cheesiest thing known to mankind because Axel said so. I got our initials engraved on it.”

“Wow, Blake Gunner.” I observed our initials, B and L, that were drawn in cursive. He took the chain and walked around me. I bit the inside of my cheek as he moved my hair to the side so that he’d put it on. His fingers grazed on the back of my neck as he clipped it. I spun around and looked up. “Thank you.”

“You’re welcome,” he said, then put the cigarette to his lips.

“Did Levi ever go to Minnesota?” I randomly asked. Blake slowly shook his head and raised a brow. I bit my lip and looked down. My thoughts diverted to earlier in the kitchen when Axel said he knew my name, then looked at Levi and his mom.

"Did Axel ever visit Illinois before you guys moved here?"

"Yeah, we all did. Once a year for the summer and then we'd stay at Aidan's," Blake replied. "Last summer was weird, though. He stayed longer."

I opened my mouth to say something but cut off when my phone rang. I mouthed a sorry to Blake as I took out my phone then walked out of the room.

"Hello."

"Hey, babe," Benny greeted as I leaned against the wall.

"Hi, you leave for the game yet?"

"Yeah, we just got here. Listen, err…I need a favor. That's if you're not busy."

"N-not at all."

"Well, my parents left for Wisconsin this morning, so Sam's all alone at home, bu—"

"He's all alone!"

"No, no, no! There are people there. I just need you to check up on him…and, well, them too," Benny mumbled. "But if you're busy, I understa—"

"No, it's cool. I'll go. Enjoy the game," I said as I walked back into Blake's room.

"Oh, thank you. You're a lifesaver and thanks again for the tickets," he said, then ended the call.

"Who was that?" Blake asked as he played with his lighter.

"Benny, he wants me to go to his house."

"Okay, I'll take you."

"Are you sure?" I asked as we walked out of the room and into the living room.

"Yeah, it's cool," he said, then put on his black denim jacket. He grabbed two helmets that were hung up and handed one to me. We walked out into the cold weather where Blake's motorcycle was.

"C-can I drive?" I mumbled. He turned to me with a confused look and eyed me up and down.

"Can you?"

"Yes! How do you think I got to the station that night of the drugs?" I asked as I put on my helmet.

"Sure, okay." He chuckled. I walked to the motorcycle then swung my left leg over it as I gripped the handles. Out the corner of my eye, I noticed Blake's stare.

"You just gonna stand there or what?"

"Sorry, just enjoying the view," he said as I sat on the motorcycle. A few seconds later, I felt the weight as Blake sat behind me. I turned the key then started the bike. Blake's arms wrapped around my waist as he kicked the side stand in. I drove out of the driveway and onto the road. At first, I turned slowly and got used to the motorcycle, but after five minutes, I cruised. A smile formed on my face as the wind sent chills through my body. I felt Blake's hand on mine as we held the accelerator. I kept my eyes on the road as he turned it. The motorcycle roared as I laughed. After ten minutes, we arrived at Benny's house. I parked the bike in the front as Blake kicked out the side stand. I removed my helmet then got off the motorcycle.

"That was fun." I grinned.

"It was. Not bad. I've taught you well." He smirked as I gave him the helmet.

"You're acting kind of weird these past few days. What's going on?" I asked as he scooted to the front of the motorcycle.

"Actions speak louder than words, baby girl," he said, then put the visor on. Without another word, he started the motorcycle and sped off. I was frustrated, so I stomped my foot on the ground. Since there was snow, I almost fell but quickly regained my balance. I walked to the front and raised my hand to knock, but the door flew open with Carter in front of me.

"Ugh, you're not the pizza guy," he groaned, then spun around. I stepped into the house and shut the door behind me.

"What gave you that idea?" I asked sarcastically.

"Well, first, you don't have pizza; second, you're not a guy; and third, you have nice boobs," he said, and I immediately covered my breasts. "Take it as a compliment." Carter laughed as he pointed at me. I rolled my eyes as I watched him sit on the sofa and scroll through his phone.

"Wh-where's Sam?"

"He's in the basement. Ugh, it's been thirty-one minutes and fifteen seconds. Ha, thank goodness, I ordered five boxes."

"Wow, that's a lot," I said as I walked toward the basement.

"Well, we're hungry as fudge," he said as I walked downstairs.

"Dude, come on, you can't be on your phone all the time. What the hell you even doing on there? Watching anime po—"

"Checking your mom out on Tinder!" Sam said as I reached downstairs.

"Damn, that hurt," Aidan said as he put his hand on his chest.

"I don't need babysitters!" Sam exclaimed, then spun around to face me. His expression immediately changed as he smirked at me. "On second thought, maybe I do need one." He grinned then walked toward me. Aidan and Liam scowled and strolled to the sofa. "Hey, cutie. If I were an octopus, all three of my hearts would belong to you."

"Damn," Liam said as he flicked through the channels.

"Err…yeah," I said.

"Pizza's here, blokes!" Carter said as he carried five boxes down the stairs. I sat between Liam and Aidan as Carter put the boxes on the coffee table. Sam came and squeezed between Aidan and me.

"Hey!" Aidan pointed out, since he was halfway off the sofa.

"Got a problem? My house," Sam stated as my eyes widened.

"N-no, here, eat pizza," Aidan mumbled as he shoved a slice in Sam's mouth.

"Hey, you're wasting good food!" Liam called out as he reached over me to get the pizza Aidan shoved down Sam's throat. Sam swallowed the whole thing, and Liam's jaw dropped. Aidan reached over for another, but I quickly stopped him.

"That hurt," Sam whined as he pointed at Aidan. "Lana, it hurt!"

"Aidan!" I scowled as Aidan threw his arms up and backed away. Sam frowned as he put his arms around me and cried.

"I was playing!" Aidan said as he looked at Sam. "He's faking it!" He pointed. I scoffed as I swung my arm around Sam's shoulder. I glanced down and noticed he pulled his tongue. Aidan opened his to argue, but I quickly leaned forward.

"Okay…let's see what's on TV," I sighed as I took a slice of pizza. Carter agreed as he flicked through the channels.

***

"Ugh, I'm bored," Sam whined as he leaned his head on my shoulder.

"Yeah, let's do something fun. This is boring," Aidan said as he turned off the television.

"Well, it's almost nine p.m. What do you guys wanna do?" I looked at my phone.

"Oh, meet me by the car in five minutes. We're going out." Liam grinned, then bolted up the stairs.

"Finally." Sam sighed in relief as he continued to play on his phone. We did as told and gathered our things. We walked to Aidan's car and got in. I sat in the back with Sam and Carter while we waited. A minute later, Liam ran to the car. He knocked on the trunk and Aidan opened. We heard things being moved as Liam put stuff in the back. He shut it then got into the passenger seat. Aidan started the car then turned to Liam with a questioning look.

"What'd you put in the trunk?" he asked as we pulled out the driveway.

"A body," Liam dramatically said as my eyes widened. "Just kidding, bro. Skateboards. Since you had yours in the trunk, I came with mine, so all I had to get were three more for them." He pointed to us. "There's this underground place I always go to after school."

After we drove for ten minutes and listened to music, we finally arrived at the underground skate ramp. I didn't want to skate, so everyone else carried a skateboard except me. We entered the place where most guys skated. A few girls lingered around, and they looked so cool.

"What's up, guys?" a voice said as I turned my head to see Tyler. He was one of Liam's friends, and he was on the basketball team, but other than that, I barely knew him.

"Hey, this is Benny's weird little brother Sam." Liam pointed to Sam, who looked around.

"'Sup, dude, you know how to skate?" Tyler asked as he fist bumped Sam.

"Hell yeah." Sam grinned as he dropped his skateboard on the ground. He followed Tyler and Liam where they went skating. I leaned against the wall and listened to the music that played through the speakers. Everyone seemed so chilled and enjoyed themselves.

"Hey, Lana," Aidan said as he skated toward me. I smiled as he stopped right in front of me then picked the board up. He stood next to me as he put one leg up to lean against the wall.

"You're not skating?" I asked.

"I did. Can't beat Liam, though. He's in the zone." Aidan chuckled as he pointed at Liam. I followed his gaze to see Liam; he was magnificent. The tricks he did were so cool, and he seemed relaxed. "Carter told me what happened before Christmas…with Parker," Aidan blurted out. I turned to see the concerned look, yet he lowered his gaze and sighed. "I knew it. That first day when I saw Parker push you into the janitor's closet, I knew it…yet I didn't do anything. I asked him, and he said it was nothing. I should've known better. I could've saved you. I'm sorry, Lana."

"It's okay. It's my fault. It's over, and it happened." I shrugged.

"I'm not leaving you alone with Parker or Austin ever again. Not only did Parker sexually assault you, but he and Austin stole the two parcels. We're in deep shit, Lana. When we get our new schedules, I'll make sure that none of them are in your classes."

"Thanks, Aidan."

"No, thank you. You're the brave one. With everything you've been through, you stuck strong. You're one of the bravest and strongest people I know," he said, then dropped his skateboard again. He stood in front of me and opened his arms. "Come on, I know you wanna. I love hugging," he said. I playfully rolled my eyes as I hugged him and placed my chin on his shoulder since we were almost the same height. After a few seconds, I tried to pull away, but he squeezed and mumbled in my ear.

"No, no, just a bit longer."

For the next hour, the guys skated. Tyler and Liam insisted on teaching me how to skate, and let's say I almost face planted if it weren't for Aidan and Carter. Sam was pretty good, especially since he tried to show off his moves to me. We went back to Benny's house pretty late and fell asleep after we watched a few movies.

***

"Lana, Lana, wake up!" Benny yelled as my eyes snapped open. I jolted up to see that I was in Benny's bed. I glanced to my side and noticed Benny's face drained of color. "Hey, are you okay? You're sweating like crazy." He wiped my forehead with a cloth.

"Yeah, I just…" I trailed off.

"Nightmare?" he guessed.

"Y-yeah…well, no, a dream that I keep on having. Well, it's not a dream since it happened," I mumbled as Benny laid down beside me. I rested on his chest. His fingers grazed through my hair as I let out a sigh.

"What was it about?"

"The night of Homecoming. When I was running in the industrial area. It was raining, and I don't even know how I ended up there. Then the part when I ran to the alley and just when I turn around to face Jack, I wake up." I sighed. "Then the next night it replays, just that part."

"Well, maybe it's trying to tell you something," Benny said. "What do you see?"

"Well, when I ran, gangs walked past me. None of them took note of me. I got closer to the alley and cars were parked," I said.

"Are there people in the cars?" Benny asked as I sat up and glanced at him.

"I-I don't think so," I mumbled, then rubbed my eyes. I yawned, then glanced around the room. I raised a brow since the sun shone through the window. "What time is it?" I asked and collapsed on his chest. He laughed as he wrapped his arms around me, then kissed my forehead.

"Well, I didn't want to disturb you, so I left you to sleep. It's now one p.m." He looked at his phone.

"What? How did I get here?" I asked as I straddled him.

"Last night I came home, and you were all passed out in the basement. So I brought you up here, put you in comfy clothes, then in my bed," he said as I looked down. I didn't even notice that I was in a pair of sweatpants and a baggy sweater. "You're quite a heavy sleeper, babe, but don't worry…I didn't look." He gave me a cheeky grin. "You can get done up here. I'm gonna go check up on the guys."

"Thanks," I mumbled as he got up and walked out of the room. I brushed my teeth with the toothbrush I used the last time I was here. Since it was already late, I decided that I'd shower when I got home and get ready for the party there. I put on my clothes from yesterday then walked downstairs where I heard voices.

"If you clear the dining area then we can have beer pong over there!" Nick said as I reached the bottom of the stairs. Most of the furniture was pushed back or out of the living room. Melissa was on a sofa as she texted on her phone while everyone else worked.

"Hey, Lana," Aidan and Tyler greeted as they walked past.

"Hi," I murmured. "Where's Benny?"

"He's in the kitchen," Aidan replied. I thanked him then went into the kitchen, where I saw tons of

Solo cups on the counters. Benny had his back faced to me while he was busy with the stove. I sat by the island and watched him. He spun around with a pan in one hand and spatula in the other. He placed the fish on a plate then looked at me.

"Hey, babe, lunch is almost ready." He put the pan on the stove then took another fish and put it in.

"I didn't know you cooked," I said as he approached me and pecked my lips.

"Yeah, well, when your dad owns seafood restaurants, and your mom loves cooking, you're bound to learn something." He chuckled.

"Okay, DJ is set up, and we'll do the lighting later. Now, where's the food we were promised?" Liam asked as he sat next to me.

"Almost done, bro," Benny replied as he took the fries out of the oven then went back to the stove. Five minutes later, we were in the kitchen eating Benny's fish and fries. It was superb, especially the fish, yet Liam stole my fries. "You guys have to go and get the drinks, right?" Benny asked Melissa and Nick.

"Yeah, we'll take Lana with us so we can drop her at home to get ready," Melissa said with a wicked look in her eye.

"And you three." Benny pointed at Tyler, Liam, and Aidan.

"We get the fireworks!" Liam cheered.

"Oh no," I mumbled.

"Wha—it's not like when we pull up the driveway fireworks will be going off in the car," Aidan said.

"Hopefully not." Nick sighed.

"Tyler, I trust you, dude. There's a lot of fireworks," Benny said.

"Tonight's going to be freaking lit. This house is gonna be packed," Aidan cheered.

"Can we have throwback songs? That'd be cool," Liam said.

"Yeah, dude and EDM," Tyler added. We talked about tonight and the events that would happen. Once we were done, I drove with Nick and Melissa. Nick said he'd drop me at home with Melissa then get the drinks. Apparently, Liam's cousin Bethany supplied them with alcohol. When we're done, he'd come and get us. Melissa explicitly stated that she wanted to be at my house when I chose an outfit.

***

When we got to the house, I wasn't surprised to see Levi, Blake, and Keene. We walked upstairs and into my room. I shut the door, then opened my closet.

"I haven't been to a party in like…forever," I muttered.

"Don't worry, I got it covered. You take a nice shower while I get ready, then I'll pick out something for you," Melissa said as she took out underwear for me. It had to be the black lingerie that Levi found in my drawer when he came here. I walked into the bathroom and locked the door.

Once I finished, I wrapped a towel around my hair. I put on my underwear, then wrapped the towel around me. I slowly put on my contacts because I didn't want to wear glasses. I walked out to see Melissa dressed in a red jacket, black dress, and white heels. Her hair was curled up as she stood in front of my mirror and did her makeup.

"Wow, you look beautiful," I said as I dried my hair.

"Thanks, and you will too. Your outfit is on the bed," she said. I took the towel off my head and walked to the bed. A black leather jacket, tight white crop top, black shorts, and the red heels she got me for Christmas was placed there.

"It's still winter." I looked at the shorts and crop top.

"Yeah, but we'll be indoors, and you look hot in black. Trust me." She grinned, then looked around my room.

"What are you looking for?" I asked.

"I just didn't come to help you out. I came because I want to see this so-called Bucket List that you and Levi created," she stated with a grin. I let out a sigh as I walked to my closet and bent down to reach the last drawer. I took out the list and stared at it with a sigh. There were a few things ticked off. Whenever Levi came, we'd finish it, but it didn't look like we'd do it since he'd leave tomorrow. I handed it to Melissa as I got dressed. As she read it, she laughed at some of the things.

The Bucket List

Levi / Lana

Bathe elephant: - / -
Whale watching: - / -
Night at the museum: - / -

Make soap: √ / √
Attend a street fight: √ / -
Go to a paint party: - / -
Be in the newspaper: - / -
Read a book before the movie: - / √
See a movie in black and white: √ / √
Volunteer: √ / √
Give blood: - / -
Donate: √ / √
Buy matching shoes: - / -
Dress in sexy lingerie: - / √
Get a tattoo piercing: √ / √
Indoor swimming pool at night: - / -
Meet Oprah: - / -
Shave head or someone else's: √ / -
Wear colored contacts: - / -
Don't fall in love: √ / -
Sleep on a haystack: - / -
Milk a cow: - / -
Drive a Harley Davidson: - / √
Bodyshot: - / √
Say 'Hello' in 80 Languages: - / √
Help homeless person: √ / √
Pose with a wax figure at Wax Museum: - / -
Climb a tree: √ / √
Professional Photoshoot: - / -
Smoke a cigarette or use a hookah: √ / √

"You can immediately point out who wrote what." She pointed to "read a book before the movie," and I rolled my eyes. She put the list on my desk, then helped me get ready. My hair was left loose, but Melissa curled it a bit. Even though I got a haircut a month ago, it grew a lot.

"What's wrong?" I asked as she looked at her phone.

"Nick's outside. He wants me to come now since they want the drinks." She sighed, then grabbed her things. "The trunk and backseat are loaded, so you'll have to get a ride with one of the guys. I'm sorry, girl," she cooed, then eyed me up and down before she left. "You look hot, though." I let out a sigh as I did my makeup, which was a soft, smoky eye. I put on the chain, which completed the outfit, then grabbed my phone. When I walked downstairs, I saw Keene on his phone. He looked up and took in my appearance. He slowly nodded his head in approval as I reached the bottom of the stairs.

"You look lovely. I like that thing going on with your eyes." He pointed to the smoky eye.

"Thanks, you look good too." I laughed as I looked at his outfit that consisted of a red baseball tee, grey tight sweatpants, and Vans.

"All right, let's g—" Levi stopped mid-sentence as I spun around to look at him. We took in each other's appearances. He wore a black leather jacket, white tee, black jeans, and high-top Vans.

"Nuh-uh, you two aren't going anywhere," Jade's voice echoed. Levi spun around to face his mother. I gripped on my leather jacket as Mom and Jade approached us.

"You two are not going. Remember last year when you two went out to a party?"

"This is Benny's party, Mom, plus it's New Year's Eve," I whined.

"Nope, unless you get someone else to supervise you, none of you are going," Jade said as she gestured to the three of us. Mom and Jade walked upstairs and left us in a pissed mood. Blake came from the kitchen with a cinnamon roll in his hand.

"What if we sneak out when they're watching their soap operas?" Levi chuckled.

"No." I shook my head because I didn't want to sneak out anymore.

"Got any other ideas, princess?"

"They say we can go if someone else takes us." I smirked at Blake. "I know just the person they'll approve of."

Chapter Fourteen

Lana

As expected, Mom and Jade were fond of the idea that Axel was with us. Blake and I found it weird and decided to question Axel and Levi while we drove to the party. They said they met at a party and quickly changed the subject. I glanced at Keene, who sent me skeptical looks. Of course, he'd know because he knew Axel and Levi.

We arrived at Benny's house and noticed the party already started. Since its winter, everyone was in the house, which only made it congested. It was easy to walk since the entry had been cleared of snow.

"Gotta admit Nielson throws a lit party," Levi said as we looked at the house with the bright lights.

"Name?" the bouncer asked.

"Levi Radcliff."

"Nope."

"Of course," Levi muttered as he stepped aside. I sighed as I stepped forward and looked at the scary bouncer.

"Lana Willson."

"Enjoy the party," the guy said.

I pointed behind me and said, "They're with me."

"One only," the guy said as I turned to look at them.

"Don't worry, I'll get in." Levi smirked as he took out his phone. I looked over to Keene, who put his arm around Levi, stating that he wasn't going anywhere without him.

"I'm not going anywhere without my brother," Axel said as he playfully hit Blake's back. I groaned as I looked at the party, then at them. They turned their heads simultaneously to a tall girl who wore a midnight blue dress and black heels. We watched as she gave her name to the bouncer, then walked in. "Love you, brother. See you on the other side," Axel said as he swung his arm around my shoulder and we walked in. "Love you, man!" he said as we entered the house. People surrounded the place, either dancing, talking, or mingling. "Well, pumpkin, we have arrived. Don't know when I'll see you but just remember…" He trailed off as girls walked past us. "Actions speak louder than words." He smirked, then followed the girls.

I playfully rolled my eyes as I walked through the crowd of people. On the way, I danced since the whole crowd jumped to the beat. I finally reached the kitchen and saw familiar faces.

"There she is!" Ethan cheered as he pointed at me with his Solo cup. I smiled as I walked over to Benny, who sat on a chair. A hard look filled his features as I sat on his lap. Ethan handed me a drink, and I thanked him.

"You're looking beautiful tonight," Benny said as he put an arm around my waist.

"Thanks." I smiled as he kissed me.

"Hey, what's with the bouncer?" Miranda asked as she sat on the counter with Marcus next to her.

"Freaking Park Town High don't like losing, so they heard we're throwing a party," Benny said.

"Yeah, this place might be crawling with them." Ethan laughed as we looked at the living room.

"Cool party, though. Love the throwback songs," Marcus cheered. As we talked over the loud music, I turned my head to see Carter walk in. He wore a gray sweater, yet there was a big mark on it as he walked to the island with a paper towel.

"Dude, what happened?" Benny asked.

"I was talking to this chick, and she dumped her drink on me," he said as he wiped his sweater.

"What'd you tell her?" Marcus asked.

"Well, we were off to a great start, then I sort of told her a dirty pickup line."

"Reminds me o—where's Sam?" I turned to Benny, who facepalmed.

"I knew I forgot something," he said as I gaped at him.

"Dude, how do you forget your own brother?" Marcus laughed.

"Never saw him the whole day. He's probably in his room." Benny shrugged as Aidan entered the kitchen with Tiffany. Miranda and I sent Tiffany a wink, and she nervously shook her head too. "Dude, have you seen Sam?" Benny asked Aidan, who gave a drink to Tiffany.

"Are you talking about that kid who walked up to me and said a creepy pickup line?" Tiffany asked. Ethan asked her what he said, and my eyes widened because I never thought the twelve year old was capable of such dirty things, then I remembered he had Carter as a friend.

"The kid's gotta step up his game. He's almost thirteen!" Carter pointed out as we looked at him.

"Oh my god. If anyone sees him, drag him to his room and shut the door," Benny said.

"That won't stop him," Aidan mumbled as Miranda let out a gasp.

"Let's dance! I love this song!" She beamed then hopped off the counter with Marcus. I stood up and pulled Benny out of his seat as we joined Miranda and Marcus. Tyler controlled the music as he jumped with the crowd. Benny and I danced in the middle of the crowd with everyone else. He placed his hands on my waist as I swayed. I laughed as we made silly dance moves with Marcus and Miranda. Everyone sang and danced as Benny pulled me closer. I spun around and swayed my hips against him, then closed my eyes. I felt his breath on my neck as I threw my head back. When I opened my eyes, I noticed someone's gaze on me. He leaned against the wall from across the room as he sipped his beer. He looked so familiar. I felt Benny kiss my neck, and I shut my eyes and danced. The song ended, and I opened my eyes to see that the guy was gone. Weird. I spun around to face Benny, who still had his hands on my waist. He gave me a quick kiss, then dropped his hands as I stepped back.

"I need to use the bathroom quick," I yelled over the loud music. He gave a quick nod as he pointed upstairs. I gave him the thumbs up as I walked off the dance floor and strolled to the stairs. The hallway barely had light, yet I noticed the tall blond walk into a room with a girl. I walked into the bathroom and locked the door. I sat on the toilet and took a piss as quickly as I could. I caught the movement as the bath curtain pulled open. I immediately closed my legs as I whipped my head to see Levi in the bathtub, shirtless.

"Man, you piss loud," he stated.

"What the hell? You almost scared the shit out of me!" I yelled. The other side of the bathtub's curtain pushed open to reveal a shirtless Blake, who laughed.

"Literally!"

"What the heck are you guys doing in the bathtub naked? Are you d—"

"No, and we have our underwear on!" Blake said as he sipped his beer.

"Are you guys drunk?"

"Not yet," Levi said as he drank his beer.

"We lost a bet, so we have to stay in this bathtub for five minutes half-naked." Blake pointed to their clothing beside the bathtub.

"How are you keeping time?"

"Carter's outside," Levi said as I bit the inside of my cheek. I remembered when Carter walked into a room with a girl. I took toilet paper and was ready to clean myself, yet I felt their eyes on me. I looked up and motioned for them to look away. Levi groaned as he pulled the curtain so they couldn't see. I cleaned myself as quick as possible then put on my panties along with my shorts. I took out my phone, then put on my camera before I flushed the toilet. Blake pushed the curtain again as well as Levi. I quickly took a photo before they reacted.

"That's going on Instagram." I looked at the photo.

"Hey!" Blake said as I put my phone in my pocket, then washed my hands.

"No, no, you still got a minute left," I lied. "Well, see you guys." I slowly backed away. As they sipped their beer bottles, I quickly grabbed their clothes and ran out of the bathroom.

"*Lana!*" Blake yelled, and I heard them behind me. I quickly looked over my shoulder to see them half naked as they ran toward me. I ran into the first room that was open, and I straightaway regretted it since it was Sam's room. Sam casually laid on his bed, surrounded by girls who looked my age and older. They were engrossed in what he said, but when I entered the room, they turned to me.

"There she is!" Sam pointed to me as I gripped the clothing.

"You're right, she is pretty," one of the girls said as they eyed me.

"Well, thank you." I dramatically flipped my hair as Blake and Levi ran into the room with their shoes in their hands.

"Are you guys gay?" a girl asked, and Blake facepalmed.

"No, she just took our clothes when we were in the bathroom," he said as the girl raised her brow.

"Dude, that came out wrong." Levi laughed.

“We lost a bet, okay? We’re not gay, and what the heck are you girls doing in Sam’s room?”

“This cute boy was just telling us about her,” another girl cooed as she pointed at me.

“There you are, princess.” Levi smirked as he walked closer to me.

“Who you calling princess? She’s my queen,” Sam exclaimed as I furiously shook my head and tossed their clothing to them.

“What the fuck? Who gave this kid alcohol?” Blake asked as he looked at the girls, who threw their hands up in innocence. I awkwardly stood in the middle of the room and noticed Sam took a picture of me. Once Blake and Levi were dressed, a girl pointed at the three of us.

“You’re all matching!” She giggled to the leather jackets. I had the sudden urge to cringe as I looked at Blake’s outfit. He wore something like Levi, except he wore a gray tee and combat boots.

“Okay, I’m going now,” I stated, then walked out. Blake and Levi followed behind as we walked down the hallway. “Where’s Keene?”

“He’s in the basement with Jaden,” Levi replied as my eyes widened.

“Jaden’s here? How di—”

“He knows most of the bouncers in Illinois, hence his awesome parties, so I called him.”

“Wow, okay,” I stated. I continued to walk until I reached downstairs while Blake and Levi went to the basement. I glanced up and saw Tiffany by the DJ; a few feet away from her was Aidan.

“Hey, Lana!” she yelled over the music.

“Hey, you enjoying the party?” I asked. She

nodded, then awkwardly turned to Aidan. A table was nearby, so I grabbed a quick drink. "Are you guys a thing?"

"No, no, we're just friends. Taking it slow." She smiled.

"Cool, but you guys are cu—" I cut off when Benny appeared next to me with a cup in his hand. When I glanced up, I noticed how his jaw was tightened. "What's wrong?"

"Ethan and I just kicked a guy out from Park Town High. It was not easy since he was drunk as fuck," he muttered then took a swing of his drink. When I looked over his shoulder, I saw the guy from earlier. He danced with a girl, yet his eyes were on me. I shifted uncomfortably, and Tiffany must've noticed.

"Girl, you okay?"

"Yeah, err…that guy keeps on staring at me, yet he looks so familiar," I said, then sipped my drink. Benny spun around and squinted his eyes at the guy. His face went blank as he pulled me closer to him.

"He's on Park Town High's basketball team," Benny stated as we looked at him.

"W-we never saw him that night of the game," I said.

"Yeah, well, he sat out because he loves to play dirty. I think his name is Quinton," Benny said as my eyes widened. That's why he looked familiar; he's from the other party.

"He's gonna cause trouble," Tiffany stated as Benny grunted.

"Yeah, well, I don't want him looking at my girl and ruining the party," he said, then walked toward

Quinton.

"Benny, wait," I called out, but it was too late since he gripped Quinton's arm.

"Look, I don't wanna start a fight, but I saw you looking at my girlfriend, and you're that Quinton guy who sat out by the game, so I suggest you leave before I fuck you up," Benny said as I stood behind him.

"You're a real sourpuss, Nielson. Hey, there's beer pong, babe," he said, then waved at me. Benny was about to punch Quinton, but Liam appeared and held him back. I noticed a crowd formed around us, and half were from Park Town High.

"What's goi—Hey, aren't you that school we beat a few weeks ago?" Liam asked as he pointed at Quinton.

"Unfortunately, and who knew that you of all people would score?" another guy said as he stood next to Quinton.

"Look who I found flirting with my boyfriend," Melissa sang as she shoved a girl from Park Town High into the circle.

"You don't belong here, so just go and crash someone else's New Year's party," Marcus piped up.

"We're not going without a fight," Quinton stated as he glared at Benny.

"Instead of a fight, why don't we make things fun?" Liam asked with a grin. Benny threw his head back and groaned while Liam placed a hand on Benny's and Quinton's shoulders. He spoke to Tyler, who turned the music down. "Yo, Ty, give us a fast beat." People backed away as I knitted my brows. Tiffany grabbed my hand and pulled me back closer to Tyler, where we got a full view of the crowd.

"All right." Quinton nodded as he took off his jacket and threw it across the room. I drank the rest of the cold liquid as a hip-hop song played. Quinton and his friend danced as everyone watched. I tilted my head at their unusual moves, then again Liam always wanted peace. Quinton was good, and he was built for it since he's quite buff and tall. The crowd went crazy, and my eyes widened as Benny and Liam danced. They were ten times better, and I wasn't saying that because he's my boyfriend, but the breakdancing was incredible.

"Shit, I'm getting some of this!" Aidan cheered as he walked past us and joined Benny and Liam, which only made Park Town High nervous. I cheered as Benny went on the ground and did a hand glide. Marcus joined, which surprised Tiffany and me as he did a backspin. The girls from Park Town High stepped forward as they swayed their hips. I laughed as Miranda and Melissa stepped forward and joined them.

"Is this some kind of *Step Up* scene?" Tiffany asked as Park Town High backed away.

"Better than fighting at a party." I laughed as we looked at our friends. They looked like they had fun. Liam and Aidan literally danced the people out of the house, and the rest of the people applauded. Tiffany went to Aidan while Miranda approached me. "You got moves, Stevens."

"They come in handy," she said, then refilled our drinks.

"Didn't know you could dance like that," someone said as I spun around. Jaden stood in front of us with a smirk molded onto his face as he looked at us.

"What are you doing here, Jaden?" Miranda asked.

"Well, hello to you too, ladies," he said then turned to Miranda. "Just helping a friend out. I ditched my own party to come here, which is way better. You two remember my party, right?"

"Yeah," I mumbled and turned to Miranda, whose eye twitched.

"And how you and Keene got so fucking drunk that you just decided to jump in my pool from the roof." He looked at Miranda, then smirked. "Then comes the fun part."

"Stop," Miranda demanded as I raised a brow.

"Right, Lana?" He turned to me.

"What?" I asked as I looked at Jaden and Miranda.

"Oh, she doesn't know," Jaden stated, then let out a dry laugh. "It's quite funny that you lost your virginity to Levi at my party yet you don't know that she lost hers too."

My eyes widened as I stared at Miranda, who looked at the ground. Jaden disappeared into the crowd, which left tension between us.

"Miranda, what happened?"

"We were drunk, okay? You were off with Levi, and Keene just wanted to keep me company since we were at a big party. I let him take my virginity."

"Why didn't you tell me?" I asked as my jaw dropped.

"Well, things were rough after we left the party, then Levi left, so I didn't think it was important." Miranda pouted as she ran a hand through her blonde hair.

"I feel like a such a bad friend for hanging out with Keene now," I mumbled.

"It's okay. He asked me so many times before we did it, and I said yes. He's not that bad, Lana. I actually prefer him over Levi."

"Sure, you do." I laughed, then looked up to see Marcus and Benny.

"Who knew our boyfriends could bust a move, huh?" Miranda quickly asked as Marcus swung his arm around her shoulder.

"You could literally see it on Liam's face that he wanted to do that for a long time and now was his chance," Benny said as he placed his hand on my back.

"It was fun. Hey, midnight's in, like, twenty minutes," Marcus said as he looked at his phone.

"We'll go help Liam and Aidan with fireworks. I don't trust them. Meet us on the back porch in ten," Miranda said, then winked at me. Benny's arm snaked around my waist as he motioned upstairs. He walked on as I trailed behind and finished my drink. It was only my third drink. When I walked into his room, he shut the door and pinned me against the door. Thank goodness my cup was empty as I dropped it.

"I'm so glad I got you when we're still sober," he whispered, then kissed down my neck and hugged my waist. I ran my fingers through his hair, then raised his face so that I'd kiss him. His hands tugged my jacket, and I helped him pull it off, then locked my arms around his neck. I moaned as he deepened the kiss. His hands traveled everywhere until one reached between my thighs. I jumped up and locked my legs around his waist as he spun around and walked to the bed. Benny hovered over me then kissed down my collarbone. I leaned back and gripped his hair, to which he groaned. He placed an arm on either side of me, then came up and left a long, sweet kiss. He straddled me, then pulled off his black baseball tee to reveal his toned, hard chest. I didn't know why, but I liked neck kisses. Benny was certainly good at it as I tilted my head to the side. When I saw his small digital clock, it showed that there were five minutes left until midnight. At the same time, I felt Benny's hands go under my body and to my bra strap. My eyes widened as I placed my hand on his chest. He immediately stopped and looked at me. "What's wrong?"

"Err…the…f-fireworks! I wanna go see them," I mumbled, then sat up. "Plus, you're the host. You should be there too."

Benny slowly nodded, then helped me off the bed. I grabbed my jacket while he put his shirt back on. I gave him a tight smile, then entwined my fingers with his as we walked to the back porch. Mostly everyone was on the back porch or kitchen while music played through the house. Benny and I stood outside while we watched Marcus and Liam set up the fireworks.

"A toast to 2016…what a shitty year," Aidan said as everyone raised his or her cups in agreement. “We lost friends, did strange things, but most important, we made new friends. Half of us wouldn’t be here together if it weren’t for the senior year we’ve had so far.”

“I’m gonna help them.” Benny pointed to Liam and Marcus, who were arguing.

“Twenty-seventeen better be lit, otherwise I’ll be disappointed as fuck,” Nick said, and everyone agreed.

“And a toast to Nielson for hosting this awesome party!” Ethan added. Carter stood next to me and handed me a drink. We cheered Benny on as he smiled at us.

“And we wouldn’t be here if a certain someone didn’t get into a car with four hot guys,” Carter mumbled beside me. I playfully rolled my eyes because they’d all be here, everyone except me. When Levi wouldn’t come for Christmas and came for summer instead, I’d be in my room on New Year’s Eve or in Dad’s office while he was on patrol. Benny stood next to me again as we did the countdown. I looked around and thought what a year it had been. At the beginning of 2016, I would’ve never thought I’d end it with these people.

“Three…two…one! Happy New Year!” Everyone cheered as the fireworks went off. I turned to Benny and gave him a small smile.

“Happy New Year.” I smiled and cupped his cheeks. As soon as we kissed, a strange feeling whirled through my stomach, and the memory of Madam Saga entered my mind. I pulled away from Benny, and he frowned. I went to kiss him again but stopped as someone called out Benny’s name.

"I'll be back," he said and walked into the house. I followed, then walked into the kitchen where Melissa was sitting on the counter swinging her legs. I stood in front of her and noticed that she took a shot.

"Happy New Year, girl! Take a shot with me," she said and gave me a drink. We took the shot in one swing, and I let the alcohol burn the back of my throat. I put the glass down to see Melissa smirk. "So…where did you and Benny disappear to?"

I thought back to what Benny and I did a few minutes ago. I nervously bit my lip as I thought what would happen if we continued.

"We almost had sex," I mumbled.

"What?" she yelled over the loud music.

"Benny wanted to have sex with me," I said.

"What?" She cupped her ear.

"We were gonna have sex!" I yelled, and everyone in the kitchen stared at us. Melissa's jaw dropped while a random guy from school walked past and high-fived me.

"All right, Lana!"

"So why didn't you?" she asked, then hopped off the counter.

"I-I don't know. We've only been dating for, like, a month," I said.

"Understandable, but Nick and I had sex way before we were even dating," she said as I turned to her. "Yeah, Kelly dared me to, so I did and…let's just say he was quite nervous. We had sex, which meant a lot to him, and then he said I'm the only girl he would ever want to be with."

"Wow."

"Maybe Benny didn't mean that. Did he say it directly?"

"Well, he just stated that he's glad that he got me when we're still sober." I shrugged. "I don't know why I stopped. I just don't want to disap—"

"I got it!" Melissa said, then pointed at my empty cup. "You need to get drunk." She grabbed a bottle of rum. Melissa was probably on the verge of getting drunk as she filled our cups and added soda. I flicked my hair over my shoulder and looked around the kitchen. I saw Axel leaning on the wall opposite us. He smirked as he raised his can.

"Cheers, pumpkin," he said as Melissa handed me my drink. Melissa and I raised our cups at Axel, then drank the fresh alcohol. I finally got used to the taste as the liquid filled my body. Melissa held up the bottle and motioned for a refill. Axel strolled to us and threw his can in the trash. He took a cup and held it out as he smirked. "Let's get fucked."

***

The party just seemed to get started after midnight. Everyone was either alive or high as fuck. I walked into a room where people played beer pong. I glanced down and saw multiple cups and smiled as I took one.

"Hey!" someone called out as I drank it. The people looked at me as if I were a freak. I looked back and forth at them as I finished the beer and put the cup down.

"Don't stare at me." I pouted.

"Then quit drinking our game. Either you play or

watch. So what are you gonna do?" the girl asked.

"Don't make me choose!" I whined, then took another cup.

"Whoa, okay, she's on our team," a random guy said as he took the cup from me and pulled me to his side of the table. I swung an arm around him and his friend's shoulder as they threw the ball. They gave me a weird look, and I grinned.

"I've been playing with balls all week," I said as they turned to me. "True story!" I said to the guy who thought I spoke bullshit. "First it was big balls, then medium sized, and now they're small."

"Good to know," the guy on my right mumbled.

"I know, right! I wonder what balls I'll be facing next."

"One can only imagine," the guy on the left added.

"Uh huh. I wanna be surprised, motherfucker!" I squeezed my arms so that their cheeks touched mine.

"That's great, err…you should go lay down or something," the guy on the right mumbled as he pried himself off me.

"You're right…I need to go find my balls," I said, then took a cup. Everyone groaned as I skipped out of the room. I drank the beer in one gulp as I walked through the house. There were a few more people from Park Town High, and they started fights throughout the house, so Benny was busy. I stared at the familiar door that I hadn't been to all night. I pushed it open and saw a few people. Since I'm quite drunk and it's dangerous to walk down the stairs, I jumped onto the wooden rail and slid down. I felt a nip in my butt as I frowned. I glanced around and saw Keene. I hopped over to him, then bent down. His eyes widened. "Do I have a splinter in my ass?"

"Err…first, you're drunk, and second, maybe," he said as I stood up straight and he stood behind me. Blake approached me with a smirk tugged on his lips. He shoved his hands in his pockets, then looked around.

"Hey, baby girl, where's your boyfriend?"

"He's upstairs, being Batman." I winked.

"Oh, then what am I?" Blake asked as he placed his hands on my cheeks.

"Mm…the joker." I giggled as I rested my palm against his chest.

"Then that must make you Harley Quinn," he whispered and inched closer as he stared at my lips. I closed my eyes, and my hand traveled down as my fingertips brushed against his muscles. My eyes shot open as I felt a pinch, and I immediately let out a squeal. I looked over my shoulder at Keene, who held the splinter.

"Got it," he said, then threw it on the ground. I spun back around to face Blake, and realization hit me that he was going to kiss me. Being the stupid drunk that I was, I yelled in his face, then walked away.

"Hey, princess," Levi said as he took my hand in his.

"What are we doing?" I asked as he pulled me toward a group.

"Playing the old classic, truth or dare." He smirked as I looked at the group. It was the worst idea ever since Parker, Kelly, Jennifer, Austin, Carter, Blake, and Levi were in the circle.

"I'll go first." Jennifer smirked as she spun the empty beer bottle that was in the middle. I eagerly watched as it landed on Austin.

"Dare."

"I dare you to strip and only get dressed when it's your turn again." She smiled. My eyes widened as Austin nodded, then took everything off. Once he was done, he sat crossed legs and covered his crotch with one hand, then spun the bottle with the other. It landed on Blake, and he immediately replied with truth.

"Weak," Keene called out from the sofa, where he smoked with Jaden.

"How long have you gone without having sex?" Austin grinned.

"I don't know, a month I guess," Blake answered, then spun the bottle. It landed on Kelly, and Blake smirked as he looked around the circle.

"Dare," she said as Blake turned to Levi.

"I dare you to give Levi a hickey," he said as Levi's eyes widened. He showed Blake the middle finger as Kelly walked over to him. She sat right in front of him, then leaned forward as she pecked his lips. We watched as she kissed down his neck and started to bite on his collarbone. I glanced up to see Levi with an expressionless look. Once she was done, she walked back to her seat, and I looked at the hickey.

"Damn, that's one hell of a hickey," Jaden called out. Kelly spun the bottle, and this time it landed on Carter. He also took a truth, and Kelly licked her lips as she looked at me.

"Is it true that you and Lana had shower sex?" she asked as my eyes widened.

"No," Carter replied as he shook his head.

"That's not what it says in the picture," Austin sang as Carter looked away.

"What picture?" Levi and I asked in unison. I watched as Austin reached for his phone, then swiped through it. He gave the phone to Levi, and I leaned over to get a closer look. I remembered that day. It was when Carter slept over. Thank goodness my back faced him, but it still disgusted me as I glanced up at him.

"You scumbag! What the fuck?" I snapped as I took Austin's phone and threw it at Carter.

"Dick move, Halls," Keene said as he shook his head.

"Who else has this?" I asked Austin.

"Well, the soccer team and half the guys in school," he responded as I glared at Carter.

"Oh, fuck you! You fucking shit!"

"Lana, calm down. You're drunk," Jennifer suggested.

"Fuck no! How dare you do that to me?" I demanded.

"It's his fault. He wanted proof!" Carter pointed at Parker.

"He doesn't need proof, and you know that!" I said, then I turned to Jennifer. "What's the size of this asshole's dick?" I pointed to Carter.

"As small as my middle finger," she replied as people laughed.

"And Kelly, how is the so-called player in bed?"

I glared at Carter.

"Ehh." She waved her hand in response.

"There's your proof!" I yelled at Parker.

"Ooh." Jaden laughed.

"I'm sorry, Lana. We only knew each other for a few days…I—"

"No, fuck you, man. No guy should ever do that!" I said, then grabbed Blake's can and threw it at the blond.

"Okay, I deserved that," Carter mumbled as he tossed the can aside.

"Yeah, and to think I let you borrow Levi's hair gel!" I said.

"So that's where all my gel went when I got here." Levi shook his head.

"Wait…you were in her bathroom?" Blake asked as everyone chattered. Blake and Levi talked about my bathroom, Carter apologized, Austin sat naked as he stared at us, and Kelly laughed her ass off.

"Hey! Everyone, calm down! But FYI…" I trailed off then pointed to Carter. "Fuck you." I then looked at Parker. "Fuck you."

"Fuck me." I pointed at Blake and Levi, then quickly pointed at Kelly. "Fuck you."

"And fuck you," I finished off with Austin and Jennifer. I said it so fast I didn't even realize what I had said. I looked around—no one seemed to notice.

"Okay, let's carry on with the game," Carter muttered as he spun the bottle. It landed on Jennifer, and Carter thought a bit. "I dare you to go and kiss Tiffany over there." He pointed at Tiffany, who was talking to Aidan.

"Easy." Jennifer smirked as she got up and walked to Tiffany. I watched as she strode between the two, then smashed her lips on Tiffany. Tiffany's cup dropped as Aidan gaped. Jennifer pulled away, and I literally heard Aidan asking, "What the fuck?" Jennifer rolled her eyes as she placed a hand on the back of Aidan's neck and pushed him toward Tiffany. I clapped my hands and cheered because they finally kissed. Jennifer sat down, and everyone cheered her on except for Kelly, who stared.

Jennifer spun the bottle, and finally, it landed on me. I felt bored, so I went with a dare. Jennifer smirked as she looked around the basement. Her eyes fell on me as she eyed me up and down. "I dare you to give a lap dance to the person on your left or right," she said as my eyes widened. Austin whispered in her ear, which only made her smirk grow. "Let's make it challenging, so whoever you pick has to be tied to the chair while you're doing it blindfolded." I didn't have to look either way to know that I had to choose between Levi and Blake.

Chapter Fifteen

Lana

It turned out word spread about the lap dance, and people made their way down to the basement. I stood in front of Benny and took in his appearance. He didn't say anything, but he was pissed. Not only were we a couple, but I was about to do a lap dance at his party.

"I'm not gonna do it, I—"

"Oh, come on, Lana, I'm freaking naked," Austin said as he stood behind the pool table.

"I don't think doin—"

"Do it. Their hands are tied to the chair so they won't get too touchy. I trust you," Benny said, then licked his lips. I let out a sigh as he leaned on the pool table. I wrapped my arms around his torso, then looked up at him. He looked down, then kissed me, and I smiled against his soft lips. The smell of alcohol fell from his mouth as he spoke to me. I pulled away and looked at him because he'd been drinking. "But you owe me, Lana Willson."

"Don't worry, I'll be thinking about you the whole time."

"Why did it have to be a la—"

"What's wrong, Nielson? Jealous that your girlfriend might give one of us a boner?" Levi asked, but I looked at Benny. His jaw clenched as he folded his arms and looked over my shoulder.

"At least she can take care of mine," Benny said as I let out a sigh.

"Okay, let's get this show on the road," Jennifer said as she stood between Benny and me.

"Wa—wait, I haven't decided yet," I muttered as she put the blindfold on.

"Well, we're making it fun," she said as she tied it from behind. We moved back as she pulled me. I couldn't see, but I heard the many voices around the room. The music stopped in the basement, and I wondered what song they might play. Jennifer stopped me, and I staggered a bit but remained still. "All right, Lana," she began as the room got quiet. "Since you're blindfolded, you don't know who's who. You're in the center of the room, and Blake and Levi are on either side of you sitting on a chair." I could hear everyone talking. "Each of them are four steps away. You decide whether you wanna go left or right. Ready?"

"Fuck no," I muttered, because I still felt light headed from the alcohol.

"Good enough for me."

The music played. I groaned because it was "Wrong" by Zayn and Kehlani. People cheered as I debated which side to go to. *Okay, Lana, just do it and get over with.* Eenie meenie miney mo…*left it is*. I turned to the left and slowly walked. That's when the room erupted in cheers mixed with murmurs, and I wondered who it was. I bit the inside of my cheek because I tried to hold in a grin as I stopped at the fourth step. My heel touched his shoe, so I knew that I was in front of him. I parted my legs and inched closer. I let out one last sigh, then swayed my hips. I placed my hands on his hips and ground on him. My hands trailed up his sides and stopped at his neck. I locked my arms around his neck as I brushed against him. He threw his head back, and I brushed my fingers through his hair. My chest was against his as I felt his head rise. He leaned his head against my temple and groaned. My eyes widened as I continued to move to the beat of the music.

"I love you," he whispered, yet I couldn't tell who it was because it came out so raspy and quiet. When Kehlani's part came on, I swiftly stood up and backed away. Whispers and murmurs spread, and I smirked as I spun around. I counted four steps and stopped in the middle as I looked at the person four steps away from me in the other chair. Whoever it was was lucky. As I crouched, I leisurely took off my jacket and tossed it aside, then crawled toward Levi or Blake, and the crowd lost it. I stopped at four, then felt around for his shoe, then stood up. I bit my lip as I spun around then placed my hands on his knees. I leaned back and made sure I brushed myself against him. I leaned back into his chest as I sat on him, then swayed my hips. I tilted my head back and felt his chin on my shoulder. As I moved against him, I felt his lips drag on my skin, closer to my neck. He left a sloppy kiss on my neck, and I instantly stood up. The song didn't end as I reached the middle. I turned to the right and made sure I was in front of Benny. Once I pulled off the blindfold, I locked eyes with him. A pissed look filled his face as I approached him. I felt everyone's eyes on us as my hand grazed up his thigh. His jaw clenched as he looked me, then my lips. I smirked as I placed my hand behind his neck and brought him close so that we'd kiss. Everyone went wild, and I sensed camera flashes. I raised my left leg and took his hand then placed it on my thigh so that he could hold me. We continued to kiss, and the song was about to end, so I pushed him back, and we ended up on the pool table. The song ended, and people cheered as we kissed. I rolled over and laid next to him while I caught my breath. Many faces towered over us, and the first I recognized was Miranda's.

"That was gold, girl!" she cheered as I sat up. She handed me my jacket.

"Thanks," I mumbled. I turned to Benny and noticed he sat next to me with an expressionless look. I cautiously entwined my hand in his, then rested my head on his shoulder. "Do I still owe you?"

"Yeah, you do. We have to finish what we just did," he said as I let out a nervous chuckle. We still held hands as we hopped off the table, then walked through the crowd. People awkwardly high-fived me on the way, which made me turn back to the two chairs. They were empty, and I thought about who said that.

"Hey, we still need to continue our game!" Kelly said as she pointed at Austin, who was still naked. I shook my head as my grip on Benny's hand tightened. As we walked upstairs, Liam walked past us and froze when he saw Austin.

"Why the hell does this look like the start of a terrible porno?" Liam asked. Austin flipped him off. Benny and I laughed as we walked upstairs and back into the living room. I pulled him into a corner to block out the noise.

"I'm sorry for earlier. I'm still a bit drunk, and I shouldn't have played truth or dare with those people." I sighed as he handed me a cup.

"It's okay, at least I got the finale," he said, then took a sip of his drink. "Come on, let's dance." He pulled me toward the crowd. Benny chugged down on his drink, then tossed the cup aside. After a few minutes, Ethan joined us as we danced.

"Can I get a refill? Pwease…" I whined as Benny squinted his eyes at me.

"Okay…I'll be right back," he said, then took the cup and disappeared into the crowd. I awkwardly stood with Ethan and tapped my foot as I watched the people dance. A throwback song came on, and I let out a huge gasp and turned to him.

"I love this song!" I balled my fists and hit his chest.

"Ouch, err…okay. Would you like to dance?" He grabbed my wrists to stop me.

"Yeah, sure, okay," I said, then pulled him to the center of the room. We danced with the humungous group of teenagers to "Starships" by Nicki Minaj. Everyone knew the song, so we jumped and sang along. "Get down on one knee and hold your hands up," I yelled over the music.

"What? Why?" he asked.

"You'll see."

He got down on one knee, then held his arms up. I grinned as I held his hands, then stepped up onto his knee. I swung around so that I sat on his shoulders. He cursed under his breath as he stood up. Ethan's hands wrapped around my ankles as I bobbed my head to the music. I threw my hands up in the air as I danced and people looked at us. They cheered as some other people joined. Everyone jumped and went crazy as multiple lights shone through the room. Some guy handed me a can of beer, and as we danced, I opened it. Some of it spilled.

"Chug! Chug! Chug!" everyone shouted as I drank it all. I dumped the can, then felt a bit dizzy from being in a full room. When I glanced up, I saw my boyfriend leaning against the doorframe as he watched me.

"Why do I have three boyfriends?" I tilted my head at the three Bennys. My head felt heavy as I leaped forward. Benny came out of nowhere and caught me in time before I face planted.

"Okay, you're done," he said as he took me from Ethan's hold. He picked me up bridal style and pushed his way through the crowd. On the way, we passed a table, and I managed to grab a bottle of brandy. I hid it in my jacket as Benny carried me upstairs. I laughed as we walked down the hall. I started to hum a familiar tune, then sang. I sang a rhyme we both knew, then looked up at Benny. He squinted his eyes at me as he looked down. I waited, then gestured with my hand for him to carry on. He let out a huge sigh as he continued the nursery rhyme that we learned when we were kids. Benny mumbled the song as we entered his room. I finished the song off as he set me on the bed. He walked to close the door, and I quickly took out the bottle and placed it on the other side of the bed. I watched as he spun around and collapsed on the bed next to me. I let out a sigh as I turned to him. I placed my hand on his chest and swung my leg over his. He gazed at the ceiling as I stared at his brown eyes. I recalled what happened earlier in this bed, which made me think of us.

"Should we continue what we started?" I asked as I sat up and straddled him. I took off my jacket as he smiled at me. He placed his hands on my bare thighs and raised a brow at me.

"Do what?" He rubbed circles with his thumbs.

I leaned down then pecked his lips. I moved to his ear and whispered, "Sex," and he turned to me.

"What makes you think we'd do that?"

"You said you're glad that I was still sober…" I trailed off as he laughed. I frowned as I rolled off him. Benny turned to me and propped his head upon his hand. I stared at him as he stroked my cheek.

"We've only been dating for a month, babe. I don't want to rush things…" He trailed off.

"But why were you trying to take off my top?" I mumbled as my cheeks reddened.

"We always cuddle and talk about everything in our underwear," he whispered, then kissed my neck.

"Oh." I looked down to see that I wore a bra

under the crop top. I laid there and thought about what an idiot I was and how drunk I got for nothing. Benny continued to kiss and leave hickeys on me as I played with his hair. His phone went off, and he looked up to read the message. He let out a groan as he slowly stood up. “What’s wrong?”

“Nick needs help with something. I’ll be ri—” I cut him off when I pulled him back in the bed. I pulled his shirt off and kissed him.

“I’m sure he’ll understand if you’re ten minutes late.” I grinned, then picked up the bottle of brandy. He laughed as we continued to make out, then shared the bottle as we talked for the next ten minutes.

***

Blake

I looked up once again to see Benny Nielson walk down the stairs and into the kitchen. I glanced at Keene, who leaned against the doorframe. He gave me a nod as I did the same, then walked upstairs. That freaking lap dance. I knew Lana. I noticed when Jennifer told her to do that dare, she panicked. Then being the surprising nerd that she was, she gave both of us a lap dance, then made out with her boyfriend afterward. Fuck Lana Willson. When she walked off, Levi and I stared at each other, then laughed at each other’s boners. Freaking hell.

I stood in front of Benny’s room. I opened the door and expected to see Lana in bed, but I was welcomed with Lana's back faced to me in her black lacy lingerie. I shut the door, and she spun around. Her angry expression changed as she noticed me.

"Blake, what are you doing here?" she whispered as she walked over to me.

"Put your clothes on. We're going out," I said as I tried to avoid eye contact.

"Where? And who's we?" She giggled, then swayed.

"Do you trust me?" I suddenly asked as I thought about the next few hours.

"I-I don't know," she whispered.

"Okay, understandable, but you're going to have to trust me for the next few hours, okay?" I held my hand out. She looked at me, then my hand. After a second, she nodded and accepted it. "You'll find out soon if you hurry up," I added, then walked to the bed and tossed her clothing toward her.

"Okay." She dragged her words, then got dressed. I tried hard not to watch, but it's kind of hard since the room was so dark and the only light was the moon that glistened out the window. The moonlight outlined her body so well as it took in every aspect of her beauty. My head whipped to the door to see the doorknob rattle. I rushed to it and locked the door, then leaned my ear against it. I heard many groans and moans.

"Who the hell is in here?" the guy asked.

"Hi, it's me! La—"

I ran and cut off Lana as I cupped my hand over her mouth. She raised a brow at me, then looked over my shoulder.

"Anyone in there? I can pick locks, you know," the girl said as she banged on the door. If we told our names, it could lead to something worse, so I thought of the first thing I heard when I walked past doors at a party. I removed my hand from Lana's mouth, then wrapped it around her waist. I closed my eyes and hoped that it'd go well as I spanked her ass. She gasped, and as I squeezed, she moaned. My jaw tightened at the alluring noise that I wish I heard often. I looked over my shoulder and watched as their shadows disappeared.

"Why'd you do that?" Lana demanded as I turned back to her.

"They had to know that someone's in here…"

"Why didn't you moan?" she asked.

"I don't moan loud. Mine is low and draggy. You would know if we—"

"But why spank me? Was I a bad girl?" She pouted at me.

"It was either kiss you, which I can't because of your cock block of a boyfriend, or…eat." I smirked.

"Eat?" She tilted her head. "How was eating supposed to make me moan? Unless it's meat, because I love meat."

"Don't worry, we'll eat soon."

"Ooh, can we eat together?" Lana asked as her face lit up in excitement.

"Yeah, we'll eat together every day."

"Yay!" She clapped her hands. "Will it be meat?"

"Something like that, baby girl."

"Ooh, baby girl. You like nicknames, don't you, Blakey boo?"

"I guess."

"Just like Levi and Axel. Hehe, I'm a pumpkin princess."

"What does Benny call you?"

"Bright eyes and babe." Her cheeks reddened as she twirled her hair.

"Well, you'll always be my bad girl, nerd, and baby girl," I mumbled.

"Where's Benny?"

"Downstairs." I didn't want to tell a drunk Lana that he's with his friends. Other than being goofy and sexy, who knew what else she's capable of?

"I want Benny," Lana whined as she tugged on my shirt.

"I'll take you to him, but not right now," I said as I backed away, yet her grip tightened as the back of my feet hit the bed.

"Why?" she asked as her hand rested on my chest. I lost my balance, which resulted in us falling onto the bed. Lana landed right on top of me as her head rested on my chest. I noticed she laughed and looked up at me. My erection hit my jeans as she crawled up so that we were eye level. She reeked of alcohol as I stared into those beautiful blue eyes.

"Hehe, you have a shiny thing on your nose," she blurted out, then poked my nose ring. Her finger traced down to my lip as I slowly opened my mouth. Her index finger was firmly placed on my bottom lip as she snickered. My hand suddenly went behind her neck as I inched closer. My other hand trailed down to her waist as I pressed her body against mine. The sound of a glass being tampered with brought me back to reality as Lana whipped her head around. She climbed off me and walked toward the window as I lay there. Shit. I was going to kiss her. She owed me a kiss, yet I didn't want to do it on her boyfriend's bed. I couldn't even do it because she had a boyfriend. I got up and stood behind Lana. She opened the window and bent down to look out. "Hello!" Lana waved. I glanced over her shoulder to see Keene, Levi, and Axel.

"Come on!" Levi said as he glanced around.

"Are you here to rescue me from this big tower?" Lana called out.

"What? Just climb down!" Keene stated. Lana huffed as she folded her arms. Even though I wanted to stay, I walked around and stood next to her.

"Dude, bring her!" Levi yelled.

"It's not that easy getting a drunk Lana to do things," I said.

"Ugh, fine!" Keene huffed. "Rapunzel, Rapunzel, get the fuck down!"

"That's not the words," Axel pointed out. I stood up and walked toward the door. I slowly unlocked it and heard the loud music.

"Okay, we can go," I mumbled, then spun around to see Lana on the windowsill with her shoes in her hands. My eyes widened as she threw them out.

"Catch me, my knight!" She laughed, then jumped out the window. I ran to the window, my heart almost dropping out of my chest as I reached it. I bent down to see Levi, Axel, and Keene sprawled out on the ground and Lana laid across right on them. They groaned as Lana raised her fist and cheered. I let out a sigh of relief as I thought about the rest of the night.

We were in Levi's car as we drove away from the party. I looked next to me and noticed Lana's frown.

"What's wrong?" I whispered. She cuddled into the blanket and let out a horrible cry.

"I want Benny!"

"Oh my God," Keene muttered as he reached into her jacket pocket and took out her phone.

"What are you doing?" Levi asked from the driver's seat.

"He's gonna notice soon that she's gone. I'll send him a text on her phone," Keene replied as we nodded.

"Where are you taking me?" Lana asked, then sank in her seat.

"Well, we have less than twelve hours together, princess. I'd like to spend it with you," Levi said as he pulled a paper out of his jacket. "We're going to do as much as we can on this bucket list."

"Actions speak louder than words," she whispered.

"Yeah, take this as a way of making up for not being there when I said I would. The times we promised but screwed up again…" He trailed off.

"Yeah, we've been planning this for a few days," I said as she looked at me.

"Oh…so what are we doing first?"

"Underground street fight. I got it covered," Axel said as he handed me the list. As I looked through it, some of the stuff was ticked off, yet what caught my eye was the *Don't fall in love* that Levi only ticked.

"We update the bucket list every second year," Lana said as she leaned her head on my shoulder.

"When did you get a piercing or tattoo?" I asked, since both ticked it. She leaned forward and flicked her earlobes. "That doesn't count."

"Well, maybe I'll get a piercing here…" She trailed off as she placed her hand on her breast. I gulped as her hand lowered as she looked at me. "Or here."

"Okay, tattoo it is," Axel said as he cleared his throat. Lana threw her head back and laughed as she looked at Keene. He gave her phone back, and she put it in her jacket.

"Keene, guess what? Guess what?"

"What?"

"Blake and I are gonna eat someday," she said as my eyes widened.

"What?"

"Yeah. Together, and I'm gonna moan." She nodded as I facepalmed.

"What the fuck?" Levi asked as he looked at me through the mirror.

"Yeah, will you moan?" she asked me.

"Maybe. It's kinda hard." I gestured to the meat.

"Yeah, sometimes you have to suck and pull," she said, which caused Axel to choke on his drink.

"Holy shit," Keene muttered.

"I like sucking all the juice out of it. Do you?" she asked with an innocent look.

"Uh huh." I laughed as Keene glared at me.

"Yay! Who wants to join us?" Lana asked.

"Oh my fuck, you're adorable when you're

drunk, pumpkin."

***

We arrived at the underground street fight that was near downtown. Lana was a bit sobered up yet remained quiet as we held hands. We followed Axel as he greeted a bunch of people. He must've been here before because people cheered him on. I looked around and saw a big cage where two men fought. Lana seemed to notice it too as she gaped.

"You do cage fighting?" I looked at Axel.

"What gave you that idea? The two men fighting in a cage?" he sarcastically asked.

"It's dangerous! You could get badly hurt!" Lana spoke up.

"Don't worry, princess, he's good," Levi assured Lana as we followed Axel. He brought us to a room with a vanity mirror, desk, and couch. Lana and I still held hands as we walked to the sofa.

"Do you always fight?" I asked as Axel took off his flannel.

"Of course, brother. You earn money by racing. I earn it by fighting…well, I used to race…" He trailed off as he glanced at Lana.

"Ooh, are you gonna win?" Lana asked, and Axel laughed.

"Pumpkin, I always win," Axel said as he got ready for the fight while we walked into the busy crowd. I didn't know how to describe Lana when she's drunk. She's very clingy; her hand hadn't left mine since we got out of the car. We got the closest we could to the cage where a fight had ended. The guy who lost looked pretty jacked up. He coughed out blood while the man who won walked around, raised his fists, and cheered. I felt Lana pull my hand back as she stared at the guy.

"What's wrong?" I asked.

"That guy just—I've seen him before," she replied. I looked at the man who walked around; his eyes landed on us as he smirked.

"Where?" I asked as he turned his back to us, which made him look familiar.

"I-I think he's the one who was in my room," she whispered. Before I'd questioned Lana, the crowd went quiet as people made way for Axel. He was shirtless yet wore his jeans with his white hand wraps. He walked into the cage where the guy from Lana's room was. The ref was there, talking to the two fighters. "What if he's watching us?" Lana whispered in my ear.

"H-he won't do anything in a crowd. Stay close." I released my grip on her hand as I pulled her in front of me, her back resting on my chest as I wrapped my arms around her waist. The fight began, and my brother was good. The guy apparently took the first punch, but Axel dodged it, then raised his leg as he did a front kick. I glanced to the right and noticed Levi's face was blank. "Hey, you okay?" I asked. He slowly nodded, then turned to Lana.

"Freaking foul!" Keene demanded as he banged his fists on the fence. The guy punched Axel by his kidney and neck. Axel staggered back as he raised his arms to block the punches. He did a sucker punch, and the guy backed away. The crowd was crazy as one side cheered for Axel and the other end for the man. He went down and kicked Axel by his ankles. He fell to the ground and coughed up blood. My jaw clenched as the guy already cheered with his back turned to Axel.

"Come on, Axel!" Lana yelled as she leaped forward and shook the fence. The referee started the countdown, but Axel wiped the blood from his mouth and got up. The guy spun around at the same time Axel raised his leg. He kicked the man in the hip, and he swayed. Axel took the chance and punched him right in the jaw. He pushed the guy against the fence and gave him many punches. I pulled Lana away as the fence wobbled. The guy had his back faced to us as he slid down the chainlink and groaned. Everyone went wild as people hit the cage.

"Take her to the car! We'll get Axel!" Levi yelled. I nodded and pulled Lana away from the crowd. Levi and Keene went after Axel as we ran out. Thankfully, we parked close to the building, so it was easy to get out.

"He's always here," Lana mumbled as we reached the car.

"What?" I asked.

"That guy, one of James's men. He was there that night I was with Miranda," she answered. Before Lana continued, we heard groans. I looked over my shoulder to see Keene dragging Axel. I ran to help as I put his other arm around my shoulder.

"Where's Levi?" I asked as we approached the car.

"Aww, you're not going to congratulate me on

my win, brother?" Axel sighed as he leaned against the car.

"Are you okay?" I grunted.

"I'm perfectly fine," he said, then spun around to open the car door.

"Where were you?" Lana asked as Levi approached us.

"Nowhere," he answered, then unlocked the car. Lana gave me a weary look as we entered the vehicle. Axel sat in the back with Lana and me while Keene drove. We drove in silence as Lana helped Axel with his bruises.

"I've never seen that dude before. Who was that?" Axel groaned.

"I don't know," Levi and I said in unison. I raised a brow as I turned to Lana.

"Well, at least you saw your first street fight, pumpkin," Axel said as he read the list.

"Yeah, thank you," she mumbled, then took a pen from Levi and the list from Axel. I watched as she ticked it off, then read the list. Her thumb grazed over *don't fall in love*, and I sighed.

"Watch out!" Levi yelled as we looked up. The car came to an abrupt stop as we leaped forward. I held Lana back as her arm wrapped around Axel's chest. We looked to see a guy in front of the car. He motioned for one of us to get out as he walked over to his Toyota Supra.

"Come on, Blake," Levi said as he got out of the car. I opened the door and looked back at Lana, who gave me a concerned look. I assured her that it was okay as I got out of the car.

"Who are you and what do you want?" I asked as

I stood next to Levi. The guy leaned on the hood of his car and smirked.

"I want to race that beauty." He pointed to the Mustang.

"What makes you think I want to race your shit-ass car?" Levi asked as he folded his arms. The guy playfully rolled his eyes as he reached into his pocket and pulled out money. He looked over his shoulder, and we followed his gaze to the road up ahead.

"Quick race down this path, y'know, some New Year's fun." He winked.

"That road leads to a park," I said.

"Then we'll stop at the park." He shrugged, then raised his hand, which held the money.

"All right, this will be easy," Levi said as the guy approached us. He pointed to the car and shook his head.

"Oh no, I want to race your car, but the girl must drive."

Chapter Sixteen

Blake

I sat in the passenger's seat of Levi's car while Lana gripped the wheel. We stared at the long road ahead of us, and I regretted it because she might be a little tipsy.

"At least it's one more thing to tick off the bucket list," I said.

"Yeah…who is he?" Lana asked as we looked to our left to see the guy in his car.

"I don't know, but it's kind of strange that he had a lot of cash on him."

"Do you think this is planned?"

"I don't know…but you'll do perfectly fine. Just listen to me, and we'll win this," I stated, then rested my hand on her bare thigh.

"Where's Levi?" Lana asked, then moved her leg, so I took it as a sign and shifted away.

"He's with Axel. They're waiting up ahead," I said. Lana let out a sigh as she gripped the wheel and looked forward. Her foot hit the accelerator as the car thundered. Keene was in the center with his arm raised. I looked at the guy to see him do the same as Lana. "Wanna do that move where the car rises?"

"Err…sure."

"Okay, when Keene says go, you're going to keep it in park for a second, then put it in reverse while pushing down on the accelerator. Two seconds later, put it in first gear and, well…the car will rise, then zip down the street as fast you can," I said, then turned to Lana. "Got it?"

"Not really, but I'll give it a shot," she mumbled, then wrapped her hand around the handle. I put my hand over Lana's, which made her look at me.

"Trust me," I whispered, then looked at Keene. Once he dropped his hand, the smell of burned rubber polluted the air. I guided her hand as it went in reverse. Everything happened so fast as I looked at the side mirror to see smoke from the tires. The car rose as the guy in the Toyota gaped at us, then drove. We landed on the ground, and that's when the race began. We zipped down the long road, and I literally heard Lana move her foot toward the clutch. "Second gear," I called out and looked over my shoulder to see the guy right on our tail. "Block him."

"Wha—we're in the lead. I do—"

I cut her off when I squeezed her thigh. She yelped and blocked the guy. After a while, she whacked my hand away and went into third gear. In a matter of seconds, we saw Axel and Levi. I smiled as they cheered and hollered. The guy was next to us as we drove full speed. I looked at him, and he did the same. Lana hit the accelerator pedal once more as we passed the finish line. I smirked and raised my middle finger at him as we stopped.

"Oh my god! We did it!" Lana cheered as I turned to her.

"You did, baby girl," I said as she gave me a smile, then pulled me in for a quick hug. We got out of the car, and Lana immediately ran to Levi. I watched as she jumped in his arms as he laughed.

"You finally did it!" he said as the guy reached into his pocket and pulled out the money.

"Not bad…as promised." He held up the money.

"Where's Keene?" Axel asked.

"Aww, shit, we forgot him again!" Levi said as he pointed to Keene who ran toward us.

"Screw you, guys. You know that." He huffed as he stood next to me. The guy was about to give us the money until we heard claps. It was hard to look around since it was dark and the only light was the headlights of the cars. The claps got louder as the guy backed away. I raised a brow as he smirked.

"Tick that off the list," a recognizable voice said. I stiffened as James appeared in front of us with two men behind. Just as expected, one of them was from the cage. His face looked swollen.

"Hey, you were the guy I beat." Axel pointed at the man who glared in return.

"What are you doing here?" Keene asked as I looked at him, then Lana. She seemed frightened as she stood behind Axel.

"Just wanted to say a quick hello." James smirked as he stood right in front of us.

"Can I have my money now?" the guy asked as

he looked at James.

"Wa-wait—you set us up!" Lana pointed at James.

"I had to find some excuse to talk to my boys." James laughed as I looked away. "You could've just done what I asked, and none of this would be happening."

"Yo, I don't know what's going on, but I want my mo—" The guy cut off when James raised his hand. One of his men behind him pulled out a gun with a silencer and shot the man in the head. My jaw dropped as he fell to the ground, blood oozing out of his skull. We watched as James spun around and approached the guy. He placed his foot on his back and looked at us.

"Not the first time some of us have seen blood coming out of someone's head," he said, and his men laughed. My jaw tightened as I looked at the body. He still had his eyes open, which made the hair on the back of my neck rise. I looked at Lana and expected her to cry, but all I saw was a blank expression as she stared at the body. Levi held a poker face while Axel and Keene looked shocked. Then there was me. I didn't know how to feel because I didn't want James to get inside my head. "I wouldn't do that if I were you." James looked at Keene, who held his phone. "Otherwise I'll just shoot you all, since you're such disappointments to me." I looked at his two men, who had pistols in their hands. James walked over to Lana, and Levi immediately stood in front of her. James smirked as he leaned in and whispered in his ear. Whatever he said put Levi off as he stepped aside and walked over to me. I watched in fear as James stroked Lana's cheek. I didn't know if she shivered from his touch or her shorts, but she closed her eyes as James put a lock of hair behind her ear. I stepped forward, but Levi gripped my arm. I scowled. He gave me an icy glare in return and shook his head. "Such a beautiful girl can do so much damage," James muttered as he cupped her cheeks. My jaw clenched as I saw the tear roll down her cheek. We watched as James backed away and snapped his fingers. The men took the dead body by each arm and pulled him. "Don't do anything stupid until we see each other again," James said as he looked at Levi, Lana, and me. "Happy New Year, and remember…actions speak louder than words." He then walked into the dark night with his two men, who casually carried the body as if he weighed nothing.

"I miss Christo," one of James's men piped up as they walked off. We couldn't see them, but we heard them.

"Same here, Mike. He's an idiot for not following," James said, and that was the last thing we heard until they were gone. Silence filled the atmosphere as we took in what had happened. I didn't know what else he wanted from us. Out the corner of my eye, I saw Lana walk forward. Her breaths were heavy as she looked in the direction James went in.

"*You can't just do that!*" she yelled as I closed my eyes. I hate to see her like that. "*Where is he?*" she yelled as I opened my eyes and raised a brow. "*What do you want?*" she cried out as Levi walked to her.

"Hey, hey, hey calm down, pr—"

"I'm not going to calm down! What the hell? We just witnessed a murder, Levi. Not just any murder, but one done by a drug dealer!" she exclaimed as Levi placed his hands on her arms.

"I know, princess. You just have to calm down. Everything's gonna be ok—"

"No, no, no—we have to tell my dad. He'll kno—"

"*Listen to me!*" Levi yelled as he shook her. She stopped and stared at him. "Your dad doesn't know that we're here. He doesn't even know that we're all together out here. We'll tell him when we get back, okay? I just need you to relax!" He raised his voice. She nodded her head as Levi dropped his arms and stared at her. I looked past them and saw something on the ground where the dead body had lain. I walked over to it and blocked out the others as I saw a paper on the ground. I picked it up and unfolded it. When I read the paper, I squinted my eyes as I thought about what S1 meant.

"I wanna go home," Lana whispered.

"You can't. I planned the whole night for us. I don't know when I'll see you again for the next year," Levi said as I rolled my eyes.

"I'm gonna miss you." Lana pouted as she wrapped her arms around his torso.

"Me too, princess, but I'll always be there when you need to talk or a shoulder to cry on."

I had to resist the urge to gag at his nonsense.

"Thank you," she mumbled into his chest as I walked to the car.

"Anytime. Love you," he said as I froze and

turned to their moment. She stared at him with that smile that I've seen one too many times. It wasn't a happy smile or a sad smile; it was a mixed emotions smile. Her only smile I'd noticed.

"Love you too," she said, then pulled away from him. "Levi, I need to tell you something about that guy and his guy that we saw in the cage they we'r—"

"Err…guys, we gotta go." Keene cut off Lana as we heard a gang approach us. We rushed to the car. Keene drove while Axel sat in the passenger's seat. Lana sat between Levi and me and leaned into his chest as he ran his fingers through her hair.

"Quick, get us out of here," Levi said as Keene started the car. I watched the gang walk past us to the abandoned Toyota. They started to dismantle it.

"Where to now?" Axel asked as he ticked off street racing from the list.

"Head back downtown. We're going to a paint party." Levi smirked as he looked at Lana. She was half asleep as Keene turned on the radio. When I looked down, I saw Lana's hand placed loosely on my thigh. I slipped my hand through hers and entwined our fingers together as we drove through downtown.

***

By the time we arrived at the party, it was two-thirty a.m. Levi called Jaden, and somehow, he talked the bouncer into letting us in, since we were underage except Axel. The place was packed with people, and their neon clothing, as well as the lights, stood out. Lana was off with Keene while Levi, Axel, and I stood away from the crowd.

"Listen, err…for what happened earlier, we keep it between us, right?" Levi asked as he looked at us.

"Yeah, we will, but you know Lana. She'll tell her dad, and I think it's right because he's been looking for James for months now," Axel said.

"I know. Something's not right. I can see it her eyes. There's something that she's hiding," he said as I rolled my eyes.

"Aren't you hiding something from her too?" I asked. He glared at me.

"Look, man, you two and Keene are the only people I trust. I want you to take care of her," Levi hissed.

"Why are you all so protective now?" I scrunched my nose up.

"Remember this." He raised his sleeve where the tiny hole was. I remembered when he told us what happened. It scared me, but I didn't think he told us everything. If Lana ever found out, she'd go nuts. We nodded in unison with confused looks. "How I got this…somehow involves her."

"How?" Axel asked.

"I don't know, but promise me that you won't let anything happen to her. She's already been through so much. I don't want what happened earlier to happen again," he mumbled as we followed his gaze to see Lana dancing. She looked so beautiful and free. Her head was thrown back as she danced while people surrounded her. No cares in the world of the things that surrounded her, that sort of look you barely saw on Lana Willson. "Well, I'm gonna find Keene," Levi mumbled as he walked off. Axel handed me a drink and I thanked him. We stood there and drank the alcohol as I thought over what happened earlier. Levi seemed calm after what happened, while Lana was the complete opposite. It made me wonder what James whispered in Levi's ear. Axel knew James, since Deputy Paul told him when I got arrested. Although I was suspicious of Keene.

"You really gonna let that guy put paint on her?" Axel nudged me as he pointed. I followed his finger and looked across the room. Lana took off her jacket, which exposed her glowing white crop top. I smirked at Axel as I drank up the cold liquor and gave the cup to him. I also took off my leather jacket and dumped it on his head, which made him groan. I walked toward Lana and looked at the guy who painted her back. He saw me, and I shooed him away as I took the brush and began. Her hair was moved to the side as I painted white stripes. I glanced down at her lower back as I thought about what to paint there. I shrugged as I began to use orange and yellow for the sun. Lana spun around with a startled look when she realized it was me. I grinned as I dropped the brush and dipped my fingertips into the pink paint. She stared at me as I placed my finger on her temples and brushed them down her jawline. She tugged on my shirt as she lifted it up and over my head. I stood shirtless as she ran her fingers over my tattoos, then picked up a brush. She painted dots around my eyes, then lines.

"I hope you didn't mess on my back," she said as I put yellow on my thumb, then dragged it down her chin.

"Nope, you look like an angel with wings," I said, and she laughed. A chill kicked up my spine as she covered her whole hand in paint and stepped closer. She raised her head as she left orange handprints on my back.

"Guys, check it out," Axel said as Lana and I backed away. We followed his gaze to see that Axel had painted a dick on Levi's back.

"Not funny, dude," Levi muttered as he looked at Lana and me.

"Yeah, you're right. It's fucking hilarious because it's glowing!" Axel exclaimed as Lana and I laughed.

"What's up, guys? That chick there just kissed me, and I feel fucking fantastic!" Keene slurred.

"What do you mean she kissed you?" I stepped closer and noticed the sweat run down his face.

"Dude, did you swallow anything?" Axel asked as he handed me my jacket. Keene breathed heavily as he pulled off his baseball tee.

"Yeah, when we kissed sh—"

"Shit. You swallowed an ecstasy pill," Axel muttered as he ran off. My eyes widened as I thought of the symptoms an ecstasy pill had. Keene tripped, but I managed to catch him as my arm wrapped around his torso. I took him away from the crowd where Axel found us and handed him a bottle.

"Dude, we gotta get you out of here. It's too congested," Axel said as Keene leaned against the wall.

"How long do the effects last?" I asked.

"Probably about three hours or so, but we have to get him out of here or else…" Axel trailed off as he gave me a worried look.

"I wanna dance," Keene slurred as he waved at the people who danced.

"Go get Lana and Levi. We have to go," Axel said as I nodded. When I walked through the crowd, I spotted Lana and Levi. A blank look filled my face as I watched them. She sat on a chair and painted his back while he painted her thighs and legs. His hand went in between her legs, and she laughed, then pushed him away.

"Guys, we have to go," I stated as I held my shirt and jacket.

"Why?" Lana pouted as Levi helped her up.

"Keene swallowed an ecstasy pill, so he can't be here."

"Oh, okay. Come on, princess, we're going to our next stop." Levi smirked as he took her hand in his. They walked past me, and I let out a sigh. I was glad that Levi wouldn't see Lana after this night. I grabbed her jacket too and followed them as we walked out of the club.

I sat between Keene and Lana yet regretted it since she was wide awake and he sweated.

"Am I in the north pole? It's fucking freezing!" Keene yelled out as he closed his window.

"You were sweating just a few minutes ago!" Levi said as he drove.

"You know I'm starting to think that everything we do on that bucket list has a consequence," Axel pointed out as Lana ticked off paint party.

"What gave you that idea? Was it the guy who

got shot or Keene getting drugged?" Lana sarcastically asked.

"I feel sick," Keene mumbled as he rested his head on my shoulder.

"Dude, we're almost there. Hold on," Levi muttered as he drove faster. After a few more minutes, we finally arrived. We got out of the car, and I grinned as we read the sign.

"If you haven't realized, Levi, it's closed," Lana stated as we looked at the indoor pool.

"Oh, come on, princess. This is an old one, and the only security they have are gates." Levi shrugged as he helped Keene.

"So we're gonna break in?" Lana demanded.

"Sshh! Don't say it like that. It's just we're visiting at the wrong time." Axel grinned as he swung his arm around her shoulder.

"If we get caught, it's all on you," Lana said as she pointed at Levi.

"Oh please, princess, have you ever gotten caught?"

"Not really," she mumbled as I smirked.

"Exactly." Levi shrugged as we stopped at the entrance that only had a locked gate.

"Shit," Axel muttered as he shook the gate. As my brother tried to pick the lock, Levi walked around the building. Keene leaned against the wall and sang a random song as Lana looked out for anyone. I watched as Levi ran back to us with a wicked look.

"There's a ladder that leads up to the roof," he said, then pointed inside and onto the ceiling where there was an opening.

"Someone climb, get in there, and open for the rest of us," he said as Lana snorted.

"You do realize whoever opens that window will land in the pool."

"Uh-huh."

"I'll go." Axel grinned as he took off his clothes.

"Are you sure?" I raised a brow at him.

"Yes, brother, it's not like I'm jumping off a cliff." He laughed, then tossed his clothes to me. I let out a sigh as we watched him walk off and around the corner. We looked inside and above by the center of the pool as we waited for him. Two minutes later, we saw someone drop into the pool with a big splash. I bit my lip as I watched him come up for air and out of the pool. Axel pushed the button, and the gate unlocked. Levi and I opened it as we rushed inside. Keene was clearly happy since he jumped in with his clothes on. I took out my phone and checked the time to see that it was three a.m. I glanced up and saw Axel and Keene in the pool while Lana stood a few feet away from the pool. Her jacket was off as well as her shoes, which displayed the paint on her body. I slowly bit my lip as I took a picture of her. She turned to me as I held the phone up and blocked her face. I laughed as I continued to take photos of her.

"Aren't you getting in?" I asked as I took off my clothes.

"I don't know," she whispered as I unbuckled my belt.

"Come on, princess!" Levi yelled behind her. I watched as he ran toward her, picked her up, and dived into the pool with her. Lana glared at Levi as he splashed water on her. Keene came up behind Levi and jumped on him. Lana turned to me and gestured me to come in. I playfully rolled my eyes as I jumped in and swam toward her.

We played in the pool for the next ten minutes, and my thoughts drifted off to when Lana and I were in the park and had a little picnic before Homecoming. I remembered when she told me she loved to swim. The guys jumped in the pool while Lana swam back and forth. I rested in the center as I watched her. She stopped and floated on her back, and I took the chance to swim toward her. Her clothes were off by now; all she wore was her black lingerie. Her eyes were closed as her hair spread out. I managed to get off all the paint on my body, but Lana still had hers. I cautiously placed my hands on her back to keep her up.

"Is this that Troy and Gabriella moment when they were in the pool?" Lana asked as she opened her eyes.

"If you want it to be." I laughed as I put my one arm around her waist.

"How come all of your paint is gone?" She looked at my face and chest. I shrugged as my eyes diverted to her painted thighs. "Can you help with mine?"

"Sure," I mumbled as I moved down and poured water on her thighs, then wiped off the paint while she did her arms. My eyes lingered up her body to her underwear. I swallowed the lump in my throat and continued. After that, she stood up and faced me. She placed her hands on my cheeks and stroked them with her thumbs.

"You still have some on your nose." She chuckled as I looked at her face.

"You too…everywhere, actually." I laughed as my hands cupped her cheeks. I wiped the paint with my thumbs as I swam closer. She looked up at me as her hands went to my shoulders. I ran my fingers through her wet hair as the palm of her hands touched my chest. My hands traveled down to her neck as I closed my eyes and leaned in.

"Oh, fuck," Levi exclaimed as Lana pushed me away. I looked at her only to see her look at Levi and Axel, who got out of the pool.

"Cops," Axel said as I turned back to Lana. I helped her out of the pool and looked back to see Keene float like there's no tomorrow. I cursed under my breath as I swam and supported him.

"Come on, dude!" Levi demanded as he stood at the edge of the pool and held a hand out. I pulled Keene toward Levi, and he helped Keene out of the water. I quickly got out and grabbed my clothes.

"This way!" Axel called out as we followed him with our clothes in our hands. We ran into the changing room, and Levi immediately shut the door behind him. Axel spotted a window and ran toward it, then opened it. I helped him while Lana got dressed.

"We know you're here!" someone called out from the pool as we opened the window.

"Quickly," Axel whispered as we made way for Lana to go first. A panicked look filled her eyes as I took her hand and helped her up and out of the window. She only wore her shorts as she held her top and shoes. Once everyone was helped to the window, I went through. Just in time, too, as a police officer came through. The changing rooms were in the back, so we had to run all the way around to get to the car. As we ran into a random street, I looked ahead to see Lana slowed down.

"Why are you slowing down?" I yelled in a whisper.

"My feet hurt because of these heels! I think I'm gonna get a blister," she mumbled as I ran next to her.

"Hold on tight," Axel piped up as he stopped behind Lana and picked her up and threw her over his shoulder. I smiled at him as we continued to run, then looked up ahead. A flash of light was seen, followed by a person. My eyes widened since Levi and Keene were already ahead of us. I ran forward and warned them about the people up ahead.

"We're almost to the car, though," Keene slurred, and I almost forgot that he was still a bit intoxicated.

"Freeze! You have the rig—" The female officer cut herself off as she lowered her gun and gaped at us. "Not you again." Officer Jackson motioned us to follow her. We followed in silence as she walked in front of us. I gritted my teeth as a cold breeze swept through and onto our chests. Officer Jackson only had one set of handcuffs on her. We arrived at her car, and Levi leaned against it as she took out more handcuffs.

"You finally got caught, princess." Levi smirked as Officer Jackson put the cuffs on him.

"Who you calling princess, Radcliff?" she demanded as Levi, Keene, and I raised a brow, then spun around to see that it was only the three of us.

"Damn." I bit my lip because Lana didn't get caught—neither did my brother.

***

I stared at Officer Jackson outside of the jail cell as I went over the last event because no one else was in this cell except us. I glanced to the side to see Keene asleep on the bench. I watched as Officer Jackson got up and walked down the hall and into another room. Levi sat next to me on the floor and leaned against the wall. We've been in here for almost an hour, and I wondered what Lana and Axel were doing. She's still a bit drunk, and well he's…Axel, so anything could happen.

"Do you remember that day we watched all the *Shrek* movies with Lana?" Levi asked.

"Yeah," I mumbled as I remembered how we watched movies a few days before Christmas.

"We watch it every year, and every year I tried to figure out why she liked it so much…" He trailed off as I squinted my eyes. "She says because there's always a happy ending. Even now. Coming here and seeing what she's been through, I finally understand. She's waiting for her happy ending," he whispered.

"Well, this is reality. Not everything has a happy ending." I closed my eyes and leaned my head against the wall.

"Yeah, and when I arrived here, I thought it'd be like every other year, just her and me. When we were growing up, everyone in the neighborhood knew us as the best friends Lana and Levi," he mumbled. "Now seeing how everything has changed…how she has changed and moved on…"

"She hasn't changed. You just didn't grow up, dude." Keene yawned.

"Well, it takes time to get used to the fact that she has so many new friends. Not to mention that half of them bullied her!" Levi snapped as I opened my eyes.

"Now she's dating one of them too," Keene added as Levi cursed under his breath.

"Yeah, and him of all people. Like, what the fuck? He doesn't deserve her," Levi snarled.

"Then who does?" I asked, because I deserved her; I wanted her.

"Not me. I love her. She's my other half, but look at me. I can't give her anything." He stared at me with a panicked look. "As much as I love her, I've learned to control it and only see her as a best friend. I'm not independent, and for that, there's never gonna be an us. There's never gonna be the same Levi and Lana that everyone knew," he whispered.

"Blake deserves her," Keene spoke up as my eyes widened.

"What?" Levi asked as he turned to me.

"Yeah, the dude's whipped. Can't you see it? They have a lot in common," Keene said.

"Whoa. I've been so busy trying to not hate Benny that I didn't realize that you liked Lana," Levi confessed as I sighed. "I'm suddenly intrigued. What do you like about her?"

"What's not to like about her?" I asked. "She's

funny, caring, beautiful. I mean, have you seen her eyes? Those electric, mesmerizing blue eyes that always draw me back and are mysterious, which only makes me want her more. I want to figure her out, the real Lana Willson. It's in there somewhere."

"Whoa," Levi commented.

"Told you he's whipped as fuck." Keene giggled as he pointed at me.

"What's the closest encounter you've had with her?" Levi asked.

"At the cottage with that drug dealer. I kissed her."

"Man, bad timing and place, dude," Keene pointed out as I rolled my eyes.

"Do you think she likes you?" Levi asked as the corner of his mouth lifted.

"I don't know. One time we're talking like best friends, then the next we're fighting."

"Look, I've known her for four years now, and I see that she's a person who likes to crush all their feelings into this one big ball of emotions, then when the time is right, she reacts," Keene began. "Whether it's cheerful, depressed, wrecked, or terrified…it's like sometimes she doesn't even know what's going on or what to do."

"Man, that pill really does have an effect on you," Levi commented after a while.

"He's right, though. That's what makes Lana so mysterious. She'll be smiling, but you don't even know if it's real or not." I sighed. "She's magnificent at acting, but not as herself."

"Yeah, it's kinda sad because you'll think she'll

be happy, then something happens or comes up and then…" Levi trailed off, yet I could only imagine what he thought of. It could be when Levi and I raced or when we found out that Parker sexually harassed her. That ruined me. I couldn't believe it. When I beat him, I was acting on the sudden urge to hurt him so badly.

The conversation soon died down as we heard many footsteps approach us. I glanced up to see Officer Jackson walk toward us with two people behind her.

"All right, you three, I don't want to hear from you again. Just be glad I'm in a good mood and that it's a new year," she said as my eyes narrowed.

"Who bailed us out?" Levi asked as we stood up and walked to the gate.

"The one and only!" Lana's voice echoed as she cheered. I took in her appearance and noticed that she had bare feet and wore Axel's flannel.

"Lana, does your father know that you're out so late?" Officer Jackson asked as we walked out of the cell.

"Not really, Miss Jackson, but I heard you're in a good mood, so…" She winked.

"Yes, but if I see or hear of the five of you, I won't hesitate to lock you all up."

"Will do, Miss Ja—did you know that there's a song with your name, Miss Jackson?" Lana asked as we walked down the hall.

"I thought she was sober," Levi grunted as he glared at Axel.

"We made a few stops before we came to get you guys." Axel shrugged as we watched Lana. She swung her arm around Officer Jackson's shoulder and belted out the lyrics to Panic! At the Disco's "Miss Jackson."

"Okay, I think we need to go." I grabbed Lana and guided her out of the station.

"What the hell?" Officer Jackson stated as she stared at us. We were finally out of the station, where I let go of Lana and watched as she skipped to the car and continued to sing.

"Where are her shoes? And why is she wearing your flannel?" Keene asked as we walked to the car.

"Her feet were getting sore, and do you really think I was going to let her enter the police station in a crop top and shorts?" Axel asked.

"Where's her jacket?"

"It's in the car, and plus, pumpkin looks cute in my clothing," he said. I rolled my eyes as we got in the car. I sat in the middle while Lana sat on my right and Keene sat on my left. Axel drove this time while Levi turned on the radio.

"Guess where we got the money?" Lana asked as she clapped her hands.

"Is it from that guy you raced?" Levi asked as he turned to face us.

"Yeah! Since I won fair and square, I took the money that fell to the ground and shoved it in my jacket pocket," she said as her eyes sparkled with excitement.

"Yeah, and the money from the fight I won, we used it to buy a bottle of whiskey and a bag of chips." Axel motioned to the bag of chips, which Keene ate.

"Where are we off to now, Captain?" Lana asked

as she straightened her posture and saluted. I laughed at her childishness.

"Tattoo parlor." Levi grinned as he read through the list.

"Aww, I don't know what to get." Lana frowned as she turned to me.

"You can get a piercing," I suggested, then remembered a few hours ago when she was drunk and hinted where she wanted a piercing.

"I think I have something in mind for a tattoo," Levi faintly said.

"Hey, Keene, guess what, guess what?" Lana urged as I gave a look.

"What?" he mumbled.

"I killed someone." She giggled, then poked my cheek. Everyone in the car fell into a profound silence as we absorbed what she had said, then laughed at the ridiculous things Lana said when she's drunk.

"You're funny, princess. How much alcohol have you consumed in the last twelve hours?"

"I don't know. Maybe four—teen beverages or something like that, but I'm still happy and alive!"

"How is that possible?" Axel laughed.

"I take my medication every day." Lana pouted as she tugged on the sleeves of Axel's flannel. Other than being intoxicated and childish, she looked cuddly. Her hair was curled up from the pool and the flannel ended by her thighs.

"What medication?" Keene asked.

"You know." She wiggled her brows at me. "Vitamin A, B, C, and all I'm missing is D, am I right?"

"Oh my God." Levi facepalmed as we laughed.

"I'm hungry!" Lana whined.

"You just ate a bag of sweet chili chips," Axel pointed out.

"Oh yeah." She chuckled, then turned to me. Our faces were inches apart as she stared at me with a sly grin and her eyelids drooped. "You know what I'd go for right now?"

"What?" I asked as she leaned in and whispered in my ear.

"A nice juicy piece of meat."

Chapter Seventeen

Blake

We arrived at the parlor Keene suggested. It was open twenty-four hours, and Keene knew the people, so it was no problem. When we walked in, I took in the atmosphere. Multiple designs were advertised on the walls. Most of Axel's and my tattoos were done in Minnesota, and I've been to one parlor in Illinois, but not this one. A guy walked in from the back and took off his gloves. Apart from the tattoos that covered his arms, he had clear amber skin and stubble that covered his square jaw.

"Keene!" the guy exclaimed as he greeted him with a handshake.

"'Sup, man," Keene said, then turned to us. "You know Levi, of course. This is Axel, Blake, and Lana. Meet Isaac. He owns the place."

"So what can I do for you today?" Isaac asked as he put the gloves in the trash can and folded his arms.

"Our lovely friend here would like…" Levi

trailed off as we stared at Lana.

"I-I don't know." She shrugged.

"Don't stress, kid. A tattoo takes a lot of thinking, especially your first one. Kendra might help." Isaac looked over his shoulder. "Kendra!" he called as I stuffed my hands in my jeans pockets. The woman who entered the room, who I assumed was Kendra, wore black jeans and a maroon tank top that displayed the tattoos that surrounded her collarbone. She had short curly hair, which brought out her high cheekbones.

"Hey, guys."

"Kendra, Lana here is getting her first tattoo." Isaac gestured to Lana, who was now in her leather jacket and heels.

"Cool, follow me." Kendra motioned Lana to follow her into another room. I watched as Lana whispered something to Levi. He nodded, then followed them. I walked around the parlor and looked at the different designs. Isaac turned on music, and I smiled as Drake came on. Axel took off his shirt as I raised a brow and walked over to him.

"You're getting a tattoo?"

"We're getting a tattoo, brother." He winked as I sat down on a chair. I closed my eyes for a moment and sighed. I knew what tattoo he wanted. Last year we got a tattoo of Mom's name, Roxanne, on our left bicep. Now we'd get a tattoo of our dad's name and when he passed away.

"All right, boys, what would you like?" Isaac asked as I took off my jacket and gray tee. Axel did a little sketch of the way we wanted it. It was like the way we got Mom's name. After we argued on where we wanted it, we finally decided to put it on our left forearm. I went first as I sat on the chair and laid back. Isaac pulled his chair up and sat next to me as I held out my arm. He cleaned the area of my arm where I wanted it tattooed as I closed my eyes. As I felt the needle press against my skin, I thought of what Lana got.

After being still for forty-five minutes, the light that was on us dimmed. I squinted my eyes, only to be met by those familiar blue eyes.

"Hi." She towered over me.

"Hey, are you done?" I asked, and she nodded.

"Levi and I got matching tattoos. He's getting his done now." She looked over her shoulder and into the room where he was.

"All good, man. I'm assuming you know what to do since you got quite a few tattoos," Isaac said as he put on the see-through covering.

"Yeah, thanks." I sat up and observed the tattoo of my dad's name.

"All right, Gunner number one, you're next," Isaac sang as I got off the seat and put on my tee. Unlike me, Axel talked to Isaac the whole time while he was busy. I followed Lana to the corner of the shop where a big mirror was displayed on the wall.

"What tattoo did you guys get?" I looked through the room where Levi was. His stomach was on the seat with his shirt off while Kendra tattooed on the side of his hip. I turned to Lana, who raised her jacket. Through the see-through cover, I saw a small tattooed crown in black, and underneath it said "princess" in cursive.

"Levi suggested it. Since he's been calling me that for fourteen years." She smiled, then lowered her jacket.

"Cute, but as Sam said, you deserve to be a queen," I quoted as my mouth curved into a smile.

"You're funny, Blake." She shook her head. "What did you get?"

I held out my arm as she observed the black ink. She glanced up at me and smiled.

"Your dad?" she asked. I nodded.

"It's beautiful," she whispered as her fingers grazed over it. A flush crept up my face as I stood in front of the mirror and read it.

Damian Gunner
05-14-14

After we finished our tattoos and paid, Levi needed gas, so we stopped at a gas station. I sat in the car with Keene while Levi and Lana filled the tank and Axel paid.

"You know I'm gonna confess something…" Keene said as his whole face went blank. I sat up and looked in front to where he sat. "I once had a crush on Lana."

"No way." I laughed.

"True shit. She was sixteen and goddamn, bro. That's when puberty hit her." He cupped his hands and motioned to her breasts.

"What happened?" I laughed.

"Well, Levi was always with her, and plus I'm two years older than her. It was just a little crush," he said in a flat tone as I raised a brow.

"Wait…if you're twenty, then she's eighteen, and I'm seventeen," I sighed.

"No freaking way, you can do the math," Keene sarcastically gasped as I rolled my eyes.

"Well, yeah. When's your birthday?" he asked as we watched Lana and Levi.

"August fifth," I replied.

"You know it's weird. Levi's birthday is the nineteenth of June, and Lana's birthday is the si—"

"Sixteenth of June." I lowered my head.

"Yeah."

"So she lost her virginity to him at seventeen?" I randomly asked.

"Yep, at Jaden's party. Summer 2015," Keene mumbled. "In this very car."

A sudden chill crept up my spine as the thought of Levi and Lana having sex in here.

"Then the next day he left," I muttered.

"That's what she thinks," he said as I looked at him.

"What are you talking about?" I asked. He shook his head.

"It's not my place to tell. A lot happened after that party; he has a lot of fucking explaining to do." He glared at Levi.

"Does it have to do with the hole in his arm?" I asked.

"Nope, but it does have to do with your brother. The longer he waits to tell her everything, the more damage it's going to create," Keene stated as I gazed at him. I opened my mouth to ask him more but cut off when Levi got into the car. He started the car, then drove further away and into a parking spot. Levi got out and pulled his seat forward. Lana stood next to the car and looked at me.

"Come on." She held her hand out. I gave her a weird look as I accepted her hand. She pulled me out of the car and toward the gas station. We entered the store, and I glanced around. Besides the cashier that gave us strange looks, there was no one else here.

"What are we looking for?"

"A razor."

"What's the razor for?" I asked as we continued to walk.

"You'll see," she said, then stopped in front of the aisle and took a razor. After Lana got a few other things, we walked to the front cashier. He gave us creepy looks the whole time he served us. Lana gave him a crumpled-up bill, which must've been from the pool, and he glared at her. We walked back to the car. Lana stood in front of Levi and Axel. They stared at her while I joined Keene, who sat on the hood. I watched as she tossed the bag with the rest of the stuff she bought to Levi. He looked inside with a mischievous grin on and took out the box with the razor.

"The one with the batteries?" Levi asked as he smoked a cigarette.

"Yep." Lana smirked.

"Cool. Keene, you're getting a haircut," Levi said as he tossed the box to Keene.

"What? No, no, no. I'm not getting my head shaved by an eighteen-year-old girl." Keene scoffed as he threw the box back at Levi.

“Oh, come on, please? You do need a haircut,” Lana whined as she looked at him.

“Yeah, and I’ll get one at a barber. Not in front of some sketchy gas station,” Keene said as he jammed his hands in his pockets. They argued as I got off the hood and into the car. I looked at my phone and noticed that it was four-thirty in the morning. Axel got into the car and sat in the passenger seat while I looked at Keene. It seemed like he agreed to shave his hair off as Lana held the razor in her hand. Levi stood behind her and told her where to cut. I watched as his hand cupped over hers, and I instantly rolled my eyes.

“What’s on your mind, brother?” Axel asked as he lit a cigarette, then opened the window.

“Nothing,” I replied as I stared at them. Keene’s brown locks fell to the ground as he swore at them.

“Hey, don’t worry. She won’t see him and you’ll get her soon,” Axel assured me as I scoffed.

“You forget one thing: she has a boyfriend.”

“Stop worrying about that and just live in the moment. You’re a Gunner, and we always get what we want. I know you will; you’ll even get that kiss she still owes you,” he stated as we laughed. Once they were done, they got into the car with Lana and Levi in the back while Keene decided to drive. He had a freshly shaved head. Axel laughed as he poked it.

“Shut up,” Keene said as he shook his head and started the car.

“Where are we going now?” Lana yawned as she leaned back in her seat.

“Wherever the road takes us,” Axel answered as

he turned on the radio. I watched Levi swing his arm around her. He brought her to his chest, then turned to me. I watched as he put two fingers to his lips for a cigarette. I sighed as I took out two and lit mine, then gave him the other. He lit it with his Zippo, then took a drag. As the song played, he put the cigarette against Lana's lips. They continued to share the cigarette until Lana fell asleep on his lap.

"Dude, when are you gonna tell her?" Keene asked after a while.

"I don't know. She'll freak, though," Levi said.

"You do realize if we're not careful, she might find out, and that's worse than telling her," I muttered, then looked down at Lana, who moved.

"I'll tell her, don't worry. She's asleep now, though," Levi notified us, then caressed her hair. She continued to move, and I let out a grunt as I threw my cigarette out the window, then picked up her legs and put them on top of mine. I took her shoes off and threw the blanket over her.

"You had the whole winter break," Keene said through gritted teeth.

"Okay, I get it," Levi snapped as he glared at Keene. Everyone went silent after that except for Lana. Levi and I watched as she continued to twist and turn. She panted as she turned the other way so that her butt was right on my thighs. Her chest rose and fell with rapid breaths as Levi tried to wake her.

"*Lana, wake up!*" I yelled as she took sharp breaths. When I was about to pull the blanket off, she shot up and took deep breaths as her eyes widened. I watched in horror as she turned to me and mumbled something, yet I couldn't figure it out.

It lasted for fifteen seconds, then she collapsed into Levi's arms and fell asleep as if nothing happened.

***

After we drove for half an hour, we decided to rest. Keene stopped at a motel that seemed to be in the middle of nowhere. Axel and Levi got a room with two beds and said they'd drive for food while Lana rested. I carried Lana with the blanket wrapped around her. Keene had the key while he took her shoes.

"Here it is. Room 127." Keene sighed as he unlocked the door, then walked in. I went into the motel room and took in my surroundings. It had maroon walls and a turquoise ceiling, two beds against the wall with a table in the middle. It had pineapple covers with five pillows on each of them. There was a TV stand opposite and a desk next to it. I put Lana on the left bed and took off her jacket. I wrapped her in the blanket and placed a pillow under her head. "Hey, I'm gonna check the rest of the place out. You okay here with…" Keene trailed off as he looked at Lana.

"Yeah, I'll probably take a nap, too." I shrugged, then took off my jacket.

"Cool, see you soon," Keene said, then walked out the door. I let out a sigh as I sat on the edge of the other bed and stared at the TV. I noticed the bags formed under my eyes. I turned on the TV and flicked through the channels. It stopped by the music channel where random music videos played. I walked around and laid on the bed as "West Coast" by Lana Del Rey played. I placed my hands behind my back as I turned to look at my Lana. She looked so peaceful when she was asleep. I turned back and stared at the ceiling. My eyelids got heavier and heavier as the song played. As I closed my eyes, I felt a weight on my body. When I opened my eyes, I looked to see Lana wide awake as she straddled me.

"Lana, what are yo—"

"I can't sleep."

"Oh well, you can sleep here," I mumbled. She smiled as her blue eyes gazed into mine. Her hands went to her crop top, and I raised my hands. "Whoa, what are you doing?"

"Benny and I always cuddle like this." She giggled, then took off her crop top, which left her in her bra. I gave a stiff nod as she laid on my chest. I awkwardly wrapped my arms around her torso and brought her up so that her head rested beside mine. I felt her breaths on my neck as I turned my head. She looked at me, then placed her hand on my cheek. I bit the inside of my cheek as her hand went behind my neck and her fingers raked through my hair. "You've wanted to kiss me all night, Blake Gunner," she whispered as I stared at her lips. "What's stopping you now?"

"Nothing," I whispered, then pressed my lips against hers. While we kissed, she sat up and straddled me. I parted her lips because I craved for her, wanted her as my tongue slid across her lip. The kiss felt so different from our first one. The song echoed in the room, which made the atmosphere edgier as my hands trailed down her bare skin. I pulled her closer and placed my hand on her butt, then shifted so that I hovered over her. My hands went under her and made my way to her bra strap but immediately stopped because she wasn't sober yet and she had a boyfriend. "Lana, wai—" I stopped, but her finger wrapped around my chain as she pulled me closer and kissed me again. Her other hand traveled down to my shirt, and she tugged on it. I pulled it off, then roughly kissed her neck. Her fingers knotted in my hair as I grunted. I left soft kisses right down to her stomach and stopped at her belly button. I looked at her to see her throw her head back as I dragged my bottom lip up to her neck again. Her arms locked around my neck as I kissed her. Her hot plump lips mixed with my thin ones. Lana's one leg wrapped around me as she used her other to be on top again.

After a few minutes, we stopped, and our heavy breathing filled the room. Her head rested on my bare chest as she traced my tattoos. I had the other arm behind my neck as I went over the past events.

"Lana," I said in a low and hoarse tone.

"Hmm," she murmured, her fingertips against my skin, sending chills up my spine.

"Look, err…" I breathed out. "I had fun tonight, and I don't think we'll be having one like this in a long time so…we've had a rough past, done bad things, and even though we've known each other for, like, five months, you're one of the few people I trust, care about, and just enjoy being around with. After tonight, we're gonna have to face reality again."

"The bad sides of us have been locked away and

never spoken of, but it's slowly coming back."

"Yeah, and we can either let it define us or build us up," I said and thought about the past few months. "After everything we've been through, you have captured my heart, and I thi—I think I've fallen in love with you, Lana Willson." I looked down. Her fingers stopped as she turned and rested her chin on my chest. Her mouth curved into a smile as she stared at me with an unreadable look. "Don't look at me with those mesmerizing blue eyes and smile. That Lana smile that can get away with anything. That smile which is so strong and hypnotizing that you think it's real," I said and felt my face warm. "Say something, please," I grumbled. She crawled up, and I felt her lips brush against my ear. I stared at the ceiling as she placed her hand on my chest.

"Sometimes the heart knows stuff that the mind can never explain. Don't think, Blake. Just let your heart do all the talking," she whispered, then drifted off to sleep on my chest.

***

Lana

Tears streamed down my face as I ran in the rain. My makeup was smudged, and my pink dress clung to my body. I slowed down my pace, then ripped off my heels as I looked around. To hear the guys at Homecoming brought me to tears. I was angry, frustrated, and naïve. I couldn't believe they did that to me. And to think Parker was the one who set the whole thing up. He's a manipulative person who liked to stir up trouble. Now to stand and not know where I am because I ran off. The rain got worse as thunder echoed in my ears. I continued to run, but I didn't know where I was going. I saw a few cars as well as tall buildings and ran onto the sidewalk. My breaths quickened as I felt goose bumps on my arms. I noticed their stares and only imagined what they thought. I turned a corner for shelter and noticed I stepped into an alley. I backed away, and my body hit against the wall. When I turned my head, I was met by a man who smirked. As he opened his mouth to speak, my eyes snapped open, and I was met by a turquoise ceiling.

I raised a brow and sat up from the comfy surface. The same dream I had for the past week and I still didn't know what it meant. I looked over my shoulder to see Blake in another bed. It looked like he got up too because his hair was messy and his grey shirt was wrinkled. He looked at me, then squinted his eyes as he glanced around.

"I-I just had a dream," he mumbled.

"Join the club." I sighed and looked down to see that I was still in my party clo—wait, what happened to the party?

"Do you ever feel like something's so real then you wake and realize it was just a fucking dream?" he asked as I looked around the room.

"Yeah…wait, what did you dream of?"

"What were you dreaming of?" He raised a brow. I shook my head as I pulled the unfamiliar duvet off and grabbed my jacket. I put it on, then stood up but immediately regretted it as I felt a pain in my head.

"Why do I smell like chemicals? Where am I?" I asked as I rubbed my temples.

"We're in a motel room," Blake mumbled as he stood up.

"What? Why?" I demanded as I walked away from him. There was a door a few feet away from me. I pushed it open. I didn't know where I was and why I was with Blake. It must've been the back since it was an open area. I walked as I looked around. It must've been early morning since it was still dark, but in the distance, I noticed the purple sky.

"Whoa there, pumpkin, how many times do I have to save you?"

I instantly stopped and looked up to see Axel. I looked over his shoulder and understood why he stopped me. I would've fallen into an empty pool in which Keene skated.

"What the heck is going on?" I stepped back. Axel stared at me, then threw his head back and laughed. He spun around and pointed to Levi, who sat on the edge of the pool.

"She's sober, guys!" he announced as I shook my head, then walked around the pool to Levi. As I walked, I felt little sores on my feet. I sat next to him, then looked around at the run-down motel.

"What happened? Where's Benny?"

"Good morning to you too, princess. You're finally sobered after being so drunk, then sober, and then drunk again," Levi said. I glared at him, and he sighed. "We took you from the party, and we did a few things from the bucket list."

"What things?" I asked. He cleared his throat, then took out the paper and handed it to me. I took it and scanned through the things I remembered that weren't ticked. "No way I went to a paint party!"

"Yeah, Keene even swallowed an ecstasy pill." Axel laughed as I looked at Keene.

"Oh my god. Are you okay?" I looked at Keene, who stood in the center of the pool with the skateboard.

"Yeah, I'm fine," he mumbled.

"We also went to a cage fight which Axel fought in, street racing, indoor pool, and—"

"Whoa, are you okay?" I cut off Levi as I looked at Axel. Holy crap, so many dangerous things happened in the last few hours.

"I'm perfectly good, pumpkin."

"What else?" I put my palms flat on the ground as I swung my legs.

"Err…" he mumbled.

"Where are my shoes?" I looked down to my bare feet. "What happened to my heels? Don't tell me I—"

"Here they are," Blake said as he threw them from across the pool. My eyes widened as they came toward us. Levi raised his arms and caught them before they hit us.

"Thanks." I fake-smiled at Blake, who gave an awkward thumbs up, then walked back into the motel room. "What's wrong with him?" I narrowed my eyes.

"I don't know." Axel shrugged.

"Well, we gotta go. Still got a few things we can

do," Levi said, then stood up. I remained still as I tried to remember everything that had happened because something didn't feel right. We silently walked to the car, and I decided to sit in the front with Levi. I drank the bottle of water that Keene got for me when he checked out of the motel room.

"Okay, what do you remember last?" Keene asked from behind me.

"Err…the party obviously," I said, then smiled. "Then kissing Benny at midnight."

"Well, it's kinda good that you don't remember anything after midnight." Axel snorted as I raised a brow.

"What? Can we go home?" I whined.

"No. I got, like, six hours with you…please, princess," Levi cooed as he pouted at me.

"Fine." I huffed. Axel leaned forward and rested his arm on the seat. He sent me a dirty look as I smiled at him.

"Y'know what else happened at your boyfriend's party?" he asked. I squinted my eyes at him as he leaned in and whispered in my ear. "You gave Levi and my brother lap dances, pumpkin, and what a show it was."

I gave Axel a blank look as he smirked. I laughed, and Levi turned to me as well as Blake from the rearview mirror.

"That's a good one. I'd never give you two lap dances, especi—" I cut off when Axel shoved his phone in my face. I quickly scanned through it to see that he was on Instagram. It was Kelly's profile, and her recent post scared me. Why would she post that? It was a collage; I gave a lap dance to Blake and Levi. The third picture frightened me because I kissed my boyfriend in the same room. The caption didn't surprise me at all: *Hoe of the year goes to the Sheriff's daughter.* My eyes widened as I scrolled through the comments, which made me frown. I tossed Axel's phone back, and he caught it as I stared at the window. I hated it when I got drunk. I hated parties. Something bad always happened. I was a horrible girlfriend and, in general, an awful person.

"Are you okay?" Levi asked.

"No," I grumbled.

"Hey, at least you made out with your boyfriend after that, so it's a win-win situation," Axel said.

"I hate myself," I mumbled, then flicked through the mixtape that Uncle Griff made Levi and me when we were young. "Howlin for You" by The Black Keys came on, and I turned up the volume. The guys took it as a sign that I didn't want to speak, so we sat in the car with the music as we drove to the next thing on the stupid bucket list.

***

"Where are we going?" I asked as we walked up a hill. We drove for half an hour, then Levi stopped, which seemed to be in the middle of nowhere. No one answered me, and I sighed. I was the last one to reach the top, and I saw Levi's smirk. I followed his gaze and watched the cows as they ate grass. My eyes widened as I turned to Levi, who had a smirk molded onto his face. "Not happening."

"If I'm not mistaken, it is on the bucket list,

pumpkin," Axel mumbled beside me.

"I wrote that when I was like eight."

"But it's still on there," Levi said.

"Do you guys even know how to milk a fucking cow?" Blake asked as he stuffed his hands in his pockets.

"Nope," Levi and I said in unison.

"Yes," Keene said as we turned to him. "Don't ask."

"Lead the way, Keene Stoner," Levi said.

"Dude, I still can't believe your last name is Stoner." Axel laughed as we followed Keene to the cows.

"Shut it, Gunner," Keene grumbled as he grabbed the bucket that stood by the gate.

"Aren't we gonna get into trouble?" I looked over my shoulder and saw the farmer's house in the distance.

"Not if we hurry up," Blake mumbled. We stood in front of the cow that leisurely ate grass. I didn't like it one bit. Keene took the bucket and cautiously placed it underneath the udder. He squatted next to the cow, and I leaned in to see what he did. The cow smelled funny, or it was the shit a few feet away from us. Keene held his hand out, and Levi rummaged through the bag and took out Vaseline. He rubbed it all over his hands, then gave it back to Levi.

"Where'd you get that?" I whispered to Levi.

"You bought all of this stuff," he murmured as we watched Keene wrap his hands around two teats.

"How? When?"

"It doesn't matter. You even got this." He pulled

out a Playboy Deodorant spray.

"What the h—" I cut myself off as Levi sprayed himself. Blake watched us in amusement, which Levi noticed. He walked over to him and sprayed him too. It turned out the cow didn't like it and mooed loudly. My eyes widened as the other cows raised their heads from the grass and joined.

"Shit. Run!" Axel yelled. Keene stood up as we followed Blake and Levi, who already ran the other direction. Keene and I ran through the cows, and one almost kicked us. We continued to run for the next few minutes, and my feet ached in the heels. I stopped to catch my breath and to remove the heels. That's when I noticed that we were in a sunflower field. Most of the sunflowers died since the cold winter swept through, yet it kept me covered.

"Come on." Blake popped out of nowhere and grabbed my arm. He pulled me through the field to an abandoned barn where everyone else was.

"Well, that didn't go as planned," Keene muttered.

"No shit," Levi muttered as we walked into the barn.

"Hay!" Axel pointed to a stack of hay. Blake looked at his brother in disappointment, then shook his head.

"Sleeping in a stack of hay is on the list." Keene shrugged as he pulled his jacket off and put it on the hay.

"Yeah, I'm pretty beat." Axel yawned as he took off his flannel and used it as a pillow. The whole barn was filled with hay, so we spread out. I couldn't sleep, though, because I had too much on my mind. That dream I had got worse. Also, Levi would leave. As much as he annoyed me, I didn't want him to leave. I felt as if us two together didn't get much time alone. He'd go back to college, and I'd probably see him summer break or at the end of the year.

"Princess, you awake?"

"Yeah," I whispered, then heard footsteps.

"Follow me," he whispered as I got up. As I walked out of the barn, I noticed Axel and Keene hugged each other. Blake had his back facing me as he curled up into a ball. I walked out of the barn to see Levi run into the field. I grabbed my phone and took a picture as I followed him. The deeper I walked, I seemed to lose him, so I decided to take more pictures.

"Levi, where are you?" I called out as I put my phone back in my pocket. As I walked through the dead flowers, I tried to find him. Out of nowhere, I was pulled down onto someone. I hovered over Levi, who grinned. "Idiot." I laughed and rolled off him. We laid in the field with dead sunflowers hanging over us. I let out a sigh and turned to him. I stared at the bird tattoo on his neck, then at his eyes. "I'm gonna miss you," I confessed as he turned to me. He had a sad look in his eyes but still held a smile.

"Me too, but we'll see each other…soon." He whispered the last part, then looked up at the sky. "I hope you had an amazing time."

"Yeah, even though I can't remember half of it." I sighed, then felt his palm brush against my hand.

"Look, when you do remember," he said as I

looked at him, "just know that I-I love you, okay?"

He waited for me to say it in the same tone and same way. My eyes bored into his as the corner of my mouth turned up and responded, "Love you too."

"You know after the pool, we got arrested. Well, Keene, Blake, and I, while you and Axel were out God knows where," Levi began, and I felt his fingers entwine with mine. "It was actually the first time I enjoyed being in a prison cell. We just talked." I laughed at the thought, then a sudden reminiscence entered my mind when I sang "Miss Jackson" in Axel's flannel. "Blake's not a bad guy, you know."

"Yeah, but what's up with him?" I asked.

"I don't know. When we're hanging out, he sometimes spaces out for a while," he mumbled. "He's sorta short-tempered, but he's caring."

"Yep."

"While you were drunk, he was by your side the whole time."

"Oh."

"Yep," he added, then held my chain. "He gave you this."

"Yep," I said as he played with it.

"You do know that his is from Connecticut and yours is from Minnesota."

"So?"

"You'll understand, princess, soon." He laughed. "Wanna go home?"

***

The drive home was an hour long, and Blake offered to drive. It felt short because most of us slept. We dropped Keene off, then turned to the Gunner household. It was weird because their goodbyes to Levi were rather short. Levi and I got home, and thankfully Dad wasn't home yet from his night patrol. Our parents were still asleep, so we snuck into the house and to my bedroom. Levi showered while I helped him pack, typical that he left it for the last minute. While I put his shoes in the case, he walked out of the bathroom with a towel draped around his waist. I took out my clothes and was ready to enter the bathroom until I felt him pull me back.

"Hey, you might want to take that off now," he said as he placed his hands on my hips. I followed his gaze and saw a bandage on the left side of my hip. He rubbed his hand on it, then slowly took it off to reveal a tattoo. My eyes widened as I walked to the mirror and turned my body to stare at it.

"What the hell is this?" I demanded as I stared at the black ink on the side of my hip.

"It's a tattoo, princess. See? I got one too." He smiled as he stood next to me and leaned his body toward me. Our tattoos touched, and it formed a full crown that read Prince and mine, princess, but together it said, Princess.

"Oh my God," I gasped at the tattoo.

"It was on the bucket list since we were like thirteen, fourteen. When we saw Uncle Griff's tattoo, you immediately wanted one," Levi said as he straightened his posture and stared at me through the mirror. "Just gently wash it then use the ointment in the bathroom. It's by the sink." Levi brought me back as he touched my tattoo.

"Yeah, err…thanks," I whispered, then grabbed my clothing. I did as Levi told me and took a nice warm shower. I washed all the pool chemicals out of my hair, then walked out. I put on my underwear, then a white tank top, pink sweater, blue jeans, and white Converse. I dried my hair, took out my contacts, and put on my glasses. By the time I was done, everyone was downstairs. No one talked at the table since it's our last meal together. After breakfast, I sat in the living room with Levi as I watched him pack up.

"Levi dear, what about your dirty laundry?" Jade asked as she came into the room with a bag.

"I'll leave it here, Mom. Lana will keep it for when I come again." He took it from his mother and handed it to me.

"And when exactly do you plan on coming again?" She glared at him. I sat on the La-Z Boy and strummed Levi's guitar as I watched the two. Levi gave his mother a stern look, and she threw her hands up. "Goddammit, Levi Ramone Radcliff!" she huffed, then walked into the kitchen and called her husband.

"What was that about?" I asked.

"Nothing. Mom's just overreacting." He wrinkled his nose. Out the corner of my eye, I saw Dad walk toward the front door. There were voices followed by footsteps, and I looked up to see Uncle Griff.

"Hey, guys," he greeted.

"Hey, Uncle Griff," Levi and I said in unison.

"So, Lana, are you gonna miss this idiot?" Uncle Griff asked as Levi looked up.

"Yeah." I awkwardly chuckled as they shared looks.

"Let me help you," Uncle Griff said as he helped Levi with the last few things. As I played his guitar, I heard voices from the kitchen. The only words I made out were: stay, no, future, and she.

"Lana," Levi called out as I turned my head to him. "I think I forgot one of my jeans up in your room. Can you check, please?"

I gave a short nod, then put his guitar down and walked out of the room. I still heard voices from the kitchen, but Uncle Griff's voice topped all of them.

"What the hell are your jeans doing in her room?" he asked, and I laughed as I walked upstairs. Out the corner of my eye, I saw all the adults wander into the living room. I continued to my room. My room was right above the living room, so I made out the voices. I crouched down and leaned my ear on the wooden floor to hear. I was curious.

"You're putting my daughter in grave danger, Levi!" Dad exclaimed.

"He came out of nowhere and just started talking to us. They had guns and everything. If there was something I could have done, I would have, and you all know it!" Levi hissed.

"Did you at least tell her?" Griffon asked as I rolled my eyes.

"No, she was freaking out, and when he left, she yelled out, 'Where is he?' and 'What do you want?' It was honestly scary seeing her like that," Levi replied as I squinted my eyes. Little bits of me yelling flooded my mind. Blood splattered everywhere as the person collapsed to the ground. My features softened as the memory of James came back. How Levi comforted me after I yelled and I was going to tell him everything.

I stood up and grabbed Levi's ripped jeans that hung on my door. I walked down and heard their muffled voices. When I entered the living room, everyone stopped to look at me. I held a poker face as I walked to Levi and gave him his jeans. "Thank you," he whispered, and I nodded as I sat back down. I looked at my dad, who ran a hand through his hair in frustration, probably at the thought of James. Richard and Griffon glared at Levi while Jade and Angie whispered to each other.

"Come on; we gotta hit the road." Richard broke the silence. Levi nodded as he began to lock his bags. All the adults piled out of the room, and Griffon went to help Richard load the car. I walked over to Levi and helped him.

For the next twenty minutes, the house was silent for some unknown reason. Levi didn't talk as I helped him put stuff into his car. I stood on the porch and watched as Levi greeted Uncle Griff. I gave my farewells to Jade and Richard, and they were already in their car as Mom and Dad spoke to them. They hugged each other one last time as Levi slowly approached me.

"Well, this it, princess." He walked up the porch and stood in front of me.

"Yeah, all the best, and enjoy college," I mumbled because I didn't know what to say.

"Yeah, and I promise that we'll talk and FaceTime a lot." He pulled me in for a hug. I wrapped my arms around his neck as he whispered in my ear. "Promise me one thing." I pulled away yet his hold on my waist tightened as I looked up at him. "That you'll keep working and striving to get into Yale. It's your dream school, princess." I smiled. "Also on the very first bucket list we made. So at least one of us will leave Illinois happy."

"Promise," I said as he wiped away a tear with his thumb. I looked over his shoulder and noticed Uncle Griff watched us with a stone hard look. I glanced back at Levi, who smiled at me, then let go. As he walked down the porch, the corner of my mouth tugged up in a smirk. "Goodbye, my knight in shining armor," I said. Griffon laughed as Levi spun around and gave me a sad smile. I watched as he ran, picked me up, and hugged me.

"Love you," he mumbled as my legs wrapped around him.

"Love you too," I whispered as a tear rolled down my cheek, and I thought what would happen if we saw each other again.

Chapter Eighteen

Lana

Our break was short, and it's back to school. I regret not spending a lot of time with Levi because I missed him. At least he has kept his promise, and we've spoken a lot. The past few days I spent getting ready for school, finishing work, and going on dates with Benny. He hadn't said anything yet about Levi or me when I left his party, but then I checked my phone and saw that Keene texted him that night. That was a crazy night from what I could remember, but it was also one of the best nights of my life.

"Morning, Dad." I sat at the table. He spun around and placed a cup of coffee in front of me, then sat down.

"Morning. Your mother just left. She has an early operation."

"Okay."

"Excited for school?"

"Nope."

"I know you aren't. I never was, but it's the last semester. It's crucial, Lana. Griffon will help you as much as he can, but most of it's on you."

"Don't worry, Dad. Have I ever disappointed you?" I asked, then rethought the past few years. "Wait, don't answer that."

"Yes, you have, Lana, and you know it." Dad shook his head.

"I'm sorry, Dad. I don't even remember much from Jaden's party. All I did was go with Keene, Miranda, and Levi. We were having a very good time, then…" I trailed off as I tried to remember what happened after I let Levi take my virginity in his car. We arrived at the party early, so he parked his car in the garage so it was the perfect place, I guess, all alone, away from everyone else with The 1975 echoing in the car. "Levi and I left because he wanted to go somewhere, and…from there I don't remember anything,"

Dad let out a sigh, then stood up to put his mug in the sink. I silently drank the rest of my coffee as I watched him.

"I'm just glad you're safe," he whispered, then kissed my forehead. I stood up and put my cup in the sink. I spun around when he put on his jacket. I stood in front of him and fixed his collar as I avoided eye contact. "Listen, err…Levi told me about what happened on New Year's with James." I gaped. "As witnesses, you all need to come in for questioning. We found the body."

"What? Where?"

"At the park and it wasn't pretty. He was hung upside down on a tree," Dad hissed as I closed my eyes for a moment and tried to remember his face.

"When should we come?"

"After school will do," Dad said with a sad smile, then sighed. "I'm sorry you have to go through this, honey. I just want to get him and keep you safe. Heaven knows what else he's planning."

"You'll get him, Dad. You have to, and I know you will," I said, then hugged him. Benny's car honk broke the silence as I pulled away. I looked up at Dad and watched him sigh.

"Listen, now that you have a boyfriend, I don't want any distractions, okay?"

"Yes, Daddy." I pursed my lips as I grabbed my bag and walked out of the kitchen. I got into Benny's car, greeted him, then kissed the corner of his mouth. Usually, he'd turn while I closed the door, but he stared straight ahead. I gave him a weird look as we drove.

"Do you know what I just realized?" he asked after a while.

"What?" I asked and turned to his blank expression.

"A few days ago, you gave Levi and Blake lap dances. I had a few drinks, you were drunk as fuck, and I just…" He trailed off as he slowed the car down and parked against the sidewalk. "Fuck!" He hit his palms against the wheel. My eyes widened as I looked at his hands, then him. Benny turned to me, then leaned forward as he placed a hand on my cheek. He pressed his lips against mine, and I quickly responded when I kissed him back. He leaned his forehead against mine as he looked at me, then my lips. His thumb caressed my cheek, then moved to my chin as he stared at me. "You're mine. Okay?" He pecked my lips. I smiled at him as I bit the inside of my cheek and nodded. "Good." Benny started the car again and we drove to school. The rest of the way I couldn't stop grinning and biting my lip. To think he stopped to give me a proper kiss and said I was his. I didn't want to squeal or he'd think I was weird.

Benny parked the car, then turned to me. A wide grin plastered on my face as he smirked and leaned forward. He parted my lips and kissed me as I smiled. "I just want to kiss you all day," he whispered, then slowly bit his lip. He was about to lean in and kiss me again, but I quickly spun around because I felt as if I was being watched. I put a hand to my chest and rolled my eyes when I saw Liam. Benny cussed under his breath as I got out of the car. I glanced up at the brunette, who smiled.

"Creep," I muttered as Benny approached us.

"The windows were tinted!" Liam beamed.

"Yeah," Benny and I said unison as we walked.

"Smile!" Liam caught up to us as he held up a camera, then took a picture of us. "It's for the yearbook."

"Oh wait, retake it. You never get my good side," Aidan said behind us. We spun around and watched him pose.

"What a photobomb, dude," Liam snorted as he showed us the picture. It was a perfect picture of Benny and me, but Aidan seemed to pop out of nowhere. He jumped in the background, so he looked like an idiot with his mouth wide open and arms raised. We laughed as we walked up the stairs and into the crowded hallways. I saw Miranda and Melissa by the lockers, and I went to them while Benny greeted Nick and Marcus.

"Hey, guys," I greeted as Miranda rummaged through her locker.

"Hey, guys? That's all you say?" Melissa demanded as she held her phone in her hand.

"Hello?"

"I follow this account on Instagram that shows all the raves, silent discos, and frat parties. Guess who I found on their profile?" Melissa asked as she tilted her head at me. Miranda looked at the picture and glared at me. I raised a brow then snatched Melissa's phone to look at the picture. My jaw dropped when I saw Blake and me at the paint party. "Your hands are literally all over each other."

"I was drunk, okay? Also I had a strange craving for meat," I mumbled.

"Meat?" Miranda stated as she stared at me.

"Yeah. I know, right? Weird."

"You didn't do any drugs, right?" Miranda asked, and I shook my head.

"No, just Keene, but he's okay, just bald," I replied. Melissa gasped as she started to mumble out words. A hard look filled her features as I stared into her blue eyes.

"Paint party…shaving heads. You guys did the bucket list, didn't you?" she squealed.

"Yeah, not everything though, just the important stuff." I giggled.

"Wait…I still wanna know who you dressed up in sexy lingerie for?" Miranda asked as she shut her locker then leaned against it.

"My boyfriend, obviously," I said as Melissa gave me a look.

"Really?" they asked in unison as I rolled my eyes.

"Yes! You even made me wear it to his party." I pointed to Melissa. Marcus and Benny came and stood on either side of me, and I looked up at Benny.

"Right?" I asked.

"Huh?" He squinted his eyes.

"Just say yes." I sighed as I noticed Melissa's grin.

"Yes." Benny dragged as he gave me a weird look.

"Told you." I pulled my tongue at Miranda, who rolled her eyes.

"Yo, guys, we got assembly," Ethan called as he approached us.

"Ugh, what do they want now?" Marcus groaned as he swung an arm around Miranda's shoulder.

"Discussing the semester." Ethan chuckled as he shoved his hands in his pockets. We walked to the school's auditorium as I held hands with Benny. My phone vibrated, and I pulled it out to see that Melissa tagged Blake and me in the picture. I glanced up and noticed the smirk on her lips. I scoffed and shoved my phone in my pocket. We entered the auditorium and noticed seniors had already taken their seats. I followed Benny to the center, where I sat next to him and Aidan. Miranda and Melissa sat behind us with their boyfriends, while Tiffany sat next to Aidan and Ethan sat beside Benny. Out the corner of my eye, Aidan slowly entwined his fingers with Tiffany. Miranda leaned forward as I turned to them.

"So are you two finally a thing?" Miranda asked, and we turned to look at them.

"Yes. You had your chance, Stevens," Aidan said and put his hand over Miranda's face, then pushed her away so he could kiss Tiffany. I laughed as Miranda scrunched her nose up and rubbed her forehead. Marcus grinned as he cupped her cheeks and kissed her. I turned to Benny; he was speaking to Ethan, who scoffed.

"What's wrong?" I asked when I noticed the looks on their faces.

"Coach assigned us to the freshman and sophomores with basketball," Ethan grumbled.

"At least we're getting extra credit in P.E." Benny shrugged.

"So when will you guys be doing it?" I asked.

"After school and some periods in P.E.," Ethan answered. I nodded, then glanced up at Blake, Carter, and Liam, who sat in front of us. Blake winked as he motioned to his phone that had the picture Melissa tagged us in. I rolled my eyes, then turned to the front to see Principal West. He tried to hush the students, but nobody listened. Coach Harris stepped forward and yelled. Everyone grew silent after that, and the people in the front took deep breaths as they placed their hands on their chests.

"Thank you." Principal West nodded at Coach. "Graduating class of 2017. These next few months will be the busiest time of your high school experience," he said as everyone groaned. Out the corner of my eye, I noticed Aidan pulled out a small remote. I watched as he pressed a button, then the projector behind Principal West turned on. He continued to talk as Aidan hit another button. My eyes widened as everyone laughed at the picture of Principal West by the beach in a Speedo. Liam spun around and high-fived Aidan as they cheered. Principal West turned around and glared at the projector while Mr. Bronx and Coach Harris snickered. "Turn it off!" he yelled, but it went to the next picture, which was Coach and his pet fish Max. People laughed as they took out their phones and recorded. Coach glared at the image, then yelled louder than Principal West. I nudged Aidan, who sighed, then pressed another button. Instead, it changed to a picture that made the guys whistle. Last year, Miss Rosa was gone for a couple of months to Hawaii. Seeing the picture of her in a white bikini at the beach made the guys act like dogs. Carter stood up and raised his arms.

"The Lord is with us!" he exclaimed, then bowed to the picture. Griffon didn't find it funny as he scanned the students, then pointed with his index finger at Aidan and Liam. The final picture was of Mrs. Singleton. She was a rigorous, old fashioned teacher. Everyone laughed at the picture, which seemed to be her doing karaoke in a pantsuit. Aidan finally turned it off after everyone composed themselves. The teachers looked pissed as they glared at us. Principal West nodded as he approached the mic.

"Very well, whoever is responsible for that, it was a great laugh, and I'll let it slide since it's the first day back." Mrs. Singleton huffed. "As I said, we teachers will be looking for nominations for Valedictorian. Counselors will be available if you need help with your applications for college, and then there are finals. Now as we said before winter break, you'll receive new schedules. You'll collect them from your homeroom teacher on the way out."

I got my schedule from Miss Rosa and scanned through it. Not much had changed. I had new teachers for AP Biology and Elective classes. Instead of Calculus on Monday first period, I had AP Physics. I was happy with the days I had Study Hall but scoffed at P.E. on Friday.

"Hey, guess who's joining your Physics class?" Melissa stated as she held up her schedule.

"I thought you didn't take Physics," I said as we walked to class.

"Yeah, well, it was either this or Mrs. Singleton's Bio class, and I don't want that bitch all up in my face," she said as we entered the classroom. I stopped to see the desks had changed. The teacher's desk was still in the front, but our desks were on either side and faced each other. There was a significant gap in the middle that separated the four rows.

"Mr. Gorton, are you blind? The board is that way," Liam said. The teacher was drawing on the board. It was a sketch of the classroom and our seating plan. Each desk had a name on it, and people caught on as they went to find their desk.

"Why do we have a seating plan?" Melissa asked as I looked at the board to see that I sat next to her but in front.

"It's my classroom, and fascinating people are being put in my class," he said as we took our seats. I took out my stuff, then glanced up to see Blake and Carter opposite me. Melissa sat on my left while Erwin, who also wore glasses, sat on my right.

"Fascinating people," Melissa groaned as she watched Kelly and Austin walk in. Benny walked into the class and glanced at the board. He looked at me, then smiled as he sat behind me.

"Do you hate me?" Liam asked as Kelly and Austin sat on either side of him.

"Mr. Sanchez, I hate every one of you. Don't assume you're special," Mr. Gorton joked as he winked at Liam. "All right, class, settle down! I know you're eager to tell your friends what an excellent winter break you had, but it couldn't be better than mine, so let's move on." He wiped the board. "Get out a paper and pen because I'll explain how the semester will work. It's short, and I want to get through everything." Mr. Gorton took off his jacket and hung it over the chair. He stood in the middle of the class and glanced around. I pushed my glasses up to see him stare at Blake, who had his hands shoved in his pockets. "Blake, are you going to remember everything I say magically?"

"Sure." Blake shrugged as his lips drew into a straight line.

"Are you also going to get a degree one day magically?"

"I don't see yours anywhere."

"Oh yes, it's in my apartment on my wall, next to the other two. I'd bring it to school, but I wouldn't want suckers like you drooling over it," Mr. Gorton said as I bit the inside of my cheek. Blake threw his head back and let out a bitter laugh. Mr. Gorton rested his palms on Blake's desk, and the two glared at each other. "Listen, Gunner, you're in my class now. You follow my three simple rules." He held up three fingers. "Rule number one, you can cuss, but not louder than me. Rule number two, don't annoy me, and rule number three…I'm the teacher; you do as I say or get the hell out of my class." Kelly snorted. "Got something to say, Kelly?" His gaze locked on Blake.

"Nothing at all." Kelly faked a smile.

"For once." Melissa sighed as she rolled her eyes.

"Right, since that's cleared everyone, take notes. Every week we'll have a pop quiz. The reason I'm saying every and not once is because I might give you every lesson just for the fun of it." We groaned. "Every third week up until finals we'll have a practice test on the units we've done. We have to get through five units and revision of the whole year's work if you all want to pass." He looked around. "If you need teachers to reference for your applications, I'll be here every day after school. I'll be available on Tuesday and Thursday for Study Hall, so if you don't get anything during class, come ask me, or even after school," Mr. Gorton said as we wrote down notes. "Yes, Mr. Sanchez?" Liam looked down on his paper, then at the teacher.

"What did you say after 'take notes?'" he asked. Everyone groaned.

***

Benny and I sat down at our regular cafeteria table, and I realized mostly everyone was here. Liam stood up again and took pictures of us.

"Can't you take one of the other people?" I pointed to everyone else.

"I wanna make this yearbook good. Have a separate page just for us." Liam winked, then looked down at the picture. "Would you guys stop photobombing?" he groaned as he looked behind us. I followed his gaze to see Carter and Marcus.

"Whoa," Carter said as he stared at the picture.

"What?" Marcus asked as he looked too.

"I look good." Carter grinned then took a seat. I playfully rolled my eyes as I ate my fruit salad. I glanced up to see Aidan and Blake laugh as they approached the table.

"Where'd you get the pictures, though?" Blake asked as he sat opposite me.

"Principal West's office computer," Aidan said as Miranda gaped at him.

"Oh my god, and he had a picture of Miss Rosa." She grimaced.

"I think it's more disturbing that he had a picture of Mrs. Singleton," Ethan said as we cringed.

"We took a family picture once, and Bethany was missing. We found her in the kitchen with a block of cheese," Liam stated as he looked at us. "I think that's where it all started."

"How old is your cousin?" I thought of the girl obsessed with cheese.

"Twenty-two." He smiled, and we stared at him.

"I think she'll be perfect for Axel," Blake confessed as we laughed. Out the corner of my eye, I noticed Jennifer standing up across the cafeteria. She spoke, but nobody heard her. Parker took something out of his pocket and threw it on the ground. It made a loud crack noise, which caught people's attention.

"What now?" Aidan asked as he looked at Parker.

"Err…there has been some rumors going around, and I'd just like to, err…put an end to it," Jennifer began, and I knew what was coming. "For a year and a half, I have been stumped on my sexuality. But it's a new year, and well…I'm coming out as a proud lesbian. It's 2017. I shouldn't care what people think because this is me and I finally understand it."

A smile crept up my face as I looked around. Everyone went silent as they looked at Jennifer. It was understandable to expect a reaction because she's friends with Kelly, who quietly sat and stared at her friend. Jennifer looked around with a forlorn expression. I let out a sigh as I clapped. My friends turned to me with stunned looks. Jennifer gaped at me but immediately smiled as other people clapped too. She smiled, then took a seat. Everyone soon got back to his or her tables, and noise filled the cafeteria. I turned to Benny, who smiled at me.

"You did the right thing," he said, then pecked my lips. I felt something being thrown at me, and I snapped my head to Carter and Liam, who stared at us.

"Yo, have respect for us single blokes."

"Why do you say blokes?" Aidan asked Carter, who rolled his shoulders.

"My sister is studying in the UK, and when we FaceTime, she always says blokes. Damn, now she's growing on me," Carter explained, then looked around the cafeteria.

"When's the last time you got laid, dude?" Marcus asked.

"Obviously last night," Carter replied with a playful roll of his eyes.

"Same," Marcus blurted out, and I smirked at Miranda, whose eyes widened.

"Ooh," Blake and Carter hollered as the rest of us laughed. Marcus grinned as he swung his arm over Miranda's shoulder as she reddened.

The bell rang, and everyone rose to their feet. I swung my bag over my shoulder and walked out of the cafeteria. I followed Benny to the stairs, where he'd have Social Studies on the next floor. I kissed him on the cheek then walked down the hall to my locker. I opened my locker and took out my folder. Out of the corner of my eye, I saw Blake lean on the locker next to me.

"Hey, baby girl."

"Stop calling me that, I beg of you," I whined as I looked through my locker.

"Whatever you say, nerd."

"Listen, err…my dad wants you all to come to the station after school."

"Why?"

"Well, Levi told my dad what happened that night."

"Oh yeah, Levi told us that he would tell your

dad."

"That's funny, he didn't tell me anything."

"Well, maybe he just didn't want you to worry."

"Yeah, but it doesn't matter now. They found the body, and we have to answer a few questions."

"How do they know that it's his body?"

"Levi must've given a description."

"Do you know what I just realized? You're older than me."

"What?"

"Yeah, your birthday is in June and mine is in August."

"What year were you born, Blake?"

"1998," he replied as I facepalmed.

"Oh my god, me too. I'm like two months older than you, Blake."

"Wait. What the fuck? Then why did I tell Keene I'm seventeen?"

"Because you're shit at math or a drunk doofus."

"Probably both. I had a couple of drinks that night, but it's cool, though. I dig older chicks."

"It's just two months, not much of a difference."

"Whatever you say, baby girl."

"Please stop calling me that!" I begged as he came closer.

"Why? You don't like it, baby?" I felt his breath on my neck. "Baby, baby, baby," he repeated as I threw my head back and groaned.

"Ugh!" I slammed my locker and started walking. "I'm supposed to be calling you baby, since I'm older!" I pointed out as he walked next to me.

"You're right…" He trailed off as a smirk tugged

at his lips.

“I-I was joking. I’m not going to call you that.”

“Aww, but with the whole age thing, it’s just numbers.”

“Yeah.”

“Like distance and height, they’re all just numbers, right, man?” he asked as Carter stood on my other side. I looked over my shoulder and wondered where he came from.

“Yeah.” Carter shrugged, and I instantly felt short as the two looked straight at each other.

“Dude, she’s older than me.” Blake pointed at me.

“Bro, older chicks are cool,” Carter said as his face brightened.

“Oh my god, it’s just a couple months. What other ‘older chicks’ do you guys know?” I looked at them. Blake and Carter smirked at each other, then nodded.

“Miss Rosa!” they said in unison, then high-fived each other over me.

“That’s just creepy.”

“So you’re telling me that you are not one of the girls in Calculus who check out Mr. Bronx?” Carter asked as he looked at me.

“Yes! It’s weird. I’ve known him for, like…forever.”

“Right.” Blake and Carter dragged as they winked at each other.

“Mr. Halls, get in here right now!” Miss Rosa scolded as we walked past her classroom.

“The beauty awaits.” Carter sighed as he fist-bumped Blake, then walked off.

"So let me get this straight…we're both eighteen, right?" Blake asked as we walked to Photography class.

"Yes, Blake. Are you sure you're not high?"

"I don't know. The guys came over last night, and you know anything can happen with them." He winked as he opened the door to let me in.

"I thought you're slowing down on the cigarettes and stuff?"

"You said five a week, I've only had two so far," he said as I glanced up to see Melissa sitting with someone else. She smirked and gestured to the table in the back, being the only empty table left.

"It's only Monday." I narrowed my eyes at Blake.

"No shit, Sherlock, and tomorrow will be Tuesday," Blake sarcastically said as we sat in the back of the class. Melissa spun around and gave an innocent smile as her eyes flicked to Blake then me.

"I heard we're getting our results for that unique project," she said as Mr. Dockwell entered the classroom.

"I only sent mine in a few days ago. Change of interest, I guess," I admitted.

"Same," Blake chimed in.

"What changed your mind?" Melissa asked as she wiggled her brows at me and gestured to Blake, who was on his phone. I squinted my eyes, then shook my head as I leaned forward to tell her. Mr. Dockwell cut me off as he spoke. I leaned back in my seat as Melissa spun around.

"As promised, I said I'd give your unique assignments back. Some of you sent them over the winter break, and I managed to mark them," he said as he handed out the assignments. "I'm glad that you have understood photography terminology and used it well in your assignment."

"An A. Thanks, Mr. D!" Tyler said. Mr. Dockwell squinted at him.

"Please, class, don't call me that. Mr. Dock is fine, but not Mr. D."

"Why? Are you saving the 'D' for someone else?" Blake asked as my eyes widened. Mr. Dockwell grinned as he slowly nodded; he quickly fisted bumped Blake, then walked to the front of the classroom. "I think I like him more than Mr. Bronx." Blake laughed as I playfully rolled my eyes.

"As some of you heard from Principal West, these next few months are imperative. We have to get through a lot, and the first thing we'll be doing is a test," the teacher said as I wrote down notes. "Just a small test on the history of photography and parts of the camera." I sighed in relief.

"Indeed, since it's next Friday, I am giving you time to study. Those of you who haven't finished your assignments, do so now or fail." He walked to his desk. Melissa spun around and snatched my assignment before I'd even looked at it. I threw my hands up, and Blake laughed as he scanned through his. I watched as Melissa slowly turned around with her jaw dropped. She looked at me, then Blake. I watched as Melissa quickly took Blake's assignment, and I laughed at him. We waited for a while, but it didn't look like she'd give it back. Blake took my laptop and put in his earphones. He put one in, then turned to me with a cheeky smile. I looked down and noticed he offered me to listen. I put it in and smiled at the rock music. I watched as he put the laptop between us, then slouched in his seat as he leaned on my shoulder. I felt uncomfortable and shifted in my seat, then placed my arm on his chair. He whipped out his phone, then brought up the picture of us at the paint party.

"Should I make this my background?" he asked as I looked down.

"No way, that's just weird." I laughed.

"Aww, but I like it," he cooed as I watched him save the picture. Melissa spun around, and Blake and I looked up. "What? Haven't seen two friends hanging out before?"

"Oh no, it's cool," she said, then raised her phone and took a picture. Before I reacted, she winked at me, then spun around in her seat. While Blake chose another song, I checked my assignment. I stared at the photograph that I'd taken. It was of Levi when he ran through the field of sunflowers. I caught up with him and took a quick picture as he spun around. The corner of his eyes were crinkled as he laughed. His leather jacket blew in the wind as he ran a hand through his hair; it looked even better since it was in black and white. My phone vibrated, and I took it out to see that Melissa had sent me a picture. I thought it'd be the one she just took, but it was Blake's unique assignment. The image brought back the memory of me when I stood by the pool as he took pictures of me with the glow in the dark paint. The image itself was beautiful, especially the color of the pool in the background. I was brought back to reality when Blake rested his head on my shoulder again. I raised a brow at his song choice but went with it anyway as we listened to "West Coast" by Lana Del Rey.

***

Benny and I arrived at the station. Axel's car was already there. I took off my seat belt and opened the door. I was about to get out, but Benny pulled me back in. As I turned to him, he pressed his soft lips against mine. I smiled against his lips, then pressed my forehead against his. I didn't want to go to the station anymore. I wanted to be with my boyfriend. I wanted his soft lips on my neck and my fingers in his hair. I parted my lips, wanting to kiss him again, but I knew that if we did, I'd be late.

"Thank you. See you tomorrow," I whispered, then quickly pecked his lips. I grabbed my bag and got out of the car. As I walked through the front doors, I looked over my shoulder and waved at Benny. He smiled through the window, then waved back as I watched him drive away. When I walked into the busy reception area, I saw Miss Jackson at her regular desk. "Hey, Miss Ja—"

"I know. They're all waiting in your dad's office." Deputy Paul pointed.

"Err…thanks." I walked down the corridor. Deputy Paul gave me a firm nod as I walked past him and into Dad's office. Axel and Keene sat on the sofa while Blake leaned against the desk.

"Hey, pumpkin." Axel waved with a bright smile.

"Hi, guys." I saw that my dad wasn't here yet. I sat in front by his desk, and Blake sat next to me while we waited. None of us spoke as I thought over that traumatizing moment. At that moment in the back of my head, I knew James would do something like that. He'd do anything not to get caught but still leave little clues. Dad called each of us, one at a time, to the interrogation room. Once we finished, we returned to his office again. He decided to question us once more all together. I knew what he tried to do. To see which once spoke first so that the others wouldn't be surprised at their answer.

"Right, the sooner we get this done, the better. I want to make sure I got everything, okay?" Dad asked as he walked into the office and shut the door. "So you guys were driving, then this guy stopped you and wanted to race Levi's car," Dad began as we nodded. "Levi accepted just for fun, but then you had to drive."

"Yes," I said as Dad sat behind his desk.

"Did you win?" he asked. The corners of my mouth pulled up in a smile as I nodded. "That's my girl," he mumbled, then cleared his throat as I giggled.

"Moving on. James appeared with two guys behind him. What were they wearing?"

"James wore a suit, but the other two guys were dressed in black," Keene answered as he stood behind me.

"When the guy got shot, what happened next?" Dad asked, and I looked down.

"He stood on the man and said it's not the first

time that some of us are seeing blood coming out of a head…or something like that." Blake shrugged as I picked my nails.

"Then he approached your daughter, Sheriff, but Levi stood in front of her th—"

"Then he whispered something to Levi, causing him to back off," Blake cut off Axel. I looked up and noticed Dad stared at his notes.

"Dad, did Levi tell you what James said to him?"

"Err…yes, but let's just stick to the story, okay?" Dad said as he motioned for us to continue.

"His men had guns so we couldn't do anything. H-he, err…he stroked Lana's cheek and sa—"

"Sheriff, sorry to disturb you, but I've just been to the…" Detective Kale interrupted as he entered the room. He stopped mid-sentence, then glanced at us. "Well, well, look who we have here."

"What is he doing here?" Blake demanded as he eyed Detective Kale. No one answered as Detective Kale turned to my dad.

"You didn't tell them yet?" Detective Kale asked, then let out a bitter laugh as my dad shook his head.

"Tell us what?" Blake demanded as he gripped the chair. Detective Kale sniggered as he walked to Blake. He crouched down so that he was eye level as Blake glared at him.

"Haven't you heard, Gunner?" he asked as his eyes flicked to me, then Blake. "Sheriff Willson and I are working together, and things are finally starting to add up."

Chapter Nineteen

Lana

When we walked out of the station, my face drained of color. Detective Kale and my dad worked together to find not only James but Jack too! After Detective Kale told us that, he said we might come in for a few more interrogations. The creepy thing was he looked at me the whole time. The last thing we told him was what James said when he walked away. He mentioned two names, Mike and Christo. I knew Mike was the one in my room, but I didn't know Christo. I glanced and noticed Blake walked ahead of us. He was pissed the minute Detective Kale entered the room. I looked over to my shoulder at Axel and Keene.

"Aren't you going to talk to him?" I asked Axel.

"Do you really think he'd listen to me, pumpkin? I might be his brother, but he doesn't listen to just anybody," Axel replied as I sighed. I turned back to Blake, who crossed the road. Keene placed a hand on my shoulder and motioned me to follow him. I rolled my eyes as he gave me a supportive smile.

"Blake!" I called out as I crossed the road. Once I reached the other side, he stopped at the corner of a coffee shop. There was a bench in front of it, and he sat down. As I walked to him, I let out a sneeze. He looked up as I approached him and sat down. "You hate Detective Kale, don't you?"

"What gave you that idea?" he sneered as we stared at the station opposite us. "When I got arrested, he'd always look after me. He also talked to me because he knew my father died," Blake said, then let out a dry laugh. "I thought he felt sorry for me, but apparently he had a thing for my mom."

My eyebrows rose as I turned to him. I watched as he took a cigarette out and put it between his lips. It'd be hard to get him to stop. It was only Monday, and it was his third one.

"He didn't just talk to me, Lana. He didn't like that I was a delinquent, so one Saturday night, it was just us two in the building, and he beat me up."

"Why didn't you tell anyone?"

"Who could I tell? No one would believe me," he stated. "Then one day I was drunk as shit and knew where he was patrolling, so I went there and beat him too."

"What happened?"

"I got sent to juvie for beating a cop, obviously," Blake answered, then took a drag.

"How long did you stay?"

"A month. Momma came to the rescue and said I was dealing with a lot of grief from Dad's death."

"I-I'm sorry you had to go through all of that," I whispered as we locked eyes.

"I'm sorry you had to deal with Parker," he said. I nodded, then turned away to Axel and Keene. They spoke by the car. Out the corner of my eye, I saw Blake throw his cigarette on the ground and crush it with his shoe. He stood up and turned to me. "Come on, we'll take you home."

We rose to our feet. We walked across to Axel's car and got in. I sat in the back with Keene as we drove out of the station. Blake flicked through the radio, and I knew he was pissed, since he missed quite a few good songs.

"Heard from Levi yet?" Keene asked as he shuffled closer.

"Yeah."

"So I'm assuming he didn't tell you," Keene stated, and I noticed how Axel and Blake looked at us through the rearview mirror.

"Tell me what?" I asked as the car went silent.

"We don't even know the full story, pumpkin," Axel sighed as I tilted my head.

"Well, tell me what you know," I demanded as I thought of the other day when Levi said the things he did in California were bad and he wasn't ready to tell me.

"It won't make sense!" Blake hissed.

"Shit, sorry," I muttered. Keene awkwardly tapped my shoulder, and I turned to him. He swung his arm around the seat and leaned in to whisper.

"Levi Radcliff should be the one to tell you; it's his story," he whispered as I watched Blake rest his arm on the window.

"When?" I asked.

"Don't worry. You'll see him soon." Keene

winked at me as I narrowed my eyes at him.

"Pumpkin, do you know her?" Axel asked. I raised my head. I didn't even realize we were on my street. I leaned forward to see someone knocking at our front door. The car came to a stop, and we got out of the car. I approached the woman only to recognize that it was Linda, my neighbor. Mom somehow didn't like her; that's why she didn't want to answer the door on Christmas Eve. She gave me cookies to give her children because Linda loved to show off her five children and how she had the "perfect" family.

"Err…hello," I said as Linda spun around.

"Lana! Oh my gosh!" she squealed as she ran down the stairs and engulfed me in a hug. I awkwardly patted her shoulder as she squeezed me. Axel walked around and stood behind her as he gave me a questioning look. "I thought you were in there," she said, finally releasing her grip on me.

"I don't understand. Why are you here?" I asked.

"I was just walking my children home from school, and as I walked past your house, I saw someone trying to break in," she stated as my eyes widened.

"Why didn't you call her dad?" Blake asked.

"Well, the guy was on the tree by your window, and I started to yell. I think he noticed, so then he just jumped down and drove off," she explained as I let out a sigh of relief.

"Did you at least get a good look at the guy?" Keene asked.

"Oh no, he was dressed in black, but he seemed quite tall, like maybe six foot two or something."

She smiled.

"You said 'drove off.' What did his car look like?" Blake asked.

"Well, I don't know much about cars. I think it was black, or it could be those dark blue cars that you think is black, but it's those dark green ones, but when it's in the sun it looks black," she said as I stared at her.

"Okay then," Axel dragged out as he stuffed his hands in his pockets.

"Err…thank you, I'll let my dad know."

"No problem, Lana, just glad you weren't in there. Wonder why he wanted to go through your window." She laughed, then walked off.

"That woman is officially crazy," Axel stated as we watched her walk into her house across the street. I glanced back at my home and wondered who could've tried to break in, and only one person came to mind. James. Axel handed me my bag, and I thanked him. I slowly approached the house and unlocked it. From the corner of my eye, I noticed Blake towering over me.

"Should I let your dad know, pumpkin?" Axel asked from his car.

"Yes, please," I said, then pushed the door open. When I walked in, everything seemed to be in place. I still felt Blake's presence as we walked through the house. I stood at the bottom of the stairs and noticed he gave me an assured look. I walked upstairs, and he followed.

"What if he wasn't climbing up but down?"

"I think she would've noticed, Blake."

"Really? She doesn't seem very bright," he

stated as I let out a chuckle. We stood in front of my door, and I anxiously stared at the doorknob. I glanced up at Blake, who already looked at me. He opened the door, and I closed my eyes for a second and hoped that I didn't see another shoe. Yet everything looked the same from this morning. I put my bag down, then glanced around my room. Blake walked to the window and glided his fingers over the windowsill. "No dust." He rubbed his fingers together.

"Yeah, and I always leave my window open at least a couple inches for ventilation." I looked at the closed window. "Well, he didn't take anything."

"Yeah, because he was probably looking for something," Blake stated as he looked around the room. I walked to my wardrobe, then opened it. I searched the drawers, but I only found Levi's clean laundry, which Mom placed in there a few days ago. I took out the familiar sweatpants.

"Err…you might've forgotten about this, but I just wanted to say thank you…again." I closed the drawer with one hand and held out his sweatpants with the other.

"Thanks," he mumbled as I felt him take the sweatpants. As I lowered my arm, he gripped it. He spun me around and pulled me in for a hug. His one arm wrapped around my waist as the other went around my shoulder.

"Wha-What's this for?" I asked as he let out a deep sigh.

"You looked pale at the station. You don't deserve to go through all of this," he began. "It's hard to relive that moment, especially when James stroked your cheek and said 'such a beautiful girl can cause so much damage'…Lana, what did he me—"

"Sshh." I cut him off as I wrapped my arms around his torso and pressed my head against his chest. I didn't want to tell him. Too many were involved. As I pulled away, his arms fell to my waist. I glanced up at Blake. My eyes widened as I slowly backed away, then cleared my throat. He dropped his arms. He shrugged it off as he shoved his hands in his pockets. "I-I think it's best to leave, Blake." My voice had dropped to a whisper. He had a stone hard look on his face as he nodded.

"Yeah, they're probably waiting," he mumbled, then spun around. We silently walked downstairs and to the front door. He opened the door and turned to face me. "Will you be okay here all alone?"

"Yeah, my mom will be home soon anyway," I said.

"Okay, then I'll see you in school." He walked off. I leaned on the doorframe as I watched him get into the car. Keene and Axel waved at me, and I returned the gesture. As the vehicle started, Blake looked at me with a poker face. They drove off, and I shut the door. I let out a sigh as I walked upstairs and into my room to start my homework. I tied my hair into a bun and walked to the bathroom. I placed my glasses on the sink and stared at myself in the mirror. The bags under my eyes showed again. The dream affected me, but I couldn't get the message it tried to tell me. I finally looked away and washed my face with cold water. I was going to wipe my face but noticed there was no towel hung up. I let out a sigh as I crouched down and opened the cabinet. When I took out a hand towel, I noticed something wasn't right. I squinted my eyes because I knew that he bought another one and always left it here, but I couldn't find Levi's hair gel anywhere.

***

Over the next few days, it was the same. Homework after homework and everyone was busy with their applications. Dad hadn't said anything about James or Detective Kale. I told him about the guy Linda saw, and he almost scolded her for not phoning him. I think Blake got the message that I had a boyfriend and learned to back off. We still talked, but he always sent awkward glances.

Today when I woke up, Levi wanted to FaceTime. I got ready as quick as possible so that I could talk before school. I sat by the desk in front of my laptop with a blanket wrapped around me as I spoke to him.

"I don't think Uncle Griff likes his job." Levi shook his head as I stared at him. He laid on a bed shirtless with his earphones in as he spoke to me.

"He loves his job, he just…hates the people who disrespect him."

"Yeah, Carter told me what a prick Blake was."

"When did he tell you?"

"Oh, we talk all the time," he said as his eyelids drooped.

"Are you tired? We can chat later. It must be really early there…" I trailed off as he gave me a weak smile.

"I'm perfectly fine, princess." I smiled as I sat crossed leg on my chair and pushed my glasses up, then snuggled into the blanket as I stared at him. "I-I heard you spoke to Detective Kale."

"Yeah." I nodded, then squinted my eyes. "Levi, how do you know James?"

"How do I not know the most wanted drug dealer in the US who played my friends?"

"Wait. You know about the whole Ethan's cottage and cocaine thing?"

"Yes. Yes, I do." He pressed a hand to his cheek as he leaned on his elbow.

"Oh okay," I mumbled.

"Hey, cheer up. They'll get the bastard. Besides, you have Keene, Axel, Blake, Carter, Ethan, and Aidan protecting you," Levi pointed out as I glared at him.

"You forgot someone," I reminded him.

"Who? I did mention Aid—oh! That weird kid…what's his name? Sam!" Levi said as he snapped his fingers.

"My boyfriend, Levi…Sam's brother."

"Oh, shit, you're still with him?"

"Yes! What the heck?"

"Hehe, jokes, princess. I know you're with him. I just don't want you to be with him."

"Well, I don't care. I like him a lot." I bit my lip.

"Don't do that lip action if you're not thinking of me," he said with a wink. I rolled my eyes, and we sat and laughed for a few minutes. I stopped and looked at the screen. I didn't even notice that he stopped and stared at me. An unreadable expression filled his face, but the corner of his lip pulled up in a smile. In the background, I heard voices, and Levi looked up. The person spoke, but Levi quickly cut them off when he said my name. I raised a brow as I heard the door shut, then Levi turned to me. "Look, err…I gotta go."

"Oh, okay."

"Love you, princess."

"Love you too," I murmured. He gave a small wave then ended the FaceTime.

***

When I walked into Biology, I sighed. I enjoyed the class, but Mrs. Singleton ruined it. I sat in the back with Benny on my right. The only other people in the class that I knew were Jennifer, Carter, and Marcus.

"Did you study?" Marcus asked as he sat in front of Benny.

"Of course, she could ask any one of us," Benny answered. At the start of every lesson, Mrs. Singleton asked us random definitions. Marcus learned that the hard way when he didn't study and got detention. I glanced around the classroom and looked for the familiar blond. He already stared at me with a concerned look. I raised my brow at Carter, and he stared, then turned to the front.

"Quiet! Everyone!" Mrs. Singleton hissed as she took the eraser and hit it against the board. I winced at the noise as my eyes narrowed. She took the attendance, and I glanced at Carter, who sat right in front as he tapped his fingers on the desk. I sank in my seat and whipped out my phone.

Lana: Hey you okay?

Carter: Yeah, I'm fine.

Lana: You sure?

Carter: Yep, it's just all this homework and stuff along with the colleges we want to go to…

Lana: Agree, but you're Carter freaking Halls. You can do it.

Carter: Thanks bro.

Carter: Can I call you bro? 0___o

Lana: Lol sure.

"Miss Willson, what do you think you're doing?" Mrs. Singleton's voice echoed throughout the classroom. My head shot up, and that's when I noticed that she was right in front of me. I quickly slipped my phone in my pocket, then sat up straight.

"Nothing," I replied.

"Very well then, if you're going to lie…what is the definition of a primary structure?" she asked as I avoided eye contact.

"Primary structures…a chain of amino acids."

"Secondary?"

"An alpha helix or beta pleated sheet."

"Very good. Now, Mr. Sanders, what is a

geometric isomer?" she asked Marcus as I let out a sigh of relief.

"Err…different arrangement around a double bond," he answered as she stared at him.

"Don't tell me, show me," she demanded, then pointed at the board. Marcus quickly got up and walked to the board. He used a black marker and drew a diagram of the cis isomer and trans isomer. "For a second there I didn't think you knew what you were doing," Mrs. Singleton said as Marcus walked back to his table.

"Now, Mr. Carter Raymond Halls, what is a phosphodiester bond?" She walked to the front and stared down at Carter.

"Err…I do-don't know," he mumbled as she tilted her head. I squinted my eyes because I knew something was wrong. Carter was smart…well, when he wanted to be, and Bio was his favorite subject.

"First you don't do the homework, and now you can't answer my questions," she stated as Carter slowly nodded. "You have lunch detention, Carter. Enjoy picking up litter with Marcus."

"Why do I have detention?" Marcus demanded.

"That's wrong! It looks like a cat with lazy eyes." She pointed to the board.

"Really? I thought he was drawing you, miss," Carter said as people laughed.

"Both of you! Lunch and after school detention!" she yelled.

"No surprise there." Marcus sighed as he slouched in his seat.

The bell rang, and I gathered my stuff. When I

looked up, I saw Carter walk out, and I quickly grabbed Benny's hand as we tried to catch up with him. Since we were in the same Phys Ed class, I knew where Carter would go.

"You okay, man?" Benny asked as we stood on either side of Carter.

"Yeah, just had a long night at Blake's house, then we went street racing, so I only got home at, like, four." He yawned.

"Wow, you guys are getting pretty wasted these past few days," I said as my brows rose.

"Yep," Carter said as the corners of his eyes wrinkled up from exhaustion. Benny and I gave each other a wary look as Carter walked past us and into the boys' locker room. He gave me a tight smile then followed Carter. I walked into the girls' locker room and got changed. It turned out Melissa was not in the class anymore because she decided to do the training for first aid. At least I still had Miranda with me since I barely had her in any classes.

"All right, slackers, since you're all still in holiday mode, we're going in the weights room today. Get rid of all that extra fat that's inside from Christmas and what not." Coach waved us off as we joined our group. "Oh, and Aidan! Do not touch the exercise balls! We don't want what happened the last time to happen again!"

"Message received." Aidan saluted as we walked to the weights room. Miranda and I were in the back, and I glanced up to see Carter, Blake, and Ethan ahead of us.

"So what's up with him?" Miranda pointed to

Blake.

"We, err…he almost kissed me," I mumbled, and Miranda gasped. Nearly half of the class including Blake spun around and looked at Miranda. She glared at Blake as they continued to walk.

"And what did you do?" she whispered.

"Backed away, obviously. I have a boyfriend," I muttered.

"Mm, say it louder for some people to hear!" Miranda hissed as she glared at Blake.

"But he doesn't care. Carter told me they all went out last night, came back around four a.m."

"Wow, they must've had a lot of fun."

"Oh, we did," a stinging voice said. I looked over my shoulder and watched as Kelly forced herself between us. Her hair was platinum no more; it was black.

"Who the hell involved you?" Miranda demanded as she gave Kelly a once over.

"Me, myself and I, bitch," Kelly answered as she forced a smile.

"What were you doing there?" I asked as we reached the weights room.

"Probably being the go-to girl that she is," Miranda grumbled.

"Yeah, I taught your boyfriend that thing you like." Kelly winked at Miranda, who glared at her. "Just joking, Miranda. I had so much fun with someone else," she added, then licked her bottom lip. "I even heard he took someone's virginity," she sang, then walked into the room. My eyes widened as I sent Miranda a look. She looked as if she wanted to rip Kelly's face off, but her expression changed as we locked eyes.

"You don't think..." I trailed off, but she shook her head.

"No, it's impossible, it's probably Keene."

Chapter Twenty

Lana

We did as Coach said and did each piece of equipment. I sat on a bench where I was supposed to do chair dips, but I was tired. I looked around and saw Benny on the bench as he lifted weights. Blake was next to him and did bicep curls as he spoke to a girl. Out of the corner of my eye, I saw Miranda sit next to me. I turned to see her hair tied up in a high ponytail as she drank from her water bottle. She rolled her eyes, and I followed her gaze to where Blake lifted his singlet so that the girl could touch his chest. I turned back to Miranda, who let out a dry laugh.

"That's so not like him," I admitted.

"Don't you get it? You rejected his kiss, so he's moving on."

"Moving on?"

"Yeah, he has always been the mysterious bad boy, but now he is the player and egotistical bad boy," Miranda said, then rolled her eyes.

"A combination of both," I whispered to myself as I thought of the day when Blake told me the difference between a player and a bad boy.

"This is just the beginning. I heard he's having a party on Saturday and only certain people are invited," she emphasized.

"Wow," I commented as the girl wrote down her number on his arm. He picked up the hundred pounds and continued his bicep curls. Benny stood up and stretched, and it was a great view that showed his v-line.

"Fuck!" he yelled out as he jumped up and gripped his foot. I blinked, then glanced down to see that Blake had dropped the weight on Benny's foot. I stood up, then walked over to Benny, who glared at Blake.

"Sorry, man, didn't see you." Blake awkwardly scratched behind his neck.

"Why would you drop it, anyway?" I demanded as I wrapped an arm around Benny's torso. Blake shrugged, and I swore at him. He smirked. Coach came to us and placed his hands on his hips.

"Oh no…is your foot broken?" Coach asked as he lowered his gaze to Benny's foot.

"I-I don't know," Benny mumbled as he put an arm around my shoulder for support.

"Crap, go to the nurse. Willson, you take him, and I hope it's not broken. We got a game next week, and none of my players should have excuses!" Coach yelled as I helped Benny out of the class. Thankfully, the nurse's room was on the same floor because I didn't want to drag Benny down four flights of stairs. I pushed the door open and helped him to the bed. When I placed him on the bed, I noticed the nurse wasn't in the room.

"I'll go look fo—" I spun around to face Benny but cut off when he pressed me against the door and kissed me. The door closed behind me, and I placed my hand on his chest. He looked at me with a mischievous grin as I looked down. "Doesn't it hurt?"

"Only a bit," he whispered as he kissed up my jaw, then my lips. I wrapped my arms around his neck and deepened the kiss. His hands traveled down to my thighs, and I jumped, then wrapped my legs around his waist. He pressed me against the door, and I moaned as he left a hickey on my neck. I twirled my fingers in his hair as he groaned. He began to pull off my polo shirt, and I immediately stopped him. He looked up and gave me a questioning look. "What's wrong? Are you okay?" he asked as I got down on my feet.

"Y-yeah, I'm fine. Sorry," I mumbled as I thought of when Parker did that to me but in a more demanding way. Note to self: never make out in school again.

"Babe, are you okay?" he asked as I walked around him. Before I answered, the door opened, and I spun around. I looked at the nurse, but Benny had his eyes glued to me.

"What's going on here?" the nurse asked as she looked at Benny and me.

"He injured his foot," I said. "So I just helped him here."

"Okay, let's see," the nurse said as Benny sat on the bed. She turned to me and motioned to the door with an assured smile. I gave Benny one last look, then walked out of the room. I felt embarrassed in a way to see the look on Benny's face. He thought it was his fault, but he didn't know the story.

***

It was lunch, and I leaned against the wall. The cold wind blew in my face, but I tried to ignore it as I smoked a cigarette. It's my first one in 2017, but I really needed it. With the whole school and James thing, it's been stressful. I was at the back of the school, the abandoned part where people rarely came because it was winter. In my left ear, I heard footsteps approach me. I pushed myself off the wall and hid the cigarette behind me as I waited for the person. Ethan appeared, and I let out a sigh of relief. He approached me with a confused look.

"There you are. Benny has been looking all over for you."

"I know. I sent him a text saying I was in the library."

"This is a nice library. It's so…open," he sarcastically said. I rolled my eyes as I raised the cigarette. His mouthed formed into an "O" as I leaned against the wall. "What's wrong? It's not every day you find Lana Willson out in the cold smoking a cigarette."

"Well, when I took Benny to the nurse she wasn't there, so we…" I trailed off.

"Oh," he said as the corner of his mouth rose.

"Yeah, and well…I stopped him because I just saw Parker. We were in the same atmosphere, so maybe that's why I pictured him." I took a drag.

"That asshole. You're not the only one, Lana. I've heard he does it to other girls," Ethan said as I blew out a smoke ring.

"Then why isn't he expelled?" I demanded as I pushed myself off the wall again and turned to face Ethan.

"There's no proof, and you know Principal West is full of shit."

"I'm proof! Those other girls that he harassed are proof!"

"Does Benny know?"

"No. He doesn't know a lot of things." I mumbled the last part and took one last drag. I threw the cigarette on the ground and crushed it with my shoe.

"Parker deserves everything that's gonna happen to him one day. Don't worry, Lana. Things will get better," Ethan said as he playfully nudged me.

"I heard you guys went racing last night," I said as I put my hands in my pockets and squeezed my fists.

"Yeah, we each did a race and won. It was fun." He nodded as I smiled.

"Was Keene with you guys?" I asked as I thought of Kelly.

"Yeah, quite a few people were there," he mumbled, then stared at the ground. I nodded as the bell rang. We walked back, and I mentally thought up an excuse I'd tell Benny if he ever asked.

***

The seniors stayed after school. The class of 2012 started a thing on the top floor when their lockers got repaired. They asked for a row to keep for display. So every graduating class from 2012 on had written their names on the oldest lockers in the school. By the time I reached the top floor, there were already people lined up. I joined the line and didn't notice that Benny was in front of me. He spun around and gave me a small smile.

"Hi, how's your foot?"

"Like I said, it only hurts a bit."

"I'm sorry about earlier. I jus—"

"It's okay, I understand," he said, then faced forward. I sighed and folded my arms. I looked over my shoulder to see who was behind me. Jennifer had her hands placed on her hips as she observed the lockers. Every senior class had their locker that had been written on. I followed her gaze to see her look at her brother's class.

"Noel Brighton was part of the people who started all of this," she mumbled as her fingers grazed over her brother's name.

"How is he?" I asked, because from what Melissa told me, he was in rehab.

"He's okay. He was discharged before winter break because they've seen improvement. Now he's staying in his apartment," she replied. "Lana, err…thank you for the other day in the cafeteria. It made me feel at ease."

"No problem, but that was brave of you. Just know that people are supporting you and stuff," I mumbled, because I didn't know what to say.

"Thanks." She awkwardly chuckled as we

moved in the line. We watched as Benny wrote his name on the deep blue locker. Jennifer let out a sigh as she shook her head. I followed her gaze to see Miranda's and Marcus's names next to each other. I think she shook her head at Kelly, who forced her name between theirs horizontally.

"What's her problem?" I asked as Benny gave me the white marker.

"I don't know. Just because her dad is the principal, she thinks she owns the place and gets what she wants," Jennifer answered as I wrote my name below Benny's. Once I finished, I gave her the marker, and she held onto it as she stared at me. "Just so you know, she has a thing for soccer players." She gestured to Marcus. My jaw dropped as I nodded and backed away.

***

Benny took me home, and it seemed like we were back to normal. He said I should come to his house later and I agreed since it was Friday. I got home and changed into comfy clothing that consisted of gray joggers, a red sweater, and my white Converse. Mom came home, so I took her car and drove to Benny's house. By the time I got there, it was past five, and we chilled in Benny's room. We laid on his bed and watched a movie, then eventually fell asleep. Although for once, I didn't have the dream.

I fluttered my eyes open and noticed a blanket was on me. I glanced over my shoulder to see Benny asleep on the other side of the bed. I slowly got up and stretched to see his mother's back to us as she folded some laundry. I squinted my eyes and watched as she hummed a tune. She spun around and startled but waved it off as she smiled at me.

"Hi, Lana, I'm sorry if I woke you." She smiled.

"It's okay, Mrs. Nielson. I, err…" I trailed off as I put my glasses on.

"Aww, it's so cute that you just came over to sleep," she cooed and looked at Benny.

"Err…yeah, sleep," I said as the corner of my mouth raised.

"There's dinner downstairs if you're hungry," she said, then took the laundry basket and walked out of the room.

"Thank you," I called out. I noticed Benny got up. I turned to him and bit my bottom lip because he looked cuddly. He smiled at me and opened his arms. I laid on his chest and wrapped my arms around him. Benny's phone rang a few minutes later, and he groaned, then answered it.

"Hey, Nick," he greeted. "Whoa, yeah she's here…all right, all right we'll be there," Benny said, then ended the call. I sat up and gave him a questioning look as he got up. He put on his shoes as I did the same.

"What's wrong?"

"Nick's at Liam's apartment. They want us there." Benny shrugged as he put on his jacket.

"Okay, let's go." I put on my leather jacket, then walked out of his room. I drove since I'd go home from Liam's apartment. While we drove close to downtown, I wondered why they wanted us there so urgently. Only one thing popped into my head.

We arrived fifteen minutes later, and Benny led the way because Liam was on the top floor. We stood in front of the door, and I knocked. Nick opened the door. I raised a brow as he escorted us into the apartment. It looked very vivid with its different-colored furniture, yet it somehow matched.

"What's so urgent?" Benny asked Nick, who opened his mouth to answer but cut off when someone entered the room.

"Oh! More guests. Welcome, welcome. Would you like some tea? I'm Liam's grandma." She gave us a kind smile.

"That would be lovely, thank you," Nick replied.

"All right, come on in. I'm making cookies," she said, then walked into the kitchen.

"She's been saying that every five minutes. She has Alzheimer's," Nick said as I slowly nodded. We walked into the kitchen, and she took out a tray from the oven. My eyes widened to see that they burned. Nick turned off the oven as she stared at the burned cookies.

"I think they need a bit more time," she said, then put the tray back in the oven.

"Would you guys like some tea?" she asked, and Nick raised his hand.

"We had some, thank you," he said as she nodded, then walked out of the kitchen.

"You guys, come on!" Liam yelled throughout the apartment. Nick let out a sigh as he walked down the hall and into Liam's room. I entered his room, and I gaped at how full it was. His bed was in one corner as he sat opposite by his desk. Next to his desk was an open space but the wall was full of string and papers.

"Liam, what is this?" I looked at the pictures of the industrial area and Jack.

"We're investigating!" he cheered, then pushed up his glasses.

"Good for you, but why are we here?" Benny asked as he sat on the bed.

"We're just curious about this Jack August," Nick said as he licked his lips.

"Yeah, I've done research on him, and there's nothing. No social media and not even on his family. You guys should see how many families there are with the last name of August," Liam said.

"Well, maybe because he's a hobo," I pointed out.

"Yeah, but remember the first time he came on the news, and they had this whole background of him? Where he was born, his family, and even where he worked," Liam said as his forehead creased.

"My dad said the journalists could make up lies and stuff just to make it more dramatic."

"Yeah, but it says he was born at Provident Hospital of Cook County," Liam said, then typed on his computer.

"My mother works there," I said, then looked at his screen.

"Yeah, and I talked to her, then managed to figure out the password for their files," Liam mumbled as my eyes widened.

"Why would you do that?" Benny demanded.

"We're investigators!" Liam cheered, then raised

his fist.

"Just tell them what you found." Nick sighed as he stared at us.

"Nothing. Not a single thing about Jack August was mentioned in the last thirty years or ever." Liam sighed.

"Yeah, it just shows that the news reports false information," I said.

"Yeah, you're right," Liam mumbled, then stood up as he walked over to the wall. He took a big marker and crossed out Provident Hospital.

"Well, guess what else we found out?" Nick asked as he sat in the chair and typed. "On the news when they showed a picture of Jack August, don't you think it's funny that they had a picture of a hobo?"

"Maybe it's from his family," Liam suggested.

"Then his family would've given a picture of him before he became an alcoholic hobo," Benny said as we looked at the picture that showed up on the news. Jack August kept a poker face as he stared at the camera. His face was pale yet hard to notice from his ginger hair. He had a strong jawline and a pointy nose with chocolate brown eyes. "Wait, zoom in on his neck," Benny said as we stared at him. Nick did as told and my eyes widened when I noticed it.

"Is that makeup?" Liam pointed to Jack's face that was pale, but his neck was tanned. We exchanged looks as we took in the rest of his appearance. In the background was a sign that stated Route 28.

"That looks familiar," I said.

"Yeah, it does. I'll look it up," Nick said, then typed. I straightened my posture and folded my arms as I looked at the wall again. There was so much stuff going on that I lost count of how many strings there were.

"Don't your parents question this?" I asked as Liam stood next to me.

"Nah, they're always working, so they don't have time for me, but I got my grandma," he said with a smile.

"Holy shit," Nick muttered as we turned to him.

"What?" Liam asked.

"That picture was taken at Route 28, and the sign is exactly opposite Ethan's cottage," Nick said as we looked at Google Maps.

"What? There must be another Route 28," I scoffed.

"Nope, it's identical to the image," Nick said as he shook his head.

"Then what the hell was Jack doing there?" Benny asked.

"Do you think Ethan will know?" Liam asked.

"Sure, he'd know when a random hobo had a photo shoot opposite his cottage," Nick sarcastically replied.

"I have a strange feeling that this Jack guy isn't who he says he is," Benny mumbled as he stared at the wall.

"Maybe he's a model who just dresses poorly and hasn't shaved in days," Liam guessed as my phone vibrated. Benny and Liam argued about who Jack was while I read the text. I let out a sigh because my mother needed her car.

“Guys, I gotta go. My mom needs her car,” I mumbled as I shoved my phone in my pocket.

“I’ll come with you,” Benny suggested as I slowly shook my head.

“Then how are you gonna get home?” I asked as we walked out of Liam’s room and to the living room.

“True, I’ll just go with Nick, but call me when you get home,” he said, then kissed me.

“I will.” I nodded, then walked out of the apartment. I strolled out of the building and to the car. It was already dark outside as I got into the car.

I drove out of downtown and decided to take a shortcut. As I turned the corner, a few people came out of a bar. It seemed to be a fight, and I squinted my eyes when I noticed a familiar bald head. I parked next to the sidewalk and got out of the car to see men roughing up Keene. I ran toward him and yelled at the guys.

“What do you think you’re doing?” I demanded as I stepped between them. Keene’s eye was swollen, and he had a bloody nose. I turned to the guys, who glared at me.

“Get lost, bitch,” the one guy demanded as he shoved me out of the way. I kept my balance as I turned around and pulled on his shoulder. He turned to me with a glare as I whipped out the pepper spray Dad gave me. I sprayed him in the face as well as his friends. They cursed as the covered their faces.

“Fuck off, assholes!” I yelled as they backed away. I watched as they walked back into the bar while rubbing their eyes. I spun around to see Keene wiping the blood from his face. I noticed he was drunk as he swayed and had a dazed look on his face. “Come on.” I sighed as I helped him to the car.

***

We arrived at his apartment five minutes later, since he also had one downtown. I got out of the car, then walked to the passenger side to help him out. I swung his arm around my shoulder, and he gave me a sloppy grin as I kicked the door closed.

“Lana, guess what? Guess what?” he asked as we walked upstairs.

“What, Keene?” I asked as I pulled him up each step.

“I got meat,” he breathed out, and I held my breath as the alcohol hit my nose.

“Good for you,” I muttered.

“Yeah, I heard you love meat.” He smirked as I raised a brow.

“Err…yeah,” I mumbled as we reached his floor. “Where are your keys?”

“You have to find them.” He poked my nose as he leaned against the door.

“Keene, come on,” I whined as he smiled at me.

“Lana, come on,” he mocked as he raised his arms so that I could find his keys. I huffed as I crouched down and searched his pockets. “You’re warm,” Keene hinted as I looked up at him. I moved my hands down, but he shook his head. I stood up straight as my hands moved to the middle of his belt buckle. He smirked at me as I raised his shirt and took out his keys from his belt. “You’re hot.” He stepped out of the way so I could open the door. I unlocked the door and pushed him in. He skipped into the kitchen as I turned on the light. A few seconds later, he came back with a can of beer, but I shook my head.

"No, you had enough." I snatched the can away from him. He lowered his head and pouted as he turned the light off.

"I like it dark!" he exclaimed as I raised my arms. I cursed under my breath as we plopped down on the sofa. Out the corner of my eye, I saw him open the can and drink. I let out a sigh as I glanced around, but I barely saw anything since everything was dark. "Thank you, Lana."

"No problem. I thought you'd be at Blake's house."

"You get annoyed when you hang out with them too much," he said as he leaned forward and pressed his forehead against my temple. I felt his heavy breaths on my cheek.

"Err…Keene, what are you doing?" I asked as I tried to lean away, but he followed.

"Lana, guess what, guess what?" he whispered as he placed his index finger on my cheek and turned my face to him so that our foreheads touched.

"Wha-what?" I backed away, but he followed, which made me fall flat on the sofa. Keene hovered over me as he pressed his forehead against mine. He placed an arm on each side of me as I placed a hand on his chest. "Keene, what are you—"

"He's here," Keene whispered as I raised a brow at him. I heard the rattle of keys and turned my head to the front door to see someone's shadow underneath the door. I watched as the shadow moved underneath the door. The doorknob twisted. Keene collapsed on me. I let out a groan as I shuffled underneath him and off the sofa. I turned back to see that he had fallen asleep. I looked at the door again to see the person in front of it. He gave me a strange look as he shut the door. I gave him a once-over, and something about him seemed so familiar. He was tall with dark brown hair and chestnut eyes. He looked to be a few years older than me with his full structure and stubble.

"Am I disturbing something?" His voice sounded deep as he glanced at Keene and me.

"No, err…I was just helping him, found him at a bar," I mumbled.

"Okay. I'm Noel. I share an apartment with this idiot." He pointed to Keene.

"Wait, you're Noel Brighton. As in Jennifer's older brother," I clarified.

"Yeah. How do you know my sister?" he asked and sat on the armchair.

"We go to the same school, and I remember you when I was a freshman," I said.

"So, if you're in high school, what are you doing with an intoxicated twenty year old?" he pointed to Keene, who snored.

"Oh, I was supposed to go ho—" I cut myself off as my eyes widened. I remembered that my mother needed her car to go to work. I quickly took out my phone and read the message she left.

Mom: Never mind your dad's taking me. Don't stay out too late. Love you.

I glanced up and noticed Noel had gone into the kitchen. I put my phone back in my jeans pocket, then turned to Keene.

"Oh, just leave him. He'll wake up soon enough, then walk to his room," Noel said as he walked into the room with two glasses of water. I moved Keene's legs so that I could sit by the coffee table. Noel placed the glass down and took a sip of his. I mumbled a thank you and took the glass and drank the water. "I would give you a beer or something, but my sobriety and all that shit."

"Oh, I understand." I nodded.

"You do?" he questioned, then laughed. "No, you don't…no one does."

"Okay, then make me understand," I blurted out as I set my glass on the table.

"Well, what do you know?" he asked as he glanced at me, then the glass.

"Well…all I know is you were in rehab for being a drug addict. Your dad put you in there because he didn't want the family name going bad."

"Yeah, that's what everyone knows. I'm not addicted. I swear!" Noel stated as he stared at me with a panicked look in his eyes. "He made me do it! Ugh, I was so stupid."

"Who made you do what?"

"Do you really wanna know? Sorry if I'm bothering you. You probably want to go home."

"No, no, no. Remember? I want to understand," I said as I leaned back in my seat to show that I wouldn't go anywhere.

"Okay, well, it was senior year, spring break. I was home alone and heard a knock on the door,"

Noel began as he stared at the floor. "I answered it, and it was a few guys who told me they were there because they wanted to see my father, so I just told them to wait and that he'll be here soon.

"I was gone for a second, and when I came back, I saw them unloading stuff. That's when I got suspicious, because it was parcels. When I went for my phone and tried to call my dad, one of the guys stopped me. He told me to do what he said or he'd hurt my family." Noel whispered the last part as my eyes widened.

"This guy who threatened you…what was he wearing?" I asked as I tried to put two and two together.

"A suit, but the other three guys wore black," Noel answered as my jaw dropped. Although James only had two guys when I saw him.

"They must've talked. What were their names?" I asked.

"I don't know the guy in the suit, but I think one was named Mike and the other Christo," he answered as I paled.

"Oh. T-then what happened?"

"It was probably about three hundred parcels. Our house was pretty big, so he told me to keep them, and he'd contact me when he wanted them," Noel mumbled.

"So then how did you end up in rehab?" I asked as he looked at my glass again.

"One night I was drunk with my friends, and one of them found a parcel in the basement, and we started…" He trailed off as I nodded. "One of them snitched about it, and my dad found out. He didn't want the family name going bad, so he sent me to rehab when he found the other parcels."

"What happened to the parcels?" I asked, then slid my glass toward him, and he thanked me as he took a sip.

"From what my sister told me, Mike and Christo broke in one night and took them. You could see they'd done it before because they were so fast in doing it," Noel explained as I nodded.

"So, if your house is big and stuff, why aren't you living there?" I asked.

"My dad only cares about money and what the public will think. When I came out of rehab, he let me stay for a few days, then kicked me out." He shrugged and placed the empty glass down.

"Oh, I'm sorry," I mumbled.

"It's cool. My fault, I guess," Noel responded with a shrug. We sat in silence as I thought over what Noel said. James used other people to hide his drugs. It's like he wanted to get caught or something…

"Well, I have to go. It's getting late," I said and rose to my feet. We stood up at the same time. Noel towered over me as he smiled. He honestly didn't look like a drug addict; he seemed like a genuinely nice guy.

"Yeah, err…I'll tell Keene you dropped him off because I doubt he'd remember how he got home." Noel chuckled as I followed him to the door. "Hey, I didn't get your name."

"Oh, Lana Willson." I smiled.

"Nice to meet you, Lana. You're the first person who doesn't think I'm crazy after telling them that story," he said as the corner of his mouth pulled up.

"Well, everyone's got a story," I murmured, and he nodded. I opened the door and walked out into the cold. With one last wave, he shut the door, and I walked downstairs to the car.

***

It was late on Saturday afternoon, and we decided to stay indoors. We sat on the sofa and finished *Fantastic Beasts and Where to Find Them*, which Uncle Griff "downloaded" since he knew that I loved J.K. Rowling's books. I curled up on the La-Z-Boy and continually sneezed. I noticed she turned to me with a raised brow.

"Are you getting sick?"

"No, Mom, it's just one sneeze."

"Mm." She pursed her lips. "Where were you last night?"

"I was at Liam's apartment when I got your message, then while driving home I saw Keene and helped him get home," I explained, then shrugged.

"But Keene lives downtown," Dad chimed in as he raised a brow at me.

"Yeah..." I trailed off as his jaw tightened.

"I don't want you going there alone at night. Wait, scratch that, I don't want you going there at a—" Dad cut off when the doorbell rang. I let out a sigh of relief as Dad got up and walked out of the living room. I turned to Mom, who sent me a suspicious look. "Lana, you have guests," Dad muttered as he walked into the room. I looked over his shoulder to see Benny, Nick, and Liam come in with a box.

"Thanks, Bobby." Liam smiled as my dad wrinkled his eyes at him.

"Don't call me that if you know what's good for you, Liam," Dad said.

"Sorry, Sheriff. Can I interest you in some donuts?" Liam pouted as he opened the box.

"Just because I'm a cop doesn't mean I eat donuts all the time. It's a stupid stereotype because everyone loves donuts!" Dad huffed, then walked toward Liam. "Now give me one."

I watched in amusement as Dad and Liam ate the donuts. Benny and Nick greeted my mother, then approached me.

"Hey. What are you guys doing here?" I asked as they sat on the big sofa next to me. Nick raised his brows, then looked over his shoulder at Liam. Mom got up and took a donut. Once they were done, Mom and Dad walked into the kitchen while Liam joined us on the sofa.

"We're investigators!" Liam cheered with his donut.

"What does he mean?" I asked.

"He wants to investigate. So we're taking a drive somewhere," Benny said.

"You'll see. Now go get ready!" Liam said and gave a dismissive wave of his hand.

"Err…okay," I mumbled as I pushed myself off the sofa. They followed me upstairs and into my room. Thankfully, I was dressed and just needed to put on my shoes. While they hung out in my room, I took out my contacts and decided to wear my glasses. I put them on in the bathroom, then brushed my hair. When I came out of the bathroom, Liam held up my white Converse, which I picked out.

"You can't wear these," he said, then walked to my closet.

"Why? Are we going to the beach?" I sarcastically asked as Liam put them away.

"Nope." Benny sighed as he laid on my bed.

"Don't you have other Converse?" Liam asked as he rummaged in my closet.

"I did have black and white high tops, but y'know, they were supposed to be dumped at a junkyard." I shrugged as I walked to my closet and took out a pair of maroon Doc Martens.

"Let's just hope that they were. Oh, that reminds me, did you get rid of yours after they made such a dramatic return?" Nick asked as he looked at Liam.

"Yeah, of course," Liam mumbled as he looked at the ceiling. I quickly put on my shoes, and Benny helped me as he did the laces. When I looked down at Liam's shoes, I checked if he wore the black high tops. Thankfully, he wasn't and wore black Vans. I put on a denim jacket, then followed the boys as we walked out of my room. Mom and Dad watched TV as we passed them.

"Put on a jacket. I don't want you getting the flu!" Mom demanded.

"I'm already wearing one, Mom," I said.

"Oh well…make sure you're wearing enough layers!" She pointed to my clothing.

"I am. I have a ve—" I cut off when a car honked outside. Benny tugged on my hand as he looked at my parents.

"I'll make sure that she's warm and returned

home without the flu," Benny said, then winked at me.

"What do you mean by warm?" Dad narrowed his eyes at Benny.

"Love you, bye!" I pulled Benny out of the house before he could answer my father. We got into the back, and Nick drove while Liam sat in the passenger seat. Liam belted out the lyrics to a hip-hop song as I turned to Benny with a grin. "How are you going to make sure that I'm warm?"

"Oh, I have my ways," he replied, then kissed my hand as I bit my lip.

"Do you really have to carry that everywhere? I'm pretty sure our class doesn't want this in the yearbook," Nick spoke up as he glanced at Liam. Benny and I watched as Liam took random pictures, then turned to Nick with a grave expression.

"Relax, I have separate memory cards, one for the yearbook and the other for our pictures."

"What pictures will you be taking?" I asked as Liam raised the camera and took a quick picture of Nick's stone hard look.

"Anything that gives us a clue about Jack August," Liam mumbled as he put the camera on his lap.

"What do yo—where are we even going?" I asked as my eyes widened.

"To Ethan's cottage, because we're investigators!" Liam cheered as he raised his fist.

"Are you out of your mind? We can't go there! What if, what if—"

"Relax, Lana, it's abandoned, which makes it easier because we're investigators!" Liam assured me as Nick groaned.

"Adding the words 'we're investigators' at the end of every sentence doesn't make the situation better," Nick muttered. Liam pouted.

"You're a big meanie, Nicky," Liam said as he pressed the button to open his window. Nick let out a sigh as he looked back at the road. I let out another sneeze since Liam's window was wide open, and his head stuck out like a dog in the wind.

"Dude, close your window! You're making Lana sick!" Benny scolded Liam.

"I need some air," he yelled and shook his head.

"There's air in here, you idiot," Nick muttered as he pressed the button on his side that closed Liam's window.

"I don't want your air!" Liam frowned as he looked at Nick. "It's thick and tense, like you!"

I threw my head back and closed my eyes as Liam and Nick argued about the air. It went on for five minutes, then the car went silent; even the radio was off. I opened my eyes to see Nick drive while Liam's arms were folded as he looked out the window. Benny was on his phone, then looked up at me. He rolled his eyes, then looked down at his phone again.

"Just say sorry," I stated after a while.

"Sorry," Nick and Liam said in unison.

"I like this air," Liam stated as he turned to Nick with a smile.

"Okay," Nick said in an ominous tone as he gave Liam a smile too. Their friendship was weird, but I knew that Nick wouldn't leave Liam, no matter how annoyed he got.

Chapter Twenty-One

Lana

We arrived, and I forced myself up, then looked around. There was absolutely nothing, just a long road and brown gravel. I slowly got out of the car and stretched. On the left side of the road were a lamp post and a sign that displayed Route 28. On the right aspect of the road, a few feet away, was Ethan's cottage. While the guys walked to the lamp post, I stared at the cottage. The cottage brought back so many memories. Now to see it deserted and the "For Sale" sign up made my stomach turn. Ethan told me his dad wasn't impressed, and he got scolded for keeping it from him for two years.

"See, it's the same!" Liam exclaimed as I turned around. Nick was in the position Jack was when the photograph was taken. Benny held up the photo, and Liam looked down at his camera. I approached them and stood next to Liam as I stared at the screen. Nick held the same expression as Jack with the sign behind him, and it was identical to the original.

“Wow, that’s kinda creepy.” I looked at the photograph of Nick and Jack.

“I wonder who sent the picture in,” Benny said as his forehead creased.

“If it was his family, they chose a shitty place for a picture,” Nick said as he looked up at the sign. I stuffed my hands in my jacket pockets and looked across the street again. It’s funny; I still pictured the day when Blake forced me on his motorcycle and told me to drive. The looks on their faces showed that they were afraid. Even now when we spoke about James, they looked at me.

“Is it for sale?” Liam snapped me out of my thoughts.

“No, that sign is just up there for decoration,” Nick replied sarcastically.

“You know your sarcasm hurts sometimes.” Liam pouted as he placed his hand on his chest. Nick was about to say something as he approached Liam, but Benny held him back, then glared at Liam.

“Can you two just…not annoy Lana and me?” Benny asked as he lifted his hands to separate the two.

“He started it.” Liam huffed as he walked forward. My brows furrowed as I watched the tall brunette walk across the street and toward Ethan’s cottage. I followed him, and Benny and Nick grunted as they trailed behind.

“Liam, what are you doing?” I asked as he studied the cottage. I followed his gaze to see that the doors were surrounded by chains, but it seemed like someone had broken them since pieces laid on the ground. Liam and I looked at each other, then back at the chains.

"We're investigators," Liam whispered as he took a picture of the chains, then stepped forward.

"You are dumb to go in there!" Nick scolded as Liam pulled the chains off.

"Why would it be locked if it's up for sale?" Liam asked, then dropped the chains.

"Maybe someone has their eye on it, so Ethan's dad is keeping it locked until he can put the 'sold' sign up," I guessed.

"Then who would cut the chains?" Benny asked as he stood next to me.

"I don't know, but let's investigate!" Liam cheered as he walked in.

"Liam, get out of there! We could get into trouble!" I exclaimed as I went after him. The place looked empty without the furniture. I noticed the walls needed a paint job because I could see the shadows left behind from the posters that had been on the walls. A few things were scattered around, like a chair, trashcan, and toolbox.

"How do you guys know about Ethan's cottage?" I asked when Ethan told me that I was the first person other than the four of them to be in here.

"Kelly started a massive rumor about this place back in sophomore year. You should've seen the shit she did to try and get in here," Nick replied, then walked over to Liam, who was in the kitchen. "Dude, don't eat that! What if it's expired?" Nick stated as we watched Liam eat a bag of cookies.

"They expire in May," Liam said with a

mouthful of food. Nick stared at him in disbelief as his eyebrows drew together. I laughed as I walked away from the two and further into the cottage. The door a few feet away reminded me of the day when everything went to hell. I slowly entered the room and saw that it was empty.

I stood in the middle of the room and folded my arms. I let out a sigh, still picturing everything, the bed I laid on when they entered the room. Aidan blocked my view of the living room, but it didn't make a difference since we're almost the same height, and when Blake kissed me. Then the realization hit me that they dealt with drugs. To be honest, a part of me enjoyed it, but a full part of me realized how much emotional pain he'd put me through. I let out a dry laugh and thought about how he fucked up every time yet moved on as if it were nothing. I was done with Blake, and I noticed he's over me since he had wild parties, street raced, and slept around for the past week. I shook my head in amusement as I remembered when he told me there was a difference. Even though he's a combination of both.

"Hey, you okay?" Benny's voice interrupted my thoughts, and I spun around. I nodded with a smile as he approached me. I put my arms around his torso and pulled him in for a long sweet kiss. He immediately responded as his arms snaked around my waist and brought me closer. "Wh-what was that for?" he breathed out afterward.

"Just…you make me happy, and I haven't been like that for a while." I smiled.

"You make me happy too. Your smile is

beautiful," he said as the corner of his mouth raised. My smile grew bigger as he pulled me in for a hug again. I rested my head on his shoulder as he ran his fingers through my hair. It was true he made me happy and carefree; I felt like a whole new person whenever I was around him. I felt better.

"Yo, guys, come check this out!" Liam's voice echoed throughout the cottage as Benny and I pulled away. We walked out of the room and into the hallway, where we saw Nick in front of the bathroom door.

"Liam, what is it?" Benny asked as we stood in front of the door.

"If you want me to recheck your piss, it's not happening, bro! Remember, if it's too yello—" Nick cut off when Liam opened the door and pulled us in.

"What do you want?" I scrunched my nose.

"Guess," Liam stated with a grin as he leaned against the sink.

"Dude, it smells like shit in here. What the hell?" Benny asked as he waved his hand over his face.

"Exactly!" Liam beamed as he raised his hands.

"What?" Nick asked as he stared at Liam, and I noticed he was annoyed.

"Benny, walk to the bathtub," Liam ordered as he pointed to the white tub.

"Why?"

"Come on, just do it. We're investigators!" Liam whined as he raised his camera.

"Okay." Benny sighed. He did as told and walked across to the bathtub. Nick and I watched as Benny slowly spun around and looked at Liam.

"Liam, what did you do?" he asked as he looked at the floor.

"Nothing," Liam answered as his eyebrows rose.

"What is it, Benny?" I asked as he continued to walk back and forth. He stopped in the middle and swayed as he looked down. We followed his gaze to see the tiles beneath his feet wobble. I stepped forward and moved a tile with my foot. The one that I moved was smaller than the others. We surrounded the odd tile and stared at it.

"Well…" Liam trailed off as he crouched down. My eyes widened as he picked up the tile. It came off quickly, as if it wasn't supposed to be there in the first place. Then one by one the other tiles came out like a jigsaw puzzle gone wrong. I watched in astonishment as they picked up the tiles and tossed them into the bathtub. Once they were done, they stood up again, and I gaped at the thing below us.

"Holy shit," Benny mumbled. Below our feet lay a dusty cement floor, but what brought our attention was the utility hole cover where Benny once stood. We gave each other suspicious looks as to why there's a utility hole cover in an abandoned cottage in the middle of nowhere. Nick crouched down and grazed his fingers over the rusty metal. He tried to lift it up, but it wouldn't budge, so we crouched down to help.

"Okay. Go!" Nick exclaimed, and we lifted. As we pulled the lid up, an unpleasant smell filled the atmosphere, which was worse than the smell of the bathroom already.

"Oh my God," I said as we pushed the lid aside.

"What do you think is down there?" Benny

asked as we looked down the utility hole that was dark yet a few bars displayed, which I assumed was a ladder.

“Well, only one way to find out!” Liam responded as he swung his legs over and began to climb down.

“Are you crazy? It smells like shit down there!” I pinched the bridge of my nose.

“We’re investigators!” Liam cheered.

“It’s getting pretty old!” Nick sang as he joined Liam with no hesitation. Eventually, Benny and I joined the two because we didn’t want them to go down alone.

The horrible stinky smell filled the air as we walked. I had come to the conclusion that we were in the sewers. Liam thought it was tunnels, but as he walked, he almost fell into the gooey liquid, so we were underground by the sewers.

“Sixty-eight bottles of beer on the wall, sixty-eight bottles of beer. Take one down, pa—”

“Would you shut up?” Nick demanded as he cut off Liam.

“I’ve been singing for the past hour, and you only stop me now?” Liam asked as he looked over his shoulder where Nick was.

“I was screaming in my head, hoping that you’d stop. Now I just want you to freaking stop!” Nick groaned. Liam frowned, then dragged his feet as we walked on the side. Benny guided us while I stood next to Liam. Nick trailed behind and took in every aspect of the dimly lit sewer.

“What are you doing?” I asked Liam as he looked at his camera screen.

"Just looking at pictures," he mumbled as I leaned in to see them, but he backed away.

"Can I see?" I asked, but he shook his head. "Come on, Liam; you take good pictures." I extended my arm to take the camera. Once I got a hold of it, he pulled on my jacket to get it back. I ran with the camera and laughed.

"Lana, come on!" he whined as he chased after me. I caught up to Benny, then stood in front of him. I scanned through the pictures, and my jaw dropped. Once Liam reached us, I glanced up at him and let out a squeal.

"I knew it!" I cheered as I handed the camera to Benny. "Liam's got a crush." I gestured to the many pictures of Miranda whether she posed, smiled, ate, or walked.

"Dude." Benny grinned as he went through the pictures.

"Please don't tell her! Besides, it's just a stupid little crush," Liam said.

"Aww, why, though?" I asked as Nick caught up with us.

"There are many reasons, Lana!" he stated as his eyes widened. "Number one, she has a boyfriend. Number two, he's a soccer player, and not just any soccer player, but the captain of the soccer team! Number three, he has nice luscious hair. I mean, did you see those brown curls, bro?" he asked Nick, who stood next to him.

"Luscious?"

"And number four, he has a freaking eight pack! Look at me!" Liam exclaimed as he raised his shirt. "I got a fat pack!"

"But you play football," Benny said as he raised a brow at Liam's stomach.

"Yeah, and I eat a lot of burritos." Liam huffed as he stared at one of the pictures of Miranda and Marcus. "I envy this dude and his luscious hair."

"Do you hate Marcus?" Nick asked as he continued to walk.

"No, I just want something bad to happen to him." Liam shrugged as I laughed. As we walked, Liam continued to talk about Miranda to Nick. I smiled when he said he only showed up to homeroom because she's there. I glanced up and noticed we'd approached a corner. The smell didn't get any better the further we walked, and I wanted to go home.

"Do you know where we're going?" I asked Benny.

"Not really," he replied, then looked around.

"Wait, what? So we've been lost the whole time?" I asked as I gripped on his arm.

"Well, yeah. It's bad lighting, and it's not every day you're walking in the sewers on a Saturday night," Benny said as he raised his voice.

"You could've said something, or we should've done the smart thing and went back," I snapped. "Now we're lost!"

"Okay, yeah, I'm sorry. Let me just whip out my phone…" he exclaimed, then took his phone out. I watched him throw his arms up in exasperation. "Oh wait! There's no fucking signal!" he exclaimed, then shoved the phone in his pocket.

"Don't have to be a sarcastic prick," I hissed, then turned the corner. As I walked, I felt someone grip my arm and whip me around. I came face to face with Benny as he searched my face. A frown filled his features as we locked eyes.

"I'm sorry, I didn't mean to be a sarcastic prick and snap like that. I'm just exhausted," he admitted, then cupped my cheeks. I frowned as I avoided eye contact.

"Yeah, and I'm sorry for acting like that. It's just really smelly and cold down here," I whispered as he looked at me with concern.

"You're getting sick," he stated as he began to take off his jacket.

"No, no, no…it's okay. Then you'll get sick," I said as I stopped him.

"Are you sure?" he asked as he brought me in for a hug.

"Yes, Benny Nielson, now do your job and get us out of here," I said, and he laughed. We walked on, and Liam caught up to me. He glanced around the sewers, then stuffed his hands in his pockets.

"Do you think the teenage mutant ninja turtles are here?" he asked.

"They live in New York's sewers. We're in Illinois." I chuckled.

"Oh yeah…I forgot," Liam stated.

"Guys, look!" Benny exclaimed as he ran forward. Nick and I exchanged looks, then followed Benny while Liam took random pictures. We ran for about two minutes, which wasn't a good idea, because I sneezed. Benny stopped by a wall, and he looked up. We followed his gaze to see another utility hole, which meant a way out.

"Out of my way! I'm hungry as hell!" Liam

exclaimed as he came out of nowhere and pushed Nick aside as he climbed the ladder. "What's the time?"

"Wow, it's nine p.m.," Benny said as he checked his watch.

"Holy shit," Liam remarked as he pushed the lid open and got out. Nick and Benny told me to go next, and I gladly did. Once we were out, familiar noises bombarded my ears. When I looked around at the familiar surroundings, my jaw dropped as I realized where we were.

"What the fuck…" Nick muttered as we glanced around the alley.

"We're in the industrial area." I breathed out and noticed that the utility whole was a few feet away from the wall.

"Come on, we gotta get out of here. It's Saturday night. Who knows what happens this side at night?" Benny said as he took my hand in his and dragged us out of the alley. We walked down the sidewalk, and the sounds of car honks, shouts, and traffic surrounded us. As we turned the corner, a big crowd blocked our view. My eyes widened as I realized that there was a street race.

"Lana? Benny? What are you guys doing here?"

"I should be asking you the same thing." I eyed Carter up and down suspiciously.

"And why do you guys smell like shit?" He waved his hand in front of his face.

"I should be asking you the same thing," Liam retorted as he placed his hands on his hips.

"Well, you can't be here," Carter stated as he gave me a once-over. Before I could ask why,

Aidan and Tiffany appeared next to Carter. Aidan gave us strange looks as he took in our appearances. We weren't pleasant with our frizzy hair, dirty clothes, and awful smell.

"Hey, you want a hug?" Liam asked as he opened his arms to Aidan.

"What? No." Aidan continuously shook his hands. Liam was obviously taller than Aidan as he pulled him in for a hug and rubbed his smell on him. I grinned at Tiffany as I opened my arms.

"Lana, no," she warned and backed away. I laughed as she spun around and ran away. I followed her past the crowd and onto the sidewalk.

"Lana, watch out!" someone yelled, and I instantly froze. I didn't even realize that we'd run across the street. Tiffany was on the other side, but I froze right in the middle. I turned to my right and watched four cars idle. My eyes widened as I realized a race was about to start. When I looked at the drivers, I noticed Ethan and Keene, yet the other two's lights were so bright I couldn't see them.

"Get out of the way, bitch," the flag girl hissed as she stared at me.

"What's the magic word?" I sang, then approached her.

"Get out of the way, bitch…now," she demanded as she placed her hands on her hips. I smirked, then hugged her. She let out a high-pitched scream as she tried to pull away. "Get her off me! She smells like shit!" she yelled as Nick wrapped his arms around my torso and picked me up.

"At least I smell better than your va—"

"Whoa! I think we have to go," Benny said as he

stepped between us before we'd attacked each other.

"Yeah, get this smelly bitch-ass whore out of my face," the girl demanded, and Benny looked at her.

"Whoa, whoa, whoa. Who you calling bitch-ass whore, you du—" Benny cut off when Aidan pulled him away. As Nick and Aidan dragged Benny and me away before I slapped the girl, I held up my middle fingers, and people cheered. Nick set me down next to Liam and Benny, and I glared at the girl as she raised the flag.

"Don't worry, she's always a bitch on the streets," Carter assured us as the crowd cheered when the cars sped off.

"Yeah, but not in bed!" Jaden added as he high-fived Carter, who nodded in agreement.

"We're gonna go," Nick stated as he walked away.

"You sure? I can give you a ride in my truck," Carter suggested.

"No, it's okay. My apartment is a few blocks away," Liam assured him.

"Okay, well, see you guys." Carter shrugged as he did that handshake with Liam, then Benny and Nick. I let out a sigh as Benny entwined my fingers with his. I leaned my head on his shoulder as we walked to Liam's apartment.

***

We arrived at Liam's apartment, then took Nick's car back to Ethan's cottage to get Benny's car. Afterward, we drove to Benny's house and decided to stay there for the night. Liam and Nick always hung out at Benny's house, so they had a few items of clothing there, especially Liam, since he made himself comfortable anywhere. I immediately got into the shower and spent almost an hour trying to get the sewer smell off. I got out and tossed my dirty clothes in the basket. Benny gave me his long sleeve baseball tee and a pair of gray shorts. I dried my hair with the towel, then walked out of the bathroom and into his room. His back faced me, and I noticed he'd came out of the shower too.

"Hey, pizza should be here any minute. The guys are in the baseme—" He cut himself off as he spun around and took in my appearance. I gave him a strange look, then followed his eyes as they went down. I glanced down and noticed that the baseball tee was white and red. Then I remembered I threw my bra in the basket too. I looked up and leisurely bit my lip. I slowly approached him, then placed my hand on his chest. His hair was damp from the shower, so it was spiky.

"Like what you see?" I teased as my hand went behind his neck. I brought him forward so that I could kiss him. His hand went to my hips, then slowly under the shirt. I felt the palm of his hands go behind my back. The kiss itself was slow yet so evocative as our tongues danced. His hands went to the front, his thumbs grazing the outline of my breast as he moved up, then the doorbell rang. We pulled away from the kiss but kept in the position as I smiled at him. "Pizza's here." I stepped back, and he pouted.

"Wait…you're not going down there like that," he said. I laughed as he walked to his closet and took out an oversized black sweater. He tossed it to me and then put his hands on his hips as he watched me take off the baseball tee. I pulled the tee over my head, then looked at him. His cheeks reddened as he shyly turned away. I bit the inside of my cheek as I put on the sweater, then walked out of the room. When I walked into the basement, Nick and Liam sat by the television. I sat down on one end, then took a slice of pizza and ate it. Out the corner of my eye, I noticed Nick staring at the floor.

"Are you okay?" I asked.

"Yeah, just thinking about while we were down there. I walked behind because I took everything in. Trying to figure out how we ended up in the industrial area, in the alley," Nick responded as he looked at me in a concerned way.

"Well, it's the sewers. They could lead to anywhere." I shrugged.

"Yeah, but it's weird that they had a utility hole there in the freaking bathroom. Whoever built it chose a strange place because there's so much land open," he added as I thought it over. Benny came downstairs with his phone in one hand and a bag of pretzels in the other. He tossed the bag to Liam, who ate.

"Are you too lazy to get up and get pretzels that you have to text me from downstairs?" Benny asked as he sat down between Nick and me.

"I was busy," Liam said with a mouthful of pretzels as he gestured to the television.

"Dude, do you have a paper and pencil? I want to

see something," Nick stated as he pushed aside the snacks on the coffee table.

"Yeah," Benny answered as he got up and walked to the shelf behind us. I wrapped the blankets around me as I sat next to Nick, quite interested in where he went with everything. Benny sat down on my left as he handed Nick the paper and pen. We watched in curiosity as Nick drew a sketch of the sewers, then the tunnels we went through. It amazed me how he remembered so much and how bright it displayed. I leaned back on the sofa as my phone vibrated. I took it out and smiled when I saw a text from Levi.

Levi: Hey princess, heard you went all bitch mode with the flag girl.

Lana: How do you know? It happened like two hours ago.

Levi: I'm in this group chat with the guys.

Lana: Oh well yeah, her fault though. All she had to do was say the magic word.

Levi: Yeah, you should have seen her face afterward. She was looking for you.

Lana: How do you know?

Levi: Carter said, princess. What's with all the questions?

Lana: It's nothing. How's college?

Levi: It's good, just my dorm roommate can get quite annoying. Lol

Lana: Really? How?

Levi: Really now…what's with all the questions?

Lana: Nothing, geez, just trying to hold up a conversation.

Levi: Has it come to that where we must ask each other questions just to keep the conversation going?

Lana: I don't know. I should go. Talk to you later?

Levi: Oh, okay. Love you.

"Here's a theory," Liam said as I turned my phone off. He sat next to Nick as we looked at the sketch of the sewers. It was labeled from Ethan's cottage to where we came came out. A few tunnels led to nowhere, which frightened me on how we'd find out where they'd lead.

"What if we can't find Jack August and Detective Kale can't because he's somewhere there?" Liam said, pointing at the paper.

"Yeah, the question is how did he get there?" Nick asked as I looked at the paper.

"I don't know. I was hoping one of you could get it," Liam mumbled.

"It can't be from the alley because it's guarded by a police officer during the day and it's too dark at night to see," Benny said as he gazed at the map.

"It had to be from Ethan's cottage, since the chains were broken and the tiles moved," Nick interjected.

"If Liam's theory is correct, then where is he?" I asked.

"Only one way to find out." Liam grinned as he looked at us. "We go back down there because we're investigators!"

***

To walk down the halls on a Monday with a blocked nose wasn't how I pictured my day. After Liam's crazy idea to go back into the sewers and look for a connection there, we decided to go to sleep. Next morning when we woke up, we were lazy, so we chilled the entire day. I didn't even want to go back down there; we'd get caught.

With so many things going on in my mind, I didn't even notice that the bell hadn't rung. I passed Mr. Bronx's class, and we locked eyes.

"Hey, Lana, you seem confused, and that's not a good sign, because that means I'm not doing my job right as a teacher or uncle…" He trailed off and smiled.

"Morning, I—" I cut myself off when I sneezed.

"Whoa, you okay?" Griffon asked as he gave me a tissue.

"Yeah, it's just the little flu," I said, then blew into the tissue.

"Hey, while we still have time, I just want to let you know that next week is the last week Yale will be accepting stuff for your application," he stated, then walked over to his desk.

"Oh crap. The time went so quick I almost forgot. What else must be handed in?" I asked, then put the tissue in the trash can.

"Have you written two essays on topics of your choice and a list of activities you've done?" he asked as he read off a paper.

"Yeah, I just need to print them."

"Great, and we have your two teacher recommendations, which are Mr. Dockwell and me. The last thing is the secondary school report, which is a whole bunch of stuff."

"I'm getting that. The counselor is helping," I said, and he groaned.

"Lana, do you know how important this is? It's your future we're talking about. All of Carter's stuff is in."

"Wait. Carter applied too?"

"Yeah, he's a smart kid. Doesn't show it much in general, but you and he are both excellent students."

"Wow." I gasped. The bell rang, and people piled into the classroom. Mr. Bronx turned to his students, and I took that as a sign to leave. I tried to get to class as fast as I could, but my sneezes held me back. When I got into class, I took a tissue and sat down. Melissa greeted me as I slouched in my seat.

"Morning, everyone. Here's your tests back,"

Mr. Gorton began as he held papers. “Reason why I didn’t say good morning is because it’s Monday, which means seeing all of you again for the next five days.”

“How do you sleep at night?” Melissa asked as I sneezed.

“I sleep very well indeed, Miss Singe,” he replied as he gave my test. I let out a louder sneeze. Some people looked. I stood up and walked to the teacher’s desk to get a tissue. As I got a tissue, I sneezed again, but this time it was worse as I slouched.

“Bless you,” someone called out, and I thanked them.

“She has been blessed,” Aidan announced, then bowed to me. I gave him a questioning look as I cleaned my nose. It felt so thick and swollen as I blinked continuously.

“Who got the highest on this test?” Carter asked as I stood next to the trashcan.

“Well, you beat Lana by two questions, Mr. Halls,” Mr. Gorton replied as I gawked at him.

“Oh, Willson, this must kill you.” Blake laughed as I glared at him.

“What two questions?” I asked.

“The ones on Circular Motion and Field of Reference,” Mr. Gorton replied as my jaw dropped.

“What? But Circular Mo—” I stopped as I felt liquid fall from my nose. I leaned back and grabbed a tissue.

“Whoa, you’re looking pretty bad,” Blake stated as I felt my throat clog up.

“Thanks, I was going for that look today,” I

sarcastically responded, then sniffled.

"Lana, I think you should go to the nurse," Mr. Gorton suggested.

"What? I'm all right," I mumbled.

"As much as I'd like you to get us all sick so we don't have to attend school, I can't, so please go before you get worse," he said as his nose wrinkled up from my sick appearance. "And don't worry, I'll make sure your boyfriend brings the homework."

"That's depressing. You're still gonna give me homework," I said.

"Just get your things and go, Lana Willson, before I change my mind," he said. I let out a sigh as I walked to my desk and gathered my things. When I looked up, Benny gave me a supportive smile. He held up his phone, which meant we'd stay in touch. I smiled, then walked out of the classroom.

***

Benny

As soon as Lana walked out of the classroom, the period dragged. We took notes on Electric, Gravitational, and Magnetic Fields. It was a lot, especially since Mr. Gorton explained everything in detail. When he'd explain, I'd talk to Lana. I wanted to be with her even though she's sick.

"Yes, Mr. Sanchez?"

"What's the point of all these notes on Coulomb's Law and Electric Fields? It's not like we're gonna use them in the future. When I graduate, I'm gonna burn all my books," Liam stated, and the teacher shook his head.

"It depends on what career you want to go into," he replied.

"Still burning my books." Liam shook his head.

"Are you stupid? You do realize nobody likes you," Austin said as he turned to Liam.

"Hey! My grandma thinks I'm awesome!" Liam exclaimed as I sighed.

"So do I!" Aidan said next to me.

"Who asked you, Rowley? You're stupid as well!" Austin said as people laughed.

"Guess what? My ass is the only one in this room that gives a shit!" Aidan replied as the teacher stared at them.

"Why are you two always talking about each other's asses?" Mr. Gorton sighed.

"Because he farted out glitter once!" Austin yelled out, and Aidan shot up in his seat.

"You said you wouldn't tell anybody! And acting like a dick won't make yours any bigger!" Aidan exclaimed as I tried to hold him back.

"Whoa, whoa, even though I'm enjoying this, it's getting out of hand. One of you has to get out of my class because you're distracting the other," Mr. Gorton stated as he stopped Aidan and Austin.

"I'm not going anywhere," Aidan stated as he folded his arms.

"Me neither," Austin added.

"Then we'll let the class decide," Mr. Gorton said as he placed a hand on each of their chests to separate them. "Whoever wants Aidan to gain freedom, raise their hand?" He announced, and I shook my head as Kelly was the only one who raised her hand. "Whoever wants Austin to get out of my class, raise their hand?" He stated. Everyone raised his or her hand except for Kelly. Austin scoffed as he glared at everyone. "The class has spoken. Just go take a walk and come back when the bell rings," Mr. Gorton said as Austin walked out of the classroom.

"What? But then it's lunch," Austin stated as he stood in the hall.

"Exactly," Mr. Gorton stated and shut the door. I laughed as he walked to the board. Aidan sat down and let out a sigh of relief as we continued with our notes.

***

I took a few chicken nuggets and added them to my plate, then took the sauce with it. Marcus was in front of me, and I looked ahead to see the two last iced coffee cartons. He quickly grabbed them and added them to our trays.

"Thanks, bro." I laughed as we paid.

"No problem. So where's Lana?" he asked as we walked to our table.

"She went home because she got sick. Man, you should've seen her," I said as we approached our table to see Aidan, Carter, and Liam standing around the table.

"You lost?" I asked as I put my tray on the table, then sat down.

"I don't know. Usually, Lana sits here and then we all sort of just pile in," Liam answered.

"Well, just sit down. It's not like it's the first

time she's not here." Marcus shrugged as I sat by the wall.

"Actually, it is," Melissa pointed out.

"Whoa, it feels weird," Liam said, then sat next to Ethan. Miranda sat between Marcus and me. She looked over my shoulder and raised a brow.

"Where's Lana? I need to ask her something," Miranda said as she took out her earphones.

"She went home," I answered as I ate my food.

"Well, FaceTime her. It's urgent," she stated, then took one of Marcus's chicken nuggets. "I would, but I had Mr. George as a substitute, and he fell asleep, so I was on my phone, then it died."

"Okay," I mumbled, then took out my phone to FaceTime Lana. Liam stood behind me as we waited for Lana to answer. A few moments later, she appeared with an annoyed look and a tissue up her nose. "Damn, you look terrible," I said, and Miranda nudged me.

"Thanks for being honest," Lana responded with a sarcastic look.

"So who's at home with you?" I asked.

"My mom gave me this medication and did some home remedies, then she left because the hospital needed her," she replied with a sniff.

"So you're alone," Liam stated as he leaned his head between Miranda and me.

"Yeah, Linda came over a few minutes ago to check up on me. She's weird. She left her cat here, which is making my flu worse," Lana said, then got up.

"What are you doing? Get back in bed," Miranda demanded.

"Relax, I just need a glass of water, and I'm gonna kick this cat out. I don't like cats."

"Aww, you miss Scruffy." Blake popped out of nowhere and sat next to me.

"Not really," Lana grumbled as we watched her walk downstairs.

"Damn, you walk slower than my grandma," Liam said, and Lana turned the camera so that we saw her face.

"Yikes, you look horrible, baby girl," Blake said as I turned my head to him. "What, Nielson? Didn't know that I call her that?"

"I'm her boyfriend, and I don't want you calling her that," I hissed as Blake smirked.

"Well, she likes it. Right, baby girl?" Blake asked as he turned to my phone. Lana glared through the phone as she shook her head. I turned to Blake with a poker look on my face, and he shrugged. "Well, I like calling her that. I don't need anyone's approval," Blake stated, then stood up. I shoved my phone in Liam's hand and got up. Blake and I glared at each other as I clenched my fists.

"What the hell's your problem, dude? You can't go calling my girlfriend that. She's mine."

"She's not your fucking property, dude," Blake said, then shoved me. "Oh, and if you gotta problem with me calling her baby girl, then it might push your buttons that Levi calls her princess." My nostrils flared with rage. As Blake opened his mouth to speak, I cut him off and punched him in the jaw. He backed away and laughed. People started to notice. He launched himself at me and hit me on my temple. I shook my head and glanced up to see that he was going to punch me again. I dodged it, then pushed him onto the nearest table.

"Hey!" Kelly exclaimed as she shifted in her seat. Blake groaned as he tried to get up, but I was fast and towered over him as I threw another punch. I heard voices behind me, and out the corner of my eye, I saw a crowd form around the table. After a few punches, he gripped my fist, then lifted himself up. He knocked his head against mine, and I staggered back. He punched me in the eye but was soon held back by Carter and Aidan. I stalked toward him, but Nick and Marcus held me back. Blake and I glared at each other as a teacher stepped in between us.

"What is the meaning of this? Look at you two!" Mrs. Singleton exclaimed as she gestured to Blake's broken nose and the blood on my face. "Everyone continue with lunch, and you two…to the principal's office…now!"

Ethan grabbed the both of us and dragged us out of the cafeteria. I blocked him out as he talked about how stupid we were.

"Benny!" Liam yelled as we spun around. Liam and Miranda ran toward us with my phone, and I almost forgot that Lana must've seen the whole thing. Liam handed me my phone, then opened his mouth, but nothing came out. Miranda groaned as she looked at me, then Blake.

"Lana's in trouble. While she was walking, we saw someone in the background," she stated as my eyes widened. "Then the FaceTime ended."

Chapter Twenty-Two

Lana

My heavy breathing was the only thing I heard. My phone died when I spoke to Miranda and Liam, but in time, I spun around to see someone walk past me and down the hall. Again, the person was dressed in black, and I wondered how he or she got in. I was in the unicorn onesie that Aidan got me for Christmas. I felt like a psycho whenever I sniffed. The doors were locked, and my keys were upstairs, yet I was too scared to get them. I stepped forward, then glanced around the living room. "There's no way out!" I yelled. "If it's Mike, Christo, or James, you're gonna get caught!" I added, then ran down the hall into Dad's office. I quickly locked the door then leaned against it as I exhaled furiously.

I hoped Miranda or Liam had the intelligence to call my parents. I walked to my dad's desk and searched for a phone or something to protect myself with. Since I found no phone in the drawers, I crouched down to open the bottom one. My eyes widened as I stared at the shiny revolver in Dad's desk. The corner of my lips suddenly went dry, and my hands trembled.

The house was so quiet I heard footsteps above me. With every step, the person took, the floorboard screeched. I lowered my head to the revolver and cautiously took it, then stood up. My hands shook. I aimed the gun at the door as I took sharp breaths. I couldn't hear the steps anymore, which scared me. I put my right hand on the doorknob. I shut my eyes for a moment as I leaned my ear against the door. It's as if the rest of the world had lost its sound. I only heard me breathe, but not a single soul on the other side of the door.

I slowly twisted the knob and opened the door then looked down the hall. It was empty, yet my eyes trailed up and wondered if the person was still upstairs. I raised the revolver in front of me. As I tiptoed down the hall, my eyes flicked everywhere for any type of movement. I stopped and stood a few feet away from the front door. The living room was on my right, and the stairs were on my left. As I put a foot onto the first stair, a shattering noise erupted throughout the house. I got such a fright that my index finger twitched on the trigger. I shut my eyes and waited for the revolver to jerk from the bullet, but nothing happened. I opened my eyes and let out a sigh of relief because when a revolver was used, the hammer must be pulled back. Out the corner of my eye, I saw the front door open, and someone rushed in. My heart skipped a beat as I raised the revolver.

"Lana, whoa," Dad said as he stared at me and

the revolver. I let out a sigh of relief as I lowered the gun and walked to him. He wrapped his one arm around me and took the revolver with his other hand.

"Daddy, I'm so sorry. I'm so sca—"

"Shh, shh, it's okay. I'm here. You're safe now," he whispered as he rubbed my back. I bit my lip as tears streamed down my face. Dad assured me that it was fine while he caressed me. After a while, I slowly pulled away to see Deputy Paul and Officer Jackson walk in. "Check the house," Dad instructed them as he put an arm around my shoulder. I watched as they pulled out their handguns. Officer Jackson looked through the kitchen while Deputy Paul went upstairs. "I taught you self-defense, honey, not how to use a revolver," Dad said as he stared at it in his hands.

"I'm sorry, I just panicked. My phone died," I mumbled.

"It's fine as long as you're okay," Dad said, then pulled me in for another hug. I wrapped my arms around him and pressed my chin on his shoulder. I looked out the front door to see cop cars flash. Another car pulled up, and the man jumped out and walked up the porch.

"Sheriff Willson," Detective Kale greeted as Dad pulled away and spun around.

"Detective Kale. What are you doing here?" Dad asked.

"We're working together now, Willson." Detective Kale smirked, then turned to me. "Who was it?"

"I-I don't know. He was dressed in black. I

didn't see him," I answered, and he rolled his eyes.

"Did he say anything?"

"No, I don't kn—"

"Leave my daughter alo—"

"How did he get in? When did he get here? Was anyone wi—"

"Detective Kale, I do not give you permission to question my daughter now. As you can see, she was here because she was feeling ill. When she's better, she'll answer." Dad cut him off as Officer Jackson walked in.

"Clear," she announced, then looked at my dad and Detective Kale.

"Jackson, go with Detective Kale and scout the area. Ask around, because he or she might still be on foot," Dad commanded as Officer Jackson nodded. Detective Kale stared at me, then left with Officer Jackson.

"Sheriff!" Deputy Paul called from upstairs. "You might want to see this."

Dad and I exchanged looks, then walked upstairs. Deputy Paul was in front of my room, and my eyes widened. We approached the door, and I glanced up to see my window shattered. The glass was on the ground, and I stepped forward, but Deputy Paul stopped me. "It's a crime scene, Lana. You'll have to wait."

"Go downstairs, sweetie. There are officers there too, so you have nothing to worry about." Dad smiled.

"Daddy, you don't think it's…" I trailed off, then looked at my window again.

"I do. Yesterday, Detective Kale and I found out

the name of James's other crewmember. The one who was with him along with Mike…" Dad reminded me as I nodded. "Yeah, his name is Ernst, been working with James for ten years."

"Then who's Christo?" I thought what Noel told me. Then it suddenly clicked that Noel said there were three guys and James. So it must've been Ernst, Mike, and Christo.

"James is a dangerous man, Lana. He knows a lot of people," Dad said, then motioned me to go downstairs.

"Err…okay," I said and did as I was told while Dad spoke to Deputy Paul. When I walked out of the house and folded my arms, I stared at the officers. Half the neighbors got questioned to see if there were any witnesses. From the corner of my eye, I saw a car pull up my driveway. My shoulders relaxed as I saw Miranda, Benny, Ethan, and Melissa get out of the car. Miranda ran toward me and engulfed me in a hug. I instantly wrapped my arms around her torso as I sniffled.

"Thanks for calling my dad," I said as we pulled away.

"Of course I would. Oh my god, Lana…I swear when I saw that guy walk behind you, I got such a fright," she bawled out.

"You scared the shit out of me!" Melissa yelled, then squeezed me.

"Just glad that you're okay," Ethan said as his mouth curved into a smile. As I pulled away from Melissa, I saw Benny stare at me with a lost look. He eyed me up and down, then approached me. I looked up at him to see dried blood on his temple and a cut lip. His mouth parted as a cold expression filled his face. He pulled me in for a hug. I didn't know why, but a tear rolled down my cheek as I leaned on his chest and heard his heart beat fast. He exhaled loudly and stroked my hair.

"Fucking hell, I got so scared. I thought something wa—"

"Ssshh." I stopped him as I looked up and placed my index finger against his soft lips. "Everything's okay. I'm all right," I assured him, then slowly removed my finger.

"Yeah, you're fine. Everything's fine," he mumbled, then kissed my forehead. I held his hand, then brought him down as we sat on the porch steps. Everyone else spoke to the cops while Benny and I watched. As he looked forward, I turned to him and stared at his face. I dragged my finger down his cheek, and he turned to me. He let out a sigh as I leaned my head on his shoulder.

"What happened when you gave the phone to Liam?" I asked.

"I don't like him calling you that, and he's acting like a douche lately. You're my girl. You're my everything, and every time I see you with him or Levi, I feel like you're slipping away," Benny mumbled as I lifted my head.

"But I'm your girl. Not theirs. I don't even like that he calls me that…" I said as I placed my index finger on his chin, then turned it so that he looked at me.

"I call you babe and bright eyes, but I love to call you by your name, Lana Willson. It's a beautiful name for a beautiful girl."

"So you and Blake fought."

"Yep. Now we're suspended for the rest of the week."

"What? Was it really that bad?"

"Not really, but when we got to Principal West's office, Kelly was there. She just made things more dramatic."

"So what are you gonna do?"

"Blake and I have to do volunteering for a few hours. We got different shifts so we won't kill each other. Other than that, I'm grounded till the end of the month."

"There goes our lazy date. Now I have to watch reruns on my own." I pouted. Benny laughed as he swung his arm around my shoulder.

"I promise when this month is finished, we're not doing a lazy date, even though it's our favorite. I'm going to take you anywhere you want. Just you and me, babe."

"I'd like that," I stated as the corners of my mouth turned up. I kissed his cheek, then turned so that I'd wrap my one arm around him. I leaned against his chest, and I took in the scene in front of me.

They could only stay for ten minutes, then lunch would end. Even though Benny was suspended, his mother wanted him home as soon as possible. The rest of the day I watched TV while Dad sorted things out. Mom came home, but only for a while because she had to do a big surgery. I couldn't go in my room because they were busy. I got off the sofa and walked to the kitchen to make myself a sandwich. I found Dad, who spoke to a man in uniform. I walked to the fridge and took out what I wanted on my sandwich. As I spun around, the man shook hands with my dad, then left.

"Who was that?" I asked.

"He's putting in the security system tomorrow. Also, the guy who is fixing your window," Dad replied as I took the bread out.

"Do we really need a security system?"

"Yes, this is the second time something like this has happened, Lana. I want to keep my family safe."

"Okay," I murmured, then made my sandwich.

"Yeah, and you're not going to school tomorrow."

"What? Why?"

"You're still sick, and you just need to…have some rest, with everything going on these past few months," Dad responded as I sighed. An officer came into the kitchen with a bag, then glanced at my dad. I gave him a smile and walked out of the kitchen with my sandwich. As I walked into the living room, the doorbell rang. I groaned as I put my sandwich down, then walked to the door. When I opened it, I saw Uncle Griff with a concerned look. Outside, I didn't even notice that the sun already set.

"Sorry I couldn't be here sooner," he exclaimed, then hugged me.

"It's okay," I mumbled as he crushed me and kicked the door closed. I walked into the living room with him behind. I sat cross-legged on the sofa as I ate my sandwich. Uncle Griff sat down opposite me, then leaned back on the couch.

"Are you okay, though?"

"I'm all right."

"Even though I can see that's a lie, I'm not going to pressure you to tell me. But just remember, other than your dad, I'm the only male whose been here your whole life." Griffon let out a dry laugh. "So, if you ever need an adult's perspective, I'm here…not just as a teacher, but as your godfather and uncle."

"Thank you."

"Have you heard from Levi yet?"

"No. He's probably busy with college and stuff."

"Uh huh," Griffon murmured as I blew my nose. I stared at him with a questioning look, then put the tissue in the trashcan that I kept next to the sofa.

"Uncle Griff, what do you know about Levi?"

"He reminds me of a younger version of myself. So reckless and just…living in the moment, you know? Yet he's sort of, how do I say it?" He snapped his fingers. "He likes to have authority, but there's a small part of him that he only shows to you, Lana, and that's affection."

"Then why doesn't he tell me anything? He treats me like a child sometimes."

"He just doesn't want you to worry. If I could tell you, I would, but he said that he intends to tell you when the time is right." Griffon shook his head.

"When is the time right? When I go to college?"

"He was supposed to tell you when he was here. Yet he just stalled. Typical Radcliff."

"You said 'us' earlier. Who else knows?"

"Obviously his parents, who are dis—" Griffon cut off when the doorbell rang. He gave me an apologetic smile, then got up to answer the door. I folded my arms and huffed because whoever was behind that door better be important to interrupt. I stood up to get my phone that was charged upstairs, but Uncle Griff came into the room with two people behind him.

"Hey, Lana," Keene greeted as he gave a half-smile.

"Hi…Keene a—"

"Pumpkin!" Axel exclaimed as he approached me, then picked me up. "You're okay! You brave little pumpkin, you're okay!"

His muscular arms wrapped around my waist as he swayed me. I placed my hands on his shoulders to stop him. He looked up with a bright smile on his face, then set me down.

"I will never understand how you choose your friends," Griffon stated as he shoved his hands in his pockets.

"Hey, Griffon. Long time no see," Axel said as he greeted Griffon with a handshake.

"Same to you, Axel." Griffon smiled as I looked at them.

"How do you two know each other?"

"Err…we met at a bar," Axel replied as Griffon opened his mouth. "Yeah, a while back, so…nice seeing you again."

"You too," Uncle Griff stated, then walked into the kitchen. We sat down, and I glanced up to see Keene look around while Axel sighed. I awkwardly played with my sleeves and sniffled.

"Blake couldn't be here. He's grounded," Axel said as I nodded. "Your principal is a real prick, you know that?"

"What happened?"

"Blake wasn't even supposed to get suspended, but since Katrina is his daughter and they dated, he obviously suspended him," Axel scoffed, and I laughed at the name.

"It's Kelly, dude," Keene corrected.

"Whatever." Axel shrugged. "We would've come earlier, pumpkin, but I was busy with classes, so…"

"You go to college?" I tilted my head.

"Yeah, my friend Tamia said I should start, so I did."

"How is she?"

"She's good, still sassy, but you gotta love that about her."

"You two a thing?" Keene asked Axel with a lopsided grin.

"Nah, we've known each other since we were kids, like you and Levi." Axel pointed at me.

"That must be fun," I mumbled.

"Yeah." Axel smiled as he looked at the ground.

"Can I use your bathroom?" Keene asked.

"Of course. You've been here so many times, so I don't need to show you the way," I said. Keene smiled, then walked out of the living room and upstairs. I turned back to Axel, who anxiously played with his fingers.

"My brother told me why he got suspended and how Benny was going on about…" Axel started as my mouth twisted. "Can I still call you pumpkin?"

"You call me pumpkin like it's my name," I said and watched as his face reddened. I opened my mouth to speak but stopped when I heard Dad and

Griffon yell in the kitchen.

"A drug dealer is after my daughter, Griffon! Those four boys who didn't do their job had to pay, and since James knew Lana, he will try and ge—"

All of sudden, it went quiet, and Axel and I locked eyes. He smiled as I got up. Axel stood up and gripped my arm; I looked up to see him shake his head. Out the corner of my eye, I saw Uncle Griff enter the room with his wallet in his hand. Keene walked downstairs as Uncle Griff took out cash.

"Angie won't be back till late, so…" He gave Axel the money. "Take her out for a while, have pizza or something."

"What about Dad? Is he okay?" I tried to walk into the kitchen, but Griffon stopped me.

"He's okay. We're just gonna talk," Griffon said.

"And he's okay with them taking me out?" I pointed at Axel and Keene.

"Yeah, we trust them." Griffon nodded with a smile plastered on his face.

"Err…okay. I'll just go and change," I said, because I still wore my onesie.

"Oh no, you look fine, pumpkin. You look cute and warm, plus it's at night. Nobody's gonna notice."

"You don't have to go upstairs. Here," Keene stated as he handed me my phone and black combat boots.

"Boots with a unicorn onesie, nice," Griffon commented as I put on my shoes. When I was ready, I wanted to say goodbye to my dad, but Uncle Griff said it wasn't a good time. I gave him a weird look, but he rolled his eyes and shooed me away with Axel and Keene.

It was strange to drive with two guys who were twenty and twenty-three years old at night. I didn't know where we were going, but I wasn't even hungry. Griffon watched me eat my sandwich, so I knew he wanted me out of the house.

"Where are we going?" I asked.

"You'll see. We're first gonna get your adrenaline pumping, then eat," Axel said as he looked away from the road, then turned to me.

"Adrenaline pumping? I have the flu. I sound like a blocked drain," I groaned.

"Don't worry, it'll be gone in no time," Keene assured me from the backseat.

"I hope so. I got so much stuff to do."

"Don't worry, pumpkin, you'll get in there. They'll be stupid not to accept you."

"Yeah." I forced a smile. After we drove for another twenty minutes, we finally arrived somewhere near downtown. I got out of the car, and the wind blew in my face. "Where are we?" I asked and looked at the old concrete building where people entered.

"You wanna see some entertainment?" Axel asked as we walked. I didn't answer but followed him with Keene behind me. We didn't go through the front entrance where everyone else did but rather the back. I entered the building and noticed the people around us were much older than me. I followed closely behind Axel because I got weird looks from people, but I didn't blame them since I was dressed strangely.

"You're fighting," I stated as we walked past the cage where two guys roughed each other up. Axel told us to get a good spot while he got ready. Since it was Keene and me, it was easier to get space in the front. We managed to squeeze right in front, a few feet away from the cage. I didn't like it one bit. The guy who lost was knocked out, and I barely saw his face from all the blood. People cheered, and I turned my head to see Axel enter the cage. He was shirtless as he put the mouthpiece in. I looked at his opponent, and my eyes widened. The guy was twice the size of Axel. His veins stuck out of his skin to show how muscular he was.

"Go, Axel!" I cheered as they approached each other. As the referee spoke to them, Axel glanced at me and winked. The referee raised his arm as Axel and the other guy took their positions. I let out a shaky breath when the referee lowered his arm and backed away. Everyone erupted in roars and threw profanities at the competitor.

The other guy punched Axel in the face. He was about to hit again, but Axel dodged it and punched him in the stomach. It didn't seem to affect the guy as he instantly hit Axel's temples, left and right.

"Oh my God," I breathed out when I noticed the blood drip from Axel's mouth. The guy wrapped his hand around Axel's neck, then shoved him against the fence. People went wild as they hit the fence too. I watched in horror as the guy continuously punched Axel.

When the guy was about to knock him again, Axel dodged it and hit him in the hip. Using his other fist, he punched the man in the jaw. Axel raised his leg and put his foot on the guy's chest, then shoved him away. The guy did an overhead kick, but Axel dodged it. Keene and I cheered as Axel jumped up and kneed the guy in the face, making him fall to the ground.

Axel continuously punched the man as I cheered. The man dodged one of his punches, then pushed Axel off him. He got up, and Axel marched toward the guy, then threw him against our side of the fence. Keene took my hand and pulled me away as the man sat against the fence. Axel held onto the fence for support as he kneed the guy in the face. It was tense since the guy had his back to us, and I watched the blood splatter everywhere. When the guy had enough, the referee pulled Axel away. He walked around the cage and cheered; people shook the fence and praised him.

"Come on," Keene yelled over the noise as he took my hand. We walked out of the crowd and toward a room. Keene opened the door, where we found Axel on a chair with his feet propped up on the table. "Dude, congrats," Keene said as we entered the room. Axel turned to us with a smile plastered on his face.

"Especially when you jumped and kneed him in the face, it was awesome!" I exclaimed as I stood in front of him.

"So do you feel better?" he suddenly asked.

"Well yeah, a bit. I still have the flu, though, but I-I don't know. It was just exciting." I smiled as he cleaned his face.

"Well, you look better," Axel pointed out, then smiled.

"I'm gonna get the car, so when I honk, you guys must come," Keene said as he took Axel's car keys. I watched as he walked out of the room, then shut the door. When I turned to Axel, I noticed he struggled to clean his face.

"You need help?" I asked. He lowered the towel and gave it to me. I took it from him and slowly patted the cuts on his face. I sniffled, which made a weird noise from my nose. My eyes widened in embarrassment as Axel laughed.

"Here." He took a tissue and covered my nose. I gave him a strange look, but he insisted. I blew my nose in the tissue while he held it. We laughed at the noise, then Axel put the tissue in the trashcan. A car honked in the distance, and I straightened my posture, then gave the towel to Axel. He stood up and smiled at me.

"Where are we going now?" I asked as we walked out of the room.

"I'm hungry, and Momma's making dinner." He grinned, then swung his arm around my shoulder as we walked to the car.

"What about the money Uncle Griff gave you?"

"Pumpkin, Momma's food is ten times better than takeouts."

***

We arrived at the Gunner household, but I didn't want to be here. "I'm home, beautiful family!" Axel announced as he turned on the living room light. Blake entered the room, and his eyes landed on me. I noticed his left eye twitched. He looked at Keene and Axel, then approached his brother.

"What the hell is she doing here?" Blake demanded as he stood right in front of his brother.

"I wanna go home," I whispered to Keene.

"Relax, brother. I texted Momma, and she said it's fine if pumpkin joins us for dinner. Besides, doesn't she look adorable in that outfit?" Axel asked as they turned to me. Instead of looking away, I stared at Blake and saw his black eye and bandaged nose. He eyed me up and down, then sighed.

"I'm sorry, baby—"

"Don't you dare call me that. I don't like it, and my boyfriend doesn't like it."

"I like it," he said blankly. I stepped forward and was ready to lecture him like he did with me, but Axel came between us and Blake smirked. From the corner of my eye, I saw Mrs. Gunner walk in from the kitchen.

"Momma, pumpkin's here."

"Who is?"

"Lana Willson, Momma." Axel frowned, then swung his arm around my shoulder.

"Well, the food is almost ready," she said as I gave her a kind smile.

"You need help, Mrs. Gunner?" Keene asked.

"Sure, thank you, Keene." He followed her into the kitchen. Axel let go of my shoulder and stood in front of me. I looked into his brown eyes and noticed the smile.

"I'm just gonna go clean up quick. Don't kill each other while I'm gone." He faked a smile at Blake. He walked down the hall, and I folded my arms. Blake walked toward me. As I turned to him, he picked up his pace and forced me against the wall.

"What the hell are yo—"

"Pretty hot that you got balls to hold a gun, GG." He pressed his chest against mine. He raised his one arm and placed it on the wall as he towered over me.

"I thought you knew by now I'm no good girl," I muttered.

"Oh, I know. I just wanted you to say it." He leaned down to my ear. "You've been a naughty girl lately, but you're my bad girl," Blake whispered as I shuddered. "You might be a nerd," he said as his other hand went down to my thigh and stroked it, "but you're a very bad girl." As I felt his bottom lip flick my earlobe, I shoved him away.

"Food's ready!" Mrs. Gunner announced from the kitchen. I glared at Blake and pushed myself off the wall. He swung his arm around me, and I tried to remove his arm, but he wouldn't budge.

"But my brother's right. You do look fucking adorable in that onesie, baby girl," Blake whispered in my ear, then dropped his arm. To sit was hard since Blake wanted to sit next to me. We walked around the table like idiots until Keene noticed something was up. He approached the table and asked if I wanted to sit next to him. I naturally accepted since I trusted him. So I sat next to Keene with Axel opposite me, Mrs. Gunner on end, and Blake next to Axel. Even though Blake was far away from me, I still noticed his smirk.

"Lana, I heard what happened earlier today, and

I'm sure you're tired of hearing people pity you, and you seem just fine," Mrs. Gunner said as I chewed my food. "Have you heard from any of the universities you applied for yet?"

"Yeah, I know from ones here in Illinois, but I'm still busy with my Yale application. It's the school I really want to get into."

"All Blake's applications have been sent in," she said as we turned to Blake, who stared at his mother.

"There's a lot of work they want, so I have till next week," I said.

"Oh, well, hope you get in. You're a smart girl."

"Dude, where you going?" Keene asked Blake.

"Minnesota." Blake grinned and poked his food with a fork.

"Or the University of Illinois, Blake. They really like you," Mrs. Gunner added.

"I got time," Blake said as his smile faded.

"Okay now, I'd like to know why my one son looks like he'd been kicked by a donkey several times. I know my other son got suspended, so what happened to you, Axel?" Mrs. Gunner gestured to the bruises that formed on Axel's face. "Don't tell me you've been in a cage again?"

"Told you, Momma. He's not my brother. He misses the zoo, so he's always fighting in a cage with another animal." Blake sipped his water.

"No! I'm winning, Momma. Even ask pumpk-Lana."

"Is this true, Lana?"

"Yes, he's very goo—" I cut myself off as she stared at me. "It's not good for you."

"But I enjoy doing it."

"I don't enjoy seeing my son coming home every second night with a new bruise," she pointed out as Axel sighed. "Baby, you don't need that money. You have a job, you're going to college now, and you have a roof over your head. Why would you still want to fight?"

Axel shrugged and continued to eat. An awkward silence stretched in the room as we continued to eat. Blake didn't seem phased as he picked at his food while Keene was on his second plate.

"May I use the bathroom?" I asked.

"Of course, down the hall. Second door on your left." Mrs. Gunner smiled.

"Thank you," I mumbled, then walked out of the room. I used the bathroom as quick as I could yet it was hard since I wore a onesie. Once I was done, I zipped up the thing again and washed my hands. When I looked into the mirror, I noticed a shadow underneath the door. I closed the faucet and spun around. I looked down at the door and walked toward it. The shadow didn't move, yet I noticed its legs. I rested my palm against the door and listened. "Blake, if that's you, you're not funny," I said as my breaths quickened. I twisted the doorknob and pulled the door open. I felt paranoid because there was no one. I shook the thought away and walked out of the bathroom. While I walked down the dimly lit hallway, I had a strange feeling that someone watched me.

Chapter Twenty-Three

Lana

The next morning, Mom made breakfast, then went to work. Dad went to the station but left me in the hands of Linda. I wasn't in the mood to talk, yet she didn't mind since she spent the time looking for her cat. Dad was only gone for an hour, then came back. He told Linda to leave since she was obsessed with her cat. I also decided to take a shower earlier since I wanted to get out of the onesie and into a comfy pair of sweatpants and one of Benny's sweaters. The doorbell rang as I sat down with a bowl of popcorn, ready to watch *Footloose*. I let out a groan as I got up and walked to the door. When I opened it, I was surprised to find Blake. I gave him a once over; he looked good in his black ripped denim jacket, band tee, black jeans, and combat boots.

"Blake, what are you doing here? Aren't you supposed to be doing co—"

"I need to talk to you." He cut me off as he

backed away. I gave him a strange look, then walked out of the house and onto the porch. Since the sleeves were long on Benny's sweater, I pulled them as I folded my arms. "Do you like Benny?"

"What sort of the question is that? Of course I do." I laughed.

"Do you know what he has done to you?"

"Blake, what are you…where are you going wit—"

"Answer the question."

"Y-yes, but it only happened like three times. Most of it was teasing."

"Yeah, but he still fucking did it," Blake hissed as I stared at him.

"He changed for me. He promised he'd never do it again, and he's living up to his promise, unlike others who just don't give a fuck," I snapped.

"I said I'm sorry. What more do you want?" he quietly asked as his eyes bored into mine.

"For you to mean it and let us have at least a week where we don't fight," I said. He laughed, bitter and dry, as he placed his hands on his hips. His eyes landed on me, and he stared. His features softened as he eyed me up and down.

"I like you, Lana. I like you a lot; I'm falling for you so fucking hard," Blake confessed as I stared at him. "Even though when we're together it's not in the best situation, I just like having you around. I enjoy your presence. I like it when you push your glasses up, when you bite the inside of your cheek when you're nervous. Yeah, I noticed that. When you stare at me with a blank look on your face, it…gives me time to get lost in those mesmerizing blue eyes of yours."

"Blake, I—" He cut me off as he cupped my cheeks and continued.

"Please just give me a chance. I'll treat you so much better, baby girl. You of all people deserve a happy ending, and I'll be glad enough to give it to you," he whispered, then pressed his cold lips against mine. His eyes shut as he kissed me. Mine were open as I looked at his bruised eye and realized what he's doing. His lips began to move, so I blinked, then pushed him off me.

"No! What the hell? You can't…you can't just do that, Blake," I said as he gripped my wrists and stared down at me. As I looked up at him, his nostrils flared with his nose ring. He breathed hard and frowned.

"Look me in the eye so I know that night meant nothing to you. In Benny's room, in the car, at the pool, and the motel," Blake demanded as his grip tightened on my wrists. We suddenly stopped, and I stared at him because I knew that nothing happened at the motel. Blake's facial features softened while he searched my face; he chewed on his bottom lip and nodded. "Well, you know what?" Blake laughed. "They meant the world to me, Lana Willson." He let go of my wrists. "Why can't you see that I like you?" He backed away. "You know I'm going crazy for you and everyone else knows that except for you!"

"I do see! I know that you have feelings for me. I see how you look at me and the countless times you try to kiss me. I do see, Blake. It's just…I don't feel." I mumbled the last part, then looked at him.

"I'm sorry, Blake. I just…you keep hurting me."

The atmosphere was tense around us as I stared at the floor. I wanted to get inside and curl up into a ball and cry.

"What is wrong with you, huh?" he burst out as I backed away. "He's going to end up hurting you, Lana! You're so fucking blind and gullible!"

"You're the one who always hurts me! He changed! He cares about me, and he changed for me!" I yelled.

"Fucking bullshit!" Blake shouted, then hit his fist against the wall. My father came outside and looked at us. Blake huffed as I sniffled. We locked eyes, and mine turned glossy as his raged with anger.

"What the hell is going on here?" Dad demanded.

"Blake was just leaving," I whispered, and he rolled his eyes.

"Hey, don't you freaking roll your eyes at my daughter! Get the hell off my porch!" Dad exclaimed as he stood in front of me.

"Whatever," Blake muttered, then walked off the porch to his motorcycle. I folded my arms as I watched him get onto the bike. As he drove off, I looked at my dad. He gave me an assured look, and I nodded, then stormed into the house.

***

The next week was spent in silence since Benny wasn't at school, so I buried myself in my books. I spent time with Miranda, Melissa, and Tiffany but never told them what happened with Blake. I never told anyone, but I knew I had to tell Benny sooner or later. Blake and Benny came back to school the following week, and everything went back to normal. Especially Blake, since he skipped classes and slept around. A rumor even went around that his house was used to have regular sex.

It was after school and the second to the last day that I could send my stuff for Yale. I gathered all the work to go to Mr. Bronx and the counselor. Benny leaned on the locker beside me and scrolled through his phone.

"You ready?" he asked as I searched my locker for one last form.

"For?" I raised a brow.

"My basketball trials. Coach is evaluating me for this one college. We talked about it yesterday."

"Oh, I forgot. I'm sorry." I facepalmed and backed away from my locker.

"Yeah. It's always that, isn't it…" Benny nodded and turned away.

"What?" I asked as I gave him a once-over.

"I never see you, babe. At lunch and after school, you're always busy. The only time I get to see you is five minutes before class."

"Benny, you know that I can't help it. I'm busy thinking about my future here." I pointed to the file with all my Yale stuff.

"Yeah, but what about our future? You never have time for us anymore," Benny murmured, then pushed himself off the lockers. "But you make time for him…" he added as he leaned on the lockers opposite me. I gave him a questioning look. He grunted and took his phone out. I paled when I saw the picture of Blake and me when we were at the paint party on New Year's.

"Benny, I was drunk. I didn't even kno—"

"Do you know how worried I was when you weren't in my room? Then you sent me a text saying how you're going home, but no, you went with them." He raised his voice.

"They took me, and I was dru—"

"Yeah, it's okay because you were drunk. Out with someone else, but it's okay because you were drunk. Kissing another guy, but it's okay because you were drunk. Whenever Lana Willson is drunk, the slut comes out," Benny hissed.

"Wha— screw you!" I exclaimed as my jaw dropped. "When I was sober, the first thing that went through my mind was you! I wanted to be with you! I never cheated on you. Do you think I'd do that?"

"Well, considering he likes you…I just don't want to fucking lose you!"

"You won't. It's just school is always my first priority, Benny, and it's not my fault that you're grounded," I said. He laughed.

"Well, sorry for not wanting other guys calling my girlfriend names like that," he yelled, which echoed down the empty hallway.

"Whatever you say or do won't stop him! Stop letting him come between us," I shouted.

"I should stop?" he rhetorically asked, then gave me a once over. "You know what? I'm just gonna go. Call me when you have time for us."

"I always try to! School always comes first, and

you know that!" I yelled as he walked down the hallway. He held up his middle finger as my lower lip trembled. "Fuck you too, Benny Nielson!" I yelled as he walked around the corner. I tugged on my hair, then spun around. I came face to face with a clueless Carter, who looked at me, then down the hall where Benny walked.

"Is everything okay?"

"No! Ugh, why are guys so fucking confusing?"

"I don't know how to respond to that one." Carter awkwardly chuckled.

"Carter, what do you want? I need to go see…" I trailed off but stopped when he handed me a file.

"Here's your test. Thanks for letting me borrow it," he said. My left eye twitched as I thought Benny and I could've ignored the whole fight if he came sooner.

"Thank you," I said, then shut my locker.

"Well, good luck," Carter said, then gave me a supportive smile.

"Thanks." I sighed, then walked down the hall to the counselor. It took an hour to get everything in order, then check if everything was okay. Uncle Griff didn't need to come, but he came for support. Once we finished, the counselor said she'd get back to us when she heard any news.

I let out a sigh of relief as I walked out of the school doors and took in the fresh atmosphere. My expression changed when I remembered that Benny was my ride home and he was probably gone. He's so immature, I had to always be at his games and cheer him on, but he didn't care about my future. I huffed as I gripped my bag straps and walked down the stairs. While I decided which way to go, out the corner of my eye, I saw someone wave. When I turned my head, I saw Marcus Sanders on the soccer field. He seemed to be calling me. As I walked onto the field, I noticed he walked toward me. Yet what made my eyes pop was the fact that he wore a t-shirt, with a pair of running shorts and Nike shoes. I raised a brow at how Liam knew he had an eight-pack, but I didn't. It was clearly visible through that t-shirt.

"Hey, Lana," he panted.

"Err…hi, Marcus. What are you doing here?" I asked.

"I just come and practice sometimes." He gestured to the soccer ball he had next to his feet. "And you?"

"Oh, I was just finishing some work."

"Cool." He nodded as I did the same.

"Yeah, I should probably get going," I mumbled.

"Yeah…wait, you're walking?" he asked as I spun around. I turned back around to see that he put on a sweater. He picked up the ball, then smiled at me. "I'll give you a lift home."

"Thank you." I nodded and followed him.

"Come on; I just gotta go grab my things," he said as we walked off the field and toward the building. "So Lana Willson was about to walk home. I'm assuming something happened between you and Benny?"

"Wouldn't you like to know?" I warily eyed him.

"Well, I saw Benny storming past me into the halls. He slammed the door by the gym, so yeah, just had a feeling." Marcus shrugged.

"Yes, we did, but it was childish," I mumbled.

"It was bound to happen, though. Sometimes at lunch when I ask him where you are, he just grunts," Marcus said as I frowned.

"Have you and Miranda ever fought?" I asked as we entered the building.

"Yeah, there was this one time when I came over to her house, and she opened the door to see my hands were empty. I gave her a questioning look, and she held her phone up," Marcus began. "I looked at my phone to see that she'd sent a message saying that she wanted tacos, but I didn't see the message since I was driving, so we argued about that."

I laughed because Miranda would do such a thing.

"Then there was another fight that lasted days," Marcus mumbled as I looked at him. "It was about her mother; I didn't want Miranda staying home alone when her mother was drunk. She told me not to worry, but I didn't listen."

"The only reason her mother drinks is because she still loves Miranda's dad." I remembered the night when Miranda and I went to go get her.

"Yeah, I understand, but fifteen years later…you'd think she'd move on by then," Marcus said as we approached the door for the boys' locker rooms.

"Well, Miranda told me that he made her jubilant. Also, he loved to play games, especially baseball," I stated.

"Baseball…that's why she wanted me to teach her how to play," Marcus said as I tilted my head at him.

"Maybe one day when she sees him, she'll know how to play," I suggested.

"Yeah…then I'll try my best," he said, then opened the door. "I'll just be five minutes."

***

Fifteen minutes later, I walked through my house and put my bag on the ground. I thought the ride home with Marcus would be awkward, but we talked about Miranda. At least there was something to say. I walked into my dad's office to tell him that I finally sent all my things in for Yale. I entered the room to see papers scattered everywhere.

"Dad?"

He peeked his head up from the desk, then stood up. He straightened his posture and walked to me with a fearsome look. From that one look he sent me, I knew there was some exciting news.

***

I drove fast yet cautious down the streets on my way to Blake's house. I texted Aidan, and he said he was there with the other guys. Even though I didn't want to see Blake, it was urgent. I parked by the street and got out. As I walked up the pathway, music blared through the house. I knocked on the door as loud as I could and waited. As I took out my phone, the door opened, and I glanced up to see a shirtless Blake in front of me. As I opened my mouth to speak, a girl walked next to him and placed her hand on his chest. She was in her underwear.

"Who's she, babe?" she asked as I looked at her and Blake.

"No one you need to know," Blake said as he squeezed her butt.

"Okay. I'll see you at Jaden's party this weekend, right?" she asked. He nodded, then pulled her in for a kiss. I patiently waited as I watched the two open their mouths as if to see who could swallow each other first. Scruffy was sniffing the ground. While they made out, I looked around to see a toy that belonged to Scruffy. An idea popped into my head as the corner of my mouth pulled up. I took the toy, then waved it in front of Scruffy's face. He jumped, and I moved it around, then placed it next to the girl's foot. I bit my lip to prevent myself from laughing as Scruffy launched at the girl's foot and bit it. She let out a squeal and bit down on Blake's bottom lip.

"What the fuck?" he demanded.

"Aww, Scruffy bit you," I cooed. "It seems like he doesn't like you, and if Scruffy doesn't like you, then Axel won't like you."

"Who's Axel?" the girl demanded, and I tried so hard not to laugh as she glared at Blake.

"Get out," Blake grunted as he pushed her out the house. I stepped aside as I watched her walk out into the cold in her underwear. When I turned to Blake, I noticed his stare on me. He opened the door more and stepped to the side. I walked in and scrunched up my nose at the mixed odors.

"Lana, what are you doing here?" Ethan asked as he looked at Blake and me.

"I-I need to talk to you guys." I looked at Carter and Aidan, who entered the room. "It's quite urgent."

Aidan nodded, then motioned us to follow him. I quickened my pace so that I was in front of Ethan and far away from Blake. Even though Benny and I fought, we were still together, right? I mean it was one serious fight. The music played as we walked past the living room. I saw Keene, Jaden, Axel, and a few other guys smoking in a room. We walked down the hall, and I scrunched my nose up from the moans. The only place that wasn't occupied was Mrs. Gunner's room. I wrapped my arms around myself and waited for everyone to settle. They looked at me with questioning looks as I avoided eye contact.

"Do you remember the guy who shoved the bag at you?" I asked.

"Yeah, he had black hair and brown eyes. Why?" Ethan asked.

"What did James tell you about him?" I asked Aidan.

"He just told us that he's dead. He didn't want to be part of it all, so he just…backed out," Aidan replied as my jaw clenched.

"Well, my dad told me his name is Christo Aimar," I said, then looked at Blake. "Do you remember that night when we saw James and one of his men said they miss Christo?"

"Yeah…where are you going with all of this? He's dead," Blake stated.

"No…my dad just told me that he might not be dead," I whispered as their eyes widened.

"What do you mean he might not be dead? James told u—"

"Well, he might've lied to you. My dad just came back from visiting all the morgues in Illinois, and they've never heard of Christo Aimar before," I said.

"Wait, but your dad told us that he came to confess, and then two days later he was reported dead," Carter spoke up.

"Yeah, he came to confess, then went back home. Dad questioned his family, and it's like they barely knew him," I mumbled, then bit the inside of my cheek.

"Wait, so who reported him dead?" Ethan asked as he looked down at me.

"That's the thing I don't get…his family reported him dead and was facing too much grief to answer any more questions."

"Well, James is not just a drug dealer, he's also good with identities," Aidan said as we looked at him. "For all we know, Christo might be alive and right in front of us."

"So he might be alive and still in Illinois?" Blake asked as he looked at Aidan and me.

"Yeah, and I agree with Aidan. He might still be working with James," I said, and I noticed their nervous looks. James was not done with any of us. The silence stretched between us as the only thing to be heard was the loud music. Out the corner of my eye, I noticed Blake got up from his mother's bed.

"Well, that's a bummer," he stated, then swayed a bit.

"What's gonna happen now?" Ethan asked as he looked at me.

"My dad will probably question you guys again if anything comes up."

"Anything else?" Blake asked as he placed a hand on the doorknob. I slowly shook my head, and he smiled. I watched as he opened the door, then walked out. Carter and Ethan followed, but Aidan stayed.

"What do you think James is planning?" Aidan asked as he stared at the ground.

"I don't know. I just hope that nobody gets hurt. How did you know that he's good with identities?"

"Well, when we had the cocaine, I kept in contact with him the most. One of his men told me; I think it was Ernst."

"Does Tiffany know you're here?" I asked as I thought about the things that happened in the house.

"Yeah, I just came to hang out with my cousins and friends," Aidan mumbled.

"Okay," I said, then walked out of the room. I turned back to see Aidan with his hands shoved in his pockets as he stared at the ground. He had his thinking face on, so I decided to close the door and leave him to think. I walked down the hall and into the living room. It was filled with people who smoked, talked, or snorted drugs off the table. Some guys even did it off girls' bodies.

"Lana!" Jaden exclaimed as he motioned me to sit next to him. I slowly shook my head, but he tilted his head. Jaden Reid was bad news. Not just his wild parties, but also the fact that he was another version of Parker made me uncomfortable. I felt someone pick me up by the arms and carry me to Jaden. The guy forced me down on the sofa right next to Jaden, who snorted drugs using a rolled-up dollar bill. “How are you doing, Lana Willson?” He tilted his head back and pressed one nostril. I noticed the sweat on his forehead, either from the drugs or the crowded room. It made his ebony skin tone glow, and I glanced down to his biceps.

“F-fine,” I said as he turned to me.

“You want some? Looks like you need it.” He offered me the dollar bill.

“Jaden, back off, dude.” Blake’s voice stopped me. I turned my head to see Blake opposite us with a beer bottle. “She’d rather have this.” He smirked, then held up the cigarette. I stared at the cigarette, then him. I’d only had two cigarettes this year so far. Which made me wonder how many Blake had. Yet by the look of his house, I could tell he hadn’t lived up to his New Year’s Resolution to cut down on cigarettes. “You need it, baby girl. Don’t try to deny it. I can see it in your eyes,” he said, then held up his lighter. I bit the inside of my cheek as I looked at it again. Benny entered my mind and the fight we had earlier. I took the cigarette and put it between my lips. I took the lighter, lit the cigarette, and inhaled. I closed my eyes as I let it rest between my lips. I heard Jaden howl like an idiot beside me. As I exhaled, I open my eyes and leisurely tilted my head back. “That was hot,” Blake pointed out as I looked back at him.

“I hate you.” I put the cigarette to my lips as

Blake smirked.

"If you hate me, then why are you still wearing the chain I got you?" he asked, then lowered his gaze. I'd never taken it off since Levi left. It became an effort to take it off then clip it back on, so I decided to leave it on all the time. It was under my clothing, but it was still visible. I exhaled the tobacco into Blake's face, and he opened his mouth, inhaled, then blew it out. A girl approached Blake in nothing but a shirt. It barely even covered her butt as Jaden drooled.

"Thanks," she said, then gave him money. He took the money and put it in his back pocket.

"So this is like a whorehouse?" I blurted out, then dumped the cigarette in the ashtray.

"Indeed. Carter calls the girls, and I call the guys. It's a brisk trade, as you can tell." He pointed to a couple that couldn't wait and decided to do it in the hallway.

"Does your mom know?"

"Nope. Since she's got a hectic job as an assistant for this rich-ass company. They wanted her to go to Greece with them, so she's been gone for the past week." He smiled as I stared at him. Jaden gave him the dollar bill as the guy next to Blake separated the drugs into lines. Jaden got up and was escorted out of the room with a girl while I watched Blake. He crouched down and put the dollar bill near his nose. We locked eyes, and he suddenly froze. He cursed under his breath, then sat up properly. "Don't look at me like that. Like you care," Blake hissed.

"I care as a friend," I mumbled as he gave the

dollar bill to the other guy, who took it without hesitation and snorted the drugs.

"I don't want to be your friend," Blake said as he shook his head. "I wanna be more than that."

"Did you ever do it?" I looked down at the drugs.

"Nope," he said, then drank his beer.

"Why are you doing this to yourself?" I asked as he chugged down the beer.

"Isn't it obvious? I'm getting over you. Since you're so self-centered, I should just move on," Blake replied, then rolled his eyes.

"I-I'm not self-centered. I'm just…confused. I think I'm happy, then I'm not," I mumbled, then looked at the table.

"Isn't that sad," Blake stated, then rolled his eyes.

"What's wrong with you? One minute you're calling me baby girl, then the next you say I'm self-centered?" I raised my voice.

"I'm tired, Lana. Tired of everything that's been happening, tired of you. I just wanna fucking move on," he breathed out, and I scrunched my nose up as the alcohol hit it.

"If you're tired and want to move on, then you never really liked me, Blake," I muttered and stood up.

"Where do you think you're going?" he demanded. He tried to stand up but almost fell from being drunk.

"Away from you!" I exclaimed, then walked toward the door. I felt someone grip my arm and whip me around. I looked up to see Blake attempting to look at me as his eyelids drooped. I glanced over his shoulder and realized people looked at us.

"I'm sorry, baby," he whined as I pushed him away.

"Fuck off, Blake."

"Aww, you're ruining the party, Lana," Keene said, but I ignored him and walked toward the front door. Somehow Kelly was there too, and she sent me nasty looks. Only then I noticed quite a few people watching me. Carter called out to me, but I ignored him and pushed my way out of the house. I got into the car as quickly as possible. The music played in the house again, and I let out a pathetic scream, then banged my fists against the wheel.

Chapter Twenty-Four

Lana

When I got out of the car, I made sure to slam the door. Out the corner of my eye, I saw Benny get out of his car, but I continued to walk.

"What are you doing here?"

"Look, I'm sorry. I didn't mean to go all out on you like that. I didn't mean anything I said. I was just angry," Benny apologized as I turned to him.

"But you still said it! And you know what a sensitive person I am." I frowned.

"I didn't mean it! You know when I'm pissed I say the first thing that rolls off my tongue without even thinking," he added as I took out my key to unlock the door. "I'm sorry…we can't stay mad at each other forever. I just wanna talk, please? I'm just afraid to lose you."

I ignored Benny as I walked into the house. The alarm went off. Next to the door was the keypad, and I quickly typed the pin in to disarm it. When I turned around, I saw Benny on the porch. His mouth moved, but I shook my head and slammed the door. I leaned against it and still heard Benny. I didn't want to talk to anyone because it had been a very long day.

"Please, Lana, I'm so sorry. I didn't mean to go off on you like that," he said as I sank down into a sitting position. "I know that you want to get into Yale. You've buried yourself in books this past week, and I was worried. I didn't want you to go back on the pills." I shut my eyes. "Please, I'm sorry. I also didn't mean to call you that. I was just angry when Kelly showed me the picture. I just missed you a lot."

A tear rolled down my face as I silently cried. My throat ached, my head throbbed, and I wanted to drop. I cupped a hand over my mouth to prevent any sound.

"I'm so sorry, Lana. Please, I jus—I just don't want you to stress so much. Please open the door, and we can talk…" He trailed off as I sniffled. It seemed like everything that happened came out. All the anger, fear, sadness, depression, and shame that I'd felt the past few months flooded through my mind. The only words that echoed in my head were that it was all my fault. I couldn't hold it anymore, so I cried with my eyes shut. "Fucking hell, don't cry, please. I promised myself I wouldn't make you cry ever again. Please, Lana, I'm so sorry," he whispered. "I just want to hold you."

"No." I finally wiped the tears with my sleeves. Even though I needed that right now, I didn't want to face him. "Just go, please," I added, then pushed myself up.

"Lana, we can wor—"

"*Just fucking go!*" I screamed as tears streamed down my face. I didn't care if I sounded like a psycho as I cried so loud. It was hard to swallow since the lump in my throat grew bigger. While I sobbed, everything went mute. My mouth was open, but no sound came out, yet the tears flowed. I pushed myself off the door and slowly walked upstairs. I got to my room, then shut the door and made sure to lock it. Then I collapsed onto my bed and cried into my pillow. Even though I had amazing friends and family, I felt alone. I felt like no one would understand what I went through and thought I was a depressed freak who looked for attention. I squeezed my pillow and thought over the past few years and how everything that had happened was my fault. I was done; I was tired of it all. It was the kind of tired that sleep would never fix.

***

Sophomore year was the most sensational year of my high school experience. I sat on a bench behind the school and watched everyone outside since the weather was beautiful. It was a few days before spring break, and I met a girl, Miranda. I supposed we're friends since I met her in the restrooms when I hid from him.

Him. Benny Nielson. All he ever did was tease, humiliate, and bring me down. I never did anything to him. I pushed my glasses up and looked around to see him march toward me. My eyes widened as I took in his appearance. He was angry. Except this time, he seemed so full of rage that he'd do it again. It was freshman year when he slapped me after school. That's the first and what I'd hope the last time he'd done that to me.

"Do you know what I just found out, nerd?" Benny hissed as he towered over me.

"Wha-what?" I asked as he put an arm on either side of me.

"Ethan fucking Baxter became captain. It's your fucking fault! I deserve to be captain! You just had to be there yesterday and cheer him on! You just had to motivate him back in elementary school!" he exclaimed, then pushed me off the bench. I landed on the ground with a thud, then shut my eyes and groaned. I heard movements. I opened my eyes to see Benny. He crouched down and slowly stroked my hair. "Why haven't you ever noticed me? Why weren't we friends back then?"

"Wh-Why do you do this to me?" I croaked out as my bottom lip trembled.

"I hate myself for doing it. I'm so fucked up and alone. I hate myself so much that I tried to commit suicide! How fucking crazy is that?" He laughed yet I noticed a tear roll down his cheek. "Where is he?" he demanded, then placed a hand on either side of me.

"I-I don't know what you're talking about," I cried out as his face neared.

"Radcliff! Levi fucking Radcliff! Where is he?" he yelled in my face. "Where is he so he can give me what I deserve?" he demanded, and I thought back to when Levi and Keene beat up Benny.

"Where is he so he can finish the job once and for all? We're all so fucking happy, right? Where is he?" he demanded and banged his fists against the ground.

"I don't know," I cried.

"Where is he?"

"I don't know!"

"Where is he?"

"I don't know!" I *exclaimed, then shot up in my bed.*

I glanced around the room and noticed it was dark. I touched my face and felt dried-up tears. I laid back on my pillow and thought of the dream I had. It felt like a nightmare because it wasn't a dream; it happened. Only one thing entered my mind when Benny gave me all the letters he wrote over the years. The one from sophomore year that he wrote days after Levi and Keene beat him up and days after he cut.

I slowly got up and turned on my desk lamp. I stretched my arms and walked to my closet. I took a pair of sweatpants and searched for a comfy sweater. I opened the bottom drawer and stared at the clothing Levi left. He didn't even wear half of the stuff, only rocked in white tees and black jeans. I took out his black crewneck sweater and put it on. I got back into bed and raised it to my nose. I closed my eyes and took in the smell. It still had his strong masculine aroma mixed with aftershave. I frowned because I missed him.

I went to my contact list, and my thumb hovered over his name. I quickly dialed his number but realized how late it was. On the second ring, he answered, and I gripped his sweater. I heard him clear his throat, and suddenly I didn't know what to say. I didn't even know why I called him.

"Princess?" His voice sounded sincere and groggy, which meant that I woke him. I didn't know what to say, so I ended the call and put my phone on the table. I facepalmed at what I was about to do. I didn't even know what to say. I was snapped out of my thoughts when my phone turned on, and the light shone. I turned my head and picked up the phone to see a message from Benny. He sent two messages, and I decided to check the first.

Benny: Even though we're not on best terms right now, I just wanna say goodnight. I just wanna say I'm sorry and that it's all my fault. I'm just really sorry, and I hope I didn't wake you.

Benny: I can't sleep, all I'm thinking about is you. I need you so bad, and I'm so sorry I just didn't want you to get so hooked on the books that you'll look at pills or cigarettes again. I know you'll get into Yale, they'll be stupid not to accept you. I'm with you all the way, and I let you be the first few days because Miranda told me not to worry, but now I am.

I let out a groan as I put my phone back and pulled the blanket over me. I saw Benny every day, yet he missed me. I guess I missed him too in a way. Although with everything that we went through, at least I saw him. He didn't even know the real value of missing someone.

***

I sat in the passenger's seat of Carter's truck and stared at my phone. Since Carter lived five minutes away from me, I asked him for a ride. I continued to read the messages Benny sent me. I haven't replied to them naturally because I didn't know what to say. It'd be funny if I responded with "'K" since he took the time to think up those words. I sighed to myself and turned my phone off. The silence stretched between us, and I didn't like it. I turned on the radio, and a love song played. I groaned and threw my head back as Carter laughed.

"So I guess you two haven't made up?"

"Yeah."

"It looked like a big fight considering you flipped each other off," he said as I rolled my eyes. "Since it's Friday, you wanna ditch?"

"As much as I want to, I don't want to get into trouble." I sighed. We arrived at school five minutes later, and the bell hadn't rung yet. Carter opened the back of his truck, and we sat down. Tiffany and Ethan approached us while Carter took out a cigarette. He offered one to me, but I declined.

"BOO!" someone yelled behind me, and I jumped. I spun around to see Aidan on the back of the truck. Ethan and Tiffany hugged me, then Aidan jumped down to hug me. I sat down with Tiffany on my right and Carter on my left. When I glanced up, I searched for Benny. I spotted him across the parking lot by the sidewalk. He leaned against a tree with Nick, Melissa, and Marcus. I sheepishly looked away when we made eye contact. Tiffany leaned her head on my shoulder, then let out a sigh. “Now that all your Yale stuff is in…will you finally sit with us at lunch?”

“I don’t know,” I mumbled because Benny would be there. “What are your plans?”

“Well, there’s this college I applied for in Canada. My aunt lives there, so if I get accepted, I’ll probably stay with her.”

“What did Aidan say?”

“He’s okay with it, but what’s worrying me more is him. When I ask him about the subject, he dodges it all the time,” she said as we looked at Aidan. He waved at someone, and I followed his gaze to Liam on his skateboard as he returned the gesture.

“Well, he has to tell you something sooner or later.” I shrugged as the bell rang.

“Yeah,” she said as we walked to the front doors. I looked over my shoulder and noticed Benny’s frown. I bit the inside of my cheek and turned away as Carter put his arm around my shoulder.

***

The whole day we looked at each other. We did Phys Ed, and I told Miranda what happened. Not the part where he called me that word. Heck, I wouldn’t tell anyone. She was stunned and glared at Benny the whole period. Then our last period was Biology, and we did an experiment in pairs. I obviously paired up with Carter and looked to see that Britney chose Benny. I watched them the whole period, and I thought she noticed halfway when she placed her hand on his arm and batted her lashes.

Since it was Friday the day flew by. I took out books from my locker for the weekend, trying my best to hurry up. Carter waited for me by his truck since we'd go to Ethan's place and hang out. I shut my locker and came face to face with Benny.

"Hey," he mumbled, then stared at the ground. I ignored him, then spun around to walk out of the school building. I heard Benny sigh behind me, followed by his footsteps. I stuffed my hands in my jeans pockets and resisted the urge to roll my eyes. "You can't ignore me forever, Lana. Please, I told you I'm sorry." He apologized for what seemed to be the millionth time.

"I know, but how do I know that you won't say something or do something like that again?" I demanded.

"Please, I was stressed out. You're not the only one who's working hard for their future. I just really wanted you to be there because Coach was evaluating me for this one college. I needed your support."

"You could have just said that instead of going all out on me!"

"I'm sorry. I just missed you. We can talk this out. Come with us to the diner."

"Who? Your new friend?" I scrunched up my nose.

"Britney? She was just nice."

"Oh, come on, Benny, it's crystal clear she has a thing for you."

"No, she doesn't. She was just nice because I didn't have a partner in Bio because you were off with Carter."

"Carter's my friend, Benny. He's also yours."

"Yeah, but he's also the biggest player in school."

"He's only a player if you let him play you," I stated, then pushed the doors open.

"Lana, how long are you gonna keep doing this?" he asked.

"As long as my mood lasts." I threw my arms up in exasperation. "For now, I'm done."

I walked down the stairs and saw Carter in his truck smoking a cigarette. Ethan leaned against the truck with a cigarette between his lips.

"So, what? We're done?" Benny asked as I froze. Carter and Ethan heard, and they turned to me. I slowly spun around to see Benny sulk.

"I'm giving you space," I stated. "So you'll know how it really feels to miss someone that you care about."

With that, I turned around and walked toward the truck. Ethan opened the door for me, and I got in without hesitation. He got in as Carter threw out his cigarette and started the truck. We drove, and I glanced at the side view mirror to see Benny in the same position.

***

I thought we'd go to Ethan's house, but instead, we arrived at his cottage. I got out of the truck still confused as to why we were here. Naturally, we parked on the side of the cottage, but I looked opposite at the sign.

"Why are we here?" I asked. Nobody answered me as I spun around to face the cottage. My shoulders dropped as I saw Blake get off his motorcycle.

"What are you doing here?" we asked in unison.

"We can't hang out if you two don't sort out your problems," Ethan stated as he folded his arms.

"Where's Aid—"

"BOO!" the familiar voice of Aidan Rowley exclaimed beside me as he jumped up from the back of the truck. I let out a high-pitched scream because I thought someone would attack me.

"Dude, you were in the back of my truck?" Carter asked as Aidan jumped out of the truck.

"Well, duh. I wouldn't miss the chance of seeing this place again," Aidan stated as he pointed at the cottage.

"Come on. My dad wants me to check this place agai—wait! What happened to the lock?" Ethan demanded as he saw the chains on the ground. "Shit, he's gonna be pissed. Come on." He gestured to Carter and Aidan. They walked into the cottage, and I bit the inside of my cheek in the hope that they wouldn't find the utility hole.

"You're doing it again," Blake pointed out as I turned. "Biting the inside of your cheek."

I stared at him with a questioning look on my face, to which he sighed and stepped forward. He looked up at me and bit his bottom lip.

"Look, I'm sorry about yesterday. I was drunk, and I didn't mean what I said to you. Also, I'm sorry for acting like a jerk and for Kelly even being at my house," he said. "I'm also sorry for coming to your house and yelling at you like that. I shouldn't have done that right after you've experienced something so upsetting."

"When will it be the last time you say sorry?" I whispered.

"I don't know," he mumbled.

"What do you mean you don't know?" I bit the inside of my cheek.

"I-I can't explain, but I'm saying sorry in advance," he mumbled as I frowned.

"You're gonna hurt me again, and you're doing nothing to prevent it from happening? What is it?" I swallowed the lump in my throat because I didn't want to cry.

"I can't tell you, baby girl. But just know that I'm really sorry, and I really care about you," he whispered as a tear rolled down my cheek.

"Blake, plea—" He cut me off as he pulled me in for a hug. A hug or being comforted by someone sort of triggered the feelings to come out. I fought back the tears because I didn't want to be weak. I didn't want to cry again. The front door of the cottage creaked open, and Carter, Ethan, and Aidan awkwardly walked out. Ethan and Carter looked at us, but Aidan was oblivious to what had happened. I sniffled, then slowly pulled away. I quickly wiped my tears as they stood in front of Carter's truck.

"These cookies that I found in one of the drawers of the kitchen are so good," Aidan said as he held up the bag.

"Dude, what if it's expired?" Carter asked, and I

noticed that he had a box of condoms.

"What if the condoms that you left here expired?" Aidan spat out crumbs.

"Condoms don't expire," Ethan said as he squinted his eyes at the two. He turned to Blake and me with a panicked look. "Right?"

"Just go, you three! We'll meet you at the house," Blake said as I lowered my head. Two minutes later, they drove down the road toward Ethan's house while Blake and I were alone. Great. If we got into another fight, he'd leave me. "What's wrong?" he asked after a while.

"Nothing," I mumbled. I didn't know how or why, but my arms wrapped around him again, and I leaned my head on his chest.

"Don't lie. The whole day you never smile or laugh, and that's saying something because both of those things look beautiful on you." He placed his palms on my cheeks. "Who do I need to hurt?"

"No one. It's fine, but thanks."

"You know, I built you up well in these six months."

"What?"

"Before the bet, you were a nobody. You let people walk over you. Remember our conversation in there? And then we fell asleep?" He tilted his head toward the cottage.

"Y-yeah, how could I forget?" I chuckled.

"In these six months, we've done stupid, ridiculous things. I might've not done the whole bucket list with you, but we took chances. We took risks, and I managed to bring out the side of Lana Willson that nobody had ever seen," Blake said as he stroked my cheek. "Now you're standing up for yourself, not letting anyone walk over you or stop you from doing what you want."

"Levi might've shown me everything, but you, Blake Gunner, you taught me how to feel, how to control it, but you brought out the bad side of me, which I hated," I admitted, which was true, because even though Levi taught me how to smoke, Blake made me crave it. He made me addicted to things and brought out a complete opposite to the Lana Willson that everyone knew.

"Well, you try to see the good in people. I look for the bad to see if they're strong enough to defeat it," he said, then let go of me. Blake held my hand as we walked to his motorcycle. We got on, and he started the engine. As we drove to Ethan's house, I thought about what he apologized for in advance.

We arrived at Ethan's house and found the rest of them in the cinema room. Aidan demanded that we have a movie night, so we each decided on our favorite movie. I wanted Tiffany to come so that there'd be another girl, but Aidan said she had a family function. I sensed Carter told the guys about Benny and me because they tried to cheer me up. It made me think of the bet when everything didn't go to hell.

***

When I fluttered my eyes, I saw the screen in front of me. I placed my hand in front of my face and rubbed my eyes. Then I put my hand down, but the surface was smooth and warm. I raised my head to see that I was on Carter and his arm was wrapped around me while the other hung loosely. He was asleep, and I looked around to see Ethan curled into a ball on the sofa. I slowly got up, and Carter moved under me. I towered over him as he opened his eyes and ran a hand through his hair.

"Morning," he said in a raspy tone. I smiled, then looked around to see Blake awake, on the sofa next to us. Aidan was in front on the ground asleep with an empty box of pizza beside him.

"Morning," I said to Blake, who smiled and waved. Carter stood up and stretched. He looked at Aidan, then flung a pillow at him. Aidan stirred and waved us off as he turned to lay on his stomach. I looked at the time and saw that it was almost twelve. I couldn't even remember how we fell asleep, because after we watched Carter's choice of movie, we talked.

"Aidan, wake up," Blake said as he continued to throw pillows at him. One hit Aidan's butt, and he farted.

"Really?" I whined.

"That woke me up," Ethan said in his morning voice, which was thick and groggy.

"Oh no, I did it again," Aidan said as he looked at the empty pizza box. "I ate in my sleep."

I laughed as he placed a hand on his stomach with a cautious look. Ethan told us to stay for brunch, and it was superb. Aidan and I ate pancakes with Nutella. Afterward, we hung out in the basement. Aidan and Ethan played a video game while Carter, Blake, and I played pool. I'd never played it before, and I versed Blake, so Carter helped me out, but I still lost. Wow. Carter then took me home since Melissa texted me about a sleepover tonight.

I got home, and Dad was there. He asked where I was and I said to Ethan's, which resulted in no further explanation. I showered and decided on a black pleated skirt and black floral top. Levi wanted to FaceTime, and I gladly accepted. I sat at the desk with my laptop open while music played.

"Yeah, every day when we'd walk home from elementary school, the old guy from down the street with one eye came out and yelled at us. It was shit scary, man." Levi shivered.

"All the kids in the neighborhood were afraid of him." I laughed at the memory.

"Yeah…hey why did you call the other night?" he asked. I knew that topic was bound to come up.

"Err…my finger must've slipped. Sorry for waking you," I mumbled.

"Your finger slipped at three in the morning, and I heard your loud breathing. What's wrong, princess?" he asked with a concerned look.

"Nothing. I'm all right."

"I can see right through you. Now tell me what's wrong."

"Benny and I had a little argument, okay? No biggie."

"No biggie? What the hell did he do?" Levi demanded.

"Nothing. Like I said, we just had an argument," I said, then took out my phone.

"So I guess you haven't talked it out?"

"Yeah," I mumbled, then went into Instagram

since Miranda sent me a private message.

Miranda: Dis bitch tho.

I raised a brow to see that she sent a picture too that someone posted. I tapped it and saw Britney's page and her recent post. It was of her and Benny at the diner yesterday, and the caption said: *Besties.*

Lana: The hell? She spoke to him once this year!

I shook my head and put my phone down, then saw Levi sitting in his car. He lit a cigarette, so I took a screenshot. We did it all the time to each other.

"Hey, what song is playing?" Levi asked as he exhaled the tobacco.

"Err…"Robbers" by The 1975." I looked at my Spotify.

"Oh," he said, then wiggled his brows as the song played. I covered my face with my hands in embarrassment because the whole album played in his car when I let him take my virginity. I removed my hands to see Levi sing along to the lyrics. I laughed as he belted out the words, and my cheeks reddened. Suddenly, the door flew open, and Blake entered, singing along. My eyes widened as he walked over to me. Levi stared wide-eyed as he leaned into the phone. Blake stood behind me and wrapped his arms around my neck. We swayed and went with the beat of the music. The song ended, and we laughed. I stood up and walked to my overnight bag. Blake sat down on my chair and greeted Levi.

"What are you doing here?"

"Heard you're going to a sleepover. Melissa asked me to take you since you don't have a ride," Blake replied.

"Where's my daddy?" I blurted out.

"Right here, princess!" Levi exclaimed, then laughed with Blake. My cheeks reddened, and I mentally slapped myself.

"You guys suck." I pouted as I put on a sweater.

"You swallow," they said in unison.

"You spit," I stated with a smile.

"You choke." Levi smirked as I stood beside the desk.

"You blow," I said.

"You gurgle," Blake snorted.

"Not for free," I said, and they laughed. Levi spoke about Jaden and his parties while I bent to sit down. I told Blake to shift up, but he shook his head and instead pulled me onto his lap. I tried to get up, but he locked his arms around my waist. "How are your parents?" I asked since Blake took out his phone.

"They're good. My mom can't wait to come back to Illinois again," Levi responded as he ran a hand through his hair. Blake waved his phone in front of my face, and I saw the picture of Benny and Britney. I rolled my eyes and pushed his phone away. "I gotta go meet a friend soon, so I'll check you guys later."

I nodded, then looked down to see Blake's left hand stroking my thigh while the other went under my skirt. I bit the inside of my cheek as I gripped his wrist.

"Don't you want to make him jealous?" he whispered in my ear as his hand went in between my thighs. I got goosebumps as his hands touched my skin. My eyes suddenly dropped, and I leaned my head back on his shoulder as he caressed my thighs.

"Err…guys, I'm still here." Levi's voice snapped me to my senses, and I pushed Blake off the chair.

"Love you, see you. Bye," I said, then shut the laptop. I turned to Blake with a glare, but he smirked.

"You know…your dad just left when I arrived." He bit his lip. "You can make Benny so jealous; he'll be on his knees begging for your forgiveness, baby girl."

I eyed Blake up and down, then walked toward to him. I rested my palm against his chest and looked up at him while the corner of my mouth twitched up.

"Really?" I asked as he wrapped his arms around my waist.

"Yeah." He smirked, and I felt his hand go down toward my skirt. When he was about to go under, I raised my hand to slap him. With his quick reflexes, he took my hand and pulled me forward so that our chests were against each other. "Even I saw that coming, baby girl."

I huffed and pushed myself from him. I put on a black cardigan and combat boots, then grabbed my phone and bag. We walked out of the house, and I hopped onto Blake's motorcycle so that he could take me to Melissa's house.

***

Blake

I walked down the hallway on a Monday morning even though I didn't want to be here. I was pissed, which meant I'd be pissed the whole day. Momma came back from Greece yesterday, and she wasn't happy with the place, so we had to eliminate any whiff of drugs, sex, or alcohol. I turned the corner to see Carter and Lana by her locker. Friday was fun with her; it's been a long time since the five of us spent time together. She had to fall asleep on Carter's shoulder. Ethan said he should take her to his room, and we'd sleep in the cinema room, but he insisted that he didn't want to wake her. For crying out loud, she's a heavy sleeper. Carter could've left her on the sofa, but instead, he positioned her on him. I approached them and took in Lana's appearance. She wore a big black crewneck that looked familiar, blue ripped jeans, and ankle boots with her glasses. She looked beautiful in anything, and I was glad that one day she'd dress like a cutie, then a badass.

"Hi, Blake." She smiled, then hugged me. I returned the gesture and wrapped my arms around her. I loved it when we hugged.

"Hey, man," Carter greeted, and I forced a smile then shoved my hands in my pockets.

"Did you guys do the Physics homework?" Lana asked as she went through her book.

"Nope," I said.

"Yep," Carter replied. She gave me a look, then turned to Carter. I leaned against the locker and blocked them out as they spoke about the answers. The bell soon rang, and we strolled to class. We took our seats with Carter next to me and Lana opposite by the window. The teacher annoyed me. His ways and how he's so carefree.

"All right, class, take out your homework!" Mr. Gorton announced as he came into the classroom. I leaned back in my seat and sighed.

"I have your pop quizzes from last week, and most of you did well," he said. "Oh, and Liam. It's 2017. Quit writing 2016!"

"Sorry, Mr. Gorton, still have to get used to it." Liam shrugged as he took the paper.

"You are the stupidest person I have ever met," Austin stated as he stared at Liam.

"Hey, you got a little bullshit on your lips," Liam said as he pointed at Austin's mouth. Everyone laughed as the two glared at each other, and I shook my head in amusement. I turned my head to look at Lana, but the teacher cut off the view.

"Where's your homework, Blake?"

"Didn't do it."

"Is this going to become a regular thing? If so, I'm going to call your mother again."

"Again? Why the fuck did you call her the first time?"

"She called me because she wanted to know about your grades. But I think I'll call her again because you just swore at a teacher."

"You're not even a proper teacher. You let

people fight and cuss in class. I'll rather be in Mrs. Singleton's classes instead of being taught by an inexperienced teacher," I hissed and watched as Mr. Gorton's eye twitched. I smirked because I knew I'd pushed a button. Like the first day, he placed a hand on either side of my desk and crouched down so that we locked eyes.

"I don't remember asking for your opinion, but since we're sharing how we feel…I think you should get out of my class and come back when you've dropped the attitude, Gunner."

As soon as those words came out, I shot up from my seat and walked out of the class. I walked down the empty hallways and decided what to do for the rest of the period. I saw movement at the periphery of my vision. I looked over my shoulder to see Parker with a girl. I squinted my eyes as I slowly approached them. She frowned and furiously shook her head. I watched as Parker pulled her arm and turned his head. I followed his gaze and saw the janitor's closet. My jaw clenched because the little fucker still hadn't learned his lesson. The thought of him doing it to Lana once broke me. I wish we met earlier in life and I'd be the one who saved her. As he opened the door, I walked over and pulled back on his collar. When Parker spun around, the girl ran off, and I took the chance to shove him in the closet. He landed on a shelf. I huffed as I pulled off my leather jacket and nicely hung it on a hook.

"B-Blake, come on. You know we're cool, right?"

I let out a bitter laugh as I approached him. I grabbed him by the collar and shoved him against the wall next to us.

"I'm fucking pissed, and you're the right person to take it out on, Parker Collins."

***

I decided to ditch the rest of the day and went to Rodney's store. Since Axel worked there after his classes, I went there mostly to listen to music and chill with them. As I entered the store, music played. Axel was behind the counter busy with a customer while Keene sat by a table. He was on the phone when I sat next to him.

"Hey, brother…what happened to your hands?" Axel asked. I looked down at my bruised knuckles.

"Oh, I was just beating the shit out of Parker." I shrugged.

"Cool—wait, the asshole who did those things to pumpkin?" Axel asked as he walked around the counter.

"The one and only," I muttered.

"Blake's here too," Keene said as I turned to him. Keene placed the phone down and pressed the speaker. Levi spoke, and I immediately rolled my eyes.

"Where are you?" I asked because the background was noisy.

"I'm driving, and there's a shit load of traffic," he answered.

"Listen, I can't do this anymore," Axel said. "Every time I talk to pumpkin, I just feel sorry for her, and I just want to tell her."

"Same," Keene replied, then looked down.

"Dude, we all agreed that we'd tell her everything after she graduates…when I see her this summer. So just fucking wait and think before you speak," Levi said.

"We're hurting her even more—you know that," Axel mumbled as he slumped his shoulders.

"We're only doing it to protect her. The truth hurts like shit. We don't want something like that to happen again," he said, referring to when James came out of nowhere and shot that guy.

"What if someone snitches?" Keene asked as he looked at me.

"The fuck. I won't." I squinted my eyes at him.

"I'm not saying you. I mean your friends, Carter, Ethan, and Aidan. They know too."

"They won't tell. We kept cocaine a secret for two years; I'm sure we can do this for a few more months," I said, then gave Keene a fake smile.

"My battery is gonna die soon…Axel?" Levi asked, and I looked at my brother to see him stare at the phone.

"Yeah?"

"When you see Lana again, tell her I love her," he said as I balled my fists even though it hurt like a bitch.

"I thought Levi Radcliff doesn't believe in love," I interjected before Axel said anything.

"Dude, you know what I mean," Levi scoffed. "That night in the jail cell, I told you I can't give her the life she deserves."

The other side of the call went quiet, but I heard the traffic. I glanced up at Keene, who tapped his fingers against the table.

"Besides, love is a weakness. It's like a game," Levi added.

"Yeah." Keene nodded as he stared me dead in the eye. "And you two keep playing with her heart."

Chapter Twenty-Five

Lana

It's been two weeks, and in those two weeks, Benny and I communicated. Even though it tore me, we decided to give each other space and see other people. Not because of the argument we had, but because of everything from school, the James situation, the Jack situation, and what we wanted to do after high school. When he told me that we should see other people, the first thing that went through my mind was Britney. I asked about her, and he said they're friends. In my mind, I found ways to rip her face off, then when he left, I cried myself to sleep that night. I didn't want to see other people, and I saw in his eyes that he didn't want to either, but it was for the best. I told the guys, and Blake said we should go out and celebrate. I didn't know what he meant by celebrate, but we ended up at one of Jaden's parties.

As I walked down the dimly lit hallway, guys eyed me up and down and smirked. I put the thing to my lips and inhaled as I closed my eyes. I entered the kitchen, slightly dazed as I looked around. A couple made out on the counter, and I wanted to gag. *Ugh, they looked so happy. Wait till shit hits them.* It was the guys, Tiffany, and me here. I invited Miranda to come, but she didn't want to go to another one of Jaden's parties ever again since she lost her virginity to Keene. It was understandable because she had Marcus, and it'd be awkward if she bumped into Keene.

"Lana?" I spun around to see Ethan. He looked hot in his sleeveless muscle top, black jeans, and Nike shoes. A lazy smile filled my face as I locked my arms around his neck. I almost fell but felt his hand on my back. I laughed, then inhaled the smoke. He narrowed his eyes at the thing between my lips. "Are you smoking a joint?" he asked, and I nodded. "No, no, this is not how you should be getting over him." He frowned as he leaned against the counter. I leaped forward as he caught me and wrapped his arms around my waist.

"Then how? It's probably better than Benny, who's getting a blowjob from Britney," I mumbled. "I'm just casually smoking a joint, waiting for some guy to screw me…so where's Blake? Or even Carter?" I stated, then glanced around. I had a few drinks before Jaden gave me the joint. I depended on dangerous things to take my pain away.

"You've been drinking, and now you're smoking. Don't do this to yourself," Ethan said as he took the joint away. I watched as he dumped it on the ground and crushed it with his foot. "I know you're sad about this whole Benny thing, and I know that you two really care about each other."

"Sad doesn't even begin to describe how I feel, Ethan." I laughed. "About everything."

"Do you wanna go home?" he asked. I frowned because that'd be the best thing to do. I told my parents I was gonna stay with Tiffany, but both of us were invited to Ethan's house.

"Yeah, I'll get Tiffany and Aidan. You find Carter and Blake," I stated, then walked off. I went into the living room—it was packed with people. I pushed into the crowd with people's sweaty bodies. It was congested in here, and my head ached. A catchy song came on, and everyone danced. I smiled as I swayed my hips to the beat. I felt someone's hand on my waist and looked up to see a guy with dirty blond hair, brown eyes, and stubble. He sent me a wink as we danced. I turned around to lean on him but looked up to see…him. And another one who looked exactly like him a few feet away. The one I danced with gripped my hips as he forced me to grind against him. I tried to let go, but he was stronger than me. His twin walked toward us with a smirk. I spun around and pushed the one off me, then walked out of the crowd. I saw the bar not too far ahead, and I quickly walked toward it. When I reached the bar, I felt a hand grab my waist to pull me around. As I spun around, I grabbed the vodka bottle that was on the table and swung my arm. A glass shattering echoed in my ears as I realized I hit the guy in his temple. My eyes widened as he staggered a bit.

"Lana! What the hell happened?" Aidan demanded as he approached me. Tiffany was next to him as she gaped at the guy who swayed.

"Him and his..." I trailed off yet saw no sign of his twin. The guy fell to the ground, and Aidan crouched down. He stood up again and turned to us.

"He's unconscious," Aidan said, then looked around. "Let's get out of here before anyone notices."

"Aidan, do something!" Tiffany screeched as she gestured to the guy who had a piece of glass sticking out of his head.

"Should I call an Uber for him?" Aidan suggested. Tiffany and I glared at him.

"You bitch! What the fuck?" I whipped my head around to see the twin brother with a pissed-off look. He walked toward me but was held back by someone. As he turned around, Ethan balled his fist and punched the guy.

"It's your cocky-ass brother who started this shit," Ethan muttered. My eyes widened as the man tried to punch Ethan, but he took his wrist, twisted it, and shoved him away. I thought he'd land against the wall, but instead, he knocked into a very pissed-off Blake Gunner. Blake was solid as a rock as he looked at the guy. As the guy got up, Blake raised his knee and kicked him in the stomach. Apparently, the guy had friends, and they came over to help. Ethan and Aidan ran to help Blake. Tiffany and I turned to the unconscious guy on the ground with clueless looks. I tapped a random blond guy who appeared drunk as shit on the shoulder.

"Your friend, he, err...he needs help," I blurted out as the blond guy gaped at the unconscious man on the floor.

"Oh no. Should I call him an Uber?" the guy asked.

"Sure." I tilted my head. He nodded, then stared at the man as if he waited for something.

"You should call now!" Tiffany blurted out.

"Oh yeah! Good idea." The guy laughed, then took out his phone. Even though stuff like that happened at Jaden's parties, I couldn't help but get the image of Jack August in my mind. I hit him in the head too. I was snapped back to my senses when Tiffany grabbed my hand and said we should get out of here. I nodded, then followed her as we walked to the front door. As we passed, I saw Blake take on three guys who had blood all over their faces. The place looked crazy. Aidan hovered over a guy and punched him. Ethan shoved a guy against the wall, while other people started their own fights. Once we got outside, I folded my arms and leaned against Ethan's Corvette Stingray. Tiffany and I looked at the house and heard the yells. After a few minutes, everything went silent, then Jaden shouted like there was no tomorrow.

"There they are." I pointed to Aidan, Ethan, and Blake, who casually walked out of the house.

"Are you guys okay?" Tiffany asked as she hugged Aidan. Blake walked toward me with a concerned look; he pulled me into an embrace, then rested his chin on my head.

"Are you okay?" he asked, and I nodded. I didn't know why, but I felt safe when Blake's arms were around me. The past parties we went to he was by my side. At school, whenever he saw Parker, he randomly pulled me into his chest and glared at him.

"Turns out that's the Willis twins. Jaden said they're always harassing girls at his parties," Ethan explained as he clenched his fist.

"It's stupid that they're invited," I muttered as Blake entwined his fingers with mine. I looked down to see his knuckles had a purplish color. I glanced up at him, and he shrugged me off.

"Where's Carter?" Aidan asked as he looked at us.

"We thought he was with you gu—"

"There's the idiot," Blake stated, and I followed his gaze to see Carter Halls climb out of a window, naked.

"Dude!" Aidan yelled as he covered Tiffany's eyes with his hands. The rest of us laughed as Carter climbed down. He landed on his feet, then held his crotch as he ran toward us.

"Where are your clothes?" I demanded as he looked at the house.

"In the room. We have to go now!" He attempted to open the door, but it was locked.

"*Carter fucking Halls! Where are you?*" Jaden's voice echoed from the house.

"Carter, what did you do?"

"He just caught me having sex with his sister…no biggie." Carter shrugged as he hid behind the car. "Now can we please go!" he added. I laughed as I got into the car with Ethan. Aidan brought his car, so Blake and Tiffany drove with him. The drive to Ethan's house was awkward since Carter was naked, covered only by a blanket.

***

We got to Ethan's place and decided to stay in the cinema room again. I didn't drink so much, so by the time we were home, I was sober. Tiffany brought clothes, but I completely forgot mine, so I had to borrow a shirt from Ethan. We watched a movie on the screen, then chilled the rest of the night. Aidan made a fort, so the whole cinema room turned into a massive cuddle fort. Tiffany and Aidan were at the top, while Carter, Blake, Ethan, and I were at the bottom and shared a bottle of whiskey. Carter came to sit next to me; I noticed he had my glasses in his hands.

"You found them!" I cheered.

"Yeah, they were in my truck," he stated, then smiled at me. I watched as he opened them and looked at me. He slowly put them on me, then put a lock of hair behind my ear.

"Shots!" Blake's voice startled me as he stood between us, then sat down. Carter shifted away. Ethan placed small glasses in front of each of us and filled them. I bit the inside of my cheek as I thought how the rest of the night would go.

***

I let out a yawn as I opened my eyes. A few feet away were my glasses, but the thing that bothered me was the heartbeat against my ear. I slowly looked up to see Blake's lips parted as he slept. We fell asleep on the floor, so we had many blankets thrown over us.

“Psst.” I heard a voice behind me and turned around to see Carter with his morning hair. He motioned me toward him. I did because I was curious as to how I fell asleep. I slowly removed Blake’s arm from around my waist and put it on his chest. I shuffled to Carter and laid on my side. He brought me closer to him and put his arm around my torso. Our faces were inches away as I gazed into his blue eyes.

“How did I…”

“Well, after the many shots we took, you sort of had a breakdown. You cried about Benny.” He looked at my lips.

“What did I do?”

“You were talking about Britney, then you talked about how you missed him. Then you—err…” he stuttered as I sighed.

“What, Carter?”

“You called yourself a whore, which you’re totally not. We even tried telling you, then you got mad, and that’s when Blake came in,” he muttered as his eyes locked in on my lips. “He comforted you, and well, you fell asleep. You’re anything but that, Lana. You’re beautiful, funny, caring, and unique.” He placed his hand on my chin. My lips parted as he ran his thumb over my bottom lip. I watched as he stared at my lips eagerly. Everything happened so fast as he leaned forward and smashed his lips against mine. My eyes widened as Carter moved so that he hovered over me. On a side note, he’s an excellent kisser; no wonder he’s the player of the school! Yet I didn’t want to get hypnotized by his beauty or his amazing lips; he’s a player. He had sex with Jaden's sister!

Out the corner of my eye, I noticed Blake stirring. Carter sensed it too, then pulled away. He landed on the other side of me, right next to Blake.

"What the heck? How'd you get here?" Blake croaked out as he squinted at the blond. Carter shrugged with a smirk molded onto his face while I stared at the ceiling. Blake held a sour expression as he looked at me, then Carter. He laid back down and turned on his side so that his back faced us. As I licked my lips, I realized that Carter Halls kissed me. I felt his hand intertwine with mine under the blankets. I turned my head to the left to see Ethan a few feet away from me, jaw dropped. My face drained of color because he witnessed the whole thing.

Very soon, everyone else woke. Tiffany had extra clothing in her bag, so she lent me her white shirt dress that I had to zip up. Ethan told us we could use his room and bathroom to get changed while the guys used another room. Tiffany came out in a gray sweater and red pants. I gathered whatever I had from my last visit to Ethan's house, along with the shirt dress.

"Hey, are you okay, Lana?" Tiffany asked as she brushed her ginger red hair.

"Yeah, I'm good."

"Carter told me that you barely remember anything from last night," she stated as I lowered my head. "Well, now that you're sober, what do you miss about Benny?"

"I don't know. Seeing him having fun with Britney…it makes me confused. Because while I'm here suffering to get over him, he's out there having fun." I frowned.

"Don't think that. Maybe he's just trying to move on or hide his feelings from everyone." She pulled me in for a hug. "Aidan told me that when he went to Benny's house to hang out with them, Benny was up in his room," Tiffany said as we pulled away. "Nick went to check if he was okay and…"

"Wha-What happened?" I croaked out.

"I don't know, but Benny never came down that night," she said, her face filled with confusion. Afterward, Tiffany left the room, and I showered. Once I was done, I put on my underwear, then the shirt dress. It was still a bit cold outside, but I decided to put on my black woolen tights later. I walked out of the room to see Blake's back faced toward me. He wore his baggy sweatpants, which meant that he still had to shower. As I walked, he spun around, and that's when I noticed the cigarette.

"Heard you were looking for me last night." He stepped forward, then exhaled the smoke. "Heard you wanted to screw me."

"I was drunk."

"Not an excuse," he said, then pressed the cigarette on Ethan's desk. He reached underneath for the trashcan, then cleaned it up. He turned back to me and ran his hands down my arms. "You still wanna make him jealous, baby girl?"

"We're not even together anymore."

"Still." He cupped my cheeks and pressed his forehead against mine. "You want him to see what he's missing out on."

"Why are you doing this?"

"I realized we'll be using each other in our own way. I'll finally get you out of my system by just doing it, and you'll get Benny back for being with that bitch," he whispered, and I bit the inside of my cheek. "Plus, you'll be mine before time runs out." I gave him a questioning look, and he chuckled.

"How are we going to make him jealous?" I asked as he eyed me up and down. If I looked at myself in the mirror, I'd see myself as desperate because, yes, I did miss Benny since I saw the good in him. He changed for me, and he made me happy. I was too stubborn to admit it, and now he's gone. The only way to get him back was to make him jealous, to do it.

"I'll start off slow," Blake stated, then wrapped his left arm around my torso and rubbed my back. It wasn't so bad—his other hand glided down the back of my body until it landed on my butt. He gave a tight squeeze, and I exhaled loudly. "I'll do stuff like this…" His left hand went to my waist. He kissed up my neck, and I leaned my head to the side and shut my eyes. "Then when we're alone…" I felt his fingers on the back of the shirt dress. He zipped down the dress, and I let it fall to the ground, which left me in a bra and panties. I watched as Blake went down on his knees and kissed down my stomach. His hands wrapped around my thighs as I got goosebumps. He stopped and grazed his finger over the scar I got when Axel threw the bottle at me. Blake kissed the scar, then continued to run his fingers along my skin. He kissed my hips, then stopped again as he looked at my tattoo. Blake firmly gripped my hips, then stood up. He lifted me up and gently put me on the bed. As Blake hovered over me, my fingers got lost in his hair, and he grunted. He kissed down my neck and on my collarbone. His hand went to my tattoo, and I felt his thumb rub the ink. "When we're alone, I'll make you feel like a queen." He tapped my tattoo. I raised my head and pressed my lips against his because I wanted to feel his hard lips against mine. He responded quickly when he kissed back and pressed his chest against mine.

"Blake," I breathed out, then arched my back so that he'd kiss around my bra. "We're just doing this, right?"

"Yeah. We're helping each other out here, baby girl." He exhaled deeply, then continued to kiss me. I felt his hand going down to my underwear and brush it. He left a hickey on the side of my neck, and I moaned. I felt his hands go under my body, and his muscular, tattooed arms wrapped around me. He buried his face in the crook of my neck as I wrapped my legs around his waist.

"Lana! Come on, I'll drop you off!" Carter exclaimed as he knocked on the door. Blake grunted on my neck as he left another hard, sore hickey. "Lana? You in there?"

I let out a sigh as Blake raised his head and looked at me. His jaw clenched as he eyed me. I placed my hand on his cheek and shook my head. "I'll be down in a minute," I replied as Blake rolled his eyes and got off. I stood up and watched as Blake ran a hand through his hair. I put on my tights, then Tiffany's shirt dress. I walked to the mirror and looked at myself. I didn't look pleasant at all. I had bags under my eyes, my hair was messy, and I had two hickeys on either side of my neck. Blake walked up behind me and put my glasses on for me. He wrapped his arms around my torso and rested his chin on my shoulder.

"My nerd who's also my bad girl," he said as we looked at each other in the mirror. I lightly chuckled, then took in my appearance again.

"Blake, what's wrong with me?"

"Nothing, baby girl, you're perfect," he whispered. "We're just fucked up people who hate getting hurt by the people we care about."

***

I let out a yawn as I rummaged through my locker. I was up all night with Levi on the phone. It was good to talk to him; he made me laugh at the memories we had when we were young. I saw Carter approach me. Ethan gave me a ride to school today since Carter didn't answer his phone. I turned to him with a questioning look, but he hugged me.

"Hey, sorry I couldn't take you to school this morning. I overslept." He avoided eye contact. I nodded, then turned back to my locker. "Lana, err…about that kiss at Ethan's house. I was jus—it was sort of an in the moment type of thing. I couldn't help myself and…you know what I mean? I do it all the time."

"All the time, huh?" I stated, then bit the inside of my cheek.

"Yeah, so…" He trailed off, and I finally turned

to him. We awkwardly stared at each other, and I watched as he ran a hand through his blond locks. He looked over my shoulder, and I followed his gaze to see Miranda and Melissa walk toward me. "I'll leave you ladies alone," Carter stated, then walked off. I admitted I had a little crush on Carter at the start of senior year because one, he was my date to Homecoming, and two, he slept over, and we bonded. After everything that happened after that, the little crush drifted away.

"Oh my god. You'll never guess who I just saw getting out of Kelly's car," Melissa stated as she and Miranda stood on either side of me.

"Who?" I asked as I pushed up my glasses.

"Britney," Miranda replied as she chewed her gum.

"And I care how?" I raised a brow. Melissa grinned as she looked over my shoulder. Miranda and I followed her gaze to see Britney, Kelly, and Jennifer walk down the hall. Kelly and Britney smiled with evil looks, but Jennifer was engrossed in her phone.

"She's my replacement?" Melissa asked as she looked at Britney. "I've seen chicken breasts better than her boobs."

We laughed as they walked past. I shook my head, then shut my locker so I could lean against it. Miranda and Melissa started to say how Britney stuffed socks in her bra to make her boobs look big while I looked around. I watched Britney as she stopped in front of Benny. He didn't show any interest in Britney but kept his eyes locked on me. Only when her hands wrapped around his neck did he look down at her. The bell rang, and I watched the two. She stood on her tippy toes, then kissed him. I huffed as I pushed myself off the locker and walked to class. I had Biology, and it was on the other side of the school. I gripped my books as I squeezed past people to get there. The halls were crowded, so I decided to take a shortcut upstairs. The hallway was empty, and I smiled. I stopped dead in my tracks when I saw Blake arguing with Parker. Blake looked pissed, but Parker grinned immensely. "Blake," I whispered and looked at Parker.

"Lana, get to class," Blake grunted.

"Yeah, listen to your little boy toy, Willson." Parker faked a pout at Blake, then tilted his head. "He might get angry."

"Shut up, Parker," I demanded. He smirked at me.

"Make me," he whispered.

"I don't make shit," I responded as he bit his lip.

"Always so feisty, Lana Wil—" Before Parker finished sentence, Blake opened the janitor's room and pushed him inside. My eyes widened because I saw a teacher walk out of her classroom, so I quickly stepped into the janitor's closet, then shut the door.

"Are you high?" Blake asked as I turned to Parker. He laid on the ground with a lousy smile on his face.

"You already know," Parker sang as he held up the peace sign.

"Blake, we should go," I whispered because I wasn't comfortable in the familiar place.

"Yeah, listen to your little bitch, because what has she ever done? Besides everyone?" Parker asked. I clenched my fists as I tried to remain calm. Parker was a manipulative person who raped me. He's the first person I hated and would never forgive. "You look quite stressed, Willson. You know I'm here for you if you need anything, and I mean…anything." He opened his jacket.

"Blake," I said as my breathing quickened.

"Yes?" he asked as we glared at Parker.

"Beat the shit out of him," I grumbled and noticed the smirk on Blake's face.

Chapter Twenty-Six

Lana

I sat opposite Blake as we waited for everyone to take their seats. I glanced down to where his hands were to see that they were bruised. After he beat the crap out of Parker, we decided to ditch the period and make out behind the school. A few people saw us, but we didn't care; it was a way to relieve the stress. I looked at him and mouthed a thank you. He nodded. I noticed Benny walk past me with a sad smile. I stared at him. He walked behind me to sit in his assigned seat.

"All right, class, listen up!" Mr. Gorton exclaimed as he clapped his hands. "Austin, get off your phone." I turned to see Austin's grin as his head lowered.

"I'm not on my phone."

"Don't lie to me. Nobody grins like that," Mr. Gorton muttered as everyone laughed.

"Are you even suitable to be our teacher?" Kelly asked.

"Why'd you ask that, Kelly? I speak to everyone like this so they're comfortable, because I know that none of you like school."

"I'd rather be in Mrs. Singleton's class than be here," Kelly hissed as she stood up.

"You'll be doing everyone a favor," Melissa stated as Austin got up too.

Mr. Gorton mumbled something, but I didn't hear it as they walked out of the classroom. As he handed out booklets, Liam rushed in with an exhausted look. Mr. Gorton gave the boy a questioning look as he walked to his seat.

"I was jus—my grandma—she wanted a foot massage, so I gave her one. Then I got ready for school, and she asked me again because she forgot I gave her one, so yeah, that's why I'm late." Liam chuckled.

"No need for an explanation, Mr. Sanchez. An apology would've been sufficient," Mr. Gorton said as he gave Liam a weird look.

"We're writing an essay!" Aidan groaned as he looked at the paper.

"I know, right! It looks like I'll be reading essays next weekend," Mr. Gorton mumbled as he leaned against his desk.

"Yes, Mr. Halls?"

"How long must this essay be?" Carter asked as I read through it.

"Well…it doesn't give the word count, but just imagine it as a woman's skirt," he said as he looked at Carter. "Long enough to cover everything but short enough to keep things interesting."

The guys in the class laughed as the teacher

smiled. I rolled my eyes and pulled my skirt down because I noticed Blake licked his lips in my direction.

After we took notes for another half an hour, the bell rang. Everyone got up to go to his or her next class. Blake and I walked out of the class together, but I heard Mr. Bronx call Blake. I held my books in my hand and watched as Mr. Bronx approached us in the middle of the hallway. I felt something dig into the back of my skirt, and I whipped my head around to see Blake. Once the hallway cleared, Mr. Bronx looked at us. Blake's finger was still in my skirt, which Mr. Bronx noticed, then awkwardly coughed.

"I guess we need to play more of Griffon's Games, huh?" He chuckled as Blake let go of me.

"What do you want?" Blake asked, and I nudged him.

"Blake, you barely show up to my class, you don't fill in the answers for the pop quizzes, and you disrespect me," Griffon started. "You're barely passing my class, and I don't want anyone to fail. Even Liam and Aidan are doing well since I help them in Study Hall, but you…" Griffon trailed off, and I imagined being in a room with Liam, Aidan, and a very frustrated Mr. Bronx. "So I spoke to your mom." I noticed Blake's jaw clenched. "She agrees that you need a tutor."

"I want Lana," Blake stated, and Mr. Bronx laughed.

"That isn't your decision to make. Carter already agreed to help you."

"I want Lana," he repeated with an emotionless

look.

"Well, too bad, you're never gonna get her," Mr. Bronx stated as they stared at each other. He was a bit taller than Blake, but with the looks on their faces, I knew they were trying to scare each other. "Just for these next few weeks before finals, Blake. Then you won't have to worry about me if you graduate. That's a big if."

"Fine, whatever," Blake muttered, then took my hand and dragged me down the hallway before I even looked at Mr. Bronx.

"Why do you hate him so much?" I asked as he pulled me to our next class, which was Photography.

"I don't hate him. I just don't like how he teaches. He irritates me and acts intimidating."

"He's always been intimidating."

"Yeah, intimidating for you, and it's weird."

***

After school, I got a ride with Carter to Blake's house. He didn't want Carter to tutor him without me. I didn't know why, because I'd be a distraction. We sat in the kitchen by the island. Carter was next to me while Blake was opposite us. Blake wrote answers while I worked on my laptop. Carter had his arm around my chair as he scrolled through his phone.

"I fucking hate equations!" Blake snapped as he threw his pencil on the table. Carter and I got a fright and looked at him.

"Dude, you're not bad. You know all the

equations for Mechanics. Now you need to know Electricity, Waves, and Optics." Carter shrugged as he took Blake's book and observed it.

"Yeah, once you know all of that, it gets easy," I admitted.

"I'm not stupid! I see what I'm doing!" Blake exclaimed as he hit his books. "It's just…I don't want to do it."

"But you have to. How are you gonna graduate and get into college?" I asked.

"I already have two colleges waiting for me to make my decision and I'm pretty sure I'll pass if I don't get one thing," he emphasized.

"Just do the questions, dude. I saw that chick Katherine Taylor at Jaden's party. She came over last night." Carter smirked, and I rolled my eyes. The last name Taylor rang a bell. At Thanksgiving dinner, with Mr. Bronx and Dad, they spoke about a Misty Taylor and how hot she was. She had five kids, and maybe Katherine Taylor was one of her children.

"How is she?" Blake asked as he studied me.

"Is that even a question? We did it over and over, all the time." Carter laughed, and I noticed Blake's grin.

"All the time, huh?" I blurted out. Carter turned to me with a questioning look, but I looked at my laptop. He nudged me with his knee; I ignored him. Carter continued to do it, and I nudged him too. Blake seemed unaware of us since he was in broad focus. My thigh got numb, so I raised it. He didn't notice and nudged me again, but this time harder…

"Oh, shit, sorry! That is not how I wanted to

slam you there," he exclaimed, since his knee was still near my inner thigh.

"Yeah, because you do it all the time, huh?" I stated as I put my leg down, but his leg was still by me, so my leg was on his thigh. Blake gave us a questioning look but shook his head as he continued. Carter raised a brow at me, and I smirked. Since our legs were all over each other and our shoulders touched, I snuck my hand to his thigh that was under mine. His eyes widened as he awkwardly coughed, then looked down to his books. With my right hand on my laptop and left close to Carter's thigh, Blake didn't notice anything. My hand moved closer until I felt something hard. My eyes widened, and I bit my lip to prevent a laugh.

"L-Lana?" Carter exhaled deeply as Blake looked at him. "Can I search something on your laptop?"

"Sure." I smiled. Carter turned it to him and typed by my notes. I read what he wrote, and my eyes widened.

I'd do you right here right now on the island, Lana Willson. Fucking stop.

I lightly chuckled as I took the laptop and typed a response back.

Oh, but I do it all the time.

As he read the text, I lightly patted his boner,

then removed my leg from his thigh. I got up and washed my hands in the sink. Heaven knew how many girls touched his jeans. Carter smirked at me the whole way as I walked back to my seat. Mrs. Gunner entered the kitchen in a maroon Bodycon dress and black heels. Her hair was up in a tight bun, which brought out her hoop earrings.

"Mrs. Gunner, you're looking stunning tonight." Carter let out a low whistle.

"Yeah." I smiled as Blake turned to her.

"Thank you, Carter and Lana." She smiled.

"Where you going?" Blake asked as he eyed his mother suspiciously.

"Out with friends, Blake Monroe Gunner. I barely get to do that since I have two sons eating the whole time, so I have to work hard," Mrs. Gunner replied.

"Momma, you know I don't like my middle name," he groaned as Carter and I snickered.

"It was your great grandmother's name, Blake!" she exclaimed, then took something out of the fridge.

"Yeah, yeah. What is that?"

"Since I made your red velvet peppermint swirl brownies the other day, Axel told me to make his favorite. Pumpkin and cream cheese muffins!"

As soon as those words fell from Mrs. Gunner's mouth, Carter and Blake turned to me. Out the corner of my eye, I saw Axel enter the kitchen with Scruffy. Once Axel spotted me, he smiled and raised his arms.

"Pumpkin!" he cheered and walked toward me. He saw his mother, then the muffins. "I wasn't finished…pumpkin! And cream cheese muffins!"

"Mm." Mrs. Gunner pursed her lips. Axel took in the appearance of his mother, then squinted his eyes.

"Where are you going?"

"Ask your brother; I'm going," she muttered, then walked out of the kitchen. "And Axel, don't eat all of those muffins! Share with Lana, Carter, Blake an—"

"Got it, Momma!" He cut her off.

"This is magnificent," Carter moaned as he ate the muffin. I took one, and so did Axel, but he fed it to Scruffy. Once he finished, he put the leash around his neck, then petted him.

"You're finally walking the dog, huh?" Blake asked.

"I always do!" Axel pouted, then looked at Scruffy. "Come on, Scruffy, they don't like our company. I'm sure the bitches at the park will."

I laughed as he walked out with Scruffy. Blake and Carter finished their session an hour later, and Carter offered me a ride home, but I declined. I helped Blake clean the kitchen, then he'd take me back. I closed my laptop and got ready to go when I heard Blake approach me. I spun around, and he pushed me against the counter with his hands firmly placed on my hips. I held onto the table for support as he looked at me.

"Let's get one thing straight. If we're gonna do this, we can't see or do other people," Blake said as I stared at him. "That Katherine Taylor chick called me twice, and I told her I'm off with someone way better. So it'd be nice if you don't think twice about one of my best friends," he grumbled. "Got it?" Blake lifted me up. I nodded, but he shook his head and laughed. He placed me on the counter and pressed his forehead against mine. "I know you, Lana. You're sneaky, and so is Carter." He kissed me. The first kiss was short yet sweet. I looked down at his lips because I wanted more, craved more, and it was as if he read my mind. His tongue slipped inside my mouth. I wrapped my arms around his neck and pressed my body against his. I felt his arms wrap around my torso protectively. He lifted me up again, and I instantly wrapped my legs around him. Blake pushed me against the wall, and I picked up that he was trying to get to his room, but we continued to kiss. Kiss, feel each other, and wanting to rip each other's clothes off and take out our frustrations on each other. Take out everything that had happened for the past few months and…have fun. He pulled away and placed his hands under my skirt, then squeezed my ass. As he walked down the hall, I gripped his hair and kissed down his jawline. We entered his room, and he kicked the door closed. Blake laid me down on the bed, and I kicked off my boots as he turned around. As he went to his speakers, I glanced around his room. Everything was so neat and in place, completely different than mine. While he had old CDs on his shelf, I had books cluttered everywhere. I turned back to see him pull off his shirt and turn on the speakers. He plugged in his phone, and I bit my bottom lip as a heavy rock song played. He hovered over me and left a gentle kiss on my lips. I placed a hand on his cheek and looked into his brown eyes. They seemed darker than usual, yet so engaged. I saw the hunger in his eyes as he looked at my lips like Carter did the other morning. He placed his hand under my thigh and turned us so that I was on top of him. I straddled him and took off my sweater, then the tank top, which left me in my red bra. I placed an arm on either side of him and pressed my lips to his. Blake's hands were all over me, by my sides, up my back, and down the backs of my thighs. I pulled away and looked down at my skirt. I pulled it down by my thighs and saw Blake sit up. He spread his legs so that I'd sit on the bed. He pulled my skirt off and tossed it aside, then he took his jeans off and smirked down at me. A grunge song played as I laid on the edge of the bed. Blake hovered over me and buried his face in the crook of my neck. I felt his lips against my skin as I rolled my eyes back. I tried to run my hands through his hair, but he gripped my hands and pinned them against the bed as he pressed against me and kissed my neck. My heavy breaths turned into moans as I tried to touch him, but his grip tightened on my hands. He came up and pressed his forehead against mine. He finally let go of my hands. He ran his fingers through my hair as we continued to move against each other. I wanted to do it, and I could tell he did too, but something held us back.

"Dude!" someone yelled, then banged on the door. "*Blake!*"

"Fuck," Blake muttered as he got up. I pouted because the person ruined the moment. I got up, and Blake threw my clothes at my face. I gave him a questioning look as he put his clothes on. I got dressed as Blake turned off the music. Once I was done, I casually sat on the bed as Blake opened the door.

"Dude, what the fuck, are you dea—oh, hey, Lana!" Keene exclaimed as he looked at Blake with wide eyes, then me.

"Hi, Keene," I mumbled, then stood up.

"What are you guys—*oh!*" Keene beamed as he looked at us, then wiggled his brows.

"No," Blake and I said in unison.

"Come on, Lana, I'll take you home," Blake added as he grabbed my hand. He took me out of his house so quick that I didn't even get time to say goodbye to Keene.

***

School was weird; Blake avoided me most of the time, so I hung out with Miranda and Marcus. I didn't know what happened to the whole group; it's as if when two people fought, it affected everyone. I sat at our regular lunch table since Benny got invited to sit with Britney.

It was the last period, which was Physics, and I walked down the hall. As I turned the corner, I felt someone grip my arm and push me against the wall. I groaned, then glanced up to see Blake.

"What do you want?" I asked, then pushed him away.

"Look, I'm sorry for yesterday. It's just…Keene doesn't know what we're doing, and I'd like to keep it that way," Blake whispered as his eyes softened.

"Yeah, I get it," I whispered, then looked down.

"Here's your laptop," he said, then gave me my bag.

"Thanks." I took it. Blake cupped my cheeks, then put a strand of hair behind my ear as I looked at him.

"I just want to kiss you right now," he whispered, then looked down the hallways. There were barely any people since everyone had gone to class.

"Blake, we ca—" He cut me off and kissed me. I stood on my tippy toes to deepen the kiss. His arms wrapped around my waist to keep me in place as his tongue ran across my bottom lip. I heard footsteps behind us, and I pulled away to see Ethan stare at us. I forcefully pushed Blake's arms off me and backed away. I continued to walk since the second bell rang; I heard Blake's footsteps as he caught up with me.

"Hey, are you okay?" he asked and entwined my fingers with his. I let out a sigh, then turned to look up at him.

"Blake, how long is this gonna go on? Or when is it over?"

"When Nielson learns to man the fuck up," he answered without hesitation.

"I-I don't get you. First, you admit your feelings for me, then you want to make him jealous, yet you also want to get me out of your system. I feel bad because you seem fine with everything," I mumbled. Blake let out a sigh and stopped us. He placed his hands on my shoulders as he stared at me.

"Look, I've realized that he makes you happy. For the past few weeks, you haven't smiled. It's the fake smile because you try to hide the fact that you miss him. I see it in your eyes how jealous you are of Britney. I see how he makes you happy, how he makes that smile reach your eyes. I don't know how he does it even though he's just going to hurt you, but you see the good in him," he said, then walked. "Besides, I'm all right. It was just a little crush. Now I get to make out with you until he mans the fuck up."

"Just a little crush..." I whispered to myself, then strolled behind him. Everyone piled into the class, and I sat next to Melissa. While I opened my books, Melissa elbowed me. I turned to her, and she pointed across the room. I followed her gaze to see Britney next to Liam, where Kelly sat. Poor Liam. "Why is she here?"

"Since Kelly and Austin moved to another Physics class, Britney moved in here," Melissa replied as I stared at her. She looked around the room, then in my direction, but waved at Benny, who sat behind me. I huffed and folded my arms as I turned to Mr. Gorton, who wrote on the board. Once the class was settled, he gave us the work. We answered questions, and I'd glance over to Blake. He looked like he knew what he was doing since he had his headphones on while he worked. The rest of the period was spent in silence as everyone else did his or her own thing until Ethan walked into the classroom with a sorrowful look. I raised a brow as Principal West walked in too. Mr. Gorton stood up, and my eyes widened when I saw Detective Kale step in. The whole class went silent as we stared at the men in front.

"Sorry to disturb your teaching, but Detective Kale here needs to talk to some students, and he says it's urgent," Principal West said.

Mr. Gorton leaned against his desk while Detective Kale scouted the classroom. I felt Aidan kick my chair, and I looked up to see Blake and Carter stare at me. "There's my favorite delinquent." Detective Kale smirked as he looked at Blake. Blake's jaw clenched as he glared at Detective Kale. Principal West raised a brow, utterly oblivious to the situation, while Mr. Gorton cleared his throat.

"Well, you're interrupting my lesson, Detective, so please hurry up," he stated as Detective Kale nodded.

"Carter Halls, Ethan Baxter, Aidan Rowley, and Blake Gunner, please come with me. If you fail to cooperate, there's always another way," Detective Kale said, then pulled out handcuffs. The guys stood up and silently walked with Detective Kale, and I wondered why they couldn't be called down to the office instead of being embarrassed in front of everyone. Then again, Detective Kale didn't like Blake. As soon as they walked out of the room, the class erupted in whispers and murmurs. I folded my arms and bit my lip because I wondered what Detective Kale had in store for them.

***

Blake

When I walked down the familiar hallway to the interrogation room, I stared at Detective Kale. I knew he worked with Sheriff Willson, so he should have all his evidence. He opened the interrogation room and motioned for us to go in. He held the door as I went in last.

"How's your mom, Blake?" he asked, and I ignored him as I walked into the room. He closed the door and left us in the room. I sat next to Ethan and looked at the dimly lit room. There was a big glass opposite us where other people listened in while someone interrogated us. There were no windows in the room, just a table and five chairs. Detective Kale walked back into the room with files in his hands. I looked around to see a camera in the right corner of the room.

"Ethan Baxter, Blake Gunner, Carter Halls, and Aidan Rowley." Detective Kale grinned as he sat in front of us.

"I thought we were done with this," Aidan muttered as Kale went through files.

"On September 27th, you all were arrested for hiding drugs in Mr. Baxter's cottage on Route 28," he began. "You were forced to by James Cornelius."

"Cornelius," Aidan snorted, and we turned to him with a look of *too soon*.

"It's stated here that you all confessed about being James Cornelius alleged helpers in hiding all of his cocaine. Apparently, things went wrong, and an anonymous call was sent to the station to rat you guys out," Detective Kale continued.

"Thanks for the reminder," I sarcastically said.

"My case deals with a missing person. Sheriff Willson has been trying to get James Cornelius for the past six months when someone by the name of Christo Aimar came to confess. Later it was reported that he was dead."

"Well, he might not be dead," Carter stated.

"I know. So Sheriff Willson and I have decided to work together. And that's when everything started to make sense." Detective Kale smirked as he stood up and walked around.

"What are you talking about?" Ethan asked. Kale slammed a file down on the table in front of us. In big bold letters was the name "Christo Aimar," followed by his picture.

"He was the guy who shoved the parcels at you that day, right?" he asked as we stared at his photo. It was him. I never forgot a face. His black hair was slicked back as he held a poker face. His brown eyes glared at the camera, yet the day we saw him he looked frightened.

"Yeah," Aidan replied.

"Mr. Cornelius is well known for threatening people to get what he wants. He has a lot of men around the country, yet we've managed to catch quite a few of them in recent months. But he's also good at impersonating."

"What the hell does this all mean?" Aidan asked. He then slammed down another file next to Christo's. It was the guy he was looking for, Jack August. He sat down, then held up the two papers.

"Christo Aimar was reported dead. Mr.

Cornelius told you he was dead to scare you. The morgue had no record of him. Mr. Cornelius threatens families. That's why we couldn't get anything out of Christo Aimar's family when he was supposedly dead."

"So? He could still be alive," I said. Kale smirked as he held the papers.

"Look at each of their faces and pick out the similarities," he said, and we did as I stared at Jack, then Christo. At first, there was nothing since Jack had ginger hair, and Christo had black hair, but their eyes were the same. I tilted my head, then noticed that they had the same jawline. Same nose, same thin lips, and same expression. Jack had a weird skin tone since his face was pale, but his neck was the same color tone as Christo.

"This is Christo Aimar, a.k.a. Jack August," Aidan whispered.

"So Christo Aimar was undercover as a homeless guy named Jack August, and he might still be alive?" Carter asked, and Detective Kale nodded.

"And so Christo's real family couldn't say anything because they were threatened, and Jack's family is fake…" Ethan trailed off.

"Yeah, Jack's family was a fake. They were in on it too. That's why they couldn't give proper answers," Detective Kale replied.

"So where is Christo? Why are you here questioning us when you should be out there looking for James and his men?" I asked.

"We're working on it, Gunner, but we can't seem to get why Mr. Cornelius needed that specific identity," Detective Kale muttered, then looked at us. "Anyway, thank you for clearing that up. Now that we're certain, things will really get going."

Chapter Twenty-Seven

Lana

When we hung out that afternoon at Ethan's house, nobody talked about what happened with Detective Kale even though I asked countless of times. They said they'd tell me when the time was right, but I didn't know what that meant.

Over the next few days, Blake and I became more public. It got tiresome, but the thought of Britney and Benny made me jealous. Then the strangest thing happened. Benny came over and tried to apologize again, but I couldn't, yet I saw the desperation in his eyes. I spoke about Britney, and he said she tried to get in his pants. I would've taken him back right then and there because I missed him, but I couldn't because Blake was up in my room. We hadn't had sex because I didn't want to and he respected that, but every time we were so close. Then I thought Benny was over me, but the next day was Valentine's Day, and I received gifts throughout the day. It'd be a range of things like flowers, my favorite foods, and stuffed animals. I didn't use any of the stuff because I felt guilty, but my parents did. Dad took the food, while Mom bought vases for all the flowers. It went on for another week, and it even reached a point where my parents waited by the door for the delivery guy. I couldn't handle it anymore, so on Saturday afternoon I was at Keene's apartment, sharing a cigarette with Blake while the guys watched sports. Again, when I got there, I asked what happened, but they completely ignored me. Blake handed me the cigarette, and I snatched it, then pressed it in the ashtray. Carter, who sat on my right, placed a hand on my thigh as he gave me a questioning look. I abruptly stood up and walked in front of the television that was on the wall.

"Lana, what are you doing?" Noel asked.

"I can't take it anymore!" I yelled, then turned the television off. "Tell me what happened!"

"Lana, not no—"

"No! Now! I want to know; I need to know!" I exclaimed as they exchanged looks while I stood and folded my arms. Aidan nodded, then stood up. He took my hand and dragged me down the hall with Carter, Blake, and Ethan. The part that really bugged me was that Keene and Noel knew, yet I didn't. Once we were in Keene's room, I folded my arms and stared at them. They looked at each other, but Blake sighed.

"Is your dad still in Illinois?" he asked.

"N-no, he left for Idaho this morning. How did you—"

"He said we could tell you once he's gone,"

Aidan mumbled, then stuffed his hands in his pockets.

"Now tell me. Why did Detective Kale need you?"

"He just wanted us to confirm Christo Aimar's fake identity," Ethan said.

"Fake identity? Who was he undercover as?"

"Remember I told you that James is good with identities?" Aidan said, then lowered his head.

"So who was Christo?" I croaked out, because by their expressions I knew it was bad.

"That homeless dude, Jack August," Carter replied as I paled. I balled my fists as a chill crept up my spine. Blake noticed it and raised a brow as he stepped forward. I backed away, then looked at Aidan.

"Wh-Where's Christo?" I whispered.

"We don't know," he replied as I tried to control myself.

"I-I'm just gonna go to the bathroom," I stuttered, then walked out of the room. As soon as I was in the bathroom, I locked the door and leaned against it. I looked at myself in the mirror and stared at myself. I killed Christo Aimar…that's why James was after me. I killed one of his men. That's why when he and his men walked away on New Year's, Mike said that he missed Christo. My breaths quickened as the different scenarios ran through my head. I let out a gasp as I stood in front of the sink.

"Lana, you okay in there?" Keene asked as he lightly knocked on the door.

"Y-yeah," I breathed out, then opened the faucet.

I took my glasses off, then stared at myself in the mirror. Tears filled my eyes because what if they found Christo dead? I opened the mirror cabinet and looked at all the pills. Most of them were Noel's since he got home from rehab. The corners of my mouth went dry as I heard the knocks on the door get louder. I quickly went through the bottles and saw the same pills that Parker gave me. I took some out, then hid them in various places of my clothing.

"Lana!" Blake yelled as he banged on the door. I swallowed one, then put the bottle back and shut the cabinet. My breaths became hard as my head spun. I was in so much trouble. I needed to tell Benny. I unlocked the door and literally fell out of the bathroom. Ethan caught me and wrapped his arms around my torso to hold me up.

"Lana, are you okay?" Carter asked as he looked at me.

"I-I think I'm having a panic attack."

"O-okay, just calm down. Breathe," he said as Ethan dragged me into the room. The guys ran up and down, but it made the situation worse, as I felt dizzy. I pushed myself off him to walk but regretted it as my legs buckled. Sweat ran down my forehead as the room spun. My eyelids drooped as I fell forward into Carter's arms, then blacked out.

***

When I opened my eyes, I felt a pain in my head. I let out a groan as I slowly sat up on the bed. As my vision got clear, I saw Keene next to the bed while Ethan sat in front.

"Whoa, relax," Keene mumbled as he held my hand. I watched as he took a glass of water from the table and gave it to me. "For your head." He then gave me aspirin. I drank the water, then swallowed the tablet. I noticed I was on Keene's bed while the afternoon sun shone through the window. Ethan and Keene exchanged a look. I narrowed my eyes.

"What?" I managed to rasp out.

"Before you woke up, you kept mumbling out Benny's name and that you need to tell him…Lana, will you ever forgive him?" Keene asked.

"I-I don't know," I whispered, even though I wanted to.

"Remember when we found out that Parker…" He trailed off as I nodded. "Well, the first thing that went through Blake's and Levi's minds was that you were a whore, which you're not, but then you forgave them a few days later," he said. "It's been three weeks, Lana. You're fucking miserable without him."

Keene was right. I did forgive Levi and Blake when they thought Parker and I were fuck buddies. I hated when Keene was right.

"Benny's not doing well, either," Ethan chimed in as my eyes lit up. "He constantly asks about you in basketball. Coach yells at him most of the time, and he told Britney to fuck off. Right in front of everyone." I had the tiniest victory dance in my mind. That moment when Levi and Blake thought that of me and when Benny said that to me, a tear rolled down my cheek.

"Do you think I'm a slut?" I asked and looked at Keene and Ethan.

"No!" they said in unison.

"That day at my house Carter kissed you, and it was Blake's idea to make Benny jealous. He talked you into it. You're just the victim, Lana," Ethan said as his hands tightened into fists.

"But this must stop," Keene stated as he squinted his eyes. "This thing that you and Blake are doing. It's getting out of hand, and none of you realize who will get hurt in the end."

The room went quiet after that as I looked at my socks. I knew Keene was right. The door creaked open, and I turned my head to see Blake, Carter, Aidan, and Noel enter the room. I shifted as I looked at Blake, who watched me the whole time as he sat next to Ethan. Aidan and Noel stood while Carter sat on the edge of the bed and cautiously placed his hand on my leg.

"Are you okay?" he asked. I nodded, and he smiled. Carter looked down, and I followed his eyes to see my glasses. He opened them and leaned forward to put them on me.

"Thank you," I interrupted him as I took my glasses and put them on. He nodded, then turned his back to look at the guys. Ethan muttered something under his breath, then looked at Blake and me.

"You two have to stop this," Ethan said, and I noticed Blake's eye twitched.

"It's not healthy for either of you, and it makes Lana very depressed," Keene added, and I looked down in discomfort.

"Okay, whatever," Blake said as I looked up. We stared at each other, and I clenched my fists. I couldn't believe I let him do that to me; I couldn't believe I let him talk me into doing such things. I couldn't believe we used each other and he was so quick to call it off.

"Lana?"

"Yeah?"

"Good. Now you just need to tell us why you freaked out like that."

"James is after you," Aidan said as his eyes flashed with fear.

"H-how did you—"

"It's quite evident. We didn't deliver all his cocaine; neither did he." Aidan pointed to Noel. "So he's after you since your dad is after him."

"Killing two birds with one stone," Noel added. I squirmed.

"Can you take me home?" I asked Carter.

"Sure," he replied, then stood up and walked across the room to get my boots.

"Wait," Blake called. I turned to see him pull something out of his pocket. "What the fuck were these doing in your jeans pocket?"

I stared at the pills. I slowly looked up at Noel as my cheeks reddened. "I'm sorry."

"I-It's okay," he stated. I then felt Carter's hand on my thigh, and I turned to him.

"Are your nightmares happening again?" he asked with a concerned look.

"They never stopped." I laughed. I saw the nervous look on Carter's face when I said that. He tore his gaze away from me and looked at the other guys. I pushed myself off the bed and got up. Keene automatically stood up as he held his arms out, but I stopped him and said I'd walk. I put my boots on, then walked out of the room as I tried to block out their whispers.

***

When I walked up the porch with Carter behind me, I realized I still hadn't spoken. He didn't say anything or pressure me to talk. I spun around to face the blond and thank him for the ride home.

"Do you want me to come in? Y'know, we can cuddle…friends cuddle, right?"

"Your definition of cuddling is entirely different than my definition of cuddling, Carter Halls." I laughed. "But I'll be okay," I added, then opened my arms to hug him. He chuckled, then wrapped his arms around my waist and lifted me. I laughed as he set me down on the rail and pulled away. I rested my hands on his shoulders for support as he held onto my hips. We were eye level as we stared into each other's blue eyes.

"Is this the part where we kiss?" he asked. I put my index finger on his chest, then shoved him away.

"Never happening, Carter," I said, and he pouted.

"I thought that was our thing. Y'know, I kiss you, then you tease me down there…" Carter said as his eyes flickered with eagerness.

"No way," I said.

"Aww, I thought that's our sexual tension friendship." He smiled.

"Sexual tension friendship, that's a mouthful to say." I laughed as he helped me off the rail.

"Yeah, but you'll get used to it." He smirked as I

opened the front door.

"Bye, Carter, see you Monday." I backed into the house.

"Goodbye, my lovely sexual tension friend. I'll miss you." He fake cried and walked away. I laughed, then closed the door. I heard my mother on the phone in the kitchen. My foot kicked something, and I looked down to see a box. I crouched down and picked up the box. I sighed when I saw the usual address. I took the box and walked upstairs to my room. I placed the box on my bed and opened it. My eyebrows rose when I saw a brand-new pair of black and white high tops Converse. Obviously, my old ones were the ones I wore when we buried Christo's body, but we had to get rid of them. Now Benny bought me a new pair?

"Lana," Mom called out as I held the shoes in my hands. I heard her footsteps behind me as I looked to see what else was inside the box. There was a little note, and I picked it up and read it.

I miss the midnight conversations we had; I miss you coming to my house just to sleep because you were more comfortable here than alone in your room. I know I said we should see other people, but I fucking can't. I can't move on. I miss you; I fucking miss you and will do anything and everything to get you back.

"Aww, I was hoping for tulips today." Mom

sighed. I spun around and glared at her. "I'm joking, sweetie. When are you going to let him in? He's going crazy with all these apology gifts." Mom gestured to the different stuffed animals and chocolates in my room. "Remember before Homecoming I told you that you'd be breaking and fixing hearts before you graduate?" She chuckled as I put the shoes in the box. I gave a slight nod as I remembered that was six months ago. A lot happened in those six months for my mother to bring that up. "Well…mothers are always right." She took a chocolate and ate it. I glanced down and noticed she was dressed for the hospital.

"Are you going to work?"

"Oh yes, I am. Sorry, honey, I know your father said that I shouldn't leave you alone at home, but this is really urgent. You can call the girls over and have a sleepover."

"Yeah."

"Okay, I gotta go. See you later," she said, then kissed my cheek. When I heard the front door shut, I walked to my closet and took out comfy clothing. My ringtone played, and I walked to my desk to see that Benny called. I was taken back and stared at my phone as it played "Teenagers" by My Chemical Romance. It stopped for a second, then rang again. I huffed, then answered my phone.

"What do you—"

"Lana?" Sam's voice filled the phone as I raised a brow.

"Sam? Wha-What are you doing with Benny's phone?"

"He's sleeping right now, but I just…please

come back. There was this girl who came over last week, and it was so weird because she wasn't you." I immediately thought of Britney.

"Sam, I—"

"My brother misses you so much, Lana. Last night he never came down for dinner, and when I went to go check up on him, he was locked in the bathroom," Sam whispered as my lips parted. "My brother always locked himself in that bathroom for years, but then you came, and he was happy. We all were. Now we're worried about him again." He paused. "Please, Lana, I've never seen him so happy with someone before. I don't like seeing my big brother miserable and always blaming himself. I don't like standing by the door and hearing his cries." My eyes glistened. I sniffled, then heard someone in the background.

"Sam? What are you doing with my phone?"

My eyes widened as I heard Sam run. Suddenly the other side of the call went silent as I bit my lip then asked, "Sam, are you there?"

"Lana?" Benny's deep voice made me freeze.

"H-hi," I breathed out.

"Did you get my gift?" he asked as I stood in front of a window and looked at the sunset.

"Yeah, thanks, but you really have to stop, Benny. I really appreciate it, bu—"

"I won't stop until you forgive me. Until we're okay." He cut me off as I sighed.

"I forgive you, but I just…" I trailed off.

"Then what's wrong? Tell me what's wrong, and I can help. Are you home? Should I come over?"

"No, no I-I have to go," I said, then ended the

call. I ran a hand through my hair as I entered the bathroom. The bags under my eyes got worse, and my lips were chapped. Blake managed to find the pills I hid in my jeans pocket, but he didn't see the one inside my jacket pocket. I took it, then drank water and swallowed it. I looked at myself again because I wasn't in the mood for a dumb sleepover. I needed something to take the pain away. Before I showered, I made sure the front door was locked and the alarm was turned on. There was a feature where I put the alarm on for the doors and windows.

***

After I showered, I got bored and sat on the floor in the hallway with a cigarette between my lips. Uncle Griff and Dad's favorite whiskey bottle sat on my left and Dad's revolver on my right while music blared throughout the house. I had to be alert because James could appear any second. I had to be prepared, even though I deserved it. I crushed the cigarette in the ashtray and took a swig of the whiskey. The alcohol burned my throat, and I scrunched my nose and gagged. My gag turned to laughter as I thought of myself. It was my fault. None of my friends deserved it. I couldn't be a burden to them all the time and let them fix my problems. If I didn't run off at Homecoming, none of this would have happened. If I didn't accept that stupid bet, none of this would have happened. I took another sip and laughed as Levi flooded my mind. If he didn't leave me the first time without an explanation, Parker wouldn't have happened. The cigarettes, tablets, and rape wouldn't have happened if Levi stayed in touch.

"*Why do you always do this to me, Levi Ramone Radcliff?*" I yelled at the top of my lungs, then laughed. "Fuck my life." I put the bottle on the floor. As I smoked another cigarette, I took my phone and scrolled through my songs. I flinched when I heard loud knocks on the front door. I decreased the volume, put out the cigarette, then grabbed the bottle and pistol.

"*Lana, open the door!*" Miranda yelled, and I laughed, then put the gun on the coffee table in the living room. I turned up the music again, and "Drown" by Bring Me the Horizon began playing.

"*Willson, don't you fucking dare!!*"

I recognized the voice as Blake. I walked to the curtain and peeked through it. My eyes widened to see Miranda, Melissa, Tiffany, Aidan, Marcus, Carter, Ethan, Keene, and Axel on my porch.

"*I know you got more of those fucking pills!*"

I backed away from the window and drank the last remains of the liquid. As my friends shouted at me, tears filled my eyes. I thought they got the message that I wanted to be alone; I didn't want them to pity me. I turned the music off as my eyes welled up. My phone rang, and I glanced down to see Miranda's name. I took a deep breath, then answered the call.

"Lana, open the door right now. Your mom sent us to check up on you," Miranda stated calmly.

"I'm okay, Miranda. You're so sweet for always caring," I slurred as I walked around the coffee table. "But I just need to be alone, y'know.'"

"No! You need us! We can help you!" she exclaimed as I laughed.

"Thanks for the generosity, but you all have done so much for me. I can't do this to you guys anymore!" I cried, then stomped my foot.

"Lana, what are you talking about? You've been there for us. Now we're here for you," Aidan said.

"Stop it! Just go! All of you go have fun and stop fucking worrying about me. Just for one night don't worry about Lana Willson, the depressed freak who smokes, drinks, takes pills, and lies just so that people won't get hurt," I said, then threw the bottle across the room. It made a shattering noise, but I didn't care as I looked down at the coffee table.

"*Lana, the fuck was that? Let us in!*" Keene yelled.

"Just go. You're waking up the neighbors," I said as my fingers grazed over the curtains.

"*Screw them! We want to help you!*"

I yanked on the curtain and pulled it open. Since it was a big window, I got most of the porch view. Everyone stood there shocked. My head ached, and just when I thought things couldn't get any worse, Benny appeared. Tears ran down my cheek as I slowly picked up the pistol. My hands trembled as I held the phone and twirled the pistol in my hand. Their eyes widened as they yelled at me. They even banged on the window and door.

"*Lana, don't do this, please! Put it down!*" Melissa cried, and I watched as she collapsed into Nick's arms.

"It will get you all to stop worrying. You can all be happy without me causing trouble. The killer will be gone." I whispered the last part with a smile as I stood right in front of the window. I put the pistol against my temple and looked at Benny. His eyes were wet from the tears as he pressed his forehead against the window. He put his hand beside the window, and I stared at it. While Keene yelled at me through the phone, I dropped the pistol and put my hand against the window too. His mouth pulled up into a sad smile as he apologized. I shook my head, then told him that I was sorry. I backed away and slowly closed the curtains. "Please go. I won't do it," I whispered as I picked up the pistol.

"Lana, please, you're my best friend. I don't want anything to happen to you," Miranda cried.

"Put me on speaker," I said as I twirled the pistol with my index finger. "Please everyone, I appreciate that you took time out of your Saturday night to check up on me, and as you just saw, I'm doing quite well. Go do something fun and imagine, just for tonight, that I don't exis—"

"Pumpkin, don't say that. Everything's better with you."

I closed my eyes and tried to remain calm while I blocked out their protests. The porch light was on, and I saw their shadows tower over me.

"I'll see you on Monday," I whispered.

"*Lana fucking Jane Willson, I will break this door down!*" Blake shouted as my jaw clenched.

"You break that door down, the alarm goes off, and I am not going to put in that pin," I stated as I looked directly at Blake's shadow.

"Lana, please," Benny mumbled, and I heard the worry in his voice.

"*Lana, I am going to kick this fucking door down!*" Blake repeated.

"I dare you, I fucking dare you, Blake Gunner! Kick it down, come inside and use me just like you do everyone else!" I exclaimed and pointed at his shadow with the gun.

"Princess?"

My eyes widened as my breath quickened again. None of the shadows moved as I laughed.

"No, no, no. I'm losing it. I'm going fucking crazy!" I yelled, then ended the call. My mind played tricks on me; the voices in my head told me what a killer I was, that I should play James's stupid game. When I looked at the curtain, I saw more shadows. I peeked through to see Miranda yell at Blake while the rest tried to get in. My phone rang, and I spun around to see Levi's name. I slowly approached the coffee table and picked it up. I answered the call, then put the phone against my ear. The only clear thing was his heavy breathing. "L-Levi," I croaked out as tears ran down my cheeks.

"Princess…Axel just texted me. Don't do this. Please, open the door for them." Levi spoke in a neutral tone as I fought back the tears.

"I-I can't. I can't, Levi, I'm scared…you said you'd be my knight in shining armor," I whispered as I walked out of the living room.

"I am, princess. What happened? Who are you scared of?"

"I've done something terrible…"

"Shh. Listen to me. He also told me you have a gun with you. Please put it back," he whispered as I looked down at the pistol. I bit my lip because I almost did it, in front of Benny. "Princess, please."

"Okay," I said, then walked down the hall. I quickly put it in Dad's drawer, then closed the door.

"Good. Now we're just gonna talk, okay?" Levi asked as I leaned against the wall and sank down in the same spot that I was in before.

"Talk? Levi, I need you, and you keep leaving me. Why can't you ever stay?" I croaked out and remembered the times I cried myself to sleep because of him.

"It's complicated, princess, but do you remember what happened after we had sex in my car?" he asked calmly as I wiped my tears away.

"N-not really…"

"It's okay. Tell me what you do remember," he said, and I tried so hard to remember because I had a few drinks.

"After the party, we took a drive…downtown," I began and stared at the wall opposite me to try and visualize the memory.

"Yeah," he whispered, and my eyes closed as I remembered.

"A-and not just a drive but a r—race," I said, then squinted my eyes, trying to remember.

"Yeah," he mumbled as my jaw dropped. I covered my mouth as everything came back. The lights, fast cars, the bad side of downtown and the traffic light.

"Oh my god. I drove with you, and w—we had an accident." I sobbed.

"We did," Levi responded casually, then sighed as I cried again.

"You promised that it was safe, and you promised that you wouldn't leave my side, but when I woke up in the hospital, you were gone!" I scolded as it all made sense that Mom and Jade didn't want us to go to Benny's party alone.

"I know, and I am so sorry, princess."

"Why do you always leave?"

"I don't know, but my intention is to always come back and see you."

"I miss you so much, Levi."

"I miss you too, princess. Now let them in. Let them help you. What's the pin?"

"Two, seven…three and nine." I sighed in relief that he'd call.

"Thank you, princess, love you, and I'll see you this summer, okay?"

"Okay," I whispered as he ended the call. "I love you too."

The alarm went off, and I turned my head to see the door open. Blake put the pin in as Miranda ran over to me. She sat next to me while everyone ran in. She pulled me into her chest, and we cried. Ethan was to my right as he picked up the ashtray. Melissa towered over me, and I noticed her eyes were glossy.

"I'm sorry for being a horrible friend," I whispered.

"You're not our friend," she stated. "You're like a sister to us."

I gave a weak smile, then looked up to see Benny and Blake behind her. They stared down at me with unreadable expressions. I shamelessly looked away and tried to get up. My head spun as the sweat ran down my forehead.

"Please don't scare us like that again," Tiffany mumbled with a worried look.

"I'm sorry," I whispered, then leaned against the wall.

"It's not your fault, pumpkin," Axel said as he crouched down and picked me up. "Let's go get you cleaned up."

I wrapped my arms around his neck as he walked up the stairs. I heard their whispers and looked over my shoulder to see Nick and Marcus cleaning up the broken glass. We entered my room, and Axel walked into the bathroom. He sat me down on the toilet lid, and I turned to the sink. Axel crouched down so that we were eye level. My eyes suddenly dropped, and he cupped my cheeks.

"Whoa, stay with me, pumpkin. I know it's been a long day, but just stay with me," he said as my lashes fluttered. "This needs to come off," he said and tugged on my thick hoodie. I exhaled loudly, then raised my arms. I felt his fingers brush against my hips as he pulled the hoodie off and left me in my red tank top and pajama shorts. "Momma went through something similar when Dad died. I always used to help her like this," Axel said, then put a lock of hair behind my ear.

"Why can't Blake be like you?" I blurted out, then poked his nose.

"I get asked that a lot," he joked as I considered his brown eyes. "My brother can be an emotionless prick sometimes. That's because he isn't used to feelings; he doesn't know how to deal with them." He sat cross-legged on the bathroom rug. "Last time he faced a lot of emotions at once was when our dad, Damian Gunner, died. I had to play the big brother role for him and Momma," he mumbled, then looked down. "I had to be strong for them."

"Wasn't anyone there for you?" I frowned.

"Not really. My uncle's an alcoholic, and he doesn't care about us. Like Blake told you, he took our dad's motor shop and kicked us out of the house," Axel replied. "In this situation, he doesn't know what to do anymore. He can't control what comes out of him. That's us Gunners."

"Ugh, this is all my fault," I sighed as Axel's brows snapped together.

"No, it's not. The day I met Levi, it became my fault," he said as I gave him a questioning look. He glanced over his shoulder, and I followed his gaze to see Tiffany enter the bathroom with a glass of water. Axel got up and walked to the sink while she stood in front of me. I gave her a small smile, then drank the water.

"Aidan told me how all of them slept here last year and how they each took turns to stay up. I guess we're doing it again," she said as I watched Axel walk out of the room. "Liam and Aidan also figured out the security system, so you don't have to worry about us sleeping downstairs."

"Thank you. The blankets and extra pillows are in the guest room closet," I said as we walked out of the bathroom. She nodded, then walked out of my room. I turned my head to see Axel open my bed, then fluff out my pillows. A smile crept up my face because he used to do this for his mother. He spun around, and I noticed a white tee over his shoulder.

"Oh hey. I just found this big shirt in your closet for you to wear. Nice and big, so you won't get too hot when you sleep." He handed the shirt to me.

"This is Levi's," I mumbled as I stared at the soft cotton shirt.

"Oh sorry. Should I take ano—"

"No, it's okay," I said, then put it on. I flicked my hair over my shoulder then looked at Axel. He moved to the side and pointed to the bed. "Thank you," I mumbled, then slowly got in. Once I was settled, I looked up at Axel. "You don't have to be here."

"Pumpkin, it's fine. Besides, teenagers are entertaining as hell." He laughed, then kissed my forehead. I smiled, then watched as he walked out of the room. Aidan and Liam walked in with nervous looks while Keene trailed behind.

"Hi, guys," I murmured as Aidan and Liam stood right in front of my bed.

"Hey, Lana, we got this for you," Liam said as he gave me a flower, which was from one of the vases downstairs.

"This is from one of my mother's vases," I pointed out.

"We know, we just wanted an excuse to see you because they didn't want us to come up here." Aidan shrugged as Liam scoffed.

"Yeah, they thought we'd interrupt you by being too loud!" Liam exclaimed as he lifted his hands and laughed.

"I know, right!" Aidan stated.

"Well, thank you, Aidan and Liam. This is very nice." I inhaled the smell of the daisy.

"No problem, Lana. Group hug!" Liam said, then lifted me up and wrapped his arms around me. Over his shoulder, I saw Aidan drag Keene toward us. Aidan pushed Keene onto Liam's back while Aidan was behind him. I laughed as Keene cussed the two for being weird.

"Okay. Well, goodnight, Lana. We'll be downstairs if you need us," Aidan said as they pulled away.

"Do you guys have some clothing or—?"

"Yeah, we're good." Aidan waved off as he swung his arm around Liam's shoulder. Keene and I watched as the two walked out of my bedroom.

"Dude, please do not tell me you have your nightgown with you," Liam said as looked at Aidan.

"What about your choo-choo pajamas?" Aidan asked.

"Touché, brother," Liam's voice trailed off as he closed the door. I glanced up at Keene and noticed his stare. I awkwardly looked away, then pulled the duvet over me. He took his shoes off and opened the side of the bed. My eyebrows rose as he got in next to me.

"This is weird," I mumbled as he laid on his back and stared at the ceiling.

"Oh, come on. Remember that one summer when your parents and Levi's parents invited me to that lake house? There were three rooms, and you took that one, so Levi and I had to sleep in the living room," Keene started as I laid on my side. "It was hot as shit since the rooms only had air conditioning, so one night you let us stay with you."

"Even though the three of us shared a bed, we

didn't sleep. It was so hot." I sighed.

"And that time when we went on a road trip to California and hired a van. You fell asleep on me in the backseat," he said as my cheeks reddened.

"To be fair, there were a lot of teenagers in that van, and you wanted to sit in the back with the youngest."

"I was keeping you company since it was all of Levi's friends."

"What happened to all of them?" I asked because Levi had a lot of friends in Illinois, but I only saw Keene and Jaden as time went on.

"Moved on. Friends come and go, but Levi…he's like a brother to me," Keene mumbled. "You two are family to me, and I'm the older brother who has to look after you guys."

I smiled because Keene had always been there for Levi. He didn't have any family, and he saw Levi and me as his real ones because we'd known him for almost five years.

"Why did Axel text Levi?" I asked after a while.

"Because we knew that he was the only one who'd talk you into opening that door. He was the only one who'd calm you down," Keene replied as if he waited for the question.

"Thank you," I whispered as he turned his back to me, then turned the light off.

"Anytime. Now get some sleep," he said. I turned so that our backs faced each other.

It had been twenty minutes, and I couldn't sleep. It wasn't Keene's light snores or Aidan's and Liam's laughter downstairs, but the vivid images in my head from the night I killed Christo Aimar. I didn't know what would happen next. I knew James had his eyes on me. He must've witnessed my breakdown earlier and had a good laugh.

The bed sunk in, and I felt Keene move behind me. I raised a brow as I heard him exhale loudly. I felt his breath on my neck, and as I turned to face him, he wrapped his arm around my waist and pulled me so that my back was against his chest. He rested his chin on my head while I blinked.

"Sleep, Lana," he croaked out as his arm tightened around me. "Stop worrying and just relax. Tomorrow's another day."

Chapter Twenty-Eight

Lana

When I woke up, Keene was still by my side in the same position. All of us woke up late, and by the time Benny made us brunch, Mom was home. I barely spoke, yet no one asked, and I was glad. Everyone soon left when Mom said that we had to get Dad from the airport. It turned out he went to Idaho with Detective Kale because they found a dead body which was related to James, since it was one of his clients. Thankfully, it wasn't Christo, because the guy that they saw was a short blond dude. When we came home, I studied, but that didn't keep my friends from texting me to make sure I was okay. I replied to Ethan and told him to tell everyone I didn't want to be disturbed.

It was Monday, and Mom let me take her car because she wasn't going to work until late afternoon. I didn't want to go to school, but I had to, so I cruised the whole way. I got out of the car a minute before the bell rang. I held my bag and the can of soda I took from the fridge this morning because I didn't have time to make coffee. People rushed past me as I stared up at the miserable school building. I turned my gaze to see Benny, Nick, Melissa, Aidan, Miranda, and Tiffany look at me as they leaned against the wall. Apparently, they waited for me, but I stared at them until they got the message. I watched as they walked inside the building with everyone else. Once the front was empty, I drank the cold beverage then tossed it in the trashcan. My first period was Physics, and I was clearly not in the mood. I took my time to walk, and once I was inside, the hallways were empty. I walked to my locker and took out my things. Out of the corner of my eye, I saw someone approach me. I turned my head to see Britney strut toward me.

"Saturday night I went to Benny's house, and he wasn't there. I went to Nick's house, and he wasn't there either, so I went to your house and surprise, surprise, everyone was there. I mean no offense, but you give away more pussy than an animal shelter," she said, and I turned to her with a fake pout.

"You're just mad cause neither of them gives a crap about you," I said, then shut my locker.

"I told Kelly, and now everyone knows what a whore you are," Britney hissed as we walked down the hall.

"You guys are spreading rumors about me?" I gasped. "Well, at least you guys are spreading something other than your legs."

"You're such a bitch, Lana. Can't you see Benny is tired of you? They all are," she said as we turned the corner.

"I'm glad you think I care." I laughed.

She scoffed, and I rolled my eyes, then walked into the classroom. I walked right past the teacher and noticed everyone's eyes on me.

"Lana, Britney, you're late," Mr. Gorton stated as I sat down.

"Sorry, but Lana was trying to persuade me to smoke pot with her," Britney said as my eyes widened. Everyone turned to me with surprised looks on their faces.

"Liar, I'd never do business with her!" I scoffed as Carter laughed and high-fived me.

"Lana, calm down. It's Monday. Be kind to one another," Mr. Gorton said, then sipped his coffee as he looked at Britney and me.

"You know what's funny?" Britney asked. "Not you, Willson, so shut up."

"Britany, your mouth is so big I think you're talking in caps," I said as Melissa laughed.

"Lana, where are you going?" Mr. Gorton asked as I walked past Britney.

"I'm not feeling well. I'm going to the nurse's office," I stated as I spun around to look at the class.

"Should I come with you?" Carter asked as I locked eyes with Benny.

"No. It's fine. I'll be fine," I said. Mr. Gorton gave me a weird look. I sighed, then walked out of the classroom. I was sick, sick of Britney and school in general. At least spring break was soon. I walked out of the school and decided to go home since I didn't feel right. I knew that my mother would be home, so I'd be honest with her and say I wasn't up for it.

***

I decided to take a long hot shower to relieve all the stress. It relaxed me, but my shoulders ached for some reason. I walked out of my room with a towel wrapped around me. I noticed something floating in my room, and I raised a brow when I saw a heart-shaped balloon above my bed. A box was tied at the bottom to keep it stable, and I walked toward it.

"Hey." I spun around to see Benny against my door in a denim jacket, gray tee, black jeans, and Timberlands.

"Benny, I told you…"

"No, Lana, I won't stop until I know that we're okay. Everyone's asking about us," he mumbled as he walked past me and toward the balloon. I watched as he removed the box from the balloon. The balloon floated up to the corner of the room. "It's been hell without you. I can't sleep because I'm just thinking about you all the time. I just want to know if you've had long restless nights because of me. I just want to know that you think about me and I'm not the only one suffering from this. I want to know that I meant something to you."

"You do. When you said we should see other people and move on, I fucking lost it. I thought you were over me, so I tried to get over you," I croaked out and noticed he played with the box. "I can't believe I let myself drop so low. I can't believe I let Blake use me like that—I can't believe I did those things…"

"Lana, you're no—"

"I smoked and…and took random pills that made

me go fucking crazy! Benny, I put a gun to my head hoping that would make you all live in peace and stop creating problems. Ugh, what the fuck is wrong with me?" I demanded, then turned around and tugged on my hair.

"Lana! You're not the only one," Benny said as he spun me back around. "When I saw Carter and Blake around you, I got so jealous, and Britney was right there, so I tried to use her to make you jealous, but she became clingy and annoying. So I told her to leave, which only made it worse because it made me realize how much I missed you and what a big fucking mistake I made." He sighed. "I know that you're supposed to love yourself before you can love others, but I can't. I don't love myself for the stuff I've done." He opened the box. My eyes widened as I looked down to see a little ring with half a heart. "But I know that I love you," he whispered, then took the ring out. He took my hand and slipped the ring onto my index finger.

"Y-you love me?" I stuttered and looked into his brown eyes.

"Never stopped loving you, Lana Willson," he said, then took the necklace that he wore and pulled it out. That's when I noticed the other half of the heart. I smiled as I raised my index finger so that the hearts became one. He awkwardly scratched the back of his neck, and I noticed something on his wrist. He followed my gaze, then lowered his wrist. "I hate myself yet I love you so much that I just…" He trailed off as I ran my fingers over his scars. A tear managed to escape, yet I closed my eyes and kissed his wrist. "So, in a way, there's something wrong with the both of us. Like you said, no one's perfect." He lightly chuckled, and I opened my eyes to see that his were glossy.

"You promised you wouldn't cut anymore," I whispered as he wrapped his arms around my torso.

"Yeah, and you promised you wouldn't smoke anymore," he said. I had nothing to say, so I rested my head against his chest. "We all have something that releases the pain."

"Yeah," I said, then pulled away and wiped my tears.

"So I'll be downstairs while you, err…" He looked down, and I followed his gaze to see that I was in a towel. "Put some comfy clothes on."

"Okay. Why aren't you at school?" I asked as he walked toward the door.

"Oh, I just told them I wasn't feeling well." He winked, then walked out of the room. I laughed, then walked to my closet. I put on my underwear and decided on a loose sweater, pajama shorts, and gray knee-high socks. I tied my hair up in a bun, then walked downstairs. When I entered the living room, my eyes widened. The whole room was covered in blankets and pillows. Snacks were on the coffee table while *Harry Potter* played on the television. "Do you like it?" Benny awkwardly asked as he took off his shoes.

"Like it? I love it!" I squealed, then swung my arms around his neck.

"Yeah, I didn't know what food to get so…I just got all kinds."

"This is unbelievable. No one has ever gone through so much trouble as to buy these things for me, let alone do this for me!"

"Well, that's just how I show my love. By spoiling you and making you smile."

"You don't have to always spoil me. We could literally have a zombie invasion and be short on supplies, but as long as we have each other, I think we'll make it."

"Okay, I ditched school not to talk about zombies, but to watch *Harry Potter* with my gir—we are together, right?" he asked as his facial expression changed.

"Yes, of course. We bring out the best in each other, and now I have reason to smile again." I ran a hand through his hair. He leaned his head back and exhaled loudly.

"God, I missed that."

"I'll show you what I missed." I laughed, then took his hand and pulled him toward the floor. We sat down, and Benny started the first movie. I took the popcorn, then leaned back so that I rested against his chest. He put his arm around my shoulder and kissed my cheek. I smiled as a nice chill went through my body at the familiar touch. God, I missed his touch so much. I missed him so much.

"You know…these past three weeks I realized that I was a bit selfish because I just wanted you all to myself, but now being in a relationship means trusting each other, being there for one another, but it also means giving each other space occasionally." I turned to him. "And I'm not just saying that because Liam and Aidan want a guy's night soon," he added as I chuckled. "We should be able to hang out with other people but also make time for one another. That's why…I'll try to be nice—er around Blake."

"And Levi if he comes this summer?" My eyes lit up because there wouldn't be conflict anymore between the three.

"You know Levi and I will never get along. We hated each other since we were kids…but I'll try if he does," Benny said, and I smiled.

"I'll talk to him…I just want peace, you know? I just want things to go back to normal around here."

"When have things ever been normal, Lana Willson?"

"True," I mumbled, then felt his hand on my thigh.

"I love it when you wear long socks. It such a tu—"

"Ssshh." I cut him off and covered his mouth with popcorn. "Hagrid is coming," I said, then stuffed my face with popcorn while I watched one of my favorite characters.

***

Blake

It was after school, and I was in the living room with some of the guys. Tamia was here too, but she mostly spoke to Axel while I drank my beer in silence. When Lana said she'd go to the nurse's office, I knew she lied. No one would be up for school after facing something like that on Saturday. It scared the shit out of me, and when I saw the gun, my heart dropped. I was snapped out of my thoughts when Carter walked in. I rolled my eyes because he held books. He's supposed to tutor me, yet I'm not in the mood and didn't need one.

"Yo, Lana and Benny are back together," he announced, and I scoffed because Benny left before lunch.

Tamia turned to me with a glint in her eye. I raised a brow and leaned forward and motioned her to speak. "She played you."

"Nope. It was my idea. If I can't be with her, I should try and get her out of my system."

"Out of your system, meaning to be fuck buddies and shit?"

"We never fucked. Lana didn't want to! I thought by just being with her I'd see her as just another girl."

"Why did you do that? Why did you put yourself through so much pain knowing that you fell for her and that they'd get back together?" Carter asked as he leaned against the wall.

"Don't you get it? She doesn't like me that way, yet she goes for a guy who fucking hit her!" I exclaimed, then propped my feet onto the table. "But somehow, he manages to do the thing we all struggle to do nowadays, make Lana Willson smile. How does he make her happy? I don't know!" I yelled. "What the fuck is wrong with her? What does she see in him? What has he done for her? What does he have or do that I don't?"

"Don't you get it?" Keene asked as he sat opposite me. "He cares about her a lot. He changed for her; he's trying to make her into a better person!

But what do you do?" Keene tilted his head. "You influence her to smoke! To sleep around, just like you fucking do!" Keene raised his voice. "Do you know what she sees in you? She sees a selfish prick who sleeps around, not giving a damn about anything. Who plays with people and just suddenly goes off as if nothing happened."

"Don't talk shit!" I scoffed.

"I'm not! Saturday at my apartment when I told you guys it's over and you shrugged it off like she was just another bang, you should've seen her face. It was filled with disgust, naivety, and pain," Keene yelled. "So, if you want to keep being friends with Lana, I suggest you man the fuck up and stop depending on your dick and cigarettes to fix your problems."

"Oh, fuck off, Keene," I said, then shook my head. Everyone remained quiet, and I watched as Ethan sat down next to me.

"No, fuck you," he said, then walked off. I took another swig of alcohol and let it take me over. Even though I drowned in alcohol, I needed to get her out of my system. She's right, I brought out the bad side of her, but I couldn't help it. That side intrigued me.

"Dude, chill, that stuff's burning your throat," Ethan said as I chugged down my third bottle.

"This," I laughed as I looked at the bottle, "doesn't even come close to when Lana's lips were on mine, and we'd kiss."

Chapter Twenty-Nine

Lana

I didn't think that the diner would be open so early in the morning, but since it's close to downtown, it's convenient for people who worked. Mom dropped me off at the diner on Friday morning because she worked in the city and it was on her way. Blake and I hadn't spoken much since the incident on Saturday night, but I had to sometime. Yet I was surprised when he called me and said we needed to talk. When I glanced up, the waiter placed a bubblegum milkshake in front of me. I thanked him, then drank and put my hands in front of me, admiring the ring Benny got for me. Wow, was all I could say. The heart was small, which made it perfect for his half that was on his chain.

"Hey, Lana." I raised my head to see Ethan, Blake, and Keene. I smiled as Ethan sat next to me. As Blake and Keene sat opposite us, I looked outside to see that they came in Ethan's Tesla. I heard Keene groan as he leaned against the window.

"What's wrong with you?" I asked, then sipped my milkshake.

"Hangover." He took a menu and covered his face. I gave Ethan and Blake a questioning look. They seemed completely fine as they assured me Keene was okay. "So…why did you want to meet so early in the morning? Couldn't you tell me this at school?"

"I just wanted to—" Blake began, but Keene lowered the menu and gave him a skeptical look. "Needed to tell you as soon as possible."

"Okay." I shrugged.

"We need to stop," Blake stated as he gazed at me. I raised a brow, and he sighed and took out his cigarette box. "We need to stop. I've totally broken the New Year's Resolution, and I know you have too."

"We can't just stop. It takes time to get over something. Like I said, we should just slow down, then by summer we should totally stop."

"Aidan quit smoking. Tiffany didn't like it, so he slowed down, then eventually he just stopped," Ethan spoke up.

"I'm trying," Keene groaned as he pointed to himself.

"Then we should try too. You, me, Carter, Axel, and hopefully Levi when we see him this summer." I smiled and looked at Blake.

"Yeah, you're right. It won't be easy, but we'll do it." He nodded, then locked eyes with me. "Now what did you want to talk about?"

"H-how did you know I wanted to tell you

something?"

"I just had a feeling."

"Okay, well, err…" I mumbled. "Benny has agreed to make peace if you're willing to do your side too. I mean we can all be friends if you two are just nice to each other." I shrugged. Blake scoffed, then glanced around the diner. I turned to Ethan, who gave me a sympathetic look. I turned to Keene, who nudged Blake.

"Come on, Blake, for me, please? Think of it this way: there will be less drama."

"Have you spoken to Levi?"

"Yeah, he said he'd try," I mumbled, but I cut out the part where I literally begged him as I sent many texts because he didn't answer his phone.

"Fine. I'll try too, but it won't change how I see Benny."

"You promise?" I asked, then stuck out my pinky finger. He narrowed his eyes, then stared at my finger. Keene did an awkward cough, then elbowed Blake. He sighed, then stuck out his pinky finger too. We entwined our pinky fingers, and he gripped on mine a bit too hard, but I ignored it. As I pulled away, he grabbed my hand and ran his thumb across my fingers. He stopped at my ring and raised a brow at it.

"Couldn't he afford the other side? Or did you break it already?" Blake looked at the ring. I pulled my hand away and pursed my lips as Keene and Ethan laughed.

"He has the other half, you idiot."

"Right, he has the other half of your heart," Blake mumbled.

"Lana, I'm drinking your milkshake," Keene announced, then took my glass and sipped it.

"Sure, you can have it," I said, then watched as he slurped down my milkshake.

"So what are we doing on spring break?" Ethan asked.

"I'm using it for studying." I raised my hands.

"Oh, come on, Willson. You'll do great. We can go to your beach house," Blake said as he answered Ethan's question.

"You have a beach house?" Keene and I said in unison.

"Yeah…two, one here and another one in California." Blake nodded, and Ethan rolled his eyes.

"Oh! I got an idea! Let's have a road trip to that beach house in California then we ca—wait! Then we can surprise Levi!" I squealed as I tugged on Ethan's arm.

"Whoa, whoa, whoa. Calm down, Lana. I'm not even sure yet if I can have you all over. Besides, spring break is like in a week."

"Plus, Levi doesn't like surprises," Keene piped up.

"Oh yeah," I mumbled as I thought back to when we threw him a surprise party, and he was pissed.

"Well, even though I'd love to ditch today because we have P.E, we can't, so let's go," Blake said as he slid out of the booth.

"What about you?" I asked Keene as I paid for my milkshake.

"Oh, I texted a friend before we got here. He'll be here soon. Don't worry. Bye." I hugged him. I walked out of the diner and toward Ethan's car. With my bag over my shoulder, I pushed my glasses up to see Blake open the door for me. I gave him a strange look, thanked him, then got in the car. I sat in the back while Ethan drove and Blake sat in the passenger seat. As we drove to school, I thought about Ethan's beach house and how awesome it'd be if we could all go for spring break. I remembered when Miranda had a crush on Ethan; she must know about his beach house.

"Maybe we can go to the beach house that you have here?" I suggested as I looked at Ethan through the rearview mirror.

"Yeah," Ethan replied.

"Great, we'll talk to Miranda and everyone else, and we could all go for a few days," I said, because that would do us good after what had happened.

"Err…I don't know about Miranda, though," Blake said. I crossed my arms over my chest as I raised a brow at them.

"Does this have to do with when she was yelling at you on Saturday night on my porch?"

"Yes and no," Ethan replied, and I tilted my head. As I opened my mouth, the car came to a stop. I looked out the window to see that we'd arrived at school and the bell hadn't rung yet. I sighed, then grabbed my bag. I was surprised when I saw Blake open the door for me.

"Thanks," I said as I got out of the car. I pushed my glasses up and noticed his lips were up in a smile.

"No problem. See you later," he said, then looked over his shoulder. I followed his gaze to see

Benny, Nick, and Melissa near the school doors.

"Yeah, I'll see you around," I said as he turned back to me. Ethan stood next to me, and I smiled at him. "Thanks for the ride."

"Anytime," he said, and I walked toward Benny. The bell rang, but I managed to reach them in time. Benny swung his arm around my shoulder when we walked into the school building. Some people looked at us, probably to tell Britney and Kelly we were back in swing, but I didn't care. As we walked, we spoke about college. Benny wanted to go to Boston along with Nick, while I tried to go to Connecticut. Thankfully, those places weren't too far from each other, and if we got in, we'd most likely see each other. We entered the classroom and decided to sit in the back. Benny sat on my left while Marcus strolled in and sat in front of us. As we waited for Mrs. Singleton, I saw Britney enter the room. I bit my lip to prevent a smirk as I saw her gape at us.

"Keep walking." I eyed her up and down as she walked past. Benny laughed, then swung his arm around my shoulder.

"You didn't have to do that," he said, and we watched Britney huff as she sat down next to Jennifer. Carter came into the class and smiled. He sat down on my right, then turned to us.

"So I guess you won't need a ride home anymore?" He looked at Benny's and my position.

"Yeah," Benny replied as I opened my mouth. Carter raised a brow at his tone but laughed as he opened his book.

"You didn't have to do that," I whispered, and he

laughed.

***

Benny and I entered the cafeteria and finally sat at our table. A smile crept up my face when everyone joined. Things finally went back to normal.

"Oh! The gang is back together!" a recognizable voice cheered behind us. Benny and I turned around to see Liam skip toward us with his camera. We turned back, and he swung his arms around us and peered through. "I missed you, Lana."

"I spoke to you in the hallway just five minutes ago," I pointed out.

"I know, but it felt like months ago!" he said, then hugged us. "I'm just glad we can all sit together again!"

He backed away, then skipped toward Carter and hugged him. He did the same to Nick, who narrowed his eyes at the brunette. I bit my lip as Liam walked past Marcus to hug Blake.

"Don't touch me," Blake stated as he raised his hand.

"Everyone loves hugs!" Liam cheered, then pushed Blake's hand aside and pulled him into a hug. I laughed as Blake tried to push Liam.

"Yo, where are the grapes?" Aidan asked after he hugged Liam. Both looked down at Marcus, and Liam folded his arms.

"It's Marcus's turn to buy," Liam said as he hugged himself.

"Ugh fine." Marcus groaned, then stood up to

buy grapes. Once he returned with two bowls of grapes, everyone was settled.

"Oh! Before I forget, what are we doing for spring break?" Tiffany asked as she shared grapes with Aidan. Everyone conversed, and I turned to Ethan. He was already staring at me but shrugged.

"There's the festival in the city?" Liam suggested.

"No, no, no, we've done something like that already, which led to Lana getting stitches," Carter piped as my fingertips brushed over the scar by my chin. As everyone else threw in their ideas, I looked around the table. Maybe things would go back to normal. If we came up with something that we all agreed on, it would do us good. Something caught my eye when I saw Marcus going through Liam's camera. My eyes widened because he might see something. I nudged Benny under the table. He turned to me, then followed my gaze. We watched as Marcus's nose wrinkled up as he went through the pictures. The bell rang, and he put the camera down but still had a lost expression. Benny and I turned to each other with worried looks in the hope he didn't see anything he wasn't supposed to see.

***

I decided to spend my night with Benny because I had to tell him about the whole Christo thing. I was sure he knew about James Cornelius. I was on top of him while my head rested against his chest. Our legs were tangled under the blanket while his arms wrapped around me. I leisurely closed my eyes when his fingers ran through my hair.

"I spoke to Blake this morning," I said as I raised my head, then rested my chin on his chest. He looked down, then put a lock of hair behind my ear. "He agreed, and so did Levi when I spoke to him last night."

"Okay, then we'll see where this takes us." I moved so that I laid next to him. Benny turned so that we looked at each other. He placed his hand on my cheek and stroked it. I considered his brown eyes and saw how genuine they were. As I stared at them, I realized I couldn't keep the James thing a secret from him anymore. "You know…" he began when I opened my mouth to speak. "I just want to say I love you." He raised my chin with his index finger. "Like you don't even know how much."

He moved closer, then kissed me. My eyes instantly closed as I felt his plump lips against mine. His hand moved from my face, then traveled down to my hip. I felt the bed move as he slowly turned me so that I laid on my back. He pulled away, and I glanced up to see him straddle me, then pull off his shirt. I bit my lip when he came back down and continued to kiss me. I ran my palms along his bare skin because I wanted him. We stopped, and Benny rested between my legs. I smiled down at him as I ran my fingers through his brown hair.

"Thank you again for the ring." I smiled at him.

"My pleasure," he replied as he took my hand in his and twirled the ring.

"Why half a heart, though?"

"Because we need each other to be sane," he said, then took his chain and joined the heart so it'd be one. "It shows even though we're broken, together we're stable."

"How cute, Benny Nielson," I said, and he smirked.

"What can I say?" he said as he started to undo the buttons of my flannel. He kissed up my neck and wholly ignored the chain Blake got for me. I was still suspicious as to why he didn't ask about it.

I decided to stay a bit longer since Benny had to look after Sam. I didn't get the chance to tell him about James, but I realized Nick and Liam had to know too.

The following day, Benny and I drove to Liam's apartment. I bit the inside of my cheek to what seemed to be the millionth time. I was nervous to tell them everything. Benny knocked on the door, and like always, Nick answered the door. We walked in and found Liam's grandma on the sofa. She smiled at us, then returned to her soap opera.

"Why is the TV so loud?" I asked since she was only a few feet away.

"She's old, Lana. This is her Saturday thing whether there's people here or not," Nick replied, then walked down the hall.

"How does he know that?" I asked Benny as we followed him.

"We always help Liam with his grandma. This one time she was baking a pie but forgot one ingredient so he called one of us to get it since she wouldn't sleep until the pie finished," Benny explained.

"Why couldn't Liam go out with his skateboard to get the one ingredient?" I whispered as we entered his room.

"It was three o'clock in the morning," Benny said, and my eyebrows rose.

"Finally!" Liam exclaimed as he approached us, then pulled us in for a hug. "I am dying to know what news you have!"

"Okay, err…you guys should sit down for this," I said. They nodded, and I watched as Liam sat by his desk while Nick and Benny sat by his bed. They stared at me, but I didn't know where to start. "Do you know a guy named James Cornelius?"

"Cornelius." Liam snorted, and I glared at him while Benny and Nick squinted.

"Isn't he that wanted drug dealer that I saw in the newspaper?" Nick asked. Liam scoffed.

"Dude, you read the newspaper? Are you old or something? Ever heard of the internet?" Liam asked, and I closed my eyes for a moment as they went back and forth.

"What about him?" Benny asked as I opened my eyes.

"He, err, well…as a drug dealer, he's in contact with a lot of people. He's also good with fake identities." I noticed the puzzled looks they gave. "One of James's men was, err…undercover or in hiding, I'm not sure yet, but his name was Christo Aimar, and he was undercover as Jack August."

I finally looked at them, and their expressions were unreadable. Nick looked at the floor; Benny's lips parted as he stared at Liam and me. He spun around in his seat and typed on his computer.

"You mean, the guy we buried who randomly disappeared was working for James?" Nick tilted his head. I slowly nodded, then put my hands behind my back.

"And I think one of his other men was the one who broke into my house. I don't know what he wants," I mumbled.

"There's not much about James Cornelius or Christo Aimar, but there is an article where Jack August's real identity was, in fact, Christo Aimar and that they're looking for him," Liam stated as he read off his computer.

"So what now?" Nick asked.

"I don't know, but James wants revenge because I killed one of his men."

"Maybe they broke in because they wanted to plant more evidence. I'm assuming that night when we all slept over and found Liam's shoes, it was James's men?" Nick asked as he looked at me for clarification.

"Yeah, his name is Mike. All I know is Mike, Ernst, and James are alive," I mumbled. "While Christo…"

"You guys do realize that he's not gonna stop," Benny said. "He's going to continue ratting us out and bringing up more evidence."

"I know. Did you lie about the shoes only?" I asked as I sat next to Nick. Liam slowly turned in his seat and shared a look with Benny and Nick. My eyes widened as I thought what else they lied about. Liam stood up and looked at his wall with all the strings and papers.

"We, err…we don't know about my old car. We dropped it off, and the guy said he'd take care of it," Benny said as he rested his hand on my thigh.

"So? Did you check if he took care of it?" I glared at him through my glasses. Benny turned his head, and I followed his gaze to see Liam awkwardly scratch behind his neck as he whistled. "Oh, my fu—"

"We didn't have time to check the next day. We had a football game and Coach made us practice a lot." Benny held my hand.

"And the guy said he's busy, but I paid him an extra hundred to take care of it as soon as possible. Hopefully, he did." Nick mumbled the last part as I sighed.

"So now we don't know anything about the evidence?" I demanded.

"Nope, but what we do know is that we're the only ones who know that Christo is dead," Liam said as the corner of his mouth quirked up. He took a black marker and drew a line between Jack's name and wrote Christo.

"Yeah, but we don't even know where he is!" Nick exclaimed.

"That is why," Liam said as he pointed to the sketch of the sewers, "we're going back in there…because we're investigators!"

***

When I got out of Nick's car, I huffed. I didn't want to do it. The first time we did, we were lucky that we didn't get into trouble. To do it for the second time was senseless. We'd clearly get caught. I wore my new high tops Benny got me along with a white tee and baggy cardigan and gray jeans.

None of us spoke in the car, and it was understandable because I told them something big. Afterward, I also told them about the drugs that occurred at Ethan's cottage. That must've answered most of their questions.

"Hey, are you okay?" I asked Benny as I held his hand. I wrapped my other hand around his bicep and leaned on his shoulder as we walked.

"Yeah, I err…how long have you known about this whole Jack-Christo thing?"

"Only a week. I found out last Saturday."

"That's why you had that breakdown on Saturday night," he said and moved so that he was in front of me. I nervously looked down and nodded. Benny moved closer to me and cupped my cheeks so that I looked at him. A corner of his mouth lifted, and he kissed my forehead.

"Told you it's still gone!" Liam yelled. Benny and I turned to see them by the double door.

"What?" Benny asked as he removed his hands from my cheeks.

"Oh, err…we came here a few days ago just to check up on things, and the door is still unlocked," Nick replied. I turned my gaze away from Nick to see Liam casually walk in with his camera. Benny and I shared a look, then reluctantly followed them.

"Aww man! Someone took the cookies!" Liam said as he searched the empty cabinets. I shook my head in amusement as I thought of Aidan.

"Do we have to be here?" I groaned as we continued to walk down the hall.

"Yeah, when we were here, we found something," Liam said.

"What is it?"

Liam and Nick grinned at each other, then opened the bathroom door. My eyes immediately traveled down to the tiles, which covered the utility hole to the sewers. Like before, they removed the tiles while I took out the flashlights from Liam's bag. Once they were done, we stood around the manhole and stared at it. Only then I noticed the mark on the lid. Benny seemed surprised too, but Liam and Nick's grin extended.

"What does that mean?" I pointed at the lid that had the number three marked.

"I don't know, but look at this," Liam said as he showed Benny and me a photo on his camera. It was a utility hole like the one here except that was the one in the alley. "Since the alley is no longer under investigation, I managed to take a photo of the lid there," he added, and I saw the number one on it.

"This wasn't here the last time," Benny said.

"Yeah, which means that someone else was down here after we came," Nick said.

"Before and after, if you want to be specific. That's why the tiles were unsteady, and now that Lana has told us about Christo, it's quite clear that James was here and might be hiding the body down there." Liam smiled.

"Wow, Liam, you've really been thinking about this," Benny said with an impressed look.

"Yeah well, it's not every day you're an investigator." Liam nodded, then crouched down to open the utility hole. I took the hair tie around my wrist and tied my hair up into a high ponytail. Once the lid was off, Nick took a flashlight and climbed down the ladder. Benny went next, then me. I sat on the edge, then glanced up at Liam. He looked down and gave me a supportive look. I pinched my nose as I began to climb down.

We walked through the sewers for about half an hour. Nick led the way since he had the sketch of the sewers, yet I did notice that there were pathways we didn't go down. Hopefully, he knew where he was going. The sewers looked the same as the last time. The ground and floor were wet, strange noises were in the distance, and the horrible stench was in the air. I distracted myself as I scrolled through the pictures on my phone because I was bored. Benny spoke to Nick while Liam…

"Oh, Mr. Aimar! Come out, come out wherever you are!"

"Dude, he's dead. He's not going to answer you," Nick groaned.

"Oh, wait…what if he only comes out in…" Liam snickered while I raised a brow.

"Don't say it." Benny shook his head as we walked.

"August!" Liam laughed as we groaned. "You guys have such a funny friend keeping you company."

I looked down to my phone again and stopped by the picture I screenshot of Levi when we FaceTime. He was in the middle of lighting his cigarette, and it looked cool because the quality was decent. He was in his car with the city in the background. As I walked, I bumped into Nick's back, then stumbled a bit. I looked up to see that Nick and Benny stopped.

Liam stopped too and sent me a look as we watched the two in front of us.

"Why did you guys sto—"

"Ssh!" Nick whispered as he raised his hand. We followed his gaze to see that they stopped a few feet away from a corner where we're supposed to turn. I heard something snap, followed by footsteps. My eyes widened when I saw a shadow on the opposite wall. Benny reached over for a loose brick. Right when the person turned the corner, Benny raised his arm while Nick held Liam and me back.

"*Marcus?*" Benny exclaimed as we saw the muscularly built, curly-haired brunette turn the corner.

"Whoa, what the hell?" Marcus yelled as he held up his arms. Benny dropped the brick, and we stared at Marcus.

"What are you doing here?" Nick asked.

"Well, I was just curious yesterday when I saw photos on Liam's camera about this place."

"So you decided to follow us?" I started, and he slowly nodded, then turned off the flashlight from his phone.

"So why are you guys here in the sewers?" he asked, then covered his nose.

"Well, we're here because…" Liam began as he looked at us for help.

"Lana dropped something here, and we're helping her look for it," Benny answered with a poker look.

"You lost something in the sewers?" Marcus asked as he raised a brow.

"I'm quite clumsy," I said with a lopsided grin.

Marcus slowly nodded, then looked at his surroundings.

"So what did you drop here?" he asked, then spun around. Benny, Nick, and Liam turned to me, their eyes widened as they pointed to Marcus with questioning looks.

"Err…m-my designer pink bag." I said the first thing that came to mind.

"Designer pink bag?" Liam asked, and I glared at him to play along.

"Yes! Remember!" I said through gritted teeth.

"Wow." Marcus nodded.

"Yep," Nick said, then caught up to Marcus. I figured we'd continue to walk to the other utility hole since we couldn't look for Christo's body anymore. Yet I had the strange feeling that Marcus was on to us.

"Ugh, look at him," Liam said as he stared at Marcus, who had his back to us. "Marcus Sanders and his luscious hair, eight-pack, all in everyone's business."

I laughed as Liam shone the flashlight on his back, then put his middle finger in front of the light so that it showed on Marcus's back.

"Well, just be glad that he didn't find those photos of Miranda," I said.

"Yeah, holy crap. I would've been beaten up by a soccer player with good hair."

"Just…keep the memory cards away from each other." I sighed as we reached the utility hole that led to the alley. I checked my phone, and it was four p.m. I wanted to go first, but Liam stopped me, then whispered in my ear.

"Let him go first. Whatever is up there will take him." Liam and I snickered as we let Marcus go first. He didn't complain since he wanted to get out of the fetid place. As he climbed up, Liam poked his hair and Nick smacked his hand away before he'd notice. Once we were out, we walked out of the alley, then to Liam's apartment. Nick and Marcus's cars were still at Ethan's cottage, so they took the bus, then they'd walk from there.

We were back in Liam's room, and I sat on the bed while Benny used the bathroom. Liam was on his wall, which seemed to grow bigger and more significant since it had to do with James Cornelius and his men.

"Marcus is getting suspicious. Remember that day when Detective Kale questioned him about the pills he found in the alley?" Liam asked as he spun around and looked at me. I nodded, then tilted my head. "Well, when Detective Kale left, he kept looking at us."

"Well, I told Nick before he left that he should just have a little talk with Marcus," I said. Liam nodded, then returned to his desk. My phone rang, and I took out my phone to see that Carter called me. Weird, he rarely called me.

"Hello?"

"Lana! I need your—hehe—never mind." He giggled, then burped. I scrunched my nose up since I heard music in the background.

"Carter? Where are you?"

"I can't remember…but what I do remember is that you're so fucking gorgeous. Like WHOOAA—"

"Carter, you're drunk! Tell me your surroundings, and maybe I'll come and get you."

"Err…I see a bed and a girl," he replied, and I facepalmed. "I always see that! What's wrong with me, Lana?" He hiccuped, then continued. "I sleep around, but I wanna change! For myself, my friends, for you, and college! I don't wanna be known as Carter Halls, the sex god, in college! I want to change for the better."

"Well, you can change, Carter. Everyone can because sometimes change is good."

"You're right. Love you, my sexual tension friend!" he cheered, then ended the call. I stared at the phone for a moment, then realized Carter was still at the party, drunk off his ass. I stood up, ready to go, but realized that I didn't even know where the party was.

"What's wrong?" Liam asked.

"Carter's just really drunk, and since we live the closest to each other, I think I should be the one to take him home," I said, then sniffed myself.

"Oh, cool. He's at Blake's house," Liam replied, and I raised a brow. "Blake's having a party because his mom is gone for the weekend."

"Oh," I mumbled, then sniffed myself again as Benny entered the room.

"Here," Liam said and tossed me his cologne.

"Oh, I'm okay, thank you," I said.

"No offense, but you smell like shit." Benny smirked, and I playfully punched his shoulder.

"Fine," I groaned, then sprayed myself with Liam's cologne. It wasn't too strong like Blake's or Carter's, and it had a sweet scent to it. "I have to go get Carter from Blake's house, then go home for dinner."

"Oh, okay. Do you want me to take you?" Benny asked as I hugged him.

"Yes, please," I said. We greeted Liam, then walked out of his room. His grandma was nowhere to be found, so we left, then walked down to the car.

As Benny drove to Blake's house, I couldn't get Carter out of my mind and what he said. It's nice that he wanted to change before college and my guess…become more mature. I sometimes admitted in Physics he was more focused than me even though I was the one who wanted to become a physicist.

When we arrived at Blake's street, I heard the music. So many cars surrounded the house that Benny had to drop me in front of the house. He offered to come inside, but I assured him that it was okay. I saw Carter's truck and reminded myself to drive it. My feet ached by the time I got to the house since I walked a lot today.

"Name?" a bouncer asked, and I instantly groaned. The door was wide open, and I saw right through the house.

"There you are!" a guy exclaimed as he stepped out of the house and looked at me. I stared at him because I didn't know him, but something about his presence made him familiar. The guy swung his arm around my shoulder then brought me into the house. Once we were inside, I dropped his arm and turned to him.

"Who are you?"

"Look, I don't even know you, but you might

know my brother." He looked over his shoulder. I followed his gaze, and my eyes widened as I realized it was the Willis twins. The two at Jaden's party and the one I knocked out when I hit a bottle against his temple. I slowly backed away from him because I didn't know which one was which, since they were identical. "Look, we're here for the party, and Jaden just wanted me to make sure that you're here," he said, then pointed to Jaden, who was making out with a girl on the sofa. "You are Lana Willson, right?"

I nodded, then oddly walked away from him. I came here for one reason only: to find Carter. Yet how did Jaden know that I'd be here? I slowly walked down the hall and passed each room to hear if it was busy. By the third door, I stopped, then leaned my ear against it. I cautiously twisted the doorknob, then opened the door. A dark room met me, and the only available light was from the curtain. As I walked into the room, the door shut, and I quickly spun around.

"Carter?" I gasped as someone approached me.

"Hey, there, beer pong babe." My eyes widened to see Quinton's face. I didn't understand why he was here. Blake and Benny hated him.

"What the hell are you doing here?" I asked. Other than being a humongous pervert, he reeked of alcohol.

"Snuck in." He shrugged, then walked closer to me. "Turns out my girlfriend is somewhere around here looking for me while I look for her and well…I'm tired of waiting."

He reached out to wrap his arm around me, but I

shoved him back, then stepped to the side of the room. He cussed, then launched himself at me. I quickly ran to the door, but he grabbed me and tried to get me onto the bed. I screamed, then elbowed him in the stomach. While he recovered, I looked around for a weapon to defend myself. The room was dark, yet I saw an outline of something big. I walked to it and picked it up. It was quite heavy as I spun around and swung my arm. Everything happened so fast as I heard a thump, then watched as Quinton fell onto the bed. I put the object down and slowly walked to him. He laid on his stomach as his shoulders rose and fell. I quickly walked out of the room, then shut the door. As I continued to look for Carter, "Howlin for You" by The Black Keys came on, and I instantly smiled, remembering when Levi would say that it's our song. Since Carter was nowhere on the first floor, I decided to look in the basement. I'd seen Jaden, and he smirked at me. I saw Tamia and Axel in the kitchen, and they seemed anxious when they saw me, but I hadn't seen Blake, Keene, or Ethan.

As I walked downstairs, I heard laughter, and the music was much softer than it was upstairs. I turned my head and instantly froze. My gaze fell to the floor but slowly traveled up as I took in everything. There he was in his Vans high tops, dark jeans, and white tee that made the tattoo on his neck stand out. His laughter was poison to my ears as I watched the corner of his eyes squint and dark hair fall in his face. He stood in front of Blake, who sat on a sofa while they laughed. Keene sat on the end with a cigarette. As he dumped the ash in the ashtray, he looked at me.

"Lana?" Keene blurted out, and immediately everyone turned to me. My bottom lip trembled as I saw him, all muscular and tall. So brave and happy, who helped me stop my suicidal thoughts when I thought everything went downhill, so carefree and right *here*.

"L-Levi? What are yo—when did you get here?" I whispered as we locked eyes. Levi looked at me, and I watched as he opened and closed his mouth, but nothing came out. I saw Blake smirk as he drank his beer.

"Oh, baby girl." Blake laughed as he looked at me then Levi. "He never left."

The song, *our* song, continued to play like nothing happened. Sometimes I wished I was like music, a change in mood, but there's a start and an end, and no one's there to stop me unless forced. No one moved as they all stared at me. I guessed I was out of place compared to them, who either had a bottle or can of beer in their hand, cigarette at the corner of their lips, or swayed in their comfortable clothing. The heavy guitar riffs bounced around the room and went through everyone, including Levi Radcliff. I didn't want to look at him, but my throat closed up for a second when I caught sight of his guitar and other items that belonged to Levi. From what Blake said and the items that sprawled across the room, I concluded that Levi lived here, but I didn't want to believe it. He could've lived with anyone else in Illinois, Keene, Jaden, Aidan, Carter, or Ethan, but he chose Blake Gunner over *me*.

Acknowledgments

The acknowledgments have become the hardest part for me to write. With a book, it's planned and fiction—therefore I know what to write. When it comes to acknowledgments, there are so many things going on, and I hope that I won't forget something.

Flawed, the second book in Caught by the Bad Boys, is very deep. There are specific topics revealed about the characters that readers weren't aware of in the first book. I included that, not only because it's part of the plot, but because it brings out the primary goal I'm trying to get across. We can't judge people based on their looks or what we've heard because everyone's been through something that affected their well-being somehow.

For the confidence I gained in writing such sensitive topics, I'd like to thank the power of social media for making this a matter to speak about more frequently. There are many people out there who are going through similar situations that my characters are going through. It is great that it's being spoken about nowadays rather than being hushed or ignored.

I want to thank my parents who always supported me and were mildly open about these things. They've given me the chance to live comfortably and helped me reach my goals, one day I will repay them for everything that they've done for me. I'd also like to thank my sister, who eagerly waited by my side to read and motivated me to continue writing, and the rest of my beautiful family who supported me.

Everyone on Wattpad who started it all! I wouldn't have been where I am or accomplished so many things at such a young age if it weren't for your engagement. I'll never forget the messages I receive thanking me for writing such a heart-wrenching story with complicated characters. This book is for you.

I want to thank Limitless Publishing for giving me the opportunity to publish my work through them. You've all been wonderful to work with, and I hope we work together again with future books! My editor, Toni Rakestraw, who taught me so many things and helped me throughout the story to make it flow satisfactorily.

To all the YA books and thrilling TV shows I've seen over the years that inspired me to write a complex piece. If it weren't for your tips and guidance, I would be stuck in the first book!

About the Author

Raathi Chota's writing first began as a hobby and after growing in popularity, her gift for storytelling took off. Since gaining over ten million reads with her first novel on Wattpad, Raathi found her true calling. Being a regular high school student in Australia and a dedicated writer, her imagination knows no bounds. She enjoys random adventures where she knows she will find inspiration. Her stories are general fiction that is packed with young adult, thriller, mystery and romance themes. Raathi's stories are page-turners leaving you yearning for more. She gained over twenty-five thousand followers across Instagram, Twitter, Wattpad, and Inkitt combined. She recently began the second book on Wattpad and additional chapters on Inkitt where it gained its popularity and began trending on their website.

Facebook:

https://www.facebook.com/Raathi-Chota-1627159178043333/?modal=admin_todo_tour

Twitter:

https://twitter.com/Raathi07

Goodreads:

https://www.goodreads.com/author/show/16429704.Raathi_Chota

Wixsite:

https://raathichota.wixsite.com/blog

Instagram:

https://www.instagram.com/raathi07/

Wattpad:

https://www.wattpad.com/user/Raathi07

Inkitt:

https://inkitt.app.link/RA_Raathi_Chota

Join our Reader Group on Facebook and don't miss out on meeting our authors and entering epic giveaways!

Limitless Reading

Where reading a book
is your first step to becoming
limitless...

LIMITLESS PUBLISHING Reader Group

Join today! *"Where reading a book is your first step to becoming limitless..."*

https://www.facebook.com/groups/LimitlessReading/

Printed in Great Britain
by Amazon

83663117R00349